Affair & Honor

"There is an old saying

that things don't happen,

they are made to happen."

John F. Kennedy

AFFAIR & HONOR

BASED ON THE TRUE STORY

a novel by

BATT HUMPHREYS

FIRST TRADE PAPERBACK EDITION, MAY 2015
Copyright © 2015 Batt Humphreys

Affair & Honor
by Batt Humphreys
Published by Yellow Dog Press

This book may be purchased for educational,
business or sales promotional use.

For information:
Yellow Dog Press
154 South Creek Farm
Bonneau, SC 29431
or at:
BattHumphreys.com

ISBN-13: 9780692411865
ISBN-10: 0692411860

Library of Congress Cataloging in Publication record applied for.

For Laura and Meghan
I am rich in love.

FOREWORD

MUCH HAS BEEN WRITTEN OF two of America's more fascinating Presidents, Abraham Lincoln and John F. Kennedy, with a lot focusing on their deaths. For each generation, the timelines of our lives are marked by events that stopped the world by the enormity of their impacts, for me those include JFK's assassination, and later the morning of 9/11. They are events that changed the course of history and in the time/space warp of speculation, we will always wonder how the world would be different without the effect of three gunshots in Dallas or four planes on a September morning.

The beginning of Affair & Honor was formed in a casual conversation while touring part of what had once been The Fort Sumter Hotel in Charleston. A gifted storyteller led me through a tale of a young naval officer who was having an affair with a woman suspected to be a Nazi spy. The punchline was Jack Kennedy slept here. It led me down the rabbit hole of research and the larger context of Kennedy's entry and service in World War Two.

Many can cite the events of Dallas, even more in recent decades of his extramarital affairs. Few, and almost none of the generations following the baby boomers, know of Kennedy's heroism and medals for actions in the South Pacific. It is a story worth sharing.

There are much better biographical works on the whole of Kennedy's life, in particular I liked and read much of Nigel Hamilton's *JFK: Reckless Youth*. Researching the historical record was enhanced when the John F. Kennedy Presidential Library offered a wealth of documents and access online. I have made every effort to portray JFK's experience prior to and in the South Pacific with as much accuracy as possible.

As in Dead Weight my first novel, Affair & Honor uses a fictional reporter to connect the true parts of Kennedy, his friends and siblings to the greater scale of the war. In this case the reporter is based on the writing style of Ernie Pyle, in my opinion, one of the best war correspondents in history. For those who know of him and his writing, there is one very clear homage to his most famous piece. Some readers might also recognize subtle nods to some of my other favorite writers.

This print edition would not be possible without the support of contributors to the Affair & Honor Indigogo campaign. I was thrilled that former readers and friends believed in both the author and story enough to help bring it to the page. In particular Tim Laffin rises to the level of a true patron in this project. For every single person who has supported this effort financially, spiritually, and through your ongoing friendship.. I cannot thank you enough.

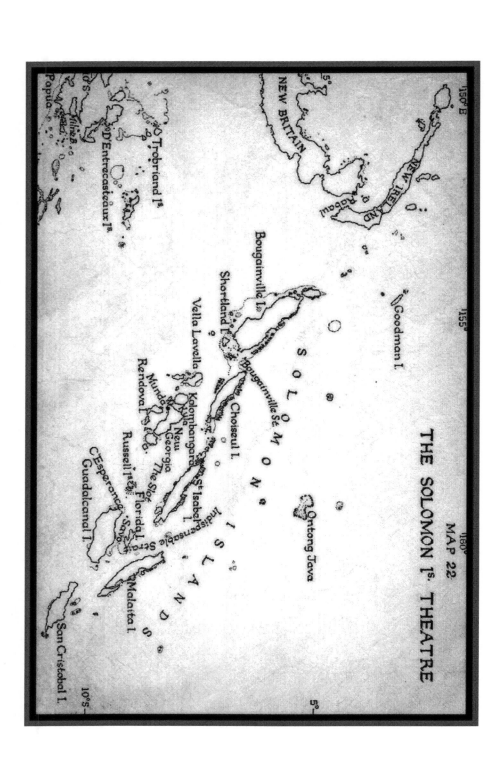

MAP 22

THE SOLOMON Iˢ. THEATRE

CHAPTER 1

IF THE WORLD WAS CREATED in six days, the seventh was Sunday south of Broad in April. Azaleas bring a heartbreaking beauty to Charleston. Framing the historic homes their blooms seem preordained. For one season she becomes a blushing young beauty offering a color of promise, if not a tease.

From St. Michaels late churchgoers stroll to the street. Either way they turn, to Meeting or Broad, their path takes them down the intersecting boulevards that define the city. Her white steeple was once painted black, with hopes that it would obscure the church from British artillery. Now another war brings young men to this old town.

A white MG comes fast around the corner, downshifting into the turn and accelerating before it straightens south. A few people scurry to the safety of the curb. The naval officer driving throws a salute to a man he barely misses.

Down the block a man stands at the corner of Ropemaker's Lane. He wears a dark suit and a fedora pretending to read a newspaper. It's a Washington newspaper. He's as unobtrusive as Godiva on a horse.

As the car passes he turns and raises the paper slightly, to a matching dark suit two blocks down. They form a pair of somber bookends with stately homes in between. Neither tourist nor neighbor, it's hard to disguise the FBI.

I stand on the opposite side. My tailor is better. I wear a double breasted suit. The war effort is rationing wool and it will be the last new suit for awhile. So make it three suits advertising out of towners. We all stand out among the locals sporting seersucker on Easter morning.

The two G-Men and I are tracking the same game. They're trying to nab a spy, said to be seducing an ambassador's son. I'm just trying to grab a headline. My name is Sam Marlow. I write for the New York Herald Tribune.

Funny how an affair with a married woman can incite the press. Not so funny when the peephole reports of Walter Winchell bring in the Federal Bureau of Investigation. In war, they say loose lips sink ships. In this case, it seems more than lips are loose. It's hard to say whether it's the salacious sex scandal or the issue of national security that brings scrutiny to every action of naval ensign John Kennedy.

Of sex, you could hardly find a more fitting female protagonist in this public passion play. She is Inga Arvad. To call her beautiful would be trite. Her newspaper photos depict a Danish woman wearing a smile that opens hearts. Her eyes then steal them. As she drives past every man on the street enters slow motion. They stop to watch transfixed, unable to look away, uncaring of the wrath he may incite at his elbow. If you're in a suit and not seduced you either are not a man, or perhaps, you're J. Edgar Hoover.

Inga went from beauty queen to newspaper woman in Denmark. In some combination of those skills she landed rare interviews with Adolf Hitler in 1935. The next year she was Hitler's guest at the summer Olympics. Her photograph with Hitler at the Games and circulation in close Nazi circles went from unseemly to a security issue when the world went to war. But security seemed secondary to Hoover. Those events were six years old. Sex and spies were kicked to the level of a full investigation when linked to young John. It gave Hoover all he needed to go after the Kennedys.

Two blocks down the street the sports car swings right then executes a U-turn pulling smartly in front of a huge mansion. I begin walking in their direction. A servant steps to the curb, formally dressed for a warm spring day and takes the door on the lady's side. Kennedy exits streetside, pauses to straighten his jacket, before making a light leap at the curb to offer his elbow. I envied the ensign.

The couple walked up and into the house as I approached a gated entrance enclosing an elaborate garden.

"Good afternoon, sir, welcome to the Calhoun Mansion," a greeting with meaning from the servant. He was well dressed and large.

"Good afternoon," I replied and continued walking towards the house.

"Do you have an invitation, sir?"

I did not. He knew I didn't. He probably knew every person by name on the party list and that didn't include me. I couldn't fool him, so I played him straight.

"I don't have an invitation. I'm Sam Marlow, a reporter from New York. That naval ensign who just entered is John Kennedy, the ambassador's son. The woman, depending on who you believe, is a Nazi spy or his latest hot fling. I'd like to speak with him and promise you as a gentleman, that I won't swill the free liquor and will refrain from pinching any of the local ladies."

That stopped him for a second, then he smiled, "You're staying with Mr. Stoney on Murray Boulevard."

"Yes. How did you know?"

"Small town Mr. Marlow. In the future if you don't have an invitation just drop a name. It always works in Charleston."

We both smiled and I walked past.

A brick inlaid courtyard fanned out leading to two separate ornate stairways each mounting to the same entrance. Separate stairs for separate sexes, a design of older days to prevent a scandalous glance of an ankle. At the door a butler in white gloves held a silver tray of small cocktail glasses.

"Saint Cecilia punch, sir?"

I ignored my earlier promise and picked one up as I entered.

The entrance hall was large enough for a small polo scrimmage with a domed ceiling that reached seventy feet above the floor. I had to remind myself that once this was one of the wealthiest cities in America not just some backwater in the state of South Carolina. The drink was not something you would order at a bar in Manhattan, a punch of some sort that managed to blend spirits and a dash of champagne, no doubt mulled with history. The history was bittersweet but the drink was good.

People strolled through the house attended by a small army of servers carrying trays of drink and food. Upstairs I heard a voice singing an upbeat and timely number carried on the music of a small orchestra. The singer was good but for the moment my eyes were after a white jacket cutting through a drawing room. I followed.

The couple flowed through French doors and onto a broad veranda that overlooked the gardens. Arvad looked admiringly at the trimmed boxwoods and intricate walkways then turned, with her back to the banister, as Kennedy leaned towards her. She caught my eye and stiffened. He caught the change and turned towards me.

"The beauty of Nature and her graces interrupted by..." Kennedy spoke but he was not smiling. "Are you one of those Feds? Your suit seems a few pay grades above the norm."

"Sorry to spoil the moment," I felt like the lowest form of gossip voyeur, "I'm Sam Marlow with the New York Herald Tribune."

"Another scribbler prying into private lives. Mr. Marlow, what a mean way to make a living."

"Ensign Kennedy, I'm actually not interested in your private life per se or your relationship incarnate. Winchell has done a far better job than I would with your so-called exploits."

"He has indeed. Then you might explain the point of this pleasant conversation."

"I'm not interested in the *what* Mr. Kennedy. I'm interested in the *why*."

"The why would seem rather obvious Mr. Marlow."

He glanced from Arvad to me. She turned her eyes towards mine. Both smiled. I took a step backwards. It would take a whole box of harpies to counter the charm this couple could amass.

I laughed, "Point taken. I'm neither blind nor unaffected. However, the *why* I'm talking about is why now? Her associations were already known, but the surveillance didn't begin until you were involved. Who's the actual target here? Inga Arvad? Or John Kennedy?"

Kennedy glanced across the veranda towards a table surrounded by several wicker chairs.

"Mr. Marlow, let's have a seat and talk for a bit."

We walked to the furthest edge of the porch. Beyond, the rail Italianate columns stood in the gardens. Kennedy pulled a chair out for Arvad.

"Mr. Marlow, if we're to be social, let me introduce Inga Arvad."

She raised her hand, "Mr. Marlow, a pleasure to meet you, so nice to be an object of your interests."

Her voice was slightly accented, just enough to know that she was Scandinavian, just enough to know that any accent in these times could be enough to draw unfavorable attention.

I took her hand. She was not timid with her grip, "A pleasure to meet you," I returned a smile. By comparison, I felt like I had teeth missing, "Hoover's depictions of you with horns do not do you justice."

She laughed. I began wishing Kennedy would leave.

Instead, he began, " Mr. Marlow..."

"Please, call me Sam."

"And you call me Jack. Then Sam, what is your interest here?"

"Call it balance. There seems to be a lot coming from the Winchell-Hoover-Washington side that seems a little too connected."

Kennedy leaned back in his chair and looked over the railing into the garden.

"There's no reason why I should discuss any of this with you. There is no conceivable gain and much to risk. But you're the first person outside of a very few in Washington who seem to see beyond the scandal. So let's talk with the understanding that none of this conversation is to be quoted or attributed directly to me."

"Understood."

"Then, ask your questions."

It was my turn to pause.

"Let's start with how you met."

He laughed. There was a hint of mischief in his eyes.

"I have this sister we call Kick.."

Kathleen 'Kick' Kennedy the second daughter and fourth child of Joseph and Rose Kennedy was a breakout beauty, a darling of the debutant world and educated at Queen's College in London during papa Joe's time as ambassador. She left school to take a job at the *Washington*

Times-Herald. Washington was a social merry-go-round before the war and Kick commanded a well heeled circle on the party circuit. Beautiful and spirited, her hair a warm, sandy color with the fiery green eyes of the Kennedy clan, Kick and Jack were two of a kind. "Late last fall I wrote Kick and told her I was coming to Washington, I'd finally gotten an assignment from the Navy and was to report for duty at the Office of Naval Intelligence. As soon as I got there she was throwing parties, introducing me to friends. Inga was staying with a friend, Page Huidekoper, who was also a reporter for the *Times-Herald .*"

Inga leaned into the conversation, "I had just landed a job with the paper writing a feature column called, '*Did You Happen To See...?*' My boss, Cissy Patterson, told me to get an interview with young Kennedy. I did."

Arvad's column was little more than a people piece in the paper. Washington attracts a broad range of interesting characters. She had a knack for getting interviews and making them interesting. It wasn't the interview with Kennedy that raised her to national interest. In fact the column that made Inga the talk of Washington wasn't even hers. The ink heard 'round the world was Walter Winchell's.

"Your piece on Jack came out last November. No offense but it was fairly innocuous. You spoke of father and son, a Harvard education and extolled the virtues of his book, '*Why England Slept*'. How did things go from that to Winchell's piece almost two months later?"

Kennedy stepped in, "War broke out Sam. That changed a lot of things. Our office went to a twenty four hour work day. That's just naval intelligence. Every branch ramped up. Intelligence is critical to war planning. Other branches had a different focus. The FBI turned their priorities and power on espionage. "

"Which brings us to Inga."

"I don't find that amusing, Mr. Marlow." She bristled, "I am not a spy."

"My apologies, I was not suggesting you are. How did this begin?"

"With a photograph."

Inga described how Kick discovered that her ex-roommate and current co-worker at the *Times-Herald* Page Huidekoper discovered an old photo in the newspaper's 'morgue' of Hitler and Arvad during the Olympic Games.

"Page joked around the office that I must be some sort of spy. It made me angry. I was doing the same type articles in Germany that I'm doing here, I just happened to get interviews with very important people. If I got an interview with President Roosevelt, would I be considered a spy in Berlin? That's no small talk in a time of war. I wasn't sure what to do so I marched into Cissy's office and asked."

You don't get to be the first woman heading a major daily newspaper in the United States by being timid, or stupid. The story as described by Inga, reduced to its simplest state, sounded like office gossip to impugn a rival either professional or romantic with the potential of an eligible bachelor like Jack at stake. But throw in photos of Hitler a week after the beginning of a world war and the game gets serious. For Cissy Patterson it wasn't just a schoolgirl squabble. Her newspaper had taken a strong isolationist stand while the rest of the country was moving towards, then entering a war. It was the wrong time for her paper to be thought of as harboring a spy. She had to take action.

"Cissy called Page into her office then took us both by the elbow and we walked down to the field office of the FBI. We both gave statements, separately."

"Then what happened?"

"It seemed pretty simple to me by stopping rumors before they started I thought we'd clear up the whole mess."

"That doesn't seem to be the case."

"Soon afterwards, there were signs we were being followed. Of course the Washington gossip mill flourished. We continued seeing each other, even used Kick as a chaperone, but tongues kept wagging."

On January 12th the gossip mill made national press in Walter Winchell's column.

"*One of Ex-Ambassador Kennedy's eligible sons is the target of a Washington gal columnist's affections. So much so she has consulted her barrister about divorcing her exploring groom. Pa Kennedy no like.*"

Winchell had released the hounds. His column is one of the most consumed in America reaching fifty million people. What he fails to supply in facts he fills with innuendo. In the mid-thirties Winchell and Hoover became friends. That bond was cemented when Winchell helped, some say flipped, Louis 'Lepke' Buchalter's, of Murder Inc., arrest for the FBI. Their relationship served each according to need. Hoover knew that information was power. The Bureau supplied the information, he turned it into personal power. Some might call it blackmail. In this case fanning the flames of a scandal through Winchell, made Jack Kennedy a tool to use against his father. One fact rang true in Winchell's report.. *"Pa Kennedy no like."*

Joseph P. Kennedy went from Ambassador to the Court of St. James to persona non grata with Roosevelt. He opposed American intervention in the war, sided with Chamberlain and pressed for appeasement with Germany. In the days before the Battle of Britain he pressed again for an unauthorized meeting with Hitler. When the bombing of London began his dispatches to Washington became more frequent and by some accounts nearly hysterical. The Ambassador was so rattled by the bombing at night, that each evening he would leave London to take refuge in the country. Running against sentiment for the war and running from the bombing every night, Kennedy's demands to be recalled to Washington increased. In October of 1940 the British ambassador in Washington was informed by London that the American ambassador was about to release an article to the press indicting the Roosevelt administration. The article was scheduled for release four days before the presidential election. Joe Kennedy was blackmailing the President of the United States. It worked. Kennedy was recalled. Now Roosevelt had a war on his hands. Joe Kennedy was back home but being held well outside any position in the new administration. Blackmail can work two ways. This time Kennedy was feeling the heat.

Jack spoke, "Winchell's little mention had an immediate impact. They shagged my ass down to South Carolina because I was going around with a Scandinavian blonde. And here we are."

Kennedy stood up, "If you'll excuse me, my back gets a little stiff when I sit too long. It's been a pleasure talking with you Sam. Perhaps we can pick up the conversation later. There are few amusements in this small town but this early spring weather is lovely and I promised Inga we would explore the rites of Spring."

With that he smiled and turned his eyes on Inga. I heard Stravinsky starting in my head then snapped to before the dance scene began.

"I hope so. We barely touched on anything beyond the scandal and as I said that's not my primary interest."

"You staying in town?"

"Murray Boulevard."

"They try to keep me busy on the base but perhaps we can get together one evening."

Inga stood, "Sam, hope to see you again."

They locked arms moving down the veranda turning into the house and out of my line of sight. I leaned back against the rail and pulled out a cigarette, lit up, and sucked in a lung full. Kennedy wasn't what I'd expected. The family was famous and rich with all the trappings that ensue; the best education, well traveled and circulating in tony society. In short it would be easy to dislike any single member if not the family as a whole. But you actually want to like the guy. He's assured but not smug. In his eyes there's a humor and mischief that appeals to either gender. I was musing on a second meeting when a woman stepped out of the house. She seemed slightly overdressed as if for an evening out to an upscale affair. She walked towards me with purpose, approaching with chin down and eyes up. The look was intended to be coy. It was working.

"Would you offer a lady a cigarette?"

It was too easy, "Have you seen one around?"

She raised an arched eyebrow. Her eyes were feline and I could almost sense the sheaths retracting over the claws. Then she laughed, like she meant it, like she needed to.

"Funny stuff city boy. There are plenty of ladies around here or plenty who pretend to be, but I would bet you somewhere behind the doors of the 35 rooms in this old house some of those ladies are letting their knickers down while we stand here gabbing. Now how about that cigarette."

I reached into my coat and pulled out my case. She took a cigarette. I was quick on the light.

"Platinum, huh? You must make pretty good money for a newspaper man."

Déjà vu.

"How did you know?"

"Small town Mr. Marlow."

"I'm feeling claustrophobic already."

"How do you think your pal Kennedy feels?"

I hate repeating my questions, so I tried a new and brilliant approach.

"What's your name?"

"Ashley Chambliss. Tough questions Mr. Reporter you got another?"

"I thought you Southern girls were supposed to be coquettes."

"Ooh la la, you drive me crazy when you speak the French monsieur."

I was going down fast. She was stubbing her cigarette in a planter.

"These people are so tacky they've decorated this place like a bordello."

"So you know the owners?"

"Kind of," she leaned way over the balcony. Suddenly the gardens weren't the most attractive view from the veranda.

" I lee-of o-vah tha-yah," laying on a thick Southern accent and pointing towards another large house down the street.

"Local girl."

"Too local."

Upstairs I heard the orchestra starting up.

"Oh, gotta run."

"Why.."

"You mean, 'We were just getting started?'"

She was fast.

"I'm the singer, upstairs, but then you never made it that far."

"I heard you. You have a lovely voice."

"Flatterer."

"You were bold enough to ask for a cigarette. Might I be bold enough to ask to buy you a drink after you're finished here?"

"My God that proposal sounds like something that would come out of a nitwit Southern boy."

"Fine, we'll do it my way. Drink?"

"Deal. Fort Sumter Hotel at five."

And she ran back through the same door she'd exited.

I fell back against a column. I was exhausted.

CHAPTER 2

A CHILL WIND BLEW UP CONSTITUTION Avenue. It was Sunday evening. It might just as well been high noon on Tuesday. Lights were on at the Department of Justice. Lights were on at the War Department. Lights were on at the White House. War turned Washington into a town that never sleeps.

Deep inside the building J. Edgar Hoover sat behind his huge mahogany desk. It was raised like a dais in a king's chamber. In a comfortable chair next to the desk was Associate Director Clyde Tolson.

"Seems they're thinking of arresting her." Hoover tossed a letter of a single sheet across the desk.

Tolson picked it up and read out loud.

"Report all information in your files.. hmmm... whether a Presidential warrant of apprehension should be issued."

"She's no good to me in jail."

"Do we have anything that absolutely indicates she's a Nazi?"

Hoover's voice boomed the length of the office and down the hall.

"Hamm and Lott get in here!"

Footsteps came pounding as two agents entered at the far end, walking in lockstep down the long approach to the Director's desk.

"Sit down boys."

They pulled two hard backed chairs in front of the desk. Both were tall well built men but sitting lower and in front of the boss they both looked like schoolboys.

"Give me a run through on what we've got on Inga Arvad."

The two looked at each other and Hamm started.

"Born Denmark 1913.."

Hoover cut him off, " Not that far back. Let's at least start when she was old enough to go after the Gestapo."

"Began working for the largest newspaper in Copenhagen in 1935. She met and became friendly with Hermann Goring's fiancé. That got her invited to their wedding. Then she got busy weaving quite the little social network. She met Himmler and Goebbels. It was Goebbels who got her the interview with Hitler."

Hoover held up a hand.

"You're telling me that at the tender age of 22 this little Mata Hari worked her way into Hitler's inner circle. If she's not a spy she's wasting a hell of a talent. Go on."

"She actually interviewed Hitler twice. He said that she was a perfect example of Nordic beauty. For her part," he looked down at a note in his folder, "She said, 'You immediately like him. He seems lonely. The eyes, showing a kind heart, stare right at you. They sparkle with force.' "

"Ha! Ask the Poles about force. Ha! Ask the French about sparkle. They sparkle like bubbles in their silly little wine. Go on."

"After the interviews with Hitler she was invited to attend the Olympic Games in '36 in Berlin. That's where they were photographed together."

"That it?"

Lott took over.

"On the personal side. She's been married twice. Beginning at seventeen she eloped with an Egyptian diplomat. That went away quickly. At twenty one she married a Hungarian movie director by the name of Paul Fejos. Not much of interest on him, but while married she took up with Axel Wenner-Gren."

"Clyde there's a familiar name."

"Seems everybody wants a piece of him besides the 'lady' in question who still receives his support. The IRS is after him for setting up his own offshore bank in the Bahamas. He spends time there with the Duke of Windsor toasting the Nazis. He's one of the richest men in the world and tied into a lot of shady deals. Oddly he was financing a film project for Mr. Inga in Peru that led to a foundation being set up in New York. Some think that's a front for propaganda at best. Strange these little circles, but Wenner-Gren's been linked to Goring as well. Thought is he may be involved with the Germans in opening a South American front. Naval intelligence doesn't like the looks of his yacht the *Southern Cross* which is the size of a destroyer and thinks he might be using it to service German U-boats. He spent a little time down Mexico way throwing money around and maybe backing a little coup attempt against the president. Swell guy, snappy dresser. He's on everybody's blacklist."

"So that's the history. This married woman of worldly ways comes to Washington and sets her sights on a lowly ensign who happens to be the son of a former Ambassador. Meanwhile she's trotting about town doing society interviews on every major player her isolationist newspaper can land. What have we got on her and Kennedy?"

Hamm sat up like a good dog, "We've got men on them pretty much around the clock. With Kennedy in Charleston we have to keep an extra detail down there. Since surveillance began they have spent time together in both DC and Charleston, one or the other traveling."

"So you know where they are but what have you got?" Hoover sounded stern.

"We're following standard protocol, intercepting mail, tapping phones, interviewing third party subjects and occasionally recording in residence."

"Well???"

"He calls her Inga Binga in his letters."

"What?? Ha! That's rich."

"Their letters are fairly intimate. They talk like lovers," he looked down at his file, "January 19 from Mrs. Fejos to Ensign Kennedy."

> *The first time I missed anybody and felt lonely and as though I was the only inhabitant in Washington.*
>
> *Loving —knowing it, being helpless about it, and yet not feeling anything but complete happiness. At last realizing what makes Inga tick.*

"Cut the hogwash!" Hoover exploded, "I want to hear something useful."

Hamm flipped through his notes, his hands stopped on one page and his eyes lit up. He cleared his throat.

"January 26, from Mrs. Fejos to Ensign Kennedy."

> *The further the train pulled away, the less visible was the young handsome Boston Bean. … There was the good old feeling of stinging eyes and a nasty pull at the heartstrings, which always show up when too great a distance is put between us.*

> *I slept like a log. At midday we arrived to the Capital of the United States. To that same Union Station, where I went on January the first 1942 as happy as a bird, without a care, a fear or trouble in the world –just in love--- remember?*

> *"Have you started making the baby yet," was a question asked me today. Guess by whom?*

"Baby!!! Holy Crap. A married woman, an officer in naval intelligence and Grandpa Joe Kennedy. Now you're talkin' boy go on."

"Another letter January 27, Arvad to Kennedy."

> *Distrust is a very funny thing, isn't it? I knew when Kick got a letter today why you haven't written to me. There was a peculiar feeling at the realization, that the person I love most in the world is afraid of me. Not of me directly but of the actions I might take some day. I know who prompted you to believe or rather disbelieve in me, but still I dislike it. However I am not going to try and make you change – it would be without result anyway – because big Joe has a stronger hand than I.*

"Great! She knows Daddy calls the shots. But Papa Joe is going to lose his hand if his boy ends up a daddy."

"Anything else on that?"

"Tape recordings at the Fort Sumter Hotel February 22nd it was learned that the subject was quite concerned about pregnancy from previous visits. Kennedy had little comment."

"Excellent work. That could be useful. So I suppose the recordings indicated intercourse?"

"Ahmm yes Director, multiple instances."

"Inga Binga indeed! Photos?"

"No sir."

"You boys better see what you can get."

Hoover sat back in his chair and leaned one elbow on the armrest. He looked at Tolson then at the two men in front of him.

"In any letter, any tap or any recording is there any conversation or hint that she's trying to work him for information?"

Hoover leaned forward. Hamm and Lott leaned back as far as their straight backed chairs would allow. It was the question that cut to the chase. Neither agent wanted to say no to the Director. It was not the type of answer that helped build a career. Tolson leaned forward as well.

Both agents opened their files and pulled a single page each.

Hamm, "Telephone intercept, February 4."

> *Kennedy: "I have to work Saturday."*
> *Arvad: "When are you sailing?"*
> *Kennedy: "I don't know."*
> *Arvad: " I think soon."*
> *Kennedy: "I'll tell you when I know."*

Lott, "February 9, tape recording Fort Sumter Hotel."

> *Arvad: " You should have taken me to meet the Lt. Commander's wife."*
> *Kennedy: "It would have been unbearably boring."*
> *Arvad: " Are you ashamed of me? I thought I was more than just someone to secret in hotel rooms on your free weekends."*
> *Kennedy: "Don't be absurd. I have little desire to build social bonds with the Lt. Commander in Charleston, unless speaking of secrets, your interest is to build a relationship with the Lt. Commander for your own schemes?? He knows a lot more than an ensign."*
> *Arvad: "Jack, don't insult me. You play me like a whore and you insinuate that I'm a spy."*

Hamm, "February 22 recorded conversation Fort Sumter Hotel."

> *Arvad: "Churchill painted a rather gloomy picture of the war*
> *effort last week on the radio. Not one word of anything but*
> *defeatism."*
> *Kennedy: "Churchill is the whole reason we're in the war. He all*
> *but promised before we went in that the Japs would roll over like*
> *the Italians. Well, the Japs are having a cakewalk through the*
> *Pacific and we're getting our tails handed to us."*
> *Arvad: " The British soldiers are just no damn good."*
> *Kennedy: "The Germans have pretty much rolled up Europe.*
> *The British Empire is all but finished. Churchill knows it."*

Hoover leaned back. "Well she's certainly no patriot and her questions make her sound like a spy. How can a woman with her connections, her background, her intrigue, be as perfectly innocent as she claims? Alright boys last chance, anything more of interest?

Lott looked at his sheet. "On the subject of innocence sir, during the period since Ensign Kennedy has been in Charleston the subject has been seen to receive other 'visitors' in the evenings."

"Really?"

"At least two other men on several occasions during the two months of surveillance."

"Anyone we know?"

"One her current husband."

"My heavens. This woman is making Mata Hari look good. But then they shot her."

Hamm picked up. "On the same night February 22 young Kennedy talked on the phone with his father in Palm Beach. Young Kennedy encouraged his father to be more vocal about his beliefs on the war. Claimed by backing off he set himself up to be branded as an appeaser. Mr. Kennedy stated that the reason he stopped speaking was because it might have a bad influence on his sons later in politics."

"Sons? Plural?"

"Yes sir."

"Well I'll be damned. Papa Joe has plans for both his boys. Running Joe Junior was pretty much given but young Jack, too? Damn. I say Damn. That makes this girl's play a little more interesting."

"Sir, I would add in numerous conversations Arvad has mentioned the notion of Jack Kennedy in the White House."

"A twice married woman, suspected spy as First Lady? That won't happen. Joe Kennedy knows that won't happen. He'll put a stop to this but it'd better not be before we get the goods on them. You know what I mean boys? Where are they *right now?*"

"Charleston."

"Who's on them?"

"Agents Malloy and Hughes."

"God help us. Those two. Well you'd better get them on the horn and make sure they've got these lovebirds on a wire and tell them they'd better come up with a way to get some photographs."

Hamm and Lott stood to attention.

"Good work you two. Now get out of here."

Both smiled, turned and walked out the same way they'd entered.

Hoover leaned back in his chair, looked over at Tolson, and grinned. On him it looked like a bulldog with gas.

"Clyde we got us a real corker here. We've either got a spy or an ace to play against Kennedy anytime we like. This girl is going to be useful. Now it's nine o'clock and way past time for my Jack Daniel's. C'mon Clyde I'm buying the steaks."

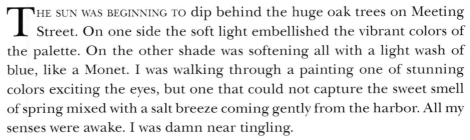

CHAPTER 3

Charleston, S.C.
April 4, 1942

T HE SUN WAS BEGINNING TO dip behind the huge oak trees on Meeting Street. On one side the soft light embellished the vibrant colors of the palette. On the other shade was softening all with a light wash of blue, like a Monet. I was walking through a painting one of stunning colors exciting the eyes, but one that could not capture the sweet smell of spring mixed with a salt breeze coming gently from the harbor. All my senses were awake. I was damn near tingling.

There was time to stroll before my cocktail appointment with Ashley. I had a feeling I could use some fresh air and a clear head before the encounter. My nose followed the breeze and I walked into the garden where Charleston formed a point that edged into the harbor like a pugnacious chin jutting into the Atlantic, one that has taken more than a few hits from history. Facing the harbor is a statue honoring the Confederate defenders of Charleston. In this case the defender is naked and holding a shield. No wonder they lost the war.

The garden has seen less honorable events. In the early 1700s a famed pirate, Stede Bonnet, known as the 'Gentleman Pirate', and dozens of his crew were hanged. Seems some of the ladies of the town took pity on Bonnet. The governor didn't. They swung off before a large crowd. Charleston takes her justice and hangings seriously.

A sidewalk built up like a parapet along the water's edge was a promenade for Sunday strollers. The hard realities of this recent war didn't seem to be affecting the afternoon ritual. I stepped across the street and picked a spot on an empty bench for a better view of the parade. There is no doubt class distinctions are both embodied and embraced by the established families. It was evident at the party earlier. It was evident now. The difference in this one park, on this one sidewalk, is that the 'members only' sign was never erected and the social dandies and daily workers share the same space. You can tell the difference in the cut of their clothes, the tilt of their nose as they pass, or perhaps the pick of the litter. Neither butcher, baker, or candlestick maker would be caught dead walking that little poodle down the street.

The effete FiFi was on the end of a leash held by a thin hand with a ring reflecting light like a beacon in the harbor. A stiff white cuff projected from the edge of his coat. He walked like he had springs in his heels that made his head seem to bob against the sky. He wore a trim light colored suit that seemed a bit tight and adorned with a brash bow tie. Walking a half step back an attractive lady feigned disinterest. She was wearing a cream crepe skirt and a red fitted jacket, her face partially covered, or disguised, by a brimmed doeskin hat. He spoke over his shoulder. Her attention was elsewhere, anywhere. As she passed she caught my eye and lingered there for a second. It would appear a number of Charleston's women marry well, but not happily.

I stood to leave my bench as an elderly couple approached. He held his left arm up at the elbow. She had her arm intertwined. They moved slowly but with feet that glided across the sidewalk like a straightforward waltz. I stepped to the side and made a sweep of my arm offering up a private perch. With his right hand he touched the brim of his fedora. With her eyes she smiled. Love does grace this town. It was time to meet Ashley.

The Fort Sumter Hotel stood opposite the harbor at the far end of the park. I set a point on the front and headed across the open green. Thirty yards out I made two dark suits sitting in shade across from the main entrance. Changing directions I cut to come up behind them. Five feet behind the bench I spoke.

"Hello boys."

One jumped. He may have been dozing. The other vaguely turned his head and fixed me with a look that was intended to impress.

"Hello Marlow."

"You know my name? Must be because I'm a famous journalist."

"Don't get silly with yourself. We get paid to know stuff."

"Like what? Like what the two lovebirds are doing for dinner?"

"That's easy. It's always the same. Steak, mashed potatoes, peas and carrots and ice cream for dessert. Room service. They do their socializing in private."

"Except for you looking through the peephole?"

"We're a little more sophisticated than that."

"Oh my. You boys better get a stiff drink and a cold shower before you listen to that 'surveillance' if you know what I'm talking about."

"Be a pedestrian Marlow, move along. Your girl's already inside."

That one stopped me. He had me. He knew it. We both smiled. I walked away.

Stepping into the hotel the temperature dropped about twenty degrees. For one fleeting moment it felt like I'd stepped into a refrigerator. The lobby was large and seemed carved out of a single granite block that emitted cool air turned by large fans overhead. My feet padded along a well worn oriental runner that came to an intersection. To the left was the front desk. From the right a piano began playing a few opening notes. The singer's voice was familiar. I'd heard it once before. I followed the song.

> *There's a saying old, says that love is blind*
> *Still we're often told, 'seek and ye shall find'*
> *So I'm going to seek a certain lad I've had in mind.*

I entered on a Gershwin line that hung in the air, an opening verse, an opening salvo. She stood across the room leaning on a piano. Behind her a backdrop of shutters carved lines of light across the room like a tiger's stripes. Her eyes had the look of a big cat at play. Her chin dropped and she smiled as she picked up the next stanza.

> *Looking everywhere, haven't found him yet*
> *He's the big affair I cannot forget*
> *Only man I ever think of with regret.*

I had been lured into a trap. By sheer will I broke eye contact when a maitre d' approached as if on cue and ushered me towards a table just far enough away for safety, just close enough to be within her spell. He pulled the chair out for me. I didn't have the strength.

> *Won't you tell him please to put on some speed*
> *Follow my lead, oh, how I need*
> *Someone to watch over me.*

The last note ended high, held and floated across the room. There was a pause, an almost stunned silence, before a half filled room erupted in applause. It might just as well been empty. That song was an arrow meant for me.

Ashley leaned forward an inch to acknowledge the audience then turned and touched the pianist on the arm with one hand using the other to sweep the room as an acknowledgement for her partner. That brought a second smattering of applause. He was a young black man, quietly dressed, wearing a dark tie. They looked at each other. Both turned their gaze towards me. I was cooked.

Her dress was different from earlier. I'd finally noticed something besides her eyes. It was emerald satin, long, low cut with straight shoulders and gathered at her waist where a white belt enclosed a span I could almost circle with my hands. One long leg reached slightly to find the floor six inches below the small stage. The other took a trip to join it. The dress did a good job of offering a lovely outline as she moved. Her walk seemed more a stalk. It was direct and with purpose.

She approached the table. The maitre d' fluttered about while pulling a chair out for her. I was standing.

"Don't be silly. Sit down Sam. You look a little weak in the knees."

"Not sure if it was the girl or the Gershwin, an effective combination."

"Why thank you suh." She batted her eyelashes as she sat, "He was a genius. To think this little town inspired something like *Porgy and Bess* almost makes you proud. Almost."

The maitre d' was still fluttering, "George, would you bring us a couple whiskey and sodas?"

"Yes Miss Chambliss."

Another patron raised a hand towards George. I saw it. George saw it, but pretended not to see it and rushed off towards the bar.

"Offer a lady a cigarette?"

I wasn't getting burned on that one again and reached in my coat for my cigarette case, pulled out two and offered one. We mingled smoke across the table.

"You seem a little quiet for a New York fellow. It can't be good for business, newspaper man short on words."

"I'm just trying to adjust myself to the pace of Charleston."

"Then you'll end up a simpering idiot and of no interest to me."

"You don't seem to be defending the home front."

"What's not to love about Charleston? If you're here for a week, or a month, it's charming, colorful and eccentric. Spend a whole lifetime here and this small space starts to feel like a cage with the rest of the world just outside the bars. Unless you're one of the few who feel the bars are what keeps the rest of the world out. The inmates are enamored by their asylum."

"But you're here."

"Visiting. My family's here. It is my home and I do love it, especially when I'm in New York or Los Angeles. You see some people seem to like my singing."

"It seems the locals like you as well."

"And the reporter from New York?"

"Smitten."

"As you should be."

George appeared at our elbows and set down a couple of highballs. I raised my glass. We clinked rims.

"To your voice and the chance to hear it more often."

She smiled and fixed her eyes on mine.

"Like at dawn and the birdsong that begins the day?"

"That might be nice."

Ashley sipped. I drank. You can say what you like for your favorite cocktails, fancy things with cute names and frills. A whiskey and soda is an honest start to an evening. It leads to honest conversation.

"What's your angle with Kennedy?"

"How do you know so much about Kennedy and my interest in him?"

"You mean how do I know he's the reason you're here? How do I know you sat with him and his Danish pastry? How do I know what comes and goes within the walls of this hotel? I hate quoting myself, 'It's a small town, Mr. Marlow.' I could write it on a napkin you could refer to for every fourth question. Those two G-men don't know half the details of their torrid little affair. This town thrives on history and gossip."

"You can call me Sam."

That stopped her for a second. She reached her hand across the table and placed it on top of mine. I didn't move it. I liked it there.

"Sam I'm sorry. Sometimes my tongue gets a little ahead of my manners. That was almost rude. There's just been so much talk about those two, it seems a little beneath a man of your talents to be down here on a gossip piece."

I picked up a napkin and pretended to read it.

"Before I ask, 'How do you know about my talents?' Would the answer be, 'This is a small town?'"

She laughed. It was a musical sound and cut through the small chatter in the room. A couple of heads turned our way. The young pianist was moving towards the piano. He caught her eye. She grabbed my hand.

"Uh oh, Steven's about to start playing. Let's get out of here. That one song was not a prelude to a little night music. It had a sole purpose."

"Anyone we know?"

"Perhaps. Come on I'm taking you to dinner."

We stood up. I tossed some money on the table. Ashley wiggled a couple fingers goodbye towards Steven. He nodded his head and began the first notes of '*Lady Be Good*'. Couple of kidders.

Outside Ashley slipped her arm through mine as we walked down the steps to the street. The two feds were still in place, looking glum. I grinned as we turned and strolled towards the river. She opened the door of a beige colored Buick convertible sedan.

"Hop in. I'm driving."

The sun was heading toward the horizon and the air had an edge of chill to it. As we pulled away from the curb she hit a button on the dash and the roof began to rise and retract.

"I know a place down on the beach that's worth a little drive to get you out of town. Some fresh air and a run through the country might be fun."

The car accelerated through traffic. She drove without distraction, eyes forward with an occasional glance in the mirror. I watched her behind the wheel. She'd hiked her skirt a bit, legs splayed slightly for better command of the pedals, hands on the wheel. The Buick didn't seem to be a casual choice. Eight cylinders with dual carburetors meant she wanted power. She worked it well.

An open car isn't the place for intimate conversation and I didn't feel like yelling. Ashley must have felt the same. Her hand went to the radio. No surprise it was set to a music station. Count Basie came out swinging. Her head went back and face erupted in a grin. The same syncopated rhythm must have gone to her foot. The pedal went down and we launched off the Ashley River Bridge.

The road quickly left signs of the city behind. Straight stretches of blacktop shot through rigid barriers of ancient oaks. Above in their branches were the early signs of the leaves that would intertwine into canopies, forming avenues of shade. Shooting through the gauntlet, the trees flashed past like dark sentinels guarding their stretch of highway. Some showed signs of deep scars and gashes where vehicles strayed or challenged. The victors were still standing.

Soon the sentries fell behind. The road became a long thin causeway charting a course through an estuary. Sea air flooded the car in the rich odors of the earth and of the sea all mingled by the tide filling the flat spaces. Seagrass was waving in the breeze. I leaned back in my seat and closed my eyes. There may be many approaches to the sea; some flat and long that allow you miles to enjoy the transition from land to ocean. Others bring you to a brink, a precipice where you stand and look out. But close your eyes and your nose travels a direct route, arriving first. It was always that way with me as a child en route to the shore. The first smell of salt air from far away made my heart race, apace with all other senses, until we reached the ocean. Tonight I felt the same thrill.

My eyes opened as the car began to slow. We were entering a small beach town. A few clusters of cottages along the road. Ahead I could see the ocean. We turned to drive parallel to the beach and approached a large building built up and attached to a long pier that ran at least fifty yards beyond the breakers. She pulled into a space almost directly in front of steps to a restaurant. It seemed the season was still a bit early.

"Folly Beach sir, famous for bootleg whiskey, a short stay by George Gershwin and occasional appearances by Glenn Miller and Tommy Dorsey. Looks like tonight you and I might be the headliners."

We walked up the steps and through a pair of French doors. A maitre d' approached looking like he'd seen more exciting nights. He smiled when he saw Ashley.

"Good evening Miss Chambliss. If I'd known you were coming I could have gotten a real crowd in here."

"Sometimes it's just better to slip in unannounced."

"Yes ma'am. As you can see any table you like ma'am."

"How about by the window."

We walked through the place. A small three piece band was banging out some little melody. They saw Ashley and all smiled. A young couple was clutched on the dance floor. Their feet were nowhere near the rhythm. Their minds were someplace only two can go.

"Two whiskies and sodas please."

The words were out of my mouth almost before we were seated.

"Yes sir."

"Well there's little doubt about what you want," Ashley grinned as the maitre d' walked away.

"That was just the cocktail order."

"You seemed to relax a bit coming out here."

"Maybe it was the sea air. Maybe it was the woman driving. Both are a bit intoxicating."

"My seems like the reporter boy's getting his vocabulary back."

"Wait until the whiskey gets here. I may become positively effusive."

"Then let's get back to my question about Kennedy."

"Are you interviewing me?"

"Just trying to get to know you. Why are you interested in him?"

"Well, it's not the affair with as you said, his 'Danish pastry'."

"You would prefer maybe his 'little strudel'?"

"That's Austrian."

"So is Hitler. So maybe she is a spy."

"Funny. You and Hoover ought to get together. But getting away from little treats sprinkled in sugar, my interest in Kennedy is more about his interest in this war rather than his amour, if you'll excuse the phrase, it almost rhymes."

"Clever. Almost being the key phrase."

"Kennedy has a reputation as a skirt chaser. Must be hereditary. I would doubt any interest in Inga is likely to last more than a fortnight, especially with the pressure he's likely to be facing from his father. It would be interesting certainly, if Hoover could actually prove that she's a spy but I doubt that. I think Hoover sees a chance to use her against Joe Kennedy."

"That's my question. Neither you, nor your columns over the last months have been the kind of inside-Washington-gossip pieces that this feels like."

The waiter slipped up quietly with our drinks. But not quietly enough to prevent interrupting. They seem to have a knack for that. I picked up my glass and raised a toast, leaned back and took a sip. My eyes wandered outside. My thoughts followed.

"The fascinating thing about the Kennedys right now is their politics on the war. Joe Kennedy all but ran out of England a coward. He ran from the First World War. He's running from this one. His isolationist play fell flat. He's on the outs with Roosevelt. Number one son Joe Junior, follows in father's ideological footsteps as an isolationist, but signs up with the Navy and is in flight training. Number two son writes a book about England's failure to prepare for war. Now he's an ensign stuck on the sidelines with a married woman and two gumshoes listening in on his amorous evenings. Where is he going? That's what I'm interested in, not what he's doing here and now."

"The Fighting Kennedys. That sounds like a campaign poster."

"It might very well be, but this war is going to come between the Kennedys and their next campaign."

I paused and took another sip of my drink. This time the waiter seemed to be looking for a sign and was at the table before my drink was down.

"Would you like to order dinner sir?"

"Ashley you know this place. Any suggestions?"

"It's a bit early for shrimp so let's start you with she-crab soup. Then I think a dozen local oysters and followed with a small filet mignon. If you would, Jamie, please bring us a glass of champagne with the oysters and ask Andre if he still has a bottle of Chateau Latour for the steaks."

"Yes ma'am." He made pronto for the kitchen.

"Sounds delicious. My trust was well placed."

"You should never doubt that. But on the subject of the local food, everyone seems to love the she-crab soup here. The local oysters I'd put up against some of the best on either coast. And steak, it just kind of feels like a steak and Bordeaux kind of night."

The soup came out quickly. It was rich and thick.

"The old story about this soup around Charleston is that William Howard Taft was visiting Mayor Rhett some thirty years ago. The Mayor asked his butler to 'dress up' the soup. He added crab roe for color and flavor. It's hard to find a restaurant or a local home that doesn't serve it now."

"I don't suppose Taft was too worried about the abundance of butter and cream. It's delicious."

Oysters and champagne followed, two of my favorites. It was cheap, it was uncivil, but I tossed her a leading question so she'd have to carry the conversation.

"You have a lovely voice. You apparently travel, perform and I would imagine have a good following wherever you go. How did that start from living in Charleston?"

"My mother's fault. She was a singer, opera actually. A small town girl who had roles with the Metropolitan. She was in the chorus of *La Boheme* once when Caruso played Rodolfo. I heard Caruso's voice before my father's. He was always playing in the house. She performed and toured, but all of the places she performed never meant as much to her as Charleston. So she returned. I was to be the protégé. Sent to Juilliard to study, some actually thought I had talent. Then one night I went to Harlem. Ella Fitzgerald was at the Savoy. A switch flipped. Opera was work. Jazz was a passion. Which do you prefer Sam?"

"I always found work to be overrated."

The waiter's timing was getting better. He showed up with the Latour, a '29 which was a far better bottle of wine than I would have expected. He uncorked and poured. It was magnificent.

"This is a nice place, but a Latour '29?"

"Charleston has a long history of importing and hoarding good wines. At one time Madeira was not only the *preferred* beverage, it was sometimes the *only* beverage because the water was unfit to drink. Andre keeps a short list of good wines for good customers."

"Yay for Andre. We held glasses in salute then clinked together."

The chef did a nice job with the steaks, asparagus on the side with Hollandaise. Sometimes simple is best.

"And you Sam? What mysterious influence created the writer?"

I hit the highlights. With the taste of the wine and the face of a woman who became more beautiful with each instant of candlelight, I was feeling like the least interesting topic in the room.

"My father was, or is, an attorney of note in New York. I suppose like you, I was to follow in the footsteps. Enrolled in Harvard, a few years *before* Kennedy mind you, heading towards a degree and law school I found myself less interested in the law and more interested in those who cover the law. Mencken was a mentor, not just for his reportage, but for his prose in the Scopes trial. It's a rare thing for the two to mix. The Leopold and Loeb trial was an odd mix of reporting and involving the press in the trial process. Then there was the Lindbergh kidnapping trial. Even Mencken called it, 'the greatest story since the resurrection'. It was part trial, part circus and as such it was a circus maximus. I was already on the street, skipping law school and covering the trial of the century."

"So to our families, we're both just little lost lambs."

"Baa, baa, black sheep."

We were sitting in a Hollywood booth that faced out toward the ocean. Ashley dropped her napkin on the table and slid around to sit next to me, putting her hand on top of mine as our shoulders touched. We sipped more wine and shared some stories of our time in New York. We were lucky. The band was on break. The place was almost empty. Waves were breaking on the beach outside.

Ashley spoke.

"The wine is making me bold."

That line came out of nowhere.

"Feeling fearless?"

"Depending on what I may confront."

"Easy there paperboy. I'm talking patriotic duty."

"I'm not sure what you're talking about."

"Sub spotting, out there in the ocean. You never know when a periscope might pop up. Let's walk out on the pier."

"Sounds dangerous."

"You may very well be in moral danger."

"You mean mortal danger?"

"Nope."

She stood up. The waiter appeared out of some hidden corner.

"Would you have Andre put that on my bill?"

"Now wait a minute.."

"I said I was taking you to dinner. Take notes next time."

There was no arguing. I dropped some money on the table for a tip. We walked out a back door directly onto the pier. Outside were no lights, no moon. It was a long walk into darkness. The tide was coming in. For the first twenty yards we could reference the white of the breakers against the beach. Then it was a matter of following the slight distinction of shade between the pier and the sea. The spring breeze off the water held more than a chill. I pulled Ashley closer to me and we walked slowly arm in arm. A rail was all that stopped us from walking off the edge and into the surf. She leaned an elbow against the wood and shivered slightly.

"It seems the only danger here is a risk of frostbite."

I slipped my coat off and wrapped it around her shoulders. My arms were still up when she turned slightly, there seemed to be little choice but to finish the embrace. She was so close in the darkness that I could barely see her face, but I could feel her warmth against me. The sea air was mixed with the scent of her hair and cologne, one so light it seemed a part of her.

"Are you afraid of the dark?"

The voice was almost smiling.

"Just the unknown."

"Then you should know this."

She pressed into me as her head raised and her lips found mine in the dark. I thought the Latour was nice in a glass. It tasted better on her. The kiss lingered. I could think of no better circumstance that could be achieved on a dock. She pulled away slightly, so slightly that we still touched. I kissed her lightly on the top lip.

"It may take me awhile to know that fully."

"Take your time writer boy."

She spun in my arms so that we both faced the ocean. There's something about combined body heat against the cold. Looking outward there was little definition between sea and sky. It was a perfect night for German submarines working off the coast. Ashley had been joking to lure me to the pier but the threat was real. U-boats were thick up and down the Atlantic taking a horrific toll against merchant ships. Our chance of spotting one tonight was about as good as spotting the lights of London some four thousand miles away.

"You're not thinking about the sweet taste of my lips right now are you?"

Intuition had raised a periscope more perilous than a German sub.

"For the briefest of moments I imagined a flash of light, of fire across the water. A ship under attack. Europe under attack. The world under attack. Maybe just the product of my vivid imagination. We could stand on this shore gazing at the Atlantic or on Malibu and look to the Pacific. Two wars are closing in on this country."

"I'm not sure I like where this is going."

"It's just beginning. Millions of Americans are going to have to fight or first Europe will fall and then the Pacific. We either win, or perish. Jack Kennedy is just one person, one story. Every home in this country will either send a son or know someone who has. Every town will muster its young and soon every window will hold a candle. They are all going."

Again she turned in my arms. I could feel her breath on my face.

"And so I imagine, are you."

CHAPTER 4

Charleston, S.C.
April 5, 1942

I N DAWN'S EARLY LIGHT I was remembering the night before. The sun was edging above the horizon red and brilliant. The Rising Sun. War has robbed the day of its innocence.

Standing on the pier last night with the whole of the country behind me the war seemed closer. The perspective can change once you get outside Manhattan to that larger place where America really exists. But in Manhattan, in the smoky newsrooms, with shouts and tickers and the occasional bell announcing a headline *that* is where the image of war is being shaped. My colleagues in their comfortable offices know as much about the fighting soldier as a general in the War Department. This war is too large to grasp as a whole. Last night overwhelmed on the edge of a pier it seemed to me that the story of the war is what is seen through one man's eyes. It could be the foot soldier on the front lines in Europe, it could be the welder in a shipyard, or it might just be a Senator's son. The rest of the press corps could compete for the big headline. In my mind the story Americans might want to hear would come from the mouths of their boys doing the fighting.

All the thoughts of the morning weren't on war. Some were on the opposite. Driving home last night Ashley offered a brilliant balance to her well honed wit. She listened while I spoke of armies and navies, planes and ships, battles a half world away. Then she spoke of two wars in Charleston and the graves of the soldiers, some lying over a century beneath their granite headstones, some only decades. It was where I was heading this morning.

Any glimpse of Charleston is going to be imprinted with the steeples that rise above the city. It's no small reason they've deemed themselves the 'Holy City'. Each peak that reaches towards heaven marks the spirits of the living and the dead. Find a steeple find a graveyard. Not a difficult task.

Ashley had suggested Church Street. I turned the corner of Broad at the top of the street and stopped. The sun had risen slightly. Large clouds behind the steeple were painted in pink framing St. Phillips. It was a church set down a row of buildings that would be called ancient in America. Some might see such beauty as a sign. The signs are always there. It's simply a matter of looking.

This church was started in 1710. A hurricane and Indian war delayed the first service until 1723. According to church record the next decade and a half was followed by fires, hurricanes, epidemics of smallpox, yellow fever, slave uprisings, Indian attacks and threats of war from the Spanish. The church had good reason to have two graveyards. The strictures of local society are such that to be buried in the church graveyard you had to be born in Charleston. Otherwise you were buried across the street. Even John C. Calhoun, seventh Vice President of the United States and US Senator was buried on one side of the street. His wife born in Charleston was buried opposite, next to the church.

Some cemeteries are hallowed ground, Gettysburg and Flanders Field. Others historic ground as this one in Charleston. Azaleas color the corners of the brick and iron enclosed space. Tree branches overhang dangling wisps of Spanish moss. I walk through stopping, stooping to read inscriptions worn by hundreds of years. It's amazing to see inscriptions that start in the late 1600's. Some bear names of those on sacred scrolls of the nation; Edward Rutledge on the Declaration of Independence; Charles Pinckney on the Constitution. There are also the monuments to men of war. General William Moultrie offered the British an early and rare defeat in the Revolution. Other names less well known except to their families, their cause and to God.

Alfred Manigault
Born in
Charleston, So.Ca.
Died in
Military Service at
Winnsboro, So. Ca. 1780
Aged 24 years

J.E. McPherson Washington, Lieut. Confederate States Army
Died at Monterey, Highland Co., Va.
August 25,1861
Aged 24 yrs

Edward Percy Guerard Jr.
Sept 7 1888 – Dec 12 1915
27
Drafted, full powered, into the
Overseas service of the infinite

Three sons of Charleston, three different wars and three different tales with the same ending writ on their headstones. Each carried to the grave his own impression of the battles survived and the one he didn't.

I slipped back from a stoop into a seat leaning against an old, worn crypt. Soft light was filtering in through the trees and I let my mind wander through the wars. Two of these men died defending their homelands. One died so far from home in a war that measured casualties in the millions. In three different centuries, each war with its own tactics, its own new war machines. The end was no different from either a lead musket ball on a sunny day or gas drifting across trenches in a landscape blasted, cold and desolate. My eyes were half closed, images from a different time and place projected on a half screen of a graveyard on a spring morning. In the corner of my vision a flash of white but of which world? I tried to focus. It moved again between two monuments. I jumped.

Laughter, either haunting or taunting, "Looks like you've seen a ghost there paperboy."

"Dammit Ashley! You can't be wandering around here like Hamlet's ghost!"

"Can't think of a better place for a ghost. Seen any of my people around here?"

I tried to rise from the ground with as much dignity as possible, brushing a bit of dirt and grass from my seat. Ashley walked towards me smiling, taking my hands and leaning inwards to kiss my cheek. She was wearing a brilliantly white blouse and dark slacks.

"Is it possible that you wore that white blouse with the notion you might spook a poor suitor?"

"Why sir," she went with the eyelashes again, "You must think I'm devious."

"Mischievous is what comes to mind."

"Did you find anything helpful here?"

"Contrary to popular belief dead men do tell tales. Though these were unspoken. I believe these young men will help me find the voices in the stories I seek."

"Sounds rather solemn so early in the morning," she held out her hand, "Come on. Let's go have breakfast."

We walked up Queen Street past homes and shops intermingled. Some needed a bit of paint and polish, or perhaps it was a perpetual stage of arrogant shabbiness. Across the corner an attractive hotel looked promising. We headed that way.

"Thought we'd have breakfast at the Mills House," Ashley walked through a door opened by a man in liveries, "Ever been here before?"

"Not in this lifetime."

The lobby had the familiar look of solid, century old buildings anywhere plenty of marble and brass, somewhere between hotel and bank. I nodded to an old woman perched in an armchair as we passed.

A young boy was walking past with newspapers underarm. I tossed the kid a dime and grabbed a paper as he walked past. All in one fluid motion. He was a pro. The headlines were inescapable, the Philippines were about to fall and the Japs were moving on to Bataan. The Germans not suited with just strategic bombing but seemed to be striking some of the Britain's most revered historical sites. We couldn't get a win and I began to wonder how soon Roosevelt would begin to feel the reality of the world closing in. Like Churchill when London was coming down around him. I slammed the paper shut and stuck it under my arm.

"Guess you didn't make it to the funny pages."

"They should start putting them on the front page. Might give folks something to look forward to in the morning. There doesn't seem to be much positive coming out of this war."

"That my friend would be where you come in."

We took a table in a courtyard warmed by the morning sun and colored with the spring flowers placed just to brighten the mood. Grim made a comeback when the waiter approached.

"Good morning, sir. Miss Chambliss. I apologize but must inform you that while it's not mandatory we are beginning to reduce our menu offerings due to rationing efforts and to help our men in uniform."

"We certainly understand," Ashley began, "I'll just have black coffee."

"I'll be slightly less patriotic. Would you bring me a soft boiled egg, dry toast and black coffee."

"Yes sir." He walked away with an order that wasn't enough to even write down.

"So last night was a last splurge?" I asked.

"Maybe. It will be a little while before rationing really impacts Charleston. Some are just trying to get used to it early. Others like my mother, poor dear, are a little confused about the whole process. She proclaimed this morning that we'd better use it all before the Yankees come to take it away. By the way you're invited to sup-puh. Not to be confused with din-nuh."

"What's the difference?"

She continued with her thickened accent, "Well, Suh, down he-uh din-nuh is served at mid-DAY. It's ow-uh big meal. Sup-puh is in the evening. Cocktails at five-thirty."

The last line in plain English.

Our Spartan breakfast arrived and we talked over coffee not of the war front but the home front and families.

"Oh to me it seems so dull. This little town and these small circles. My family has been here fo-evah. My real name is Ashley Huger Middleton

Chambliss. Seems every time families cross breed here the poor child carries an increasing length of lineage. And all those names carry an obligation to associate with those who consider themselves 'Charleston society'. You saw some of them yesterday at the party. The same people at the same parties season after season. Sometimes like yesterday I go into this trance like state. I'm singing and looking out at the people and realize that except for the music and the dress these are the same people, of the same families, at the same parties that stretch back a couple centuries. I wonder sometimes if they are actually alive or if we're all just caught in some circular scene that plays again and again and again through time."

"You don't seem to relish the role."

"I love my family and their eccentricities but never really cared about fitting in. We grow up in private schools, trained to be 'ladies' and 'presented' at the St. Cecilia Ball. Most of my girlfriends follow that track like a religion or a profession. I was always a little bit different. Music was always important but I spent a lot of time outdoors growing up down on our little plantation riding horses, hunting and fishing.

"Our little plantation? You poor dear what happened to the 'big plantation' the Yankees get it?"

"Yankee boy hush yo mouth," she laughed, "I suppose that sounds a bit smug. In perspective our place is a few hundred acres on the Cooper River. It's not one of the storied places with thousands of acres and a huge plantation house. What about you city boy?"

"An odd coincidence occurred to me last night. While you were studying at Juilliard I was living in the same neighborhood."

"Where?"

"Riverside Drive and Tiemann. It's an old building facing the Hudson."

"Really? Practically on the same block and you had to come all the way to Charleston to meet me. Was that the same building where Chaplin lived?"

"Actually I live in Chaplin's old apartment."

"I'm sure those walls have some tales."

"I try to keep them talking."

"Where are your parents?"

"In New York on the East Side. I tried to put some distance between us. In a sense, as you say, it's a small town. My father's legal interests were largely in the financial sector. He represented some of the notable investment houses in New York. It worked well for him and paid a bit better than criminal law. Our 'little plantation' is a small farm on Long Island. My father practiced law but loves horses. He raised a few steeplechase winners with the help of Tommy Hitchcock."

"You're name dropping."

"Just the facts ma'am. Since no son can follow too closely in his father's footsteps, I spent more time playing polo, though not quite at the level of the Hitchcocks, senior or junior."

"You know that whole group winters down here in Aiken."

"So I've heard."

"Now *you're* being smug."

I leaned forward, "Which is why we get along so well."

We were about to spend the whole morning talking when I got the notion I might consider doing a little work and get some sort of a story back to New York. It wasn't going to be Kennedy copy because I needed to track him down for another conversation. That was something I needed to figure out soon.

"What do you know about Kennedy's whereabouts?"

"I know he and a few other officers have rented a house out on Sullivan's Island. I'll see what else I can find out by this evening."

"Thanks. I had a thought about a story. Isn't the Coast Guard base somewhere downtown?"

"Over on Tradd Street. We can almost see it from the house. The base commander's been to the house for drinks. I'll have my father call over and let him know you might stop by."

"I guess there are some advantages to living in a small town."

"Glad to be of service to our brave war correspondents."

"Then think you could get me in with Admiral Nimitz?"

"Not unless he anchors in Charleston harbor."

"I think he's a little tied up in the Pacific."

We walked out to the street like we had breakfast at the same hotel every morning.

"See you at five-thirty, suh."

"Thank you ma'am. You really will get in touch with the base commander?"

"He'll be expecting you."

She left me standing amazed on the street corner.

The 'sub sighting' expedition of the night before raised the real prospect of a story. I walked down to one of the local newspaper offices to see if they'd let me look at some back issues. The *Evening Post* was from a lineage of papers that covered the shelling of Fort Sumter. My guess was that they'd have more than a passing interest in another war delivered on their waterfront.

History left her mark on the exterior of the offices. Like so many places downtown clinging to the past the paper's outside seemed to suggest that any attempt to modernize would simply be, tasteless. The inside suggested otherwise. Stepping through the door the reception area was large and attractive. The outer roughness continued inside but the rough brick walls and wooden beams offered an atmosphere of aged elegance. A half wall of polished wood was topped by glass framed panels separating the reception area from the newsroom. Beyond the glass I could see my world; rows of desks and typewriters, reporters on the phone and a low cloud of cigarette smoke. A smartly dressed man approached from inside and opened the door which released the sound of pounding keys and the clatter of a teletype.

"Miss Chapman," the man began, then looked at me, " Oh, sir, I'm sorry if I interrupted."

"No apologies needed. I just walked in."

"Ahh, I'm Tom Waring the editor here."

"I'm Sam Marlow with the *New York Herald Tribune*."

He walked forward and extended his hand.

"Mr. Marlow so nice to meet you. I heard you were in town."

I didn't ask.

"How can we help you here at the *Evening Post?*"

"Well I was considering a piece on the Nazi sub attacks nearby and wanted to have a look at a few back issues to see if anything recent was of interest."

"Oh my God," he exclaimed, took three steps and grabbed me by the elbow, "Come with me."

He whisked me through the doors to the newsroom so fast that my last look back into the lobby was an image of Miss Chapman with her mouth agape and one finger in the air.

"Come into my office."

He pulled me through the newsroom where a couple of reporters looked up out of curiosity, then went on about their business. Waring's office was halfway down the newsroom. Like the front, it was a half wall with the top glassed in to allow a clear view of the mania on the other side. Once he closed the door it became a sanctum.

"Funny you should show up looking into a local angle. Perfect timing. Perfect."

The office was fairly orderly for an editor, or at least the ones from my experience. Past editions of his newspaper were hung on neat racks like suits in a store. He started fanning through them.

"Aha! Here it is."

He pulled a paper out and laid it across his desk and with the same movement swept up a pipe that he shoved into the corner of his mouth. Then he stood back pointing at the headline.

"The SS *John D. Gill* just a few weeks ago. She came through Charleston on March eleventh. Reported she was being tailed by a submarine. Just after noon the next day she was given the clear and sailed out headed for Philadelphia. She was a huge oil tanker over 500 feet long carrying crude. Just after nine o'clock that night she took a torpedo into her amidships near Frying Pan Shoals northeast of here. Forty nine men were on board. Twenty three died."

He handed the paper to me. I'd never heard the story. One ship on a long list of merchant vessels sunk. At this point hundreds a month were falling prey to the German U-boats. This was a large ship said to be the largest sunk off the coast of the Carolinas. The cargo exploded. The crew of the merchant ship showed the stuff of heroes. That was my story.

Waring was just putting a match to his pipe when I came bolt upright out of my chair. His eyes bugged out a bit.

"Tom this is amazing. Simply an amazing story. Thank you. I was heading down to the Coast Guard base anyway. Now I have a target."

"Our pleasure. If any such story can make a national paper like yours, we're all the better."

"I'd really like to stay and talk.."

"Please, I can see it in your eyes. You've got a story. It's a crazed look good reporters get. Wish I saw it more around here."

The Coast Guard base was a short distance across the peninsula on the Ashley River side. I was at the gate after a brisk fifteen minute walk. The guard gave me a wary look.

"I'm Sam Marlow with the *New York Herald Tribune* here to see Commander Williams."

"He's expecting you, sir. Head to the main building by the dock. They'll direct you to his office."

I walked on a base that had the appearance of a small naval facility. Vessels tied to the dock were painted in a similar gray to help conceal them at sea. It appeared that most of the cutters were out. Ships at dock could do little work against the Germans. I was shown into the Commander's waiting room. It was standard issue; metal chairs, metal desk and metal cabinets. A seaman walked out of the office.

"Commander Williams will see you sir."

The Commander's office was just as hard looking as the waiting room. So was the Commander.

"Mr. Marlow. Welcome to Charleston. We don't see too many New York reporters down here."

"Maybe better reporters would find better stories about the Coast Guard."

He smiled at that one. I could recall few stories in the papers in recent months that made any mention of what some in the military might call the 'home forces'. With a history that goes back to the late 1700's, the Coast Guard didn't become a branch of the military until 1915. With Europe falling and the Japanese overrunning the Pacific many people didn't see the threat close to our own shores.

"We appreciate your attention and happy to help as I can but you understand that I can't discuss details of our operations."

"Understood, sir."

"Fire away with your questions."

"Reading the local papers, it would seem you've been a bit busy of late."

That got a laugh.

"The Jerries don't want us in this war and seem to be doing their damndest to sink everything going to support the effort. It's hard to keep track and I wouldn't want to try to guess the numbers of the ships sunk and men and materials lost, but I can tell you one thing, it's a brave man who steps on deck and heads out into those waters."

"Are your crews doing a lot of rescue operations?"

"More than we'd like. That means Jerry's got a kill. We prefer hunting him before he strikes us. We chase sightings, drop charges, get an occasional chance to strafe him from the air."

"What about the *John D. Gill*?"

He leaned back in his chair. It creaked. No oil for rusty chairs during this war.

"That was a bad one. The ship reported a U-boat tailing it as it sailed up the east coast. We ordered her in here. Patrols went out hunting and found no sign. So we sent her on her way. The sub must have been waiting and nailed her with a torpedo northeast of here. They say you could see the flames from Wilmington beach. We sent a cutter up for survivors and brought most of them back here to Charleston. Some were in pretty bad shape."

"Newspaper reports mentioned one sailor on the merchant ship that was noted for his bravery."

"Able Seaman Cheney, he's here."

"Could I talk with him?"

"He's got some bad burns but can talk. He's up the street in a hospital. The Coast Guard doesn't have medical facilities."

"If possible, could I talk with one of your men who was on the rescue?"

"That would be good. SEAMAN CLARK!" He yelled to the outer office.

"Yes sir." Clark appeared in the doorway.

"Check the roster for March 13 and find a seaman who can talk with Mr. Marlow."

"Yes sir."

We talked in a roundabout way of the Coast Guard's challenge. They had thousands of miles of coast to cover and millions of square miles of sea. The Germans had the definite advantage. It was beginning to show in the numbers. U-boats began their hunt for ships in open sea in 1939 and became more aggressive year to year. The Commander wasn't giving me hard numbers, but did suggest that unless something changed the Germans were on track to triple their kills this year. Like every other front facing the military, it wasn't looking good.

I heard two sets of footsteps coming up the hall in double time. Seaman Clark appeared with a young looking petty officer.

"Petty Officer Third Class Charles Hutchings, *sir.*"

"At ease petty officer. This is Sam Marlow, he's a newspaperman from New York and has come all this way just to talk to you."

His eyes got wide. The Commander smiled.

"I want you to walk Marlow up to the hospital where able seaman Cheney is. You can talk on the way."

"Yes *sir.*"

"And petty officer if I read anything in the *Herald Tribune* bad about the Coast Guard you'll spend the next six months scraping barnacles off ships."

"Aye sir."

Petty Officer Third Class Hutchings led the way. He was either able or enlisted early because he looked barely eighteen.

"How old are you petty officer?"

"Nineteen sir."

"Where you from?"

"Rome, Georgia sir."

"Where's that?"

"Northwest Georgia, sir, little spot where that Sherman fellow kind of started his march to the sea."

"Seems both of you ended up here."

"I suppose so sir."

"Why did you join the Coast Guard?"

"I'm the youngest of five sons. My father didn't stop us from signing up but said we'd have to each pick a different branch."

"So you got the Coast Guard."

"Sir, the Coast Guard got me is the way I look at it."

"You made petty officer pretty quickly."

"Things seem to happen pretty quickly these days. Once you get past seaman training, if you know what you're doing, you can move up pretty fast. "

We were walking back up the peninsula passing a small lake surrounded by a broad walkway, framed by palm trees and handsome houses. Two little boys played by the edge of the lake their black mammies sitting on a nearby bench watching closely. On the water a boat was under attack. The boys lobbed rocks high to splash on either side.

"Bombs away," from one young voice.

"Opening machine guns," from the other as he picked up a handful of pebbles and sprayed them across the boat.

Their young voices had a frightening echo of reality. I hoped this war would end before their young commands might become real.

The hospital was part of the medical school just beyond the lake.

"The seaman was brought here for his burns. It was closer than the naval hospital."

Cheney was on a second floor wing. There were several men strolling the hall in various wraps and bandages. It looked like able seaman Cheney wasn't the only victim of Nazi subs spending time on the ward.

"He's down here in the end room. Got himself a corner room with a view. Had to have a room with a telephone what with the White House calling and all."

We walked in. Cheney was propped up in his bed. His head wrapped except for his mouth and eyes. His arms were covered in bandages and resting on a stack of pillows. Underneath each. When he saw Hutchings he raised one arm an inch. It was the best he could do.

"Hutch."

The Petty Officer raised a half salute.

"Cheney. How's the nurses?"

"Couple kind of cute ones. Don't do me a damn bit of good. Can't grab a thing with these arms all wrapped up like this."

"President call today?"

"Nope reckon he's a bit busy."

Two kids, kidding. One was being awarded one of the war's first medals.

"Cheney, this here's Mr. Sam Marlow with the *New York Herald Tribune* he wants to ask you a few questions about the *John D. Gill* ."

Dateline: Charleston, S.C., April 5, 1942
Sam Marlow/New York Herald Tribune

You don't have to travel far to find a hero in this war because the front is a lot closer than you might think. This old town is facing new invaders. They come in the night prowling just off the shore, hunting like a pack of wolves on lone prey with few defenses. German U-boats are taking a terrible toll on our merchant fleet.

In Charleston I found both the war and a hero.

Able seaman Ed Cheney Junior lies in a bed in a Charleston hospital wrapped up like an Egyptian mummy and wise cracking with nurses like, well, an able bodied seaman. But he's a lucky seaman like twenty six others on his ship who survived after being torpedoed in the dark of night. Twenty three of his crewmates died. That number might have been a lot higher, except for the young man bandaged in white and propped up before me.

On March 11th the SS John D. Gill was headed up the coast with a load of Texas crude bound for Philly. They saw a sub tailing and pulled into Charleston for the night. The Coast Guard sent out a plane and a cutter to search for the boat but it takes a pretty dumb Jerry to show himself during the day. On March 12th the Gill headed back to sea.

Seaman Cheney says at 10 o'clock that night he and one of the young fellows from the engine room were having coffee in the mess. The young wiper was wondering out loud what he'd do if the ship was ever hit by a torpedo. Ten minutes later he found out.

The torpedo hit amidships and knocked them out of their chairs. All hands scrambled to the deck. To stern the crew of navy gunners was sighting down their weapon hoping to get a shot at the sub.

The torpedo hit released a gusher of oil. The good thing about Texas crude is that it has a high component of gasoline. The bad thing for the Gill is that a life preserver tossed overboard had a self-igniting carbide flare. The sea erupted in flames.

All prepared to abandon ship except for the navy gunners who still wanted a crack at the Jerries. Seaman Cheney managed to get one life boat into the water and leapt into the fire, swimming underwater to push the boat out of the flames. He called to survivors and lead them beyond the inferno. Then he swam back through the fire to help those who couldn't make it.

Most of the survivors were badly burned but they still had to row beyond the reach of both the flames and ship so they wouldn't be pulled down when she sank. For hours they watched the Gill drop lower into the water. The fire burning around her so bright it could be seen 25 miles away on the shore.

At dawn the Coast Guard found the survivors. Both crews watched as the Gill disappeared beneath the surface.

President Roosevelt called able seaman Ed Cheney. He's going to receive the war's first Merchant Marine Distinguished Service Medal.

Funny thing, able seaman Cheney doesn't think he's a hero.

I risked wearing out my welcome and swung back by the *Evening Post* to file my story back to New York. The risk didn't seem too great.

"Mr. Marlow so nice to see you back," Miss Chapman rose from her seat. Both a welcoming gesture and an opportunity to see a little better. She was a platinum blonde but the color didn't seem to have leached her brains. Her one piece dress was cut for attention which I doubt she lacked in an office full of reporters.

"Good afternoon, Miss Chapman. Is Mr. Waring about?"

"Yes, of course. He's on deadline. I'll buzz him. Please go in."

I walked through the door as Waring walked out of his office.

"Sam that was pretty quick. Get what you needed?"

"Cheney was great. I didn't want to stay too long. He's still pretty beat up. I ran back by my room and the story pretty much wrote itself. I was wondering if I could use your teletype to send it to New York."

"Certainly. But here, hand me your story. I'll get someone to type it for you. Let's wait in my office."

Miss Chapman did the honors. Waring and I talked more about the *Gill* incident and other reports on Coast Guard action around Charleston. I had a notion that there would be more stories and asked him to let me know if he heard of anything. There was a light knuckle on the door.

"Story's off to New York Mr. Marlow. It was a very touching piece," she looked out the window. "Wish some of our guys could write like that."

"Hmmm," Waring place his pipe in his mouth, "That's not light praise Sam. Don't let the hair color fool you. She's a pretty sharp critic."

"Why thank you, Miss Chapman. That's very kind."

I smiled. She smiled. I started wondering what a newspaper job might pay in Charleston. Waring caught my eye, and my drift, and laughed.

"Sam I believe you've got a cocktail engagement."

"How did you know? Let me guess, it's a small town."

"Evening cocktails at the Chambliss house is a standing invitation. We'll see you there

"Then see you in a bit."

A fast walk across Charleston is a waste of too many beautiful images but there was no time for a stroll. I was staying in a carriage house next to the home of some family friends. The Stoneys lived on Murray Boulevard, the avenue that runs along the Ashley River and forms one part of what locals call the Battery. It's a street lined by some of the city's most beautiful homes. That's saying a lot in Charleston. It was no surprise to discover that Ashley lived around the corner on East Battery in a home that had already struck me as beautiful even before I knew she lived there.

I was back in my room in fifteen minutes. The day seemed like a whirl, from a graveyard in the morning to the Coast Guard, hospital, newspaper and now off to cocktails. I showered quickly put on a new suit, fresh shirt and was knotting my tie when there was a banging started up on my door.

"Marlow, he-ah son. You in there?"

It was my host Thomas P. Stoney. Like most of those who lived along these streets, Thomas P. came from a long and colorful family in Charleston. He was a two term mayor. His namesake had left the family history behind and went to California in the 1800s. Well educated, he tried and failed as a miner. Then took up law. He went one step further and married a northern girl. When the War of 'Northern Aggression' began he came back to South Carolina and fought with his brothers. Equally as daring, his wife convinced the captain of a blockade runner to help reunite her with her husband. She sailed a dangerous passage to arrive behind Southern lines. The Thomas P. outside my door was a man of short stature and patience.

"Marlow, he-ah son. Open the door."

I did.

"Looks like you're just getting up son. You writers can't sleep all day and get anything done. He-ah. Heard you were invited to the Chambliss house for drinks. Let's walk together."

He headed out like a banty rooster, head forward and feet working to keep up. I grabbed my coat and ran to catch him. Thomas P. was a friend of my father's. Some association and lifetime brotherhood that grows out of boy's boarding schools. When they grew older they stayed connected through horses. The Stoneys at the time owned a plantation called Medway with a thoroughbred track. Sometimes my father would send his horses down for the winter.

"Marlow, he-ah." He looked around to see if I'd caught up.

"I told your father I'd keep an eye on you. Now you better watch yourself with that Chambliss girl. She's broke a string of boys here in Charleston."

That made me smile for some reason, "Yes sir, I'll try to."

He was walking like a New Yorker. We were at the house in minutes. Approaching along East Battery the Chambliss home was one of few that had an adjacent extra lot that was used as a free standing garden. A high pink wall led to the house three stories high of the same eye catching color. Each floor opened out to a large veranda that overlooked the harbor. I wanted to be up on that veranda. Stoney approached the door without slowing his step. His knuckles were knocking before they touched the thick wood of the door. It opened on the first rap.

Ashley was standing halfway up the stairs. Her dress hung from her shoulders, squared and cascading downwards, stopping to accentuate each wonderful curve that was offered teasingly by a cut here, a drape there. It was a light colored satin. She wore red lipstick. Somewhere beside me there was a buzzing that was Thomas P.'s voice.

I couldn't hear it. Ashley's voice rang like a bell.

"Why Mr. Stoney, Mr. Marlow welcome."

"Ashley honey, where's your father I need to talk to him."

"Mr. Stoney you know where my father is, second floor parlor."

"Marlow, he-ah, stop looking like you've never seen a girl before. I warned you."

Mr. Stoney bounded up past Ashley and disappeared around a curve in the staircase.

"He warned you?"

"He warned me."

"Smart man that Mr. Stoney. Come on up Sam. Welcome to the oh-so-social Charleston."

We walked up the stairs together. She took my arm and we walked into a large parlor that opened onto the veranda. The parlor faced the harbor. The room extended back to show an adjacent dining room. Food was set on the table for an informal buffet. I could see ham on one end, a leg of lamb on the other, in between were various greens, pickles and a couple large plates of biscuits. On a highboy were several decanters of wine.

Scattered about all the rooms were people in stages of posing, as in a Toulouse-Lautrec painting. Tom Waring saw me and raised his hand. The other hand was around Miss Chapman. Nice. They walked our way.

"Sam you left without taking the copy of your article this afternoon. I took the liberty of reading it. Miss Chapman was correct. It's a fine take on a story that no one here even considered."

Miss Chapman smiled.

"You filed already?" Ashley asked, one eyebrow arched.

"Told you the morning was inspiring."

"I'd love to read something that gained the approval of the esteemed Miss Chapman."

This time the other eyebrow went up. She was working them effectively.

Waring reached into his coat pocket, "Here's the copy you left, Sam."

It was intercepted by two well manicured fingers.

"Thank you Tom. If you'll excuse us for a moment, we'll step outside."

She took my elbow and steered me through the tall French doors that opened to the veranda. We were near the front of the house and closest to the harbor. The view was spectacular.

"See something you like?"

I looked towards her.

"Take my arm for a minute."

We turned towards the harbor and looked out at Fort Sumter. It was where a war began. Somewhere out there enemy submarines were posing a threat that was real and present. But for now it was just a beautiful harbor at sunset.

"What are we doing?" Ashley asked.

"Pretending. Pretending that there is no war. Pretending that all that matters is you and me. Pretending that this scene could be repeated on a regular basis."

The moment had me. I turned towards Ashley. We leaned towards each other, lips almost touching.

"Marlow, he-ah boy."

We had paid no attention. Mr. Stoney was standing with another man at the other end of the porch.

"I warned you. You Yankee boys got no defense against our Southern girls."

Ashley almost bent over double laughing. She grabbed my hand and headed towards the other men.

"Sam, you should probably meet my father."

My face flushed.

"Mr. Chambliss, I assure you sir, I meant no disrespect to your daughter."

"Sam it's a pleasure to meet you. I've heard good things about you and rest assured, I have no doubts that my daughter can take care of herself. You two carry on. Mr. Stoney and I are discussing the fascinating and never changing politics of South Carolina."

We walked back to the other end of the porch like schoolchildren. Ashley pulled up two chairs and chose one while opening the pages of the piece I'd filed earlier. She read through it once, then again. I continued to watch the light waning over the harbor.

"Nice touch Sam, a personal snapshot. It makes me want to go shake able seaman Cheney's bandaged hand. Putting a face to the war means a lot more to me than talking about huge operations beyond my poor ability to understand."

"Well on the latter point, I believe anyone would be a fool to underestimate your ability to understand. On the former point, it goes back to the graveyard experience this morning. This war will be fought and won by individuals, grunts, infantrymen, mechanics, fliers, engineers and able seamen. I suspect many of them, in a half century, will only be remembered by a cross in a field, or in a tidy corner of some pretty cemetery like St. Phillips. I think this country deserves to know the men who carry the weight of the battle."

"Does that mean you're not going to enlist?"

"How did you know I was thinking about enlisting? And if you say it's a small town..."

"Sam it was dark on that pier last night, but I don't have to see your eyes to sense the conflict inside you. You don't impress me as a man who would shirk his duty, or run from a fight, but you should consider that your most effective weapon may not be a rifle."

"I was thinking airplane actually."

"Don't make me smack you."

"In front of your father?"

"He's beyond being surprised."

"Your point is taken. I was already thinking of forcing a play on my publisher to either get an assignment overseas or quitting in order to enlist."

"Now don't get the idea that I'm advocating you do anything foolish. I have a few notions for you first."

"And I'm available for your notions on a moment's notice."

"Well one notion involves a cocktail. It's why you're here and I've been a bad little hostess."

She grabbed my hand and walked me through the parlor. She opened a door that led into a study. Bookshelves were built into the walls. In a fireplace a few small logs burned, not enough to overheat the room, but enough to cast that dancing light that worked so well with a good book and a leather armchair. Ashley closed the door behind us.

"This is my father's study. It's where he keeps the good liquor. You never leave the good stuff out for these folks around here, they'll drink you dry and head for home."

She set two highball glasses up and reached into a cabinet.

"I hope you're not disappointed, but the general presumption is that all we Southerner's drink is bourbon. In fact, in Charleston we drink just about anything. But I prefer Scotch."

She pulled out a bottle of 25 year old Macallan then poured a couple fingers in each glass, turned and handed me one.

"I hope this will do."

"Quite well, thank you."

We both slid into an armchair that faced the fire. It could become a matter of debate how many and which views might become a favorite in this house. It would be worth the process of discovery. One corner of the room was occupied by a handsome writing desk. On top sat a Remington standard. It brought my thoughts crashing back to work.

"You know, I do have to track down Kennedy. That was the story they sent me to write. What did you say about his place on Sullivan's Island?"

"Funny you should ask."

"I can do funny much better than that."

"No doubt. But funny because I had a call earlier today that might just solve the problem."

"I'm all ears."

"They are the least of my interest. However, I had a call today from the Meads in Aiken. They're putting together a party for George. He's been through Marine training and is about to ship out to the Pacific. Our families know each other, since they've been here in Charleston. They're making it a pretty big affair by bringing in a good sized band for Saturday night and they invited me to come, hoping I'd sing."

"Well that all sounds interesting but I don't see what it has to do with Kennedy."

"Patience newspaper boy. George Mead is a friend of the Kennedys. Both Jack and his sister Kathleen will be there. If that's not enough for you they're putting together a pickup polo game Saturday afternoon. I mentioned I have this friend from New York.. "

"So you're inviting me to go with you?"

"Something like that."

"Two Kennedys and a polo game."

"Yep."

I tossed back the last sip of scotch and abruptly got up. There was an instant of dazzling dizziness, a headiness of whiskey and opportunity. Reaching down to take an uplifted hand I pulled Ashley out of her chair and into my arms.

CHAPTER 5

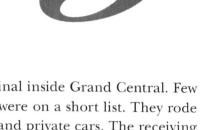

New York, N.Y.
April 10, 1942

T HE TRAIN PULLED INTO A private terminal inside Grand Central. Few knew it existed. Those who used it were on a short list. They rode in short trains, made up of locomotives and private cars. The receiving area was known as the 'Kissing Room', for a good reason. Rich men with a tryst on their minds prefer their privacy. Rich men with the FBI on their back also value a secret entrance to New York City.

Axel Wenner-Gren had more money than many countries. He carried himself with the airs of a Swedish nobleman but his wealth is as fresh as a newly printed krona. In a sense, he created one of the most powerful consumer forces in history by unleashing the domestic desires of the average housewife. Wenner-Gren put the home vacuum in her hand and opened the world of industrial products in her home. Those products evolved from vacuums and refrigerators to newspapers, banks and arms. Large stakes in the latter three can get you a seat at the Big Table.

When Europe seemed headed to war Wenner-Gren thought he could play the role of peacemaker by acting as a go-between using his contacts in Germany to arrange talks with the British and Americans. The talks never occurred. Goring called him an 'annoying and naive Swede'. Even British Prime Minister Chamberlain, seeking any route to appeasement, found him more meddlesome than useful.

Rejected by all parties the Swedish millionaire headed out on his huge yacht the *Southern Cross*. He was bound for the Bahamas. It was September 1, 1939, the same day Hitler was bound for Poland. On the day the war began Wenner-Gren happened to be in Scottish waters when a German U-boat sank the allied merchant ship *SS Athenia,* carrying women and children as passengers. The *Southern Cross* helped rescue some 380 people from the cold waters. When three British destroyers arrived on the scene they took over and sent the *Southern Cross* off under a cloud of suspicion.

Suspicion is a cloud that grows, nurtured by droplets of fact or fiction. It makes no difference which, as it becomes dark and ominous and full of portent to pour at some point. By innocence or intent Wenner-Gren fed his own cloud. In the Bahamas he became friends with the highest ranking royal suspects the Duke and Duchess of Windsor, who maintained their own Nazi sympathies.

His attempts at philanthropy fell under suspicion. When he started the Viking Fund in New York early in 1941 it was to support anthropological research. The research happened to be largely focused in South America. Some thought the Nazis were focusing there as well. To bring a circle of suspicion to completion he instilled former film director Paul Fejos as it's head. The two men shared something else in common.

Wenner-Gren stepped off the train, focused, eyes glancing to the left and right to make sure no one else was there to note his arrival. Someone waited. She had blonde hair and a secretive manner. The two walked toward each other and kissed. Voila.

"Inga, I'm so glad you could get away from Washington," he said quietly, turning her at the elbow to effect a graceful pirouette that would point her towards the private elevator, taking them both to the Presidential Suite.

"Were you followed?" he asked.

"No. They must have their rookie agents on me. They're not too difficult to slip."

"Good. Then we're alone."

As the elevator doors closed it framed a pair of Nordic perfection. From private train to private suite, the public appearance of Axel Wenner-Gren had lasted less than thirty seconds.

CHAPTER 6

T HE WEATHER IN WASHINGTON CAN change almost as quickly as the political climate. It was 9:30 and the day was already hot. Hoover arrived at the Department of Justice according to schedule. It was a routine that didn't vary. Hoover was picked up first, then Tolson. Both delivered to the office. Six days a week they would have lunch and dinner together. If anyone thought anything odd about the relationship between the two middle-aged men, few would tell. -

Hoover walked boldly down the middle of the hall. Tolson walked a respectful step behind. Walking past the area where agents worked, the Director bellowed.

"Hamm and Lott in my office. Now!"

The sound of desk chairs skidding was followed by heels on hardwood. The two agents hurried out of the doorway adjusting their coats and followed the group going down the hall. Hoover led like father goose. The line took a sharp turn left to enter Hoover's office. Each man assumed his pre-assigned seat. Hamm and Lott were at attention. Tolson poured a cup of coffee for the Director and himself then settled in his seat at the right hand of Hoover almighty.

"Boys, I have an interesting appointment on my calendar this morning. In an hour Mrs. Inga Binga will be paying us a visit. I took the appointment because it amuses me. Seems she has some 'requests' to make. Then I thought about it. A woman who is smart enough to work her way inside Hitler's inner circle, a woman who is smart enough to work her way inside the Kennedy clan, might just be a woman who could be of use to us."

The two agents looked at each other, then at the two men in front of them. It was not like the Director to share the thoughts that worked inside his head. They typically worked themselves into plans, that worked their way into webs of intrigue.

"I want to hear what you've got on the two lovebirds and what you've got between the Kennedys."

Lott started.

"On your orders sir, we contacted Joseph Kennedy to inform him that he is also a part of the investigation. Told him that certain monitoring operations were in effect."

"Ha! That conversation probably put a little purple in his face. What happened then?"

"As you suspected the word got out. We pulled the recording devices out of Miss Arvad's apartment. On March 28 Ensign Kennedy shows up in Washington. We have no recordings of their conversations that night. He returned the next day."

"Damn."

"We do have one interesting phone call intercept the next morning."

"Don't tease me son. I'm too mean to be teased."

"Yes, sir. On the following morning she called her husband in New York. She said she was quitting her acquaintance with Jack Kennedy even as she mentioned she was going to Reno to divorce him."

"So she's dropping both men although it doesn't seem to be a very exclusive club. Now that doesn't seem to make much sense."

"Seems Kennedy would agree, sir. According to a conversation between the two."

Lott began reading from a transcript:

> *Kennedy: I don't know. It's up to you whether you get divorced. I don't want to influence you in any way in getting it."*
> *Arvad: That's childish. I'm still going to get it and we decided not to see each other anymore, didn't we? So what do you have to do with it?*
> *Kennedy: You think that's correct?*

Arvad: No, it's not the wise thing and it's not the thing a Kennedy would do. I'll do it because I want to do it and I don't care if I even lose my job. I'll fix this myself. I've made an appointment to see Hoover himself to stop all these rumors.
Kennedy: What are you going to say to him?
Arvad: I'm going to say 'now look here Edgar J., I don't like everybody listening in on my phone!

Hamm smiled at that one. Lott began a chuckle that he choked off when he looked up at the Director's face.

"Anything else from that intercept?"

"Just a bit more, sir."

Arvad: I'm going to tell him that I would like to know a little bit about the whole thing myself because I hear nothing but a fantastic amount of rumors from everybody and I am after all, the chief actress in the play.
Kennedy: I doubt Hoover will admit to ordering a phone tap.
Arvad. Why shouldn't he? I'll say it's spoiling my career.. which it is.
Kennedy: I was thinking you don't know about your job. You could walk in one day and your column could be cut. There you'd be—without a job and all these other things holding over. I just want to be sure that this is what you want to do. From what you have said, I didn't have anything to do with you getting the divorce.
Arvad: You pushed the last stone under my foot, but that doesn't hold you responsible for anything. Meeting you 2 ½ months ago was the chief thing that made up my mind. As far as I am concerned, you don't exist anymore.

"Well, that seems pretty clear. She's cut bait on young Kennedy."

"But, sir," Hamm spoke up, "It doesn't seem that she has closed the door entirely."

He stood up and walked to the Director handing him a letter.

"This letter was sent from Miss Arvad to Kennedy in Charleston, it seems less an *adieu*, than *a bientot*."

Hoover looked at the letter, then at Hamm.

"Did you just speak French to me?"

"Yes sir, just to suggest.."

"Clyde he spoke French to me. Why you dear romantic fellow."

He stood up clenched the letter in his fist and slammed both to the desk.

"Special Agent Hamm English is just fine in this office. If you want to speak the language of collaborators, cowards and cheese eaters perhaps we can arrange for a closer assignment like inside occupied France. Adieu to you Hamm if you go frog on me again."

Hamm withered. Hoover returned to his seat, smoothed the letter out on the desk and began reading.

> *There is one thing I don't want to do, and that is harm you. You belong so wholeheartedly to the Kennedy-clan, and I don't want you ever to get into an argument with your father on account of me. As I have told you a dozen times, if I were but 18 summers, I would fight like a tigress for her young, in order to get you and keep you. Today I am wiser, ten years older.. twenty eight to your youthful twenty four. Nevertheless I may as well admit that since that famous Sunday evening I have been totally dead inside.*
>
> *A human breast to me has always been a little like a cage, where a bird sits behind. Some birds sing cheerfully, some mourn, others are envious and nasty. Mine always sang. It did especially for a few months this winter. In fact it sang so loudly that I refused to listen to that other little sensible creature called reason. It took me to the F.B.I., the U.S. Navy, nasty gossip, envy, hatred and big Joe, before the bird stopped. In the beginning I was just stunned darling. Then I slowly woke up.*
>
> *Once I said, "If you ever need me Jack, call me." It still holds good. If ever I can ease you a pain, physical or mental, come to me, or I will go to you.*

The Director let the letter float to his desk and leaned back in his chair. His eyes went to the far side of the room, an unfixed point on the wall. His fingers laced forming the brace of an apex atop two stubby arms supported at the elbow by the wooden arms of his chair

He spoke, looking to the same remote point.

"Either she's in love and deeply confused, or she's in total control of Kennedy. She's older than he by several years and too worldly to be a smitten sex kitten. She's..."

His voice trailed off and he looked down at Hamm and Lott sitting in front of him.

"What are you two still doing here? Nice work on the intercepts but we're not done here. Keep complete surveillance of the both of them, whether together or not."

"Yes sir." Both stood almost in salute, turned and marched out of the office.

"Clyde, what's the latest we have on the third wheel of her married ménage a trois? Oh look Clyde I just spoke French."

Tolson leaned forward in his chair.

"Axel Wenner-Gren is still active in the Bahamas and in South America. One of our informants down there suggested that any Nazi invasion would likely go first to the Upper Amazon, because it would be the devil to dig out a force that was established in those jungles. Supplies could run up the inland rivers, Bolivia, Peru and Brazil to Colombia putting them close to the Panama Canal and within striking distance of the U.S."

"So her soon-to-be ex-husband's filmmaking trip to Panama was just a front?"

"Likely."

"So he's working for the Nazis?"

"Likely."

"That's pretty much what I told the President. Here's what he thinks." Hoover handed a single page to Tolson.

In view of the connection of Inga Arvad, who writes for the Washington Times-Herald, with the Wenner-Gren Expeditions' leader, and in view of certain other circumstances (including the affair with Ensign Jack Kennedy) which have been brought to

my attention, I think it would be just as well to have her specially watched. FDR

Tolson handed the note back.

"That seems pretty clear. He's received our briefings, presumably those of the Navy and come to the same conclusion. She's to be watched."

"And since we're in the watching business I guess we'll just do as the President suggests."

The intercom buzzed on the Director's desk. A woman's voice followed.

"Mr. Hoover there's an Inga Arvad here to see you."

He remained motionless. Leaning forward he turned his head towards Tolson and smiled.

"Thank you, Miss Gandy. Send her in."

The sound of stiletto heels preceded her. The long view revealed blonde hair atop a head fixed forward, shoulders squared and arms to the side. She marched down the long approach like a sexy soldier on parade, blue eyes on Hoover and business on her mind. When she stopped in front of the Director's desk, a trailing foot fell lightly in stance with a subtle click of salute. The air carried her cologne as a calling card for the man behind the desk.

Hoover's head went back slightly affecting an air of superiority or perhaps simply sniffing the air in appreciation. He seemed like an interested bulldog.

"Mrs. Fejos what a lovely cologne."

"Thank you Mr. Director. It's 'Heaven Sent' by Helena Rubinstein an American fragrance."

"Good choice, a lovely scent and wise not to support that collaborator Elizabeth Arden."

"You seem to have an eye and nose everywhere Mr. Hoover."

"And you seem aware of subtleties that would elude most. If you were a man you'd make a good FBI agent."

"If I were a man, Mr. Director, I wouldn't have most of the skills that would make me an effective agent."

Hoover sat back.

"My apologies Mrs. Fejos. Please sit down. This is Clyde Tolson my Associate Director."

"Thank you and please call me Inga. My married name has nothing to do with this interview."

"Frankly, Inga, your married name and status have a great deal to do with this interview. Your adulterous relationship with Ensign Kennedy, your associations with Axel Wenner-Gren and Miss Arvad, others."

"Mr. Hoover, if adultery were a matter for the FBI you would be a very busy man."

"Let's be honest and blunt. Sex and war are as entwined as love and marriage. Rahab the Harlot helped bring down the walls of Jericho. Helen of Troy launched a thousand ships, so don't try to play me with the innocence of love and lust."

"I only claim to be innocent of your more evil notions that I'm a Nazi spy. Your surveillance is spoiling my career."

Hoover paused and smiled, "Now there's a familiar phrase. The question is what is your real career? You're an attractive young woman who has moved in some pretty impressive circles. I don't mean to sound cruel but your success thus far cannot be wholly attributed to the wit of your written word. So what am I to think? A woman who cavorts with a Fuehrer, a Reichsfuhrer a Reichsmarschall, a multi-millionaire, then lands in this country to take up with an Ambassador's son. That's an impressive resume."

"Now just a minute I don't think.."

Hoover stood and pounded the desk with his fist. Polite was past.

"We're at war here. This isn't a game. Your list of associations is enough to have you bundled up and put under lock and key. Don't think it can't happen. Did you ever run across Princess Stephanie while circulating in your Nazi circles?"

"No Director. I did not."

"Like you, she had friends up high. She ran in royal circles and set up a meeting with those appeasers the Duke and Duchess of Windsor with Goring. Then she took up with Hitler's close aide who was assigned as Consul-General in San Francisco. We got a little suspicious. She changed tactics and started sleeping with a high official in *this* government, a little higher than an Ambassador's son. Well I've got the Fuhrer's 'Nazi Princess' locked up where she will stay. It could happen to you, too."

Inga's posture did not change. Her eyes were an icy blue fixed on the Director. She was dressed in a black suit with a white collared blouse. It was a business suit. It was time for business.

"Why am I here Mr. Hoover?"

"Sometimes surveillance isn't enough. I wanted to see the famous Inga Arvad. If you're working for the Nazis you're shooting a bit low with young Kennedy unless he's just a 'starter contact'. If you're not working for the Nazis you've done a pretty good job on your own to construct a circle of acquaintances that could land you in some forgotten jail cell, or worse. Perhaps you should consider working for me."

"I find that notion repulsive."

"How do you find the notion of disappearing?"

"Worse."

"Then we agree that we might have some common ground and interest."

"What would you have me do?"

"At the moment nothing different."

"And what would I receive?"

"For now your continued freedom."

"How could I say no?"

"I didn't expect you to. Now Inga, if I may call you that. I want you to leave here and continue your life, your writing and your associations with Kennedy. You'll be given a contact and a means to communicate. We'll be in touch."

As she left Hoover's office, her posture gave no indication of the thoughts going through her mind. When her heels were a distant echo down the hall, Hoover turned to Tolson.

"I don't trust her, Clyde. She may very well be working for the Nazis and we just made her a double agent. But I'd rather have her close where I can watch her than out there freelancing on her own."

He lifted his head as his bulldog nose caught the scent which lingered from his new agent.

CHAPTER 7

THE ROAD OUT OF CHARLESTON is a highway of history. Route 61 seems carved through an ancient tunnel of oaks. We were a two car caravan travelling down the back path of storied plantations. The front road was always the Ashley River.

Ashley not of river, but of flesh and blood and taut spring dress was behind the wheel of her Buick. Kennedy was behind in his roadster and not liking it. Kick was beside him. She arrived in Charleston on Thursday. Kick disarmed him as only a younger sister could, teasing and toying. They looked like twins, tawny, well dressed and groomed for success. Siblings of superior quality.

Jack had no idea where we were going but didn't seemed the type content to follow. We played tag passing each other; two convertibles, two couples and two days ahead. The weekend was planned with the full knowledge that we were each racing headlong to war. That some gathered here would not return was all but certain.

Death in foreign places was not the concern for the moment. Kennedy was passing again on an open stretch. This time Ashley used the bigger engine of the Buick to keep even. The two cars were pacing each other down a two lane highway. In my peripheral vision I could see flashes of color passing by. At a slower speed one might have enjoyed the flowers in full spring blossom. Instead I looked to Ashley. She cut me a devilish grin and threw the same to Kennedy. He smiled back and shifted. It was a race.

Recklessness came to mind and was then dismissed. From the right hand side of a large sedan I saw beautiful profiles dashing in both adjective and verb and belonging to two Kennedys. The notion of danger could be dismissed. It was a dangerous rapture of youth in the lust of life.

As Kennedy shifted into high gear he gained a nose. The MG was lighter but ran like a quarter horse, quick in a sprint. The four cylinder sports car had nothing against the eight cylinder Buick with almost ten times the horsepower. Ashley accelerated to keep the car from passing. Kick was leaning forward in her seat as if getting her nose further ahead would help the car gain ground. It was all laughter and merriment until the truck appeared.

It was distant on the straightaway, about a mile down the road. At the combined speeds of both vehicles, we were approaching at about 120 miles an hour. In 15 seconds we would collide.

"Ashley, truck." My obvious observation.

"Got it." She said, as her jaw tensed.

Kennedy's face was set as well. Two stubborn people in a game of chicken. The MG was topped out. The Buick probably had a bit more but the car's weight and speed would not allow a quick burst forward. The truck was closing.

"Ashley.."

"Got it." Was all I got.

The truck was within a hundred yards. I could see the driver's face in a fury with one hand on the wheel and one on the horn. We were going to crash. My eyes turned in slow motion from the truck driver to Ashley's face. She cast a furtive glance towards Kennedy then towards the truck.

"Dammit Ashley."

My head hit the windshield as she slammed on the breaks. Kennedy made a quick hard right to cut in front of us. The truck blasted past, the horn still blowing, a Doppler shift of sound now receding. In the lead I saw Kennedy's hand waving in salute to the losers.

"Damn. Yankees always got to win." Ashley pounded the dash with her hand then burst out laughing.

"That was rather sporting of you to let him win instead of dying on the hood of a truck," I said reaching for a handkerchief to press against a small cut on my forehead.

"Oh Sam, you're hurt. I'm sorry. I should have warned you to brace yourself."

"Given the range of outcomes I'm ok with this contribution to your blood sport. Life been a little dull for you?"

"Now don't start on me, polo boy. You'll get your chance tomorrow. Last I saw it's not exactly a game for the feint of heart."

"Not quite the same as playing chicken with a truck."

"Now, now, nothing was going to happen. I just wanted to see what Kennedy would do."

I dabbed my head. On the cloth was blood.

"Sam you're bleeding."

She hit the brakes again and steered to the shoulder. I pitched forward and almost hit my head again.

"Surely you're not trying to kill me."

Her head went back in laughter that dispelled any trace of recent trauma. Hands with long lovely fingers went to both sides of my face to pull me forward. A kiss warm with passion and promise followed.

"Not my plan my friend. Not at all."

With that she reached up and kissed the cut on my forehead. Leaning back there was a trace of blood on her lips. She licked them, smiled and pushed the accelerator to the floor. We were off.

Kennedy and Kick were waiting a few miles ahead, parked under the shade of a tree. He might win the short race but would never get to our destination without Ashley in the lead. The drivers were a bit more docile as we turned westward to cut across the state. The highway was not designed to be scenic but functional. It ran parallel to a railway line that cut through small towns with cotton gins and general stores. It was a working landscape with farms and early crops showing the promise of spring. Picturesque in passing, harder in reality. Passing one field half furrowed, half still uncut, a farmer paused behind a mule and plow to watch two colorful cars pass. His hand went up to strangers streaking by. I followed his face with my eyes and returned his salute.

The landscape began to take on a different tone as we approached Aiken. Working fields became pastures. Barbed wire replaced by four board fence. There are two types of sustenance farming. One is to sustain life, the other to sustain a lifestyle. Where we rested our heads tonight there were no worries of the next meal.

Aiken was know as the Winter Colony. It was the southern retreat for the family of George H. Mead and a list of notable northern families who'd bring horses, help and hierarchy to Aiken for sport. The elder Mead had taken a family business from the brink of bankruptcy at the turn of the century to one of the nation's largest producers of paper with a tidy listing on the New York Stock Exchange. George and Jack knew each other from summers in Hyannis Port where they spent younger seasons sailing in Nantucket Sound. This winter was not spent in Aiken by the younger Mead. George was just off of six weeks basic training at Marine boot camp on Parris Island, South Carolina. He was about to head further south to the Pacific.

We drove along a hedgerow to a brick entrance leading into a gravel drive. This time Ashley gave Jack the lead. He pulled in front and downshifted as he hit the gravel and sent shards flying. We stayed a respectful distance behind to keep the shrapnel from spraying the front end of the car.

The Pillars was Mead's house, not too shabby for a second home. We parked in front of a raised portico with four columns reaching up two stories to a roof that protected both the porch and a balcony that extended from a second story entrance. Kennedy was already out of his car and walking towards ours, beginning to offer some driving tips to Ashley when the front door of the house flew open. A young man of military bearing burst out. His hair was cut short, he was tanned and muscled. Lieutenant George Mead, Jr. was a snapshot of a Marine. He took five strides, stood on the top step and pulled himself to attention.

"Ensign Kennedy. Do you not salute a superior officer?"

Kennedy spun around.

"Why sir? Is there one present?"

The two men mock marched towards each other then embraced, laughed and began a ritual of slapping and sparring with each other.

"Were accommodations at Parris Island suitable for the heir to the Mead dynasty?" Kennedy started in mock British accent.

"Oh quite. You know the winter season is all the rage for basic training. It's weeks before the snakes and alligators show up to spoil the outdoor activities."

Kick broke up the boy's club.

"George! Looks like the Marines just made you more handsome."

"Ah the beautiful Kennedy. Kick, thank God you came so I wouldn't have to be left alone with sailor boy here."

George hugged Kick and reached across towards Ashley.

"Ashley so good that you could come. This must be Sam?"

I stuck out a hand. The Marines must be issuing a new secret handshake bent on bone crushing. If that's hand to hand combat the Japs will collapse in no time.

"Sam. Good to see you. I heard you've been volunteered for the little scrimmage tomorrow."

"Very glad to be asked though I haven't played since last fall. Hope it's a friendly."

"Well that's the intent. It's local fellows most on a short leave before heading to the war. Tommy Hitchcock's here, Pete Bostwick, me, you and a few others. Now enough gabbing let's go inside and get something to eat."

Ashley linked her arm through mine as the group turned towards the house. She was pulled up short by my rooted feet.

"Sam?"

"Ashley did you know who would be playing?"

"Just the local boys Sam. You heard the man. Tommy Hitchcock is a local boy."

"He's also a legend. A ten goaler. The top polo player in America."

"Why hush my mouth. Really??"

She delivered the line with her fingers draped in mock surprise across her mouth, "We can talk about it later. Now let's go inside and have lunch like the nice man said."

George set a course guiding the group through the large open foyer. The rich have as many ways to display their wealth as they have to make it. I've seen some homes with the gilt and splendor to rival Versailles, or a French whore house. The Pillars had a graceful flow of a house created to be enjoyed. It was a sporting estate. Rooms of rich woods and leather furniture like a well apportioned club yet mixed with the handsome oils of equestrian life, with photos of a family at play. George was a prominent figure in all. Unlike the Kennedy clan of nine, the most conspicuous part of any photo was the solo son of a wealthy man. Aiken was his winter playground.

We shot straight through the house to exit on a raised patio overlooking a terraced garden, overlooking a polo field. The Buddhists believe there are seven levels to Nirvana. For a horse lover, Mead had managed it in three.

Below, the polo field ran along both sides. The midfield was directly below the patio and garden. It would be possible to watch the game from any of the three levels. Across the field, set back into a cooling canopy of trees, the barn was built to match the manor-like atmosphere of the house. Wings of stalls stretched side to side with apparent room for plenty of ponies.

Tents were being erected at the field level and on the terrace. At one end of the garden hammers and saws were laying a carpenter's downbeat building - a stage for an orchestra. The place was being decorated like a USO show, red, white and blue, with occasional highlights of Marine khaki.

Mead herded us over towards a serving table set to one side of the swimming pool. The table was set with sliced meats and cheese. A simple lunch served on Wedgwood china and silver polished.

"Ladies first," Mead gently elbowed Kennedy aside towards a chair and a brass cooler filled with ice and beer. Each grabbed one and flopped into chairs.

"What about you? Mead asked, "How's life in the Navy?"

"Miserable duty in Charleston. They shagged my ass down there because I was going around with a Scandinavian blonde. They thought she was a spy."

George's beer was tilted back for a full swig but came down abruptly upon hearing Jack's last sentence. Fast enough for a foamy geyser to erupt, followed by a guffaw that floated two terraces below. A couple of workers stopped their hammers in mid-swing to look and smile.

"I can't believe it Kennedy! Leave it to you. The world's at war and you save the country by shagging, sorry, snagging the Nazi's hottest spy. Where's your blonde Mata Hari?"

"Not so funny George. She's off getting divorced in Reno. I'm getting pressure from J. Edgar and J. Kennedy and I'm not sure which is worse. I thought I'd do the kind thing and *not* invite her so the place wouldn't be overrun by FBI agents."

"You're a giver, Jack, nothing like a few Feds to spoil a party."

"But I hadn't intended on making *you* a date for the weekend. There'd better be some girls around these backwoods."

"Just wait until tomorrow night. A little mix of Southern girls, Northern girls, even California girls, all-American girls all the time around here. None of that foreign trade."

I walked over with a plate and a sandwich and my eye on a beer. George waved me towards a chair.

"Sam, how did you end up with this motley crew?"

Kennedy jumped in, "He and the FBI followed me to Charleston. He was somewhat less obtrusive."

"That's the fact. Then somehow fate seemed to intervene. I met Ashley, dinner, cocktails and then somehow I was invited to share sandwiches with the rich and famous."

"Miss Chambliss does seem well connected," Kennedy added with a glance to another table where Ashley and Kick were settling into a conversation and lunch.

"She picked up a phone and got me into a Commander's office at the Coast Guard base. That led to a pretty good story."

"Well, if she knows any admirals who might get me a post on a warship.."

"She did mention Admiral Halsey."

Kennedy began to stand up, "Step aside Marlow, this is official Navy business.."

"Oops just kidding Jack."

He took a swipe at my head and slumped back into his chair.

"Jack you really pushing to get war duty?" Mead seemed serious.

"Damn right. You're heading out. Most of the fellows I know are going into some branch or another and no one's looking for a desk job. I'm sure as hell not going to spend this war behind a typewriter in Charleston-damn-South-Carolina. I mean no offense to the lovely Miss Ashley. It's not so much that they say 'he-ah' after every god damned remark- 'now come and see us Kennedy, hear'- but it's the abouts and oots – and the rest of the shit that convinces me we should have let the bootucks go."

"I'm surprised you haven't caused the Second Succession yet."

"There'll be none of that. We've got bigger wars to fight and we learned once that those Southern boys can fight. Think I'd rather be with them than against them."

"Seriously Jack how are you going to get war duty? Your back.."

"George," Kennedy cut him off, looking from him to me, "There are some things better left unsaid in front of our friends from the press."

I stood up. "Look Kennedy I'm not here to snoop on you. I'm here as a guest and a friend. Whatever opinion you may have of the press in general, or Winchell's form of reporting in particular, I'd appreciate it if you'd spare me the taint of association. You're not the biggest story going on here. The war is. My interest is in the part we each play. My interest this weekend isn't war, but love and that has nothing to do with you."

Kennedy stood up to face me. His eyes were locked on mine. Irish eyes and at the moment they weren't smiling. Then a twinkle. His face erupted in a smile, perfect teeth, in prominent display. He extended a hand.

"Marlow you sure you're not Irish? Brilliant point I'd like to follow you on that. This weekend is for love. War is next week."

I felt a hand on my shoulder, "So that's your objective is it?" Ashley joined at a perfect time, "I suppose I'd better prepare myself for a charm offensive."

With my right hand still in Kennedy's I let my left hand slip down Ashley's back to that delicious spot at the base of her spine. Between the two points of contact I felt an electric charge. Let the weekend begin.

"Well now kiddies now that we've got an objective. It's getting a bit late in the day. There's not a lot of idleness around Aiken. Usually a fox hunt in morning, golf in the early afternoon and a hack through the woods in the late afternoon, followed by cocktails in the evening. I think we've got time for the last two if anyone wants to ride."

"Excellent. I'd love to leg up a bit before playing tomorrow," I was ready.

"Kick?"

"George you know I'm dying to get into the woods with you," Kick threw a coy Kennedy look at him.

"Ashley?"

"I suppose someone who knows their way around a horse better look out after Sam."

"Now don't go throwing down the challenge. I'm saving myself for the match tomorrow."

"Saving yourself.. hmmm, I do hope you're only talking about your riding skills."

"Seems the game's afoot. We'll meet back down here in fifteen minutes. Your bags are already in your rooms. Top of the stairs, boys to the right, girls to the left. There will be a guard posted in between all night long but he accepts bribes."

"Jack you coming?"

"Think I'll pass George that back issue that went undiscussed. Is that pool heated?"

"Sure is."

"Then I think I'll take a few laps around the pool. It seems to help."

We were gathered again in short order. Jack was standing by the pool in a pair of bathing trunks. For a family of such means the poor fellow looked like he could use a steak. Lanky would be padding the adjective.

"Now you kids run along and have a good romp through the woods. Poor Jack will be back here swimming laps. Getting this fine physique in shape for the evening."

"Knowing you, we'll come back to find you with a mermaid," George said over his shoulder as we walked down towards the field.

The girls were ahead sporting borrowed boots and breeches. Both were wearing tweed jackets covering the lovely contour of buttocks beneath. Pity.

Below four horses were tied to a hitching post at the base of the terrace a good thirty yards from the edge of the polo field. Two of the horses had hunter manes. The other two were roached for polo. As we approached the grooms led the hunters towards two large cut stones that served as mounting blocks.

"Kick and Ashley you take those two. They're schooled know the trails and most of the jumps. Sam you and I will take the two polo horses. They should be fine on the flat and thought we might hit a couple balls after we all hack through the woods."

"That sounds great. Just swinging a mallet for a few minutes would be a big help. Thanks."

The ride out was amusing. The hunters were both over 16 hands tall and in good flesh. The polo horses were shorter. Just over 15 hands and with that lean, hard muscled look of athletes. Riding beside Ashley, I had to look up.

"You look good up there on a pedestal, be it horse or granite."

"Please refer to me as 'your Goddess'. I am Diana by day."

"And by night? Are you Venus?"

"Well there little pony boy, you're the one who was pronouncing this to be the weekend of love. But first you're going to have to catch Diana in her own element."

George and Kick were already ahead entering the bridal path at the far edge of the polo field. Ashley picked up a canter and was advancing on them. George looked over his shoulder saw her approaching and smiled. I saw his heel turn into the horse's flank and then mutter something to Kick that made her do the same. Seems the notion of a gentle ride through the woods was about to go to hell. The three of them were in a fast canter as they moved onto a wide path carved into thick woods. My horse was performing a polite little prance with her front end, obviously not intending to be left behind. One thing about a polo horse, they're not made to follow. I gave her her head. She shot forward.

We closed quickly. I could see past them down the trail where a rough log jump was built to the right with a 'go around' to the left.

Coming along Ashley I grinned and headed to the right. She spurred her horse and we headed for the jump side by side. Three strides before the jump she pushed her heels down and set her horse's head. A stride out they launched. My horse did not.

She planted her front feet a stride before the jump. I launched alone. Unfortunately it wasn't a unique experience. Being somewhat skilled in the art of the fall I cleared my feet from the stirrups as I went forward over the horse's head. Once in that suspended state where it seems you have a chance at leisure to look at the jump going beneath and the ground coming toward you, I tucked my shoulder, landed and rolled to a perfect upright seated position. Still facing in the original direction. Ashley heard the crash, checked her horse and executed a perfect pivot before cantering back. She had a worried look on her face until she saw me sitting there shaking my head.

"Well there ponyboy, I hope you do better at polo than jumping or you're in for a rough day tomorrow."

Kick and George circled up and by now the three of them were laughing.

"Sorry Sam. You hurt?" George was starting to dismount.

"Just my pride. Don't get down I'm fine. You did say the polo horses should be fine on the –flat-. I don't know too many that play polo and are cross trained for jumping."

"Well sir, I don't know about the tradition in Aiken but in most fields the grass catcher has to buy the first round." Kick joined in.

"I'll be happy to as long as I can avoid the jumps on the way back in."

I got up and went to my horse who was on the opposite side of the jump. Ashley rode behind.

"You want to go on? We could turn back."

"Oh heavens no. You missed my perfectly executed dismount. I'm fine."

The horse was standing stock still her eyes still a bit wide. Reaching to pet her neck she stiffened. She was expecting me to hit her. Ashley caught my eye.

"Somebody's beaten that horse."

"Probably some trainer. Some tend to overdo the discipline."

My hand went slowly up behind the horse's ear gently stroking. I stepped in close to her neck and petted the opposite side with my other hand. She raised her head slightly and I blew gently into her nose nuzzling that spot so soft on the muzzle.

"Lucky horse," Ashley watched and smiled.

"That's nothing, I'm saving my best for later."

"Lucky me," her smile broadened.

"Come on you two I'm looking forward to that round Sam has to buy."

Mounting up we headed off at a posting trot, moving up to an easy canter. The trail was dotted with bright flowers; bursts of colors slipping past. Overhead the trees were knitting their canopies in a bright, vibrant green that would mature to the dark green of summer. Other riders were out but few as young as the foursome riding to the Pillars where cocktails and laughter and a carefree weekend awaited them. Another group of riders approached in formal hunt attire. One man in black was wearing a top hat. He seemed a dark symbol. He rode a red horse.

A burst of laughter brought me back to the moment. I moved up along Ashley. George and Kick were cantering alongside as they led around a bend and an opening that brought us back to the opposite side of the polo field.

"Those trails run through thousands of acres of woods. You can get almost anywhere, to anyone's place here, by horseback. They're called Hitchcock Woods."

"Which reminds me. He's going to be here tomorrow. Can we hit a few balls just to warm up?"

"Thought that might be a good idea."

We were approaching the hitching post. A few mallets had mysteriously appeared while we were gone. The little mare knew what was up. She was back in her element. George and I both shed our jackets.

"Want to hit a few balls Ashley?"

"I believe I'm more interested in a highball at the moment. We're going up to change for cocktails. Don't spend too much time out here honing your game. Cocktail hour waits for no one."

A ball was on the ground next to my horse. I took a nearside back shot which managed to carry out to midfield. The little horse anticipated, spun and we were off.

"Showoff!" Was Ashley's parting word.

George tapped a ball towards midfield then unleashed a full swing that sent it a good hundred yards. He put some muscle into that swing. We spent a half hour moving balls up and down the field. It felt good. Now I was looking forward to the match instead of about playing over my head.

Riding to the rail two grooms were waiting to take the horses. Looking up the reverse view of the home was just as stunning from the flat to the terraced garden and up to the house and patio. My eyes lingered even as we dismounted.

"It's no Parris Island but it's home. I can't tell you how much I've looked forward to this weekend. We'd better make double time up the steps. Kennedy's probably already up to something."

He wasn't far from wrong. George beat me to the top by virtue of his recent training. I was sucking air by the time I got to the top and saw Jack on a lounge next to a blonde wearing something that almost resembled a bathing suit.

"Hello fellows," he smiled across the girl, "Seems the neighbors are not only friendly they're beautiful."

"Well Sally, so nice to see you and I mean that most literally. If you happen to have a few more clothes you can join us for cocktails," George seemed to put a bit of ice in his voice.

"Let's go Sam. A quick shower and let's see if we can get back in time to defend Jack's honor."

"Then you'd better hurry," Jack laughed. "Because I won't."

Even with a quick shower and change of slacks, open shirt and jacket, I was not the first poolside. Ashley and Kick were already attached to an outdoor bar, where a man in a white coat and clearly in command of his craft was at work. George was talking to a group of men in tweed jackets and boots on horseback. Jack and the blonde were nowhere in sight.

Ashley detached from her perch and started towards me with an extra drink in her hand. She wore an ivory blouse, unbuttoned at the neck which drew attention to a string of pearls. The blouse was tucked into pleated trousers with a high waist and simple belt. She was elegant.

"Thought you might want one of these." She said, handing me the other drink.

"What are we drinking?"

"The bartender seems intent on paving the way for the first weekend in May."

I took a sip. Julep. He knew what he was doing.

We turned towards the small crowd. George was there . Ashley made a slight nod in his direction.

"Recognize anyone?"

Following the direction of her gaze I caught the eye of Tommy Hitchcock.

"Holy crap," I took a long pull on the drink.

"Better be friendly, polo boy. You don't want him mad at you on the field tomorrow."

Walking across the patio I watched as Hitchcock worked the crowd. He commanded attention and admiration wherever he was. Tomorrow he would play polo as the acknowledged king of the so called 'sport of kings.' He carried a 10 goal handicap for almost two decades and led four teams to win the US National Open. That all happened after he became a war hero.

He was born to affluence and influence. It took a family friend Teddy Roosevelt to break the rules and get him into World War One. At seventeen he was flying with the famed Lafayette Escadrille. On his eighteenth birthday, he was shot down and wounded behind German lines. Hiding during the day and travelling at night he eventually reached the Swiss border and freedom. That made him a hero. But polo made him a legend.

He was barely over forty yet he stood like an elder statesman among a second generation of even young men heading to war. The War Department refused to send him back into combat. The talk was that he was going to Britain to get back in a the cockpit of a fighter.

With one hand firmly clasping my bourbon courage I stuck the other one out and walked towards Hitchcock.

"Tommy, Sam Marlow. Someone made the mistake of putting me in the little scrimmage tomorrow."

"Marlow! Well damn right. It's about time we had a chance to play together. I know your father or at least my father knows yours. Seems those two have swapped some horses over the years."

Tommy looked across the group doing hard labor on their libations. "Pete. Pete Bostwick come over here. Someone you need to meet."

Bostwick was much closer to my age and already something of a legend. A decade ago he made racing history by winning both a flat race and a steeplechase in the same day. Two weeks later he repeated the same feat.

"Pete meet Sam Marlow. He's Jack Marlow's boy. You know Jack, he and my father do some training out on Long Island."

"Sam, it's kind of strange we haven't crossed paths before. Your father turns out some good horses. I've ridden a few. As a matter of fact, I remember...."

He pulled up short on his sentence. I felt a hand slide down my back. Ashley had made her appearance.

"Now you gentlemen had better play nice with my fellow here tomorrow. He's not much use to me if you send him back all beat up."

"Tommy, Pete, this is Ashley Chambliss."

"The singer?" Pete seemed to forget horses for a minute, "I heard you were performing tomorrow night. It's about time Mead brought some decent talent to this town. I told him his party better be as good as the game tomorrow."

"You're too kind. I'll try to uphold my end of the deal. You fellows will have to do yours. Now if you'll excuse me, I'm going to steal Sam from you. He's yours tomorrow. Tonight he's mine."

We turned and walked back towards the bar. I needed a refill.

"Nice rescue. That was about to become a lengthy discussion about horses, fathers and the breedings of both. Both of those men and their abilities are far beyond anything that I could ever achieve, or perhaps even want to achieve. I am somewhat in awe, but not envious. They both live for their sports. I'm just trying to make a living."

"And that's why I'm kind of attracted to the writer boy. I like what goes on in his head. He talks pretty, in ways that make me want to hear more."

"I could whisper, if were you closer."

And she was. Her arm was around my waist, her head on my shoulder as we walked towards the wall that defined the upper terrace like the top layer of a cake. The sun was settling into the trees, visible through the leaves of early spring. A coolness came with the evening that sent the riders back to their horses. Their goodbyes echoed from the field as the group lined the wall. Then a quiet camaraderie settled each to our thoughts as the sun seemed to take its glow, and go.

Jack stood alone looking out across the fields as if there was something missing.

CHAPTER 8

HIGHWAY 40 ROLLS DOWN FROM the Sierra Nevadas towards Reno. In the rear view mirror is Donner Pass where a group of pioneers were stranded one winter and survived by resorting to cannibalism. That horrific bit of history is one most locals would prefer to put behind them. But then the point of Reno is putting a past tense on troublesome times. Like marriage.

The Riverside Hotel is six stories of red brick with Gothic Revival terra cotta detailing. It is home base for many wishing to dissolve home ties. By irony, or prescient design, it is six stories high, one for each week of residency required for a legal divorce. Demand for the comfortable corner suites is in such demand that when Clare Boothe arrived during a blizzard in 1929 she had to wait days in cramped quarters until one was available.

The Cadillac pulls to the front curb. A valet opens the door allowing a female leg to swing to the street, the other follows. They are legs worth looking at. Inga Arvad accepts the offered hand and steps out.

The sun is coloring the mountains to the north in those soft tints reserved for the west. The Truckee River runs full with the spring runoff from the hills that create a roar distinct above the background noise of the street. Pedestrians in Reno are an odd lot - a mixture of here and there, mostly there. Men in cowboy boots seem to define the locals. The rest sport a casual mix of clothe Easterners in blazers, West Coast wearing linens and then there were the two guys wearing suits and ties on either side of the Riverside's doors.

"Hello boys would you get my bags?" Inga smiles.

"We're not bellboys, ma'am."

"Well then why on earth would you be standing outside like that?!"

"Sorry ma'am, can't say."

"Don't be so coy. Please tell the Director I'll be staying in room….."

"Six-D."

"You fellows are so efficient."

"Have a good evening, Mrs. Fejos."

"Not for much longer."

Inga walked into the lobby. It was tastefully appointed to say, not a cowhide or horn anywhere in sight. The one design that was apparent was Reno's way to separate the part time residents from their money. The casino is set off to one side of the lobby and had already seeing action this evening. Directly across was a restaurant with white tablecloths showing and a maitre d' in formal attire looking through the evening's reservation book.

"Good evening I'm Inga Arvad, excuse me, Inga Fejos."

"Yes good evening Mrs. Fejos. We've been expecting you. We'll welcome you to Reno as Mrs. Fejos and bid you adieu as Miss Arvad."

"Thank you. I'm sure you're much more accustomed to this than I."

"We're here to help you in any way we can. Your room is ready. I'll have your bags sent up."

"Thank you. Can I order dinner in my room? I'm not quite up for a rousing Reno evening yet."

"Of course you can ma'am. We certainly understand. You'll probably find in a few days there's an interesting collection of folks here. Some gather regularly for dinner sharing the same table almost like a cruise ship."

"There's a Titanic joke there somewhere but I'll let it pass."

"Very good ma'am."

She took the elevator to the top floor and walked down the hall to her corner room. The suites were set for the long haul. Each had a kitchen and dining area. Inga's was smaller. She did not require rooms for servants. Her bags were already nearby where they would be unpacked; suitcases by the closet, cosmetic case in the bathroom. She began the process of settling in for her six week sentence in a town where she knew no one and where the whole purpose was to sever one tie with no real hope for the other. She had travelled light with the one exception. She brought her typewriter, hoping she might meet someone worthy of a piece for the Times Herald. She put the typewriter on the desk, pulled out a piece of hotel stationery and started a letter to the one person who seemed much more distant than the miles between Nevada and South Carolina.

The Riverside
Reno, Nevada

Jack dear.

Yes, I know, I did promise to write, and here goes:

It is evening here, and pretty ready to put the head on a pillow and go right off snoring till the sun rises again.

Because dear, even in Reno they have a sun. I wonder why they bother. A most interesting place, one you wouldn't send your worst enemy to. Not because it isn't lovely. Funnily and ironically enough, it is beautiful, with plenty of mountains with or without snow as you happen to prefer. But the place seems silly, dreadfully money conscious, and full of cowboys. The bars have uninviting names, people are bored to tears, because many of those who come out here always will be bored, and it is more conspicuous in Reno than in Chicago or New York.

Mother is coming on Saturday. She is going to be my salvation. I look very much forward to spending some weeks with her, and I shall rest, read and relax. Not a Kennedy program dearest, but one which I would love to go by for some weeks.

But here I go - egotistical as usual - only writing about the nearest subject - myself.

Often, I wonder how you are getting on, how that back of yours is behaving, and what you think of life in general. It may be tough now and then, but you know how to hold the reins and steer your horses the right way. May you never be at loss, and let me know where and when you set sail. If you feel like hearing about the West then drop a line, and I shall try to entertain you.

You do know that if you are sick, I would love to write to you, if you would like it, but let me know - that is all.

So long, someday we will have a steak, mashed potatoes, peas, carrots and ice cream again. It won't ever be like the old days, somehow the past is gone, but you have a great future, don't ever let anybody make you believe anything different.

Love from,

Binga.

The sun seemed to rise earlier and shine brighter in Reno. Being alone in a strange bed and an even stranger place is not conducive to sleep. Inga was dressed and downstairs before eight, eating breakfast and sipping coffee in a way to make the morning last. The newspaper only made her miss being back at work in Washington. From the pace of others eating in the dining room there was no rush to make it to work. The main occupation in town was waiting for a divorce. It was a tough job.

She signalled for the check, signed it to her room and walked towards the lobby. She walked without purpose or direction.

"Mrs. Fejos." The voice came from behind the desk.

"There's a message for you."

She reached for the envelope. It was blank. No name, either to or from. She had yet to tell anyone where she would be staying. Sitting in a chair in a corner away from the lobby, she lifted the lightly sealed flap on the back.

Dear Mrs. Fejos,

Welcome to Reno. I hope your trip was pleasant and your hotel comfortable. Please call me at your earliest convenience so that we might discuss a matter of mutual interest.

Sincerely,

J. Edgar Hoover

Inga crumpled the note in her fist and looked up expecting to see the FBI agents standing there. They were not. Her eyes moved from the door then back to the desk and across to the other side of the lobby. By a row of telephone booths one agent stood with phone in hand. He raised it towards her. An invitation to a command performance. She walked in his direction.

"He could have called my room."

"The Director has his own way of doing things ma'am. The person on the other end will connect you."

She took the phone, entered the booth and closed the door.

"This is Inga Arvad."

"One moment, I'll connect you with the Director."

She sat in silence.

"Good Morning, Mrs. Fejos!"

The greeting was so loud it jolted the receiver. She returned the greeting with a grimace.

"Good morning, Mr. Director, to what do I owe the honor of this summons?"

"Oh Mrs. Fejos we at the FBI are always interested in staying in touch with our newest recruits."

"I didn't expect this call so soon."

"We're at war in case you haven't noticed and waiting is not a luxury we have. We know you're in Reno for a divorce. Your soon-to-be ex-husband might have some useful information on his backer Axel Wenner-Gren. Even though we know your husband isn't the only one closely associated."

"Your insinuations are rude Mr. Hoover."

"But true..."

"Nevertheless, what do you want to know?"

"I'd like to know what Wenner-Gren was doing on his yacht in the Caribbean with those Nazi sympathizers the Duke and Duchess of Windsor. Churchill is incensed. Even he can't seem to do anything about them since they've taken up residence and title in the Bahamas."

"I don't believe Paul was on board the Southern Cross with the Windsors."

"Then if Mr. Fejos can't give you the information you might use some of your free time to reach out to Wenner-Gren himself. I'm sure he'd take your call. We want to know about the Duke and Duchess. They may be extending their royal romp to the States. If they're in bed with Hitler, like the rest of your friends, we want to know."

"Mr. Hoover I have told you once that I am not a Nazi sympathizer. As you so kindly asked for my help during our meeting in Washington I will find out what I can but you might discover that not everyone is an agent or supporter of the Third Reich."

There line was silent for a moment.

"Mrs. Fejos, I am not accustomed to being lectured on matters of national security by pretty blondes described by the Fuhrer as 'a perfect example of Nordic Beauty.' You seem to keep missing the fact that we're at war. Every German, every Jap, every person with any tie to their Fatherland is a potential spy. There are enough spies to threaten the very future of this country. We catch them every day and not all of them cruise in on luxury yachts. The captain of a U-boat thought he was so sly, he stepped off in Palm Springs and thought he'd walk into a local bar for a drink. We're not chasing ducks in the dark here Mrs. Fejos and I expect you to bring me some useful information or you may not be leaving Reno as a woman freed from a marriage but leaving in handcuffs for a federal jail."

The phone hammered down in Washington. His voice left her ear ringing. She sat in the silence of the booth looking outward. The people out there looked like they could care less about the war. But that wouldn't last. The casualties were growing daily. Soon every town in the nation would feel the pull for men and the materials of war. Everyone would contribute in their own way. She'd just been given her orders. Reaching up she grabbed the handle on the door of the booth, pulling herself up and opening the door at the same time. The same agent stood there. His eyes looked a little softer. Maybe hers did, too.

"Welcome to the FBI, ma'am."

"Is he always like that?"

"As I said the Director has his own ways. I have been instructed to assist you if needed."

"So you're not here just to follow me?"

"Not entirely, ma'am."

"Then perhaps we should have dinner and discuss plans."

"Sorry ma'am. My instructions are to assist, not engage. When you have contact with your subjects let me know and we can make arrangements."

"...assist, not engage. I can almost hear him saying that."

"Yes ma'am."

He turned and walked away through the lobby glancing not so casually from side to side to see if anyone had been observing their conversation. No one in the lobby cared except the desk manager. His eyes followed the agent as he walked away then turned towards Inga with a nod of his head. Given Reno's livelihood, he wasn't surprised that a guest was under surveillance.

CHAPTER 9

Aiken, SC
April 19, 1942

T HE MORNING BEGAN WITH THE sound of a cavalry charge. Hoofbeats
on macadam that changed to a crunch as they moved onto gravel.

"Hey you people still asleep in there? Mead, George Mead," a voice
bellowed. It came from the lead member of the party mounted on horseback, "Don't they wake up a little earlier in the Marines?"

I was still in bed. The window was open and I could feel the cool
spring morning - a prelude of the warmth to follow. The voice brought
me to my feet and to a view from behind the curtain. A small group of
morning rider were below. The leader was on a horse that didn't seem to
tolerate idle conversation. George stepped onto the portico.

"Morning Frank, you playing Paul Revere to the sunrise?"

"Just stopping by to see what time you boys are playing today. I don't
want to miss the game."

"Oh, we'll probably get started around two, polo time," stated
George.

"So you mean three?" asked the mounted leader.

"No, not that late. Just make sure you're planning to stay for the
party afterwards."

"Hope you've got enough liquor. The whole town's talking about
that!" added another.

With that the group offered a hoot in salute as they rode past Mead
and out the gate. He smiled, shook his head and walked back into the
house.

The day was afoot and I didn't want to be left behind. I was showered, dressed and downstairs in fifteen minutes. A darkness had settled over the morning. Jack and George were in the living room with a pot of coffee on the table and a newspaper in hand. As I walked in, Jack dropped it on the table. The headline read: Bataan Falls to Japs.

"The headlines are starting to report the actuality instead of preaching Victory while all we're meeting is defeat." Jack looked at the paper, "This piece quotes the Voice of America: "Bataan has fallen. The Philippine-American troops on this war-ravaged and bloodstained peninsula have laid down their arms. With heads bloody but unbowed, they have yielded to the superior force and numbers of the enemy."

"MacArthur sits safely in Australia. I doubt his personal promise of a couple of weeks ago, 'I shall return' will be of little comfort to all those troops under Japanese control now," I added.

"If Bataan has fallen, Corregidor will follow. Then what's next?" George asked while staring out the window.

"The unfortunate fact," Jack began, "Is that they appear unstoppable. Since December they've rolled up Hong Kong, plus our bases on Guam and Wake Island. In January, there was Burma, the Dutch East Indies, New Guinea and the Solomons. In February Singapore, Bali and Timor and we started an air campaign in northern Australia. They're pushing west and have all but pushed the Royal Navy to the far edge of the Indian Ocean. If this drive meets with success, the Indian Ocean would become a Jap lake and the Japanese position would approach invulnerability."

"Maybe the Japs just need to meet the Devil Dogs," Mead offered.

"You mean your Marines can fix this?"

"Seems that's the job in front of us."

"I think the Marines can make a difference but the threat, and the timing, is going to require a little more. If the Japanese drive is unstopped and Hitler is successful pushing through Turkey to the Persian Gulf then the first phase of this war would be ended in defeat." Jack continued, "The situation we're facing is grave, extremely so. The people of America must awake to the reality and extent of the war that we're fighting, or not fighting. This is a serious and long business that must be fought, and fought by troops. To fight, will mean millions killed and billions spent. To wage and win such a war, this country would inevitably go Fascist."

"Complete and total dedication to the effort I'll agree with... but I think this war can be won without destroying the Democracy." I countered, " Wilson got us through World War One without subverting the Constitution."

"World War One could be renamed in the context of this war. That was a war fought largely on two fronts both on the same continent and named, or framed, by our own particular ethnocentricity. This war already involves six continents and every color of man."

"Someone sounds like they've been corresponding with influential globe trotting war correspondents. Jack some of those lines sound like they came from Clare Booth Luce," Kick opined from just off stage.

"Well who, other than my sister, would resort to name dropping. Truth will out and I stand exposed. Yes we have exchanged a few ideas."

The mood flipped in an instant of Kennedy wit.

"Gentlemen that ends this morning's briefing. The next will be at 1700 hours, by the pool in fewer clothes and more frivolity," Jack was back on the charm offensive.

Kick and Ashley walked into the room. The three men were on their feet.

"At ease boys," Ashley said.

The women were taking control and not a moment too soon. Both walked to the tray with the coffee. The pot was empty. They looked in unison. George got the full glare.

"Ahhhh, yes.. ladies, of course coffee coming."

George got the message. He made a beeline for the kitchen. The closing door fanned the smell of breakfast. When he returned, one of the servants followed close behind and clearly had the situation under control.

"Good heavens ladies," declared the small black woman. "I apologize for Mista George, he was raised better than this. Breakfast will be on the table in ten minutes. I'll bring you two another pot of coffee. These so called gentlemen seem to only be thinkin' on themselves. Shame on you boys." She said, and the door swung closed behind her.

"That was Ruth. She runs the house. Fortunately, she lets us stay here. She loves this place and almost everyone I bring to it, including a few of my Marine buddies. If you need anything ask her. She's not as tough as she seems."

Ruth brought breakfast. It was gone quickly. There was little restraint of appetites. It would be a day for that. The morning discussion set the tone for what we knew was coming. That made today, something not to waste. George sat back sipping the last of his coffee. His plate was clean. He may have been raised the son of a millionaire but his time in the Marines taught him to appreciate the pleasure of biscuits, bacon and eggs served by someone other than a mess sergeant.

"Kids," George pushed back from the table,"We've got a few hours before this hoedown gets started. I'm going to walk outside and get some air. I'm sure a few folks will start drifting in early. Sam we need to go by the tack room and find you a pair of boots. Breeches and jerseys will be in your room by noon. I thought we might get to the horses a bit early to warm up."

"A warm up would be a good idea thanks. I may be just a little stiff from yesterday."

"You mean from falling from your horse?" Ashley had to add, "If you don't fall, you don't get hurt. Please try to keep that in mind today. I would certainly like a dance later this evening."

"I'll keep both the tip and offer, in mind."

"Lieutenant Mead.."

"Yes Ensign Kennedy."

"Where and when might the ladies arrive? Some of us will have to entertain ourselves without the benefit of a gallop across the polo field."

"Oh I'd be surprised if some don't show up uninvited.. soon."

"And for my dear and retiring sister who has very strict standards for her men, physical, mental and moral. Have you invited any fellows?"

"As opposed to my brother's standards, which are living and breathing.." Kick chimed in.

"We're a little more challenged for the fellows, you might have heard, there's a war on.. but I have invited only the finest of young Southern gentlemen."

"And if she happens to be looking for louts, we'll all be on the field," my contribution as we walked onto the patio.

Outside the air was warming. Below the terrace crews were setting up tents on the edge of the polo field. Ashley slipped her hand into mine and steered me away from the others.

"I get the notion that the hounds are about to be unleashed tonight."

"You mean the hounds of war, or the dogs of desire?"

"Lust puppies, might be more like it."

"For that I'll stay sober as a Doberman."

"My God what a dogged pursuit of metaphor."

I opened my mouth to reply but she gave me the look. I went silent as a Schnauzer.

"I want to make a point here. From that discussion this morning, from the headlines every morning and from our first discussion at the end of a long dark pier.. it seems apparent that none of us know where we'll be in a month's time. What is clear is that this weekend is something that will never happen again. Who knows who will come back from this war."

She took a step closer.

"But I'll tell you one thing, polo boy. You'd better not go out there and do anything stupid today, because it is not my intention to spend the night nursing you."

With that she leaned in and kissed me hard on the lips, before pushing me away.

I heard two distinct claps behind me.

"And the first point of the day goes to the lady."

Kennedy was by the pool. He'd already changed into bathing trunks and was standing there, a tall skinny kid, smiling.

"I thought the sailors and Marines were supposed to get the girls," George added as he stepped beside Kennedy. He, too, was in trunks but compared to Kennedy looked like Charles Atlas.

"It's the uniforms fellows. The girls love the uniforms," I tossed back.

"That's just the dressing. This is what they think about on those long lonely winter nights."

Mead actually pulled an Atlas pose on the edge of the pool. Kennedy pushed him in.

"Alas Atlas," Kennedy shrugged and executed a neat dive into the pool.

There's a funny thing about most polo games, they seem to create two worlds. One is on the field. Eight players move at incredible speed on top of beautiful horses. Risk is part of the thrill and death is not unknown. Then there's the crowd. At larger matches tens of thousands may attend. Few are barely aware of what goes on the field. They come for the show, themselves and whatever airs they can create around their sideboard lunches and silver and champagne. It sometimes seems a silly waste, though there's little wrong with a slightly inebriated debutante who lingers beyond the sixth chukker when the daylight fades as easily as her honor.

Then there are games like this one. The crowd is smaller. In this town almost everyone has some connection to horses. They know the game and they know the players. The silver along the sideboard is there, serving cocktails at a long bar open to anyone, there is no class distinction. The only impressions made today will be on the field.

Riding along the boards on the far side of the field I looked across to see the crowd in place. There was a tent at center field where I could see Ashley standing. Jack was an easier mark tall and lean with Kick as a matching part of the Kennedy clan. I was moving my mare upfield taking easy shots to warm up. The other players were doing the same. The difference; each of Hitchcock's shots sailed about three times the distance of mine.

The referee blew his whistle and both teams rode into the lineup. Tommy was on my team, Pete Bostwick was on George's side. Two other players rounded out each side.

On the first play in I caught a piece of the ball and moved it downfield, missing my second shot. Hitchcock was coming up behind and sent the ball soaring over my head and about a hundred yards towards the goal. George and I were off in a race for the ball. Coming up hard, he went for a hook. I pulled my one trick out of the bag and checked my horse. He rode past the ball and I hit a shot reaching under the horse's neck for a goal. That's how the first half went. Clean play. Clearly

Hitchcock and Bostwick were riding hard hitting long shots to feed the ball upfield to Mead and myself.

At half time, Ashley walked down to the player's tent at the corner of the field with an extra glass of Champagne in her hand.

"Good boy gets a sip of Champagne for not getting hurt in the first half."

I took the glass and threw it back in one gulp, "Boy thirsty. Girl get more after game."

"If Girl get Boy Champagne. Girl get boy."

"Boy like."

"Are we done with the Tarzan thing?"

"Yep."

A groom brought a fresh horse up to start the next chukker. I mounted and Ashley handed up my helmet. As I leaned down to take it I leaned further and kissed her, then put my heel into the horse's flank and cantered off smiling.

The fourth chukker started off with the same smooth speed, the flash of faces and sound of cheers along the sidelines. But there were some subtle shifts. The horse to horse bumps were becoming a little harder. Some of the shots on goal a little more dramatic.

So what the hell.

George was running the ball downfield and I came up hard on the side opposite his mallet and drove my pony's shoulder into his. He got his shot in but we were locked in a shoving match riding downfield at full speed. He managed to keep the line of the ball on his mallet side giving me one hard bump before leaning way out of his saddle to take a shot. His horse cut sharply to the left into mine doing what he'd been told to do, but in effect.. he rode out from under George.

It always seems like slow motion. George was suspended in mid-air for a moment, then everything went back to real time. There is a school for unplanned dismounts, one of hard knocks. Most who ride have graduated. George went straight to the automatic response of tucking his shoulder and hitting the ground rolling. He came straight up standing on his feet with the reins still in his hand. It took a second to settle in. Then he looked at the horse, who was fine.....and smiled at me then turned towards the crowd and bowed. That brought applause from the sidelines.

Tommy rode up laughing, "You might want to save some of that fight for the Japs there Marine-cowboy. You know that fall invokes the first round rule." He turned to the crowd, "First round's on George."

Mead was getting back on his horse, "Actually Tommy it's my party. All the rounds are on me."

Hitchcock rode tapping the ball a few feet forward then brought his arm fully back for a shot and yelled, "George is buying. Let's get this game done."

He unleashed a shot that looked like it came from a cannon. Eight riders took off at full gallop. The final chukkers were played like a count-down clock to cocktails. Both Tommy and Pete drew cheers and shouts from the sideboards with play that seemed impossible. The game ended as a tie.

We all rode back to the main tent and handed off our horses. There is a delightful divide between players and spectators in the post game tent. We in boots and breeches and sweat and dirt. They in fresh clothes and scents. Ashley walked within arm's reach and I grabbed her in a huge, happy hug.

"Dirty boy," she said, smiling into my eyes.

"Dirty girl?" my eyes were smiling, too.

"Oh.. in ways you can't imagine."

She let that one hang. I had no comeback because my mind was already imagining. We walked towards an area where the players were grabbing drinks and talking. Jack was in one corner of the tent, talking to a small crowd of the local finest. George was heading toward Kennedy. I put my hands around a cold beer and we walked to join them.

Tommy was in an opposite corner with a crowd of admirers. I could hear some talk of the game. I have no doubt that today's game that would be remembered and go unmatched for the rest of my lifetime. But polo is no different than any other sport. In the clubhouse after golf, in the bar after baseball, the play by play replay almost always sounds insipid. There was better gab going on.

Jack was offering his own tales of fearless horsemanship from an earlier trip to Arizona.

"Riding in Arizona was turning me into a rough rider, a real cowboy, unlike these pretty fellows you see playing their little games on the pitch. It was all going well, until I got kicked where I love and was stretched out for a few blissful minutes."

That drew a laugh and a couple of sympathetic glances from some young women who looked like they might have the nursing skills to ease his pain.

We sank into chairs as innocent bystanders. A beer after a game is about the second best sensation I can think of. My muscles were tired but not sore yet. The smell of horse and leather lingered and combined with the feel of well earned grit and dirt was a ticket to relaxation. Ashley reached out and we touched hands. The afternoon faded in a haze of conversation and an occasional outburst from the colorful people amusing themselves.

Black tie affairs always seem a farce. If you think people put on airs around a polo field, put them in a tuxedo and evening dress and see what you get. Tonight seemed worth the trouble of tying a tie, surrendering to a cummerbund and affixing cufflinks. The formality fit the end of this day and this point in our lives. If you're going out, go in style.

Leaving my room, I paused to look out french doors that led onto a small balcony then walked outside. Below the terraces, lovely by day, were even more beautiful in the evening. The upper was set with tables for dinner. Somehow, candelabras had appeared, suspended over the area offering a soft and sophisticated light. On the lower area the stage was set. The band was beginning to play under soft spot lights. Lanterns were strung over tables on the lower level and carried the line of their light all the way down to the tents on the polo field. I looked up to see a full moon rising above the trees.

"It's stunning isn't it?"

Ashley walked up behind me and slipped her arm around my waist. Her shoulders were almost bare. Thin straps connected them to the dress below. It was ivory satin. Trimmed at the top and waist with beads of a black luminescence.

"I was about to say it's one of the most beautiful things I've seen until you walked out."

"Oh my, you do know how to flattuh a girl," she said.

"There's something just brilliant about how the rich spend their money to create luxury with such ease. That looks like a Hollywood set just waiting for the star to appear," I paused, "Oh that's you. I am basking in your luminance."

"Amusing, you. In my contract I don't sing for my supper but only after it and it'd better be soon. I'm starving."

We stood for another moment looking downward. The King and Queen in review of the crowd. Ashley did a little wave of her hand. It seemed so silly. The night seemed so perfect.

Almost by Ashley's command, the call for dinner came so quickly I barely had time to finish my whiskey before being whisked to the table. Fortunately it was not one of those parties where friends, or dates, or spouses are split up to try to engender what some would mistake as more lively banter. The four of us were seated at the same table just as the first round of Champagne was served with a lobster salad. Then it began.

From a nearby table Tommy Hitchcock stood with glass in hand.

"To all our boys who fly to war. May their nerves be steady, their planes faster and their bombs on target."

That drew a round of, "Hear, hear."

George was up next.

"To the Marines who take the fight to the field. May the Japs regret the day they ever left their little island."

Jack grabbed his glass as he stood up.

"To the Navy. May our ships out-run and out-gun our enemy. May our subs strike hard from the Ocean's depths and our planes rain down death from the skies. May this country grasp the notion of total war and deliver it on all fronts. To Tommy, may your heroism from the First War carry and lead us in this one. To George, my dear friend... may the only enemy you face be native women in grass skirts. And to you all, an old Irish blessing: Until we meet again, may God hold you in the palm of His hand."

Each person at every table stood to their feet and raised their glass to the toast, or to Kennedy it was hard to tell. He had seized the moment and shaped the emotion. There were more than a few damp eyes in the crowd.

The toasts formed a sense of solidarity in the group and they now seemed to launch into the dinner and the evening with a sense of purpose. The Marine had organized an effective army of servers. Food came out flawlessly. The second course of perfect lamb was served with a perfect Margaux. That was followed by a dessert course of flan, with a small glass of Madeira. I believe three courses were all this group would sit for. Some were beginning to get up and table hop as I sat sipping coffee. The band was beginning to stir.

"Sounds like it's showtime for someone," I leaned towards Ashley.

"Yep. This should be fun. The band sounds good. We had a little meeting this afternoon to talk about songs. The group here seems well primed. I'm going to sing for about an hour. Then your mission, mister is to come and rescue me."

"Got it. One hour, then abduct the singer."

"You make that sound fun."

"I intend it to be."

She headed off through the crowd, stopping for a quick word or a handshake along the way. The band was running through an overture of some of the year's popular tunes trying to keep America's mind off the war. They started into the beginning of a good choice for tonight's opening song. Ashley timed her arrival to the mike perfectly.

Couple of jiggers of moonlight and add a star,
Pour in the blue of a June night and one guitar,
Mix in a couple of dreamers and there you are:
Lovers hail the Moonlight Cocktail.

With Glenn Miller in the background I lit a cigarette and headed towards a table where I could watch Ashley without sitting straight in front looking like some smitten fool, which I was, but I preferred to hide it. There were admirers in front who were filling that role anyway. A few couples were on the dance floor. Some couples danced with a degree of practice. Others performed moves that might best be left for home. I was just as glad to be a spectator at this event. Moving into a Cole Porter Ashley caught my eye and offered a wink across the crowd.

My story is much too sad to be told,
but practically everything
leaves me totally cold.
The only exception i know is the case,
when i'm out on a quiet spree,
fighting vainly the old enui
and i suddenly turn and see,
your fabulous face.
I get no kick from Champagne.

I took that as a cue and headed towards Kick, Jack and George and some Champagne - or better - at the bar. Jack and Kick were teasing each other about their own varied relationships. George seemed to be taking Kick's side of the exchange and I was getting a sense the Marine was starting his own charm offensive against Kick. Jack seemed to have his own objectives set on a very attractive local whom I noticed at the field in the afternoon, but who came back dressed to kill tonight. In my mind I wished them each their own pleasures and walked back towards the stage. Ashley had moved through medleys of most of the main songs and, as I might have guessed, was ending with Gershwin. She caught my eye and gave an imperceptible nod. The sign.

The way you wear your hat
The way you sip your tea
The memory of all that
No, no they can't take that away from me

It was a sentimental song to end the evening. An homage to love, in past tense. She finished the last notes of the song and I reached up to take her hand. The party stopped while everyone stood for an ovation. Ashley effected a bow and then waved towards the band. The leader stepped forward for his bow and we made an escape. She steered as politely as possible through the crowd and towards the bar. George, Jack and Kick saw us walking their way and intercepted us with big hugs of enthusiasm.

"Ashley, you are fabulous, talented and beautiful. You made this party," George was happy, a little drunk and a little less of a tightly wired Marine heading for combat.

"My pleasure, my friend. Without you this evening wouldn't have happened."

"What can I get you to drink?" George leaned towards the bar.

"A bottle of Champagne and two glasses. I've got plans."

"You're a genius," Kennedy approached the bar, "Bartender I'll have the same."

George wasn't going to be left out, "Here, here... make that three ways please."

The three men each took a bottle, the glasses and a girl by the arm. Then each went in separate directions. I steered Ashley towards the terrace steps downward to the polo field.

"You looking for a little night match, polo boy?"

"I know I'm no match for you. I just wanted to be alone, just us."

"Well technically *us* is not alone, but I'm good with those teams."

We walked to the furthest tent away from the party. I loosened my tie and took off my jacket. Ashley stepped out of her heels. I opened the wine and poured us two glasses.

"Compared to the others it may be the lamest toast of the night. But to us." I raised my glass and clinked it with hers.

She took my hand and led me towards the polo field, saying nothing, just walking. At mid-field she stopped. We were far from the lights of the party. Sounds drifted down but seemed distant. The moon was almost directly overhead.

"How many shadows do you see on the ground?"

"Two."

She pulled herself close to me and put her lips close to my ear.

"How many now?"

"One."

"Tonight that is the only world that matters."

Later when the Champagne was gone and the distant sounds were little more than whispers we walked back up stairs and into the house crossing the remains of a party well done. I walked Ashley to her door. She led me in.

"Your room is larger."

"Perks of the profession."

She dropped her shoes on the floor. I reached behind and turned off the light. The moon was still high enough to send soft beams into the room. I pulled her into the light and kissed her gently. Slowly and between caresses our clothes fell piece by piece to the ground until we were again a single silhouette in the moonlight.

In the middle of lovemaking I watched like I was someone else in the room, to see how her body fit with mine, to see the desire in her eyes, to see the furrow in her brow when her passion peaked. They were images I wanted to save to be able to pull out of a memory bank at a future time when beauty and love would be banished from the world.

Later as she lay sleeping I slipped out of bed to smoke and stare out the window.

"You look pretty good naked in the moonlight."

Her voice startled me. I jumped. She laughed.

"I thought you were asleep, how long have you been watching?"

"Long enough. And don't think I don't know what you've been thinking. Come back to bed. Remember tonight this is the only world that matters."

CHAPTER *10*

Reno, Nevada
April 20, 1942

ON THE TABLE, CANDLES WERE lit. This last dinner with her future ex-husband would be served in the privacy of her room. What some might mistake as a romantic setting was simply a more controlled environment for recording a conversation. Cocktails were just a shake away. Dinner was waiting in a silver service and scattered about the room were the listening devices that were the greatest betrayal of her marriage.

Inga looked out the window. Darkness was settling in the street below. One of the G-men was across the street. She knew another was waiting in the lobby. Two others were in the next room listening and recording. It made her a bit nervous. It made her a lot angry.

Her past infidelities had been a matter of her desires, her choices. This act of betrayal was forced by the hand of someone else. Hoover was using her for his purposes. It's not how she operated.

Neither the desire for divorce nor the affair with Jack were news to her husband. Paul Fejos was not a hapless cuckold. He arrived in America penniless and in less than two decades pressed his passion for filmmaking into a string of Hollywood successes. Frustrated by the machine that fed movie houses in the United States he began travelling the world creating documentaries of exotic people and places. Returning from Thailand he met Axel Wenner-Gren. With a billionaire as backer he travelled into the jungles of South America to locate and film the ancient lost cities of the Incas.

The circles of the rich and those connected are rather small. Fejos had already spoken with Joe Kennedy while in New York a few months earlier. Inga sifted through a short stack of letters from a husband both scorned and concerned.

> *"Well here it is, your first break in the greatest institution of newspaper writing in the US. You made Winchell's column. I'm the clown in the act and the laughs are on me. I have had enough in these last weeks. If it would have been you who was the target of the affections of the gentleman, it would be better. But that HE should be the target--that is to say that you are the one who does the running after--that is pretty sour. That my proud, always digni-fied, ramrod wife gets this fifth rate slap in the face, that hurts. I feel like hell about it."*

She lifted another that seemed to play from a different angle.

> *"There is, however, one thing I want to tell you in connec-tion with your Jack. Before you let yourself go into this thing any deeper, lock stock and barrel, have you thought that maybe the boy's father or family will not like the idea?"*

Even as a director Paul had played every actor's role in the months leading to Reno, irate and jealous, concerned and supportive and in the last note manipulative. Playing her love for Jack against his family and future wasn't even the most desperate. He used Inga's mother as a cou-rier of consequences to come.

> *"He has a detective out after you who knows when Jack comes in your apartment and where he goes; he know how many lights are burning and when the lights are turned off. He said that in two months you would be out of your job and the old Kennedy would not be sorry for you because he doesn't want his son to have anything to do with you. I hate to repeat all the terrible things he said about you..."*

It was fairly certain in that Nevada hotel on an April night that soon she would be leaving for a new life. One without Paul certainly. One without Jack, almost as certain. It seemed the only relationship likely to survive the month was with Hoover. She returned to being angry. The phone rang interrupting her pleasant thoughts on how she might get back at the head of the FBI.

"He's on his way up." The caller hung up.

Inga stashed the letters in the desk drawer gave one satisfying glance in the mirror and walked to the door just as the first knuckles fell on the opposite wood. She waited for the second knock, took a deep breath and opened the door.

Paul didn't enter. He made an entrance.

"Inga my darling. What a lovely place. What a lovely room and what a lovely woman about to become my ex-wife."

"Good evening Paul. So good of you to come."

"Why, you called. I came. Isn't that what a good husband's supposed to do?"

"Then if you're going to play to role of a good husband why don't you step over to the bar and shake us a martini?"

"From the looks all this seems to be the start of a romantic evening."

"Let's just say it's an evening to celebrate the past."

Fejos shook two martinis with the skill of Manhattan gin-slinger.

"Then let's toast to the present, before it's the past."

"Let's not use tense, to create tension."

"Then let me simply appreciate your beauty and the waning moments of this marriage," Paul offered, raising both hands and holding one martini in each.

Inga took her drink and a large first sip. The gin slipped down her throat in that way that warms and transforms. A single sip and she felt the nervousness slip away. Dutch courage is for those with nothing left to lose. She sat on the couch as if a simple verb could convey how her posture most inviting, was the opening salvo of the evening. Her hand patted the cushion. Paul Fejos was almost twice her age but responded like a puppy trained and eager. She could do that to men.

"Tell me, Paul, I hear you've traded the jungles for New York." So it began.

"One jungle for another you might say, though it's tough sometimes to tell which is more dangerous. You may have heard our friend Axel is backing The Viking Fund. You are dining tonight with the Director of Research."

"What are you researching?"

"People my dear. Ancient and interesting people and cultures. I feel like I'm just beginning a whole new life and looking into a whole new world of how cultures that evolve continents apart are all connected. What we need to understand is how."

"You've changed a lot in five years. There aren't too many men who go from Hollywood director to anthropologist."

"Humans are a much more interesting study than the fantasy world of movies."

"And what are the interests of Axel in all this?"

She wanted to get this part over with. The question brought Paul closer to the edge of the couch. It was hard not to imagine the same happening on the other side of the wall where the agents were eager to score for Hoover.

Paul leaned towards her, "You should be more attuned to Axel's interests than I. Do you still see him?"

"We haven't seen each other in some time. You should know that. You'd know if I was in New York."

"In fact I do. Do know that you've been in town to see some other fellow. You're a very busy girl managing all your men."

She was losing control of the conversation. This was not supposed to be about her outside interests. It was supposed to be about his. Though it struck her as amusing that his private eyes seemed to be just as effective in surveillance as the FBI's. One hand put the cocktail glass down and the other went to his knee.

"You're the only man of interest tonight," she stood lifting his hand to join her and kissed him lightly on the mouth.

"Now let's have dinner before it gets cold. I'm starving."

"You do still know how to whet an appetite."

The hotel menu seemed the better from several years of influx from outsiders with income and unwilling to accept both enforced residency and poor food during a divorce. Inga ordered a simple salad of artichokes and entree of beef bourguignon and a bottle of Chateau Pontet Canet, thinking if the food failed she could at least count on the wine.

Paul ate thoughtfully for a few minutes.

"You know these artichokes are from the Mediterranean, the entree and wine from France - it seems we just never seem to escape the food dictates of Europe."

"You've lost me there."

"Here's something I learned from the Incas. For thousands of years they built an empire that rivaled the reach of Rome with millions of people. They built their empire on the power of food. The whole of the civilization was dedicated to producing and distribution. A string of storehouses through the empire kept several years of food in supply. The Spaniards came and between smallpox and their disdain for the local food managed to kill an empire."

"Unfortunately, there weren't any Peruvian dishes on the menu."

"Inga please don't confuse my passion with your perfect evening. It's just that the more I travel and work in native cultures the more I think that by ignoring the knowledge of centuries we risk our future."

"I'm sure there are a number of lessons in history that could have helped to prevent this current crisis. Is Axel interested in your native foods?"

"Axel again. No, as you know my dear you don't become a billionaire dabbling in local roots. He's interested in mineral rights in Peru."

"Seems a little out of the way."

"Perhaps that's why he's a billionaire. Little things like a world war can make access to certain minerals difficult. Having an outside source could be very profitable in wartime."

"But Peru is siding with the US in the war."

"Sides don't matter when profit, not patriotism, is your motive. That's why he spends most of his time in the Bahamas as far away from the war as possible."

"But not everyone there is neutral, for example the Duke of Windsor."

"It seems for someone suspected of being a spy you certainly are intent on turning the finger towards someone else."

"What's he doing with them?" It was a bold play, but she was tired of playing.

"Jealous maybe? Perhaps his whole intent isn't to foster pro-Nazi feelings with the Duke, but more an interest in the Duchess. It seems the island is a bit dull for them and they find interesting ways to amuse themselves. Axel seems attracted to the Duchess much in the same way he's attracted to you."

"I wouldn't want to be in bed with that pair either figuratively or literally."

"Some would argue the literal, few the figurative at least on this side of the ocean. Seems the Duke isn't backing off his appeasement stand and it's become somewhat worrisome. It also seems the not-so-royal Windsors have some friendly connections with the Germans. Their homes in Paris and the Riviera are under Nazi protection. Worse than his political perspective his wife the Duchess, not The Royal Duchess, is so incensed with the royal denial that she would do -anything- to be Queen including convincing her husband to return to the throne as Hitler's King of a fascist government."

"That's not a very positive long view of the war effort."

"Let's be honest. Look at what Germany's done in less than a decade. Europe as a whole and Britain involved in a last stand that has done little to stop them. Call them pragmatists but some are looking at how the world might realign itself if Hitler wins. The Windsors and Wenner-Gren may see things a little differently from the deck of his yacht in the Bahamas. They are trying to plan a new world order that includes themselves, aligned with Hitler. If I were watching someone though I'd watch the Duchess. She's neither royal, nor rich and seems to be the one with the most to gain here."

"She's certainly a better target than some present," that statement was for others to hear.

"And what of you my dear little watched woman? What is the story of your little sailor boy? Does he have a ship to sail yet?"

"If you're referring to Jack I believe that ship has sailed. He wants to get into the war just like almost every other man I know. I told him that to me he no longer exists."

"War is an unfortunate time to be in love. Young impetuous fellows go off to fight. Things happen and they don't come back. These days there's no such thing as a merry widow."

"Nor a gay divorcee."

"Since we're on a musical theme how about a last dance?"

Paul stood from the table and took her hand leading towards a radio on the mantle. He turned the knob to the opening notes of a song that he might as well selected.

> *My heart is sad and lonely*
> *For you I cry*
> *For you, dear, only*
> *I tell you I mean it*
> *I'm all for you*
> *Body and soul*

By the end of the song her head was on his shoulder. So were a few tears. The night had not gone quite as she'd imagined. This final betrayal of Paul felt wrong. He didn't deserve to be played by her, by Hoover. There was much that would not be the same tomorrow morning. Another song started but Paul stopped. He lifted her chin and kissed her as in days of old, then led her towards the bedroom.

In the next room the two FBI agents looked at each other.

"That music's killing us. We won't be able to hear a thing that goes on in the bedroom."

"Yes we will. I put a separate recorder in there just in case. The Director never wants to miss a conversation *in flagrante delicto.*

"What is that French or something?"

"Latin you idiot. He likes to listen in on people in the act. Seems like everyone's getting something of what they wanted this evening. Except for Inga."

CHAPTER 11

Charleston, SC
April 1942

CHARLESTON IN WARTIME CAN BE a dull distraction. The week after a farewell to the men in arms. Those of us without assignment returned to pace the pretty streets and plan our escapes. Kick returned to Washington where every part of the town was wholly involved in all aspects of the war, except for the fighting and dying.

Far from where anything was happening, three plotters gathered around an afternoon cocktail in the Sumter Hotel.

"I have fond memories of this place," Jack leaned back smiling.

"This room?" Ashley met his smile.

"No. Upstairs."

"Is that over?" I thought an innocent question.

Jack paused, "Over. I'm not sure anything is ever really over. She wrote me from Reno. Wants to know when I set sail and said all sorts of motherly things about my future, my health and staying in touch."

"Motherly?" Ashley smiled.

"It's complicated."

"About the health thing.." I started.

"Sam, here's where we draw a line," Jack leaned forward, "between a friendship and anything you might put in print in the future. On the record I have no health problems. Any mention of that would scuttle any hopes I have of getting off this desk in Charleston and into the war. Between us, I've been in and out of doctors from here to Massachusetts of late, none of whom can quite make up their mind about what to do about my back. Some said surgery, some said exercise. Finally the greatest medical minds from two naval hospitals told me it was some sort of muscular strain. I'm now investing in a Charles Atlas course."

"Live clean, think clean, and don't go to burlesque shows. I quote Charles Atlas," how that came to mind I'm not sure, but it seemed worth adding.

"Well a fellow can only do so much," Kennedy laughed, "But as I begin and as you watch this body transform from a 97 pound weakling to something the women will adore.. I'm reported fit and applying for sea duty. It seems the Navy has finally hit the bottom of the barrel. They've put out a call to a couple thousand low ranking patriotic sorts who want to go to sea but who don't have any training. I'm applying for torpedo boat school. The requirements are very strict physically--you have to be young, healthy and unmarried--and as I am young and unmarried I'm trying to get in. They're setting up a training school in Melville, Rhode Island. Sixty day wonders from deskbound ensign to a man of the high seas. If I last we get command of a torpedo boat--and are sent abroad--where I don't know. "

"Bulkeley's little Mosquito Fleet?" I asked.

"So you've heard."

"Hard not to know one of the few heroes of the Philippines. He's hot copy these days for a country in need of a hero. Plucking MacArthur from Corregidor in his PT boat was no small feat, but I'm still a little leary about calling the two of them heros just because they raced to safety in the dark across 600 miles of open water to Mindanao. Ask the fellows they left on Bataan."

"The boats are fast. They get action and that's what I want. I won't debate MacArthur or the abysmal loss of the Philippines."

"I'll give him points for bravado. He's in the States on a hero's tour. He boasts he told Roosevelt that 500 PT boats would give the US control across the South Pacific. True or not, they're cranking torpedo boats out by the hundreds."

"And all I want is one. All I need is for my orders to be approved. What about you Sam?"

"Well, my chain of command works a little differently. Instead of the high notions of defeating the forces of evil and saving the world from fascism they want to sell newspapers. I told them I wanted to be assigned abroad to a combat zone. They said no. So I offered my resignation and said I was going to enlist."

That drew a furrowed brow from Ashley.

"They thought to reconsider. I told them, as I've discussed with Ashley, the notion of covering the war from the eyes of the enlisted man. There are plenty of reporters going for the big story. I think narrowing the focus might just help people at home understand what their fathers, brothers and sons are going through."

"And when do you ship out writer boy?" That one from Ashley.

"We're working with the military for an attachment with a unit."

"Any ideas?" from Jack.

"Marines."

"Mead's War."

"We talked about the Marines and their mission last weekend. It's going to be a tough slog through the South Pacific."

"Ahh... the South Pacific!! Land of native girls and fungal infections," Jack laughed.

"Better be just fungal infections," Ashley offered through narrowed eyes.

The table fell silent. Jack and I turned our eyes on Ashley.

"What?" She looked back at us.

"We were both kind of wondering where you're planning on spending the war," Jack led.

"Ponderous thoughts I've had. I didn't think I have much to offer in the role of Rosie the Riveter. And as much as I'd just love to pick up a gun and go off fighting like you manly men.. I don't have a thing to wear for combat. So I thought I'd do what I do best... sing. I'm joining the USO. If I can't fight on the front lines I can sing there. They're already recruiting for what they're calling Camp Shows. Joe E. Brown is out entertaining the troops in Alaska. My agent says they're the biggest show on earth right now and heading overseas. They're even forming what they call a Foxhole Circuit for the front lines."

"Any particular theatre interest you?"

"Well from what you two boys are saying, I'm starting to think I might look good in a grass skirt somewhere in the South Pacific."

"Outstanding service to our boys in uniform," Jack jumped in, "I'll expect nothing less than your help and support in squiring some of your beautiful USO friends when we meet sometime on those foreign isles."

"As if you'd need me, already armed with your Kennedy charm."

Jack stood.

"Then a toast, to the South Pacific to our Marines and sailors there, to those of us about to join, may God bring us victory and bring us back to this table one day."

His voice carried across the room. As we rose and joined the toast; every man, woman, customer and server, stood in salute.

New York, NY
April, 1942

Lieutenant Commander John Bulkeley saluted the statue of General William Tecumseh Sherman as he walked across Grand Army Plaza and up the steps of the equally imposing Plaza Hotel. The doorman fed him into the ornate revolving door. The door spat him out the other side into the lobby. The scene was enough to make you stop and stare but Bulkeley was no tourist. He was here for a meeting, a private lunch at the request of an ex-ambassador. Never slow to the game, the lieutenant was picking up pointers quickly on how to play politics and speak the parlance of the powerful. He walked to the desk. The naval uniform didn't seem to impress the manager.

"May I help you?"

"I'm Lieutenant John Bulkeley. I believe I'm expected."

The manager looked down his nose at a list. He was suddenly a changed man.

"Lieutenant Bulkeley yes indeed. Welcome to the Plaza. You are expected, indeed."

He looked up and snapped his fingers at a a bell boy.

"Frank take the lieutenant to Suite 1505. Enjoy your lunch sir."

"Thank you."

In the silent elevator ride Bulkeley thought of the two day trip through rough seas that brought MacArthur to safety and he to the White House, to the Plaza and to places he'd never dreamed.

The PT escape was MacArthur's idea. The Japs had a notion he was leaving and were moving to try to capture a big prize. The General decided not to wait for the safer option of going underwater by submarine. He said he didn't like being cooped up. So after a short test ride four PT boats were loaded with MacArthur, his wife, son and staff to set off at sunset. The seas grew rough and the boats became separated in the dark. The second night wasn't any better. Rear Admiral Rockwell was on *PT 34* and said it was the worst bridge he'd ever been on and wouldn't do duty on one of those boats for anything in the world. Bulkeley smiled to himself. The boats got them to Cagayan. It just wasn't the piece of cake Bulkeley had promised.

The boy knocked on the door, "Lieutenant Bulkeley sir."

The door was opened by a man wearing a tail coat and formal tie.

"Good afternoon lieutenant. The ambassador is waiting. This way please."

Butlers for lunch. What a world. He led the way through a suite the size of an apartment. A man immediately got up from a table set for lunch. He dropped a newspaper and walked towards him.

"There he is. One of the heroes of the Philippines. John, it's damned nice to meet a hero of Mr. Roosevelt's war."

"Ambassador Kennedy, a pleasure to meet you."

Joe Kennedy was taller than Bulkeley imagined. His hair was thinning in front. He was light on his feet, like a boxer or a politician, down for the moment but not to be counted out.

His smile was disarming.

"Have a seat lieutenant and let's have lunch. I ordered a couple of steaks. I eat so much damned fish in Palm Beach I grow to miss a good steak at the Plaza. Sit, sit... let's eat."

The butler served steak and fried potatoes with a salad. Simple, but Bulkeley savored every one of these meals after duty on a cramped PT boat with navy rations. Kennedy glanced at the newspaper off to the side.

"This war isn't making for very good headlines for the President. Besides saving MacArthur's ass you've done him a big favor by bringing a story about bravery and guts to the country."

The last phrase stuck in Bulkeley's mind. Joe Kennedy wasn't known for either. He'd avoided serving in the first world war and left London when the German bombs started falling.

"The mission, sir was not my idea. I just drove the boat."

"Humility serves a hero well. But let's be honest. You're brave. I'm not. To Roosevelt, you're a hero, I'm a heel. You have ambitions for your boats. I have ambitions for my boys."

"I'm not sure I understand Mr. Ambassador."

"Dammit call me Joe."

"Ok Joe let's be honest. What do you want with me?"

"Business John. Let's talk business. You want Roosevelt to build you more boats. You need to keep those PTs in the public's eye. They're not sinking any Jap battleships lately. I've got two sons. One's a pilot. The other wants to captain one of these torpedo boats of yours. One of those two boys will be president someday. Both need to see some action in this war. The public loves a hero. The public loves you. Jack has applied to your training school in Rhode Island. Are you the one who can get him in?"

"I am. But if we're talking business here. How does getting your son on one of my boats help me?"

"Simple. You put a Kennedy in command of one of your boats and the papers at home will pay attention."

"Ok. But you should understand this. We're only taking single young men and the bravest at that. This isn't a pleasure cruise around Hyannis Port. Most of the people who go out on PTs won't be coming home. Do you want to put your son at that risk?"

Joe Kennedy sat back in his chair and dropped his napkin across his plate. The lunch was coming to a close.

"Roosevelt created the risk. He got this country into the war. If he'd listened to me more then maybe we wouldn't be putting millions of our boys at risk. My son Jack isn't stupid. He knows the risks and he knows what he wants. It's the same thing I want. Just send him someplace that isn't too deadly."

Charleston, SC
June, 1942

Spring was running out in Charleston. So was patience. Jack's more than anyone's. Without Inga for distraction the desk duty compared to the quickening pace of war was making him felt increasingly left behind. He'd travelled to Melville to interview with Bulkeley, along with hundreds of others. Jack wanted PT duty and had made frequent calls to Washington and daily trips into his commander's office at the Charleston Naval Headquarters.

Finally the telegram came.

ENS JOHN F. KENNEDY 1 V(S) USNR HEREBY DETACHED PROCEED MELVILLE, RI MOTOR TORPEDO BOAT SQUADRON TRAINING SCHOOL IMMEDIATELY.

And he was gone.

Jack took the next flight out of Charleston. He called before leaving town to say, against the advice of all, he was going to swing through Washington to see Inga.

Ashley and I had taken a cottage on Sullivan's Island for a few days. They would be our last together for a while, or forever. It was late. I could hear the waves breaking on the beach a hundred yards away. Ashley was closer, much closer. We'd spent the night talking and laughing, lovemaking, walking on the beach, lovemaking... did I mention that? Now she slept peacefully, beautifully. I slipped out of bed and grabbed a pair of pants. At the door I turned to look back. Her back was towards me bare with just a sheet draped across the hips. The scene was worthy of a new Renaissance. Then I walked into the kitchen to sit and finish my last report from Charleston.

```
Dateline:
Charleston, S.C. June 19, 1942
Sam Marlow/New York Herald Tribune


    War calls all sorts to glory, just as Death
will call all sorts home. In six months time
```

those of us who seek the front lines may very well wish we were back home in a quaint southern town sipping cocktails in a posh hotel. But those who cling to those comforts will not be those who will win this war. It will be won by the sweat, suffering and sacrifice of every soldier, sailor, Marine and pilot who think less of the risk of death, than the risk of living under fascism. It will take the toil and privation of every American to make that happen. But the war will be won not by the many. It will be won by the few.

I have met a few here in Charleston. A merchant marine hero here on the homefront. There are others who can't get away from their desk jobs fast enough to get to the front lines. Over a thousand young naval officers applied to get into training at Lieutenant Commander John Bulkeley's Motor Torpedo Boat Squadron training school in Melville, Rhode Island. Bulkeley was the fellow who used his PT boats to get General MacArthur off Corregidor. His recruiting speech for skippers is a little rough: "Those of you who want to come back after the war and raise families need not apply; PT boat skippers are not coming back!" That speech didn't stop a single applicant.

One who is on his way to Melville worked in naval intelligence here in Charleston. He's 25 years old from Cape Cod. He has a brother who just earned his wings as a navy pilot. He is the son of the former U.S. ambassador to Great Britain. You can say what you want about Joe Kennedy Senior, and many have, but he has two sons willing to trade their privileged lives for their country. Mother Rose Kennedy has nine children. To a mother none are spare, but even she spelled it out to the siblings: ".. He is quite ready to die for the U.S.A. in order to keep the Japanese and the Germans from becoming the dominant people on their respective continents, believing that sooner or later they would encroach upon ours."

Even the mother of one of America's most powerful families knows sacrifice is ahead. Her son asked for duty in one of the most dangerous assignments in the war. Jack Kennedy has gotten his wish.

CHAPTER *12*

T HE GOLDEN GATE BRIDGE SOARED overhead. Every hand was on deck. This was no drill. This was goodbye. Our convoy was passing beneath. The two towers rose hundreds of feet above us in a vermillion-orange glow. It was a color in contrast to our ships painted in navy dazzle camouflage patterns. Together they could be an artistic comparison of surreal purpose, one to be more visible the other to be less. From the shore this would be quite a painting.

I stood on the bridge of the USS George F. Elliott at the captain's invitation. Below deck, from bow to stern, were 1300 Marines of the 1st Division, 3rd battalion. We watched the bridge approach, craned our necks to watch it pass over and then watched her disappear in the distance. On the water the bridge served as a gateway. We crossed from San Francisco Bay into the Pacific Ocean. It marked the transition from the lives we knew to the unknown. Young and fearless we went forth.

I'm a writer. I get paid to think such things.

The summer sun was warm on the deck and the breeze from the ocean was cool. It felt great. The captain was smiling as any good sea captain would when putting out to sea. With salt in your nostrils and a clear sky ahead we were heading out at about 10 knots bound for glory or hell, we wouldn't worry today. The men below seemed to feel the same. A cheer went up when we passed beneath the bridge. Heading into open waters some drifted back mid-ship into groups. A few clung to the rails, or heaved over them. These Marines were just out of training and almost none had seen combat. Few had seen more open water than a bass pond back home. It was kind of hard to tell whether some of the puking was from seasickness or from their last night of shore leave.

One of those below was George Mead. He sold me on the Marines when we spent the weekend in Aiken. There were plenty of correspondents in the European theater. It wasn't too tough a sell to convince the War Department that a few reporters in the Pacific theater might not be a bad idea. It also didn't hurt to pull a few strings. Mead's family had a few. I tapped Jack for a little help. It seemed to be a case of everybody using all their contacts to get into a war, instead of out.

"Nice view from the bridge. I don't ever get tired of it," Captain H.G. Patrick turned his head slightly sideways to talk to me.

"Thanks for the invitation up here."

"Interesting to have a civilian on board. Not quite what I'm used to but some of the higher ups said you were ok. If you'd like join us at the officer's mess for dinner tonight."

"Thank you, sir I'd enjoy that."

Captain Patrick took command of the ship when it was reconverted as a naval transport last year. The USS George F. Elliott was named after a former marine commandant. She was tough and with no frills as expected. Most troop transports were converted ships from one source or another. The Elliott did troop duty in World War 1 was converted back to civilian use and sailed as a passenger ship before being reclaimed by the navy for her second war. Make no mistake, she was no Queen Mary.

We were sailing straight into the sunset. Red at night, sailors delight. The seas were calm in the way that best reflect the sparkling light of the retiring sun. If you focused only on the sun and sparkling surface you could imagine it as a pleasure cruise. Open the view and the convoy of ships changed the purpose. The sea could be both beautiful and deadly - her surface a perfect poker face.

Other writers have framed it better. I thought of Joseph Conrad who'd sailed similar waters and described one war before in The Tale:

> *"What at first used to amaze the Commanding Officer was the unchanged face of the waters, with its familiar expression, neither more friendly nor more hostile. On fine days the sun strikes sparks upon the blue; here and there a peaceful smudge of smoke hangs in*

the distance, and it is impossible to believe that the familiar clear horizon traces the limit of one great circular ambush... One envies the soldiers at the end of the day, wiping the sweat and blood from their faces, counting the dead fallen to their hands, looking at the devastated fields, the torn earth that seems to suffer and bleed with them. One does, really. The final brutality of it--the taste of primitive passion--the ferocious frankness of the blow struck with one's hand--the direct call and the straight response. Well, the sea gave you nothing of that, and seemed to pretend that there was nothing the matter with the world."

Pretend was all we could do—that in this grouping of ships and armed escorts we would be safe. Into the sunset we sailed and into the ship I walked. It was time to ponder dinner and whether being pals with the captain might get a short ration of whiskey.

With some 1300 Marines and the ship's crew combined there were a lot of mouths to feed three times a day for almost three weeks. The mess crews worked around the clock and there were even shifts in the officer's mess. As long as you were eating at the captain's table, you didn't have to worry about getting your share, but by the end of the transit you could bet that fresh food would be rare and canned rations would start making the rounds. After a few days of Vienna sausages, I'd hope some of those Marines might try trolling off the aft deck.

Captain Patrick sent word for me to stop by the office in his personal quarters before dinner. You learn a new way of walking when travelling through a ship. If you go down a ladder backwards, you're derided as a landlubber. Forget to duck when you go through the hatch and you end up with a bad headache. I managed the passageway through the officers quarters and knocked on the door.

"Come in."

There's not much luxury to be found on a troop transport. It wasn't to be found here. The captain sat at a plain desk in an anteroom outside his private quarters. There were a few books and a single framed picture of a lovely woman and a chubby faced little boy.

"Attractive family captain," my way of warming up the conversation.

"Thanks. They're back home on dry land."

"Where's home?"

"She's in Austin, Texas now with family. Far from the water, far from the war and where the biggest worry is whether the Longhorns will top their record last season."

"That might be tough, or pointless if college football can't come up with a decent way to decide on a champion."

"I have a feeling this war will be ancient history before that ever happens. If you want a drink, it's in bottom cabinet under those books."

I didn't jump too quickly, just fast enough to show my lithe form in diving for a drink.

"Pour for yourself. The bottle's there more for psychological support than regular use. The limeys may still have their rum ration but sea duty in war is no place for a drunk captain."

"I hate to drink alone but it's better than not drinking at all."

"I won't think worse of you."

So I poured a couple fingers of his bourbon straight, without guilt, and sat down. I sipped and we chatted about the war in general and his recent passages as captain of the Elliott. There is no dull routine in war. He felt a lot better sailing the Pacific than the Atlantic where German U-boats were taking a much higher toll on ships.

"I guess I could ask where we're going."

"And I would probably give you as evasive an answer as possible. To the South Pacific which you might guess from our heading. To a safe, or somewhat safe, allied port and after that it would be your guess or wager as the case might be."

"A lot of bets going around below about where that might be."

"Where's the money going today?"

"Anywhere from New Caledonia to New Guinea with some long odds on French Polynesia."

"Sounds like some folks have been studying maps and throwing darts. I'd say the Polynesia wager was by someone who thought he'd signed on to a vacation cruise."

"Can you narrow it down?"

"You know I can't. But we will end up somewhere between the first two suggestions."

"That leaves a lot of islands."

"There are a lot of Japs. Throw a dart and put down your money."

Hitting on home, football and war pretty much covered the important topics. My glass was empty so we went on to the officer's mess. This captain didn't pull rank to make his meal any better than anyone else on ship. It was good and solid food. Nothing that made you think of a wine pairing but something we'd all probably dream about in a frenzied state of desire right up next to our girls and lovers in a few short weeks to come.

There's a lot of down time on a troopship. You can sleep and you can eat. Beyond that is a big open span that is filled with occasional emergency drills, card games, smoking and bullshitting with your buddies. There was plenty of time for that. Tonight I thought I'd start with a little discipline and start with doing what they were paying me to do.

Pacific Ocean, 22 June 1942
Sam Marlow/New York Herald Tribune

You might not expect to find a resident of the Lone Star state far out to sea. Seems when Captain H.G. Patrick heard Horace Greeley's command to 'Go West, young man', he hit California and kept on going. Captain Patrick is the commanding officer of the USS George F. Elliott a troop transport carrying a bunch of Marines westward to a place he wouldn't specifically mention. This ship is carrying about 1300 Marines. There are a lot of other ships with us. That's a lot of Marines going somewhere.

A convoy this size has got to attract attention. We did when we stood out from San Francisco Bay. One has to think that some spying eyes ashore relayed that information to the Imperial side of the world. They must be wondering too where all these Marines are headed, while we wonder where the Jap subs are hiding. The Elliott has thirteen gun mounts on her deck but nothing to battle the

enemy below. So we sail south by southwest and on
to our fate.

Captain Patrick sits in his office focused on
the first and less on the latter. He's sailed his
ship across the Atlantic and the Pacific before.
The Jerries are doing much more deadly work with
their U-boats than the Japs with their subs. All
on board support either their lack of initiative
or competence. But Captain Patrick and every man
on this ship knows the record of the Japs in the
south Pacific and knows that we're sailing into
the teeth of a fight. Tonight is our first night
at sea. We have three weeks to think about it.

So now I'm a war correspondent. By the time we hit port I'll have a
string of these one person reports to file. Tomorrow I'll head below to
find some marines and members of the crew. Tonight it was time for the
bunk. I had a small stash of letters that arrived at the hotel last night
before we boarded ship and saved them to read at sea. Some were from
Ashley. They would be the last thing I would read every night. Jack had
proven to be a fairly prolific correspondent. The first of his letters began
from basic training at Melville.

Dear Sam,

*No--that frantic looking figure riding that torpedo above is not
me-- it's the logo for the Mosquito Fleet, a mosquito on a torpedo,
somebody got paid to do that--but it's the way I feel these days.
Training on these PT's may not be quite the cavalry ride Bulkeley
promised. These boats are fast enough, for plywood speed boats
without armor and running on enough jet fuel to blow sky high.
The funny thing is the big weapon we wield. The boats are faster
than the torpedoes. As a matter of fact, most of the Jap ships are
faster than the torpedoes, so this should be some cat and mouse
game when we get to the fight.*

*Though no complaints here. This job on these boats is really the
great spot in the Navy, you are your own boss, and it's like sailing*

around as in the old days, though these motors take a bit of understanding as motors were never my strong point.

But until then, there are bigger worries. I'm the only one with a car here. So most nights after training we all load up and drive into Newport for dinner. On the weekends it's New York City. A couple of my hut mates are fellows from Georgia, football players, good lads but they've never seen the likes of the '21' Club. Seems most of the chorus girls in town are lonely and are quite taken by the uniform of a Navy officer. So I've taken several. The Georgia boys seem ready to give up hunting and fishing for the bigger game in NYC. Kick is still running that boys club down in Washington and doing that old column of Inga Arvad's.

Jack

I guess referring to Inga by her formal name was a sign he was moving on, or not. Her name never seems far from his conversations or letters even in a third person reference. Ashley had a recent note from Inga from California. She seemed to want to get as far away from Washington, the East Coast, Hoover and the Kennedys as possible. Though like Jack she never seemed to sever the emotional connection. Describing the quick visit the two had on his way to Melville, Inga was upset by his back and the constant pain saying, "He looked like a limping monkey from behind. He can't walk at all. That's ridiculous, sending him off to sea duty."

She sounded like a mother. When they were together there was no doubt of the sexual attraction. Mother, lover, she seemed to fill some of both roles in Jack's life, but then no one pays me to play Freud. And Oedipus was not the bedtime story I was seeking.

I picked up one of Ashley's letters. It was postmarked from Charleston. It carried the hint of her scent and I breathed deeply as I read her words and tried to imagine her voice reading them.

Dearest Sam,

I imagine you on a ship at sea somewhere on deck looking outward towards a setting sun, an evening breeze in your face and surrounded by a ship full of men. Someday, if the fates allow, the first two parts of that will be true, but you'll be surrounded by my arms as we cruise on peaceful waters in better times. We're in times we did not create, but the game is afoot and we all seem to be rallying to the cry. You are in your world of men and power to be part of a great armada of war. There is some of that I envy, that bonding that comes with war, even as it is bonded to the suffering that lies ahead. We can pull out Henry V and speak of Saint Crispian and this 'band of Brothers'. For it is you who will speak of their bravery, their fear, their heroism and humility. But I imagine you among them now, George Mead and his young raw Marines. It is a night of liar's poker and bravado real and imagined below deck in cramped quarters with cigarettes as chips. You laugh and ante and deal listening to the accents and dialects and the stories from home. The stories are the currency of your trade and your passion. By sharing them, you will make a difference in this war. America is waiting, so get writing Mr. War Correspondent.

My plans are coming together quickly. We're assembling a troupe to head that way as well. I sometimes think the layers of secrecy for these shows rivals that of war planning. It seems what we do know is that we'll base out of Australia for a while. It's close enough to hit secure zones and where plenty of Americans are based and where more will be rotating on R&R. I suppose after the Jap attacks on Darwin it makes some sense not to publicize where shows and stars (not including self) might show up.

As for you. I'm going to make this especially steamy in the hopes that some censor doesn't take a prudish pen to our lives. Every night I relive every night we've spent together. But I usually start with the night at the beach where you lost at strip poker and were down with nothing to wager except for the offer to perform..

And there... our nightly reading will end. The rest of the letter is none of your business. They were words to inspire fitful and pleasant dreams. I held her letter close to my face, breathed deeply again and fell asleep thinking of the double or nothing wager that turned that poker game around.

CHAPTER 13

Wellington, New Zealand
July 1942

THE ELLIOTT ARRIVED IN WELLINGTON in the dark of night. The Jap attacks on Australia put every allied port on edge. Blackouts were serious business that all but shut down cities at sundown.

Sleep on a troop ship comes in shifts. I was fortunate to have quarters with some of the ship's officers so I actually had a bunk of my own and was making full use of it when I heard some joker yell, "Land Ho!". It had to be a Marine from Iowa. The Navy does a bit better job of navigating than sticking some fellow up in the crow's nest these days. There was a thundering herd of feet outside in the passageway and I joined the rush topside. Reality met me there. We left San Francisco on a summer's day, crossed the equator and sailed south landing in Wellington in the middle of winter. It was freezing. Chicago might claim to be the 'Windy City' but that claim would have to stop at the equator. Wellington could declare the title for the southern hemisphere. The temperature had to be in the low 40's with a hard wind. Those who rushed to deck were soon shivering. Some heading topside were colliding with those heading back below for coats, all while the navy guys were trying to do their job of bringing the ship in to dock.

That soon stopped.

"Attention all hands. Sailors to your stations. Marines to your units. Prepare to disembark."

That sent up a unanimous cheer. The Marines had no idea where they were going at the moment but after nearly three weeks at sea in cramped quarters they were ready to go anywhere. I grabbed a coat and climbed to the bridge. Captain Patrick was there in a bridge coat. He'd been here before. I leaned off the port rail to look aft and saw a line silhouetted behind us.

"Seems like we're leading the pack."

Captain Patrick smiled, "Sometimes a bottle of whiskey invested in the right way can bring rewards. We'll follow that destroyer and the Wakefield. The rest will follow us. It'll be well into daylight before the last ship is in dock. It's not just that I'm short on patience. I don't like leaving my ship lingering out there in the strait. Jap subs love patrolling near port. It's the most dangerous part of the cruise."

"So how'd you let the Wakefield get in front?"

"You may have noticed her at sea. She's a little fancier than the Elliott. She carries General Vandegrift. He's the commanding general of this little party."

"Got it."

By the time we docked and were squared away all Marines were on deck in units in full gear and wearing their winter service uniforms. It was a tidy bunch that stepped on the gangplank and stepped foot on foreign soil for their first time as US Marines. This time there were no guns pointed at them.

"Guess I should grab my gear and head out with the rest of them."

"Guess I'll be seeing you again in a few days," the captain said looking to shore and not at me.

"Does that mean we're heading out soon?"

"I can't tell you what it means exactly, but we've got a few days to load a lot of equipment on this ship. Then we're heading back out and even we don't know exactly where yet."

"Seems like I owe you a drink from a few weeks ago."

"I believe I'll take you up on that now that we're ashore. Don't know where you were thinking of staying but you might want to get a real room for a few days. If you hurry you might be able to get a room at the St. George. It's on Manners Street. I'll see you there for dinner at 1700 hours."

"Thanks for the tip. Manners Street, God knows that's going to be a tough name to live up to with twenty thousand marines in town. See you ashore."

"Aye."

The Marines were coming off in steady streams. I fell in line and headed down the gangplank. Terra firma feels funny under your feet for the first time after a few weeks at sea few weeks and a little disorienting. There were hints of dawn as well as a few of Wellington's early risers. It would be hard to imagine sleeping anywhere near port this morning. Marines marched straight from ship to station where trains were ready to take them to a makeshift camp a few miles away. I walked alongside chatting with some of the fellows. Everyone seemed in high spirits. As the sun came up more civilians came out. I watched for about an hour, gathering impressions, then got polite directions to Manners Street. The street name still amused me.

I hit the hotel on a mission. Without Captain Patrick's advice I'd have been out of luck. The Marines were already in force, high level staff setting up camp for commanding officers. I managed to get one of the last rooms available for civilians and that was not without using a bit of pretense with the desk clerk. It was still early but there were smells drifting into the lobby that promised the prospect of a real breakfast with real eggs. It was tantalizing. It was also the first time I'd had a table and meal to myself in weeks. That camaraderie stuff can get old after awhile.

With a fresh breakfast came the first fresh newspaper in three weeks. The Evening Post was still on the stand from the night before with headlines about the New Zealand 2nd Division playing a major role in kicking the Afrika Korps and Rommel squarely in the First Battle of El Alamein. It was interesting to see the celebration of any victory. The Allies have had few. That gave me an idea.

Somewhere in the South Pacific, 11 July 1942
Sam Marlow/New York Herald Tribune

In the middle of winter in this port beneath the Southern Cross there may be the beginnings of a season of change. Not that these Kiwis are sporting cheery optimism at a war that is much more threatening to their homefront than ours, but for a change one might look at the positive.

New Zealand came under threat of a Japanese invasion early in this war. But they sent their troops off to the Allied battles in both Europe, Africa and closer in the Pacific. The country is lightly defended mainly by the old men and women who took up arms.

Then the invasion came. It wasn't the Japs but the Americans by the tens of thousands. Today I watched as US Marines walked off ships and onto the streets of this port. Children lined the curbs waving New Zealand and American flags. In the faces of the women were the smiles of salvation. With each island and nation taken by Imperial troops came stories of atrocities. These women had been living under the very real fear of falling as did Nanking, the Philippines or Hong Kong to the horrors of the invaders. Horrors.

Today was not a victory parade but a parade of purpose. There is tough work to be done but the tide may be turning. The papers are celebrating a victory of their own Kiwi 2nd Division in the desert of Egypt. They kicked a little sand in the Axis eyes. Our own Navy marked a major victory at Midway just weeks ago. We, and I mean all of us, are back in this war.

Here in this place of perfect beauty these people under threat have dared to smile when the American allies came marching. There might be a lesson here. I saw in the first paper I've held in weeks this morning that the British Parliament tried to unseat Churchill just days ago. It was an attempt to censure the PM for losses in the Pacific and Libya and led by some of the same circle of appeasers who like Joe Kennedy would rather capitulate than fight. Well, we're fighting and we're winning for a change. Churchill

`is still fighting. Closing the debate he told`
`Parliament and England:`

`"If democracy and Parliamentary institutions`
`are to triumph in this war, it is absolutely nec-`
`essary that Governments resting upon them shall`
`be able to act and dare, that the servants of`
`the Crown shall not be harassed by nagging and`
`snarling".`

`Praise the Prime Minister. Pass the ammunition.`

That and a string of other stories was cabled back to New York. Ashley got a telegram stating safe arrival and to send more steamy notes. Jack got one to get his PT boat and ass down here before the war was over. I'm quite sure that would send him into a frenzy of phone calls and pressure from Papa Joe to get an assignment a little further away from the New York nightclub scene.

With my stories filed and telegrams away, I was a few hours shy of dinner. The choice was either to surrender to that large, tempting bed all alone or a walk about Wellington. I turned my collar up and went outside.

Manners Street was keeping up her reputation but it was still daylight and several thousands of Marines had yet to find their way to the street and her pubs. As it was well into the afternoon and I'd been up before dawn it seemed a pint was within reason. I turned into the first pub I saw and noticed the reason for the early dinner appointment with the captain. A sign stated, '6 pm Closing'. I settled at a table by the window. An elderly waiter slowly approached me with eyes narrowed.

"Yank are you?"

"How'd you guess?"

"You're not from around here or I'd recognize you. You're too young not to be in uniform and off in Africa or someplace fighting. And then there's those ships that just came in."

"Yes. I came with them. My division is just behind."

"Why aren't you in uniform?"

"I'm a reporter. I'm supposed to be asking the questions."

"You're a little slow for a reporter."

I laughed, "I've heard that once before - from a local - the last time I landed in a foreign place."

"What'll you have?"

"How about a stout to ward off this cold?"

He walked away. When he came back with the beer it was my turn.

"Why do pubs close so early here?"

"I was looking for a tougher question than that from a war correspondent. Been getting that question a lot. It's just the way we do things down here. Maybe we're a little different from folks in big cities like New York. We like to have our drinks and go home to dinner and our wives. I guess up there, you like to have drinks and go out with your girlfriends then go home to your wives."

"I guess you'd have to put that moral question to a married man."

"Well, we're glad to see you Yanks here anyway. That pint's on your Kiwi allies here. Wish we'd had a few American marines alongside us at Gallipoli."

This time when he walked away I noticed that the slow gait was more of a limp. There were few who survived that campaign who didn't carry some deep scar. I sipped and stared out the window. The old guy was right. There weren't a lot of men out there between fifteen and fifty and those who were wore a marine uniform. I laid a couple of American dollars on the table for a tip or a souvenir and walked out the door. From the window I'd watched the winter sun setting. It was almost dark as I walked back towards the hotel, the lights from shops along the way were being turned on as the sun set. Almost all the stores seemed to be staffed by women. Women of Wellington meet the Marines, oh, and don't forget the sailors. I had the feeling that the local parsons might be busy in the months ahead.

Strolling back into the St. George, I thought I might be ahead of the captain. I was wrong. He was seated with a whiskey in front of him.

"Have a seat Sam. I've been waiting three weeks for this whiskey. Didn't think you'd mind if I didn't wait for you."

"Well there's a damned good reason to know a captain who's been to port before. If I hadn't known I might have waited until later for cocktails and dinner. I just found out the pubs close at six."

"They're pretty strict about it, too. They call it the six o'clock swill around here, pounding pints or whiskey before closing time. I imagine it's going to pose a bit of a problem with all the Marines in town."

"Let's hope that's the worst of their issues."

The place began filling up with Marine and Navy officers. The captain told me what he knew of the town and the islands to the north. He seemed to speak more of the Solomons and I wondered if that was chance or a subtle hint. The menu reflected the rationing of the war, but there seemed to be enough lamb in New Zealand to keep meat on the table. What left the table precisely at six were the drinks. It seemed most of the Americans in the restaurant had been there before. Ceding to custom and tradition one Navy officer stood precisely at eighteen hundred hours and raised his glass and bellowed, "To the Queen," to which all stood and offered the same toast while downing the last of their cocktails. That seemed to please our hosts.

There are many things that fuel a man's desires. This night sleep was at the top of that list. Both the captain and I walked up the stairs and headed to our rooms. It may be a tired phrase, but in this case a phrase of the tired—I was asleep before my head hit the pillow.

Camp Paekakariki

The Marines weren't wasting any time. By the time I got from town to the camp the only people around were officers and orderlies. In the hills above the camps I could hear live fire drills already underway. A jeep came racing down the road headed towards the gunshots. I waved to flag it down and got a mouthful of dust as it whipped past. Twenty yards later it slid to a stop and someone motioned for me to move fast. I did on the double. The passenger seat was occupied by a guy wearing khaki and captain's bars.

"Sorry to make you eat our dust there. It took me twenty yards before I could place your face. You're that reporter fellow that was on the Elliott."

"Yes sir."

"You might as well get up there and get used to live fire and things blowing up, too. The whole damned lot of you rookies are about to land on a hot beach facing Japs who've had a lot more practice at this than we have."

The jeep jerked forward and I grabbed the back of the captain's seat to keep from falling out. We drove past rows of makeshift huts for the marines framed in two by fours with solid sides and tacked down canvas tops. It was far from fancy but then no one here was going to be settling in.

The captain turned his head towards me and pointed in the opposite direction.

"That hill up there is called 'Billy Goat Hill'. It's a tough climb. Some say there's some similarities between that hill and some of the terrain where we're going. That's a key directive in training. Other units are split off to do mortar practice down on the flats. In a few days we're going to start some beach landing drills."

"Sounds like somebody knows where we're going."

"Somebody does. They just ain't saying."

I looked up hill and saw a flame spread across one side of the rock.

"Holy crap!"

"Flamethrowers. This ain't gonna be pretty. They say the Japs will dig into caves and fight to the death."

"They say that, do they?"

"Yep."

Time seemed of the essence here. The exercises continued all day. There was no lunch break, no meal service carried into the field. The Marines ate rations from their packs and drank water from canteens. In the short light of a winter's afternoon whistles sounded across the mountain calling the troops in. They came down from the mountain in units. They were dirty and tired with weapons slung over their shoulders. They looked like Marines who had been in a fight. The difference here was that there was no blood and no bodies. This time.

In Camp in the South Pacific
Sam Marlow/New York Herald Tribune

They are brave and beautiful these young Marines. America's finest dressed for dinner in

a field mess a half world away from home. Their appearance down either side of a rough plank dining table was uniform, but to close your eyes you could hear the voice of America. Their accents are an audible offering of the expanse of our nation. There's a Texas twang, a Georgia drawl and Iowa accent as flat as the prairies. Then there's PFC Joe Giuliano from Brooklyn. His accent is as American as it comes. The Giuliano family lives on Bay 22nd street in Brooklyn. It's a nice three story house. Joe is second generation. That leaves one story for his kids. When he gets home. When he finds a wife. His mother still cooks for the entire family. At night the smell of garlic overwhelms the scent of the sea that blows in from Gravesend Bay.

He's a rifleman. Every Marine is a rifleman. Some just think they're better. Joe didn't get much rifle training in Brooklyn. Some of the southern boys who grew up shooting squirrel for dinner like to make fun of him. That stopped when Joe and his M1903 started hitting the kill zone on targets over 500 yards. That's more than far enough to knock Nips out of coconut trees.

Joe is about as fired up a Marine as you're going to find. His only regret to being on the other side of the world is it's awfully hard to get the baseball scores. I saw a group of fellows toss the local Evening Post to the ground when they found the sport section was filled with cricket and other equally un-American games.

At the other end of the table is the platoon leader. His name is George Mead. Before the war Mead sat at fancier tables at the other end of the social set. His family has a few home addresses. His daddy is rich. If you use paper

you're in touch with his family fortune. George
senior is working in a bigger factory these days
in Washington helping Roosevelt get what he needs
to win this war. His son is taking a more direct
approach.

I met the lieutenant a few months ago at one
of their homes in Aiken, South Carolina. It was
a modest 43 room mansion with a polo field out
back. George plays a pretty decent game of polo.
Seems with his father with all that money and
friends of Roosevelt he could have found a softer
way to wage war. Instead he signed up for the
Marines and went to Parris Island. Now he's on
another island about to head to yet another. It's
the next island that will be the test because
that's where this country is going to take the
fight to the Japanese.

This platoon doesn't know too much about George
the polo player or the huge house that's his second home. There is no social class here. The only
thing that distinguishes George from the others
are the gold bars on his collar. All they know is
that the guy at the end of the table is the one
who will lead them into battle. His money can't
buy their respect. That will come when the first
bullets fly because what he does then will define
the difference between the quick and the dead.

CHAPTER 14

Melville, Rhode Island

"**S**HAFTED AGAIN!" KENNEDY SHOT OUT of his chair. He was smoking mad. He stood nose to nose with Melville's XO Lieutenant Commander John Harllee.

"I've done my training here and done pretty damn well." Kennedy yelled. "I'm supposed to be heading out with Squadron 14 for assignment."

"Take it easy, Kennedy," Harllee stood to go eye to eye, "Yes you've done well here. Your reports have all been good. Some say you're the best boat handler in the group."

"Then give me a boat and give me an assignment in a combat zone."

"I'll meet you halfway. You're getting *PT 101*. You'll remain here as an instructor to new students at the training squadron."

Jack paused for a moment and put both of his hands flat down on the desk, looking squarely into Harllee's face.

"Let me ask you Lieutenant, even assuming I'm one of your best boat skippers, are you keeping me here because I can handle a boat or because you see some advantage to keeping a Kennedy at Melville? Or better yet, what did my father have to do with this?"

"And let me tell you something Lieutenant Kennedy maybe, just maybe, this has more to do about what some think is better for the war effort and not necessarily making decisions about the war based on what Jack Kennedy wants to do. You are dismissed."

Outside the air was a cooler than Jack's hot head. Fall was coming and the grounds of the war training school looked more like a college campus. There was a touch football game starting up on the common. He looked at the teams forming and thought the game might help clear his head. Jogging back to his hut he changed out of his uniform and pulled an old beat up letter sweater over his head and went back out the door.

The scrimmage was already started when he walked up. One side was a man short. In between plays he waved his hand.

"Mind if I join?"

The fellow quarterbacking seemed to be the team leader. He also looked like he'd seen a few real games. The sides were lopsided but he wasn't sure the skinny kid waving his hand was going to be any help.

"Come on in. Where can you play?"

"Well I don't like to throw my weight around the line too much, it's kind of intimidating.. but I can usually catch the ball if it gets near my hands."

"Yeah I can see how those guards and tackles might be skeered of you," the quarterback laughed, "Take the right end."

The two sides lined up. The player opposite Jack took a long look. When the ball snapped he ran straight and rammed his shoulder hard into Kennedy before cutting towards the quarterback. Jack was knocked sideways caught his balance and ran unguarded towards the sideline with his hand up. The ball was launched like a bullet leading him slightly. Out of the corner of his eye he saw the safety closing in but not in time to block the pass. Jack was tucking the ball into his gut when two hands hit him hard, knocking him out of bounds and on his ass.

"Touch. You're down," his tackler grinned.

"Nice touch."

Jack made a gimpy jog back to the huddle.

"Good catch kid. Where's that sweater from? You play for some prep school?"

"Ahh, it's from Harvard."

"You outta college? Sorry thought you were some new recruit out of high school."

"No, I'm Jack Kennedy."

"Loo-tennant Kennedy?"

"Oh Jesus. Hey Ross, you just knocked down a loo-tennant!"

"Sorry sir, touch football around here is a little heavy on the touch part. I'm Johnny Iles from Louisiana."

"No problem Johnny. The hits might help me think straight."

"Just a little suggestion loo-tennant you might break up your pass pattern a bit. Those boys are pretty good about reading a straight line."

The game went on and Jack listened a little more and got hit a little less by the end of the day. The exercise did absolutely no good for his back but a lot for his head. It was all about tactics. Getting what you needed from this Navy wasn't about what you knew but who you knew. So Jack came up with a plan to execute an end run around his father.

Jack Kennedy had a lot in common with Senator David Walsh of Massachusetts. The senator had been a stark isolationist in lockstep with Ambassador Joseph Kennedy. That put both of them on the outside of the Roosevelt circle of friends. And like Jack Kennedy, the senator had been the recent victim of vicious accusations by the New York Post of being involved in a sensational sex and spy scandal. This one involving a male brothel in Brooklyn. Most other newspapers steered clear of direct allegations. Never to be left out of a good sex and spy story, Winchell was billing it: "Brooklyn's spy nest, also known as the swastika swishery." And just like Jack the whiff of Nazis using sex of either sort to snare high level subjects brought Hoover in like Hell's Fury. They had a lot they could talk about. He was also the chairman of the Naval Affairs Committee. Jack called and set up a lunch in Washington.

"Jack how are you?" Senator Walsh greeted him at the door of an expensive suite at the Carlton Hotel in Washington, "I thought we'd have lunch here. Too many prying eyes and ears about these days."

"If it's Hoover you're trying to avoid take my advice and check under the bed."

The senator led Jack to a table already set for lunch. The two sat in front of bowls of standard issue Massachusetts soup: clam chowder.

"I guess we have our own little experiences with Hoover of late," Walsh started. "In my case Hoover proved to be an ally in the end. His report was referenced by Majority Leader Barkley but not entered in the

Congressional record, because ummm, because of the lewdness of some of the allegations. Most of the real press reported it for what it was an absolute fabrication."

"But once Winchell floats the word out there..."

"The damage is done. I must say that after a distinguished career in public service being labelled as a person who cavorts with Nazi spies in a homosexual whorehouse is a stigma I could have done without."

"Do you think the Post was part of a plot to discredit you?"

"Your father knows better than anyone he's pretty much been run off the reservation. There are others who have opposed this war that share the notion of a 'secret society' either inside or outside the administration with a dedicated purpose to silence us in one way or another. You may very well have been part of that same plot."

"The idea has crossed my mind. It seems Roosevelt already has my father pretty much down. Palm Beach is his Elba. Using me would either be added insurance or just plain cruel."

"How is your own little scandal going?"

"Mine is so much less important than yours. I freely admit and am quite happy to admit to having a relationship with Inga. She's not a spy. Hoover will never get anything on her. The real issue is that she's a divorced woman. Between Hoover and my father poor Inga never stood a chance."

"Love and war Jack. They both have their minefields. Do I get the impression you'd like to trade one for the other?"

"As a matter of fact Senator...."

Jack returned from Washington with an ally. It was a matter of how quickly he could press the paperwork for a change of assignment and how effectively the senator could pressure Washington.

Duty on board *PT 101* was taking a turn for the worse. The seventy-eight foot Higgins boats were built for speed not comfort. All exercises were conducted above deck and it was getting colder by the day. Gunnery practice was with the .50 caliber deck guns in a freezing spray of seawater. The cold wasn't worth whining about but the drills were no closer to real battle practice than rum running from Cuba. Skippers had no torpedoes for training and the navy provided no targets for shooting.

It was cold, wet, miserable duty. To Jack it also seemed pointless. The war was moving towards a new critical phase and he was fighting for Rhode Island Sound.

Lunch with Senator Walsh finally paid off. He received a telegram from the Navy.

> *YOU ARE HEREBY DETACHED FROM DUTY IN MOTOR TORPEDO BOAT SQUADRON TRAINING SCHOOL AND FROM SUCH OTHER DUTY AS MAY HAVE BEEN AS-SIGNED YOU; WILL PROCEED VIA GOVERNMENT OR COMMERCIAL AIR TO THE PORT IN WHICH MOTOR TORPEDO BOAT SQUADRON TWO MAY BE AND UPON ARRIVAL REPORT TO THE COMMANDING OFFICER OF THAT SQUADRON FOR DUTY.*

Squadron Two was stationed in Tulagi in the Solomon Islands where the US battle for the Pacific was about to begin. Jack Kennedy was head-ed to war. He had one stop to make first.

CHAPTER 15

Hollywood, California
Summer, 1942

I NGA WALKED OUT OF THE theater. Grauman's Chinese is gaudy, like a proverbial whore in church. But the whore is the church in Hollywood. War in this town is just another subject for the movies and 'Desperate Journey' was about as far from the reality of battle as Hollywood is from the rest of the world. Nazis are no threat to narcissism. Errol Flynn battles his way with his bare fists and flight crew from a downed bomber through the enemy lines to England. Flynn as the hero. Except in the Hollywood papers - Flynn trumps the real war by making headlines with statutory rape charges. Inga wanted an interview with Flynn. If she were a decade younger she might have gotten it. Instead she was going to have to try for the inside story from one of the other actors in the movie; some guy named Ronald Reagan.

She had her own gossip column called, Rumor Has It. Her work in Washington helped. Hoover's subtle influence secured the placement. The Director wasn't just interested in espionage threats coming from abroad. He wanted any inside information on sympathizers, whether it be fact or gossip. With Winchell and Arvad he had two good operators whom he leveraged in different ways. Winchell had access and a huge readership. He made it a habit of making Hoover look good in the papers. Inga had her own ways of getting to the heart of a story. Hoover wasn't so concerned about her methods. She'd received a message from one of his agents to wait for a phone call.

"My dear Inga Binga. So nice of you to take my call."

"Why Director Hoover after all your support of late how could I not receive my benefactor? You've helped to place me in a job and apartment. There's round the clock service, or surveillance, by your agents. I guess you could say to borrow the song lyric you've got me Body and Soul."

"Body and Soul, seems like I've heard that song somewhere. Oh I remember now from the tape recording in your bedroom in Reno."

She hated him. From Reno forward she was assured that everything she did he knew about. Quite sure that every intimate moment was part of a playback reel for this chubby little pervert.

"What can I do for you Mr. Director."

"I know you're working on more information and a piece on that child rapist Flynn. Keep going there, but I want you to do what you can to get me more on that other child molester Charlie Chaplin. While you're at it see what you can get on Cary Grant and Randolph Scott. Those two spend way too much time together. Where there's smoke there's fire and those two are sending smoke signals."

"You seem to have a lot of interest in sex Mr. Hoover," she was beginning to enjoy her habit of annoying the Director.

"Oh, my dear Miss Arvad, we both use sex in different ways. You use it to gain access. I use it as a tool to manage people. The enemy uses it as a means to blackmail and manipulate people that might be of use to them. I don't believe you are so naive in this area my little one. What I do know is that you'd better use your sex or any other attractions you may have to get what I need and you'd better hurry my dear because you're getting a bit old to play a sex kitten in Hollywood."

He kept building new heights for her hatred of him.

"Oh and in case you haven't heard. Your boy Kennedy's going to war. He's coming your way first. Have a good evening. We'll be watching."

Hoover hung up.

Inga's phone rang immediately. She was still enraged by the way he treated her and grabbed the phone ready to take the offensive.

"Now listen here J. Edgar.."

"This is the operator. Collect call from a Mr. Lieutenant John Kennedy. Will you accept the charge?"

She was stunned again.

"Why yes of course."

"Inga Binga! You practicing to finally give Hoover a piece of your mind?"

"Why Jack! What a surprise!" She faked and scrambled to cover her intro.

"I finally got orders to ship out. You always wanted to know when. So here it is."

"Don't expect me to celebrate you going off to war. There's a lot I still like about the skinny lieutenant."

"Then invite him to dinner."

"When?"

"Tonight."

"You're in town?"

"One night only. I ship out of San Francisco day after tomorrow for a land of sandy beaches, coconut palms and tens of thousands of Japs. You might be the last white woman I see for awhile. Thought you might want to kiss your sailor boy goodbye."

"Why of course."

"See you at seven. I'll pick you up at your place. "

He hung up. She sat down. Her head was spinning after the two conversations and two very different emotions. Hatred for Hoover. What for Jack? The toying and teasing over the recent months of rare contact through secret channels came to a clear and final point. They can't hide from Papa Joe, or Hoover. Now both be damned.

Jack's appetite for food was was about the only dull part of his desires. He always ordered the same thing - steak, mashed potatoes, peas, carrots and ice cream. The bad back was just one of the medical issue he hid in his records. The bland menu seemed to help stave off severe attacks of gastroenteritis. Their last dinner together might also be the last healthy dinner Jack might have for many months. It was just one more reason she worried about her limping lieutenant. All along, in his letters, he was clearly aware of the realities of island duty:

> *"I understand that this South Pacific is not a place where you lie on a white beach with a cool breeze, while those native girls who aren't out hunting for your daily supply of bananas are busy*

popping grapes into your mouth. It would seem to consist of heat and rain and dysentery + cold beans, all of which won't of course bother anyone with a good stomach."

Jack picked her up at seven with military precision. He was wearing a military uniform and a new silver bar on his collar. Inga did not want to dine in. Cooking was not one of her most refined skills. Going out meant she could control the evening. Going out meant Jack would not be at her place. They had moved beyond that intimacy, the illusion that there could ever be a home or place together. She could not open herself again to those hopes. Joe Kennedy would make sure they never married. The Japanese might make sure she never saw him again. She didn't need the ghost of Jack Kennedy in her house.

This evening he was very much alive in a begged, borrowed or stolen sports car that steered straight for the Sunset Strip. Jack obviously planned his destination as the car pulled into a popular hot spot called the Zamboanga South Seas Club.

"Do you think they have steak and potatoes here?" Inga laughed.

"Probably with a slice of pineapple tossed on top. I heard they have done detailed research of the cultures and people of the Solomon Islands. I didn't want you to get the impression this was some frivolous fling for a sailor going off to war."

"Had I known I would have pulled my grass skirt out of the closet."

"I'm hoping in the evening's attire, skirts become optional."

Walking into the club was like a Marine fantasy, as if landing on a South Pacific island. There were palms and coconuts and music of a sort that might be considered Polynesian. But the main theme seemed to be....sex. The walls were painted with exotic murals - nature and nudity in extremes. Lounging, playing, frollicking, semi-sexually posed. They were all beautiful with big breasts and ample hips, looking less aboriginal in the sense of true anthropology than amorous, amoral and willing.

Jack walked in and slid his cap back on his head, "If this is what we're walking into I'm voting for Roosevelt in '44. If I find what the papers are describing, I may go Republican."

Their table overlooked the dance floor where girls in darkened hues danced in the standard issue grass skirts. There was a sparkle in Kennedy's eye and laughter and gay conversation and social gossip about friends There was no talk of war and politics or of friends in combat zones who were fighting, missing or dead. It was a night when those things did not exist. Talk of divorce and paternal impact on their love did not come to the table. This night he was the Jack Kennedy who could charm a room with his wit and if Inga wasn't by his side he could have had the choice of any girl in the room in or out of a grass skirt.

Later that night after she shared her body, in that same carefree spirit of the evening, there was no mention of obligation or future. She rose and dressed quietly. As he lay sleeping she slipped into the bathroom and sat on the edge of the tub wrote him a note to take him forward to war and the future:

My Dear Lieutenant,

I could not wake you. I could not say goodbye. There was something perfect and peaceful in your face that I wanted to keep and leave undisturbed.

Responsibility and life is just starting. Happiness and pain. Hopes and failures. Love and hatred. And as I know you, you will have plenty of it. That golden goblet which contains the elixir of life will be drunk greedily by you. But you have so much brains that you will know when to sip and when to make it bottoms up. I hope you will be happy, and as I have said so many times before, that you will get all you want.

Put a match to the smoldering ambition and you will go like wild fire. It is all against the ranch out West, but it is the unequalled highway to the White House. And if you can find something you really believe in , then my dear you caught the biggest fish in the ocean. You can pull it aboard, but don't rush it, there is still time.

Plans? I love to hear that word, because you always have a hundred. The 99 you tell me, and the one you really hope will materialize you keep to yourself. Maybe wise. Maybe right. And I believe that a person ought to live, we can't monopolize each other, even if we are the best of friends. Even lovers shouldn't and too often do.

Be brave. I don't even mind to see you a Navy-hero. But duck when the Japanese bullets aim at that handsome chest or bright head. You are just too good--and I mean good--to be carried home.

My love, Inga

CHAPTER 16

Solomon Sea
August 7, 1942

IT WAS A DIFFERENT MORNING light that broke on the deck of the *Elliott*. It followed a stormy night. It was the dawn of our invasion of Japanese held islands. We left Wellington several days ago and seemed to take a leisurely course north, until our convoy merged with another, then another. It didn't take an announcement from the brass to tell us what was happening. From either side of the ship the masts and guns and men and might reached all the way to the horizon. It looked like a city under sail, the largest city on earth and she sailed with one purpose. I would hate to be the Jap atop a coconut palm with a glass trained in our direction. If he believed in a god, it would be a good time to start praying. If he didn't, he might want to take it up.

The call to breakfast came early but there was no need to call. It's hard to sleep the night before you attack an island held by a few thousand people who have the intent of killing you.

If you were hungry the food was there. The navy mess crews held nothing back for the marines heading out. Hotcakes, bacon, steak and eggs. On any other morning that kind of food might have caused a fight to get at it. This morning a few made a hearty assault. One or two bright fellows were wrapping snacks and stuffing them in their kits. Most of us drank coffee and smoked - alone in our thoughts.

The call to muster on deck sent boots pounding. Units formed up on their lieutenants. I went with Mead's platoon. We'd done this drill before. This time was different.

A lieutenant colonel came on deck and started speaking. He was a lieutenant colonel, so you had to listen.

"Men you are leading the assault that begins the ground war against the Imperial forces of Japan. The Japs have been running this war up until this point and frankly, they've been winning. But they have not seen what I see. The determined faces of U.S. Marines..."

That brought a few cheers from the crowd. He was a lieutenant colonel, you had to cheer.

It was his version of the battle speech. It's not that I've been in battle that often, but I've heard a lot of battle speeches and if it's not Henry Fifth, then it doesn't quite stiffen the sinews, or summon up the blood.

The chatter on deck was pretty high spirited. A lot of talk about killing Japs, storming the beaches and running from one side of the island to the other. Some talked of souvenirs to send home to impress their girls. The ones who talked the least were the ones who knew what the first blood of combat would bring.

It wasn't much of a time for chatter anyway. The big guns pounded from the destroyers, sending shells overhead. The *Elliott* slowed as the landing craft came alongside. Rope ladders went over the rails. It was time to go to war.

Guadalcanal 0800hrs August 7, 1942
Sam Marlow/New York Herald Tribune

A man is but a tiny speck in war. Halfway down a rope ladder between the relative safety of the USS George F. Elliott and the Eureka boat below I looked over my shoulder to see the same scene playing out aside ships across a long line off-shore of this little island.

There were the ships. There was the island. In between was a short stretch of water. It looked like the biggest open stretch of 'hang your ass out to die' that I'd ever seen. You could hang on that rope and think about such things but not for long. A Marine boot came down on my hand and

I continued with all the other specks heading for duty and destiny.

Each of the LCPs below packed three platoons of Marines and three crew before pushing off and joining the line of assault. Two gunners were forward on .30 caliber machine guns. At the wheel was a coxswain. The Navy uses funny words. He didn't look amused. It was his boat and he had three dozen marines to get ashore in one piece.

His name is Philippe Choquet from Terrebonne Parish in Louisiana. He's a bayou boy and knows a thing or two about boats. At home they call him Philippe. On ship they call him Phil. This morning he is sir.

"Heads down Marines."

On his call we try to get small. These boats are plywood with a little armor up front. If you're standing your head and shoulders are exposed to whatever the enemy throws from shore. If you're crouched you're exposed to whatever the marine next to you throws up. Many of those fellows who chowed heavy earlier were lightening their loads.

It was hard not to look up. Wildcats off the carriers were coming in low and fast to strafe the beach. To the side other LCPs were moving in the same direction in a grim race to get to shore, drop their loads and get the hell back to sea. The .30 cals up front were chattering away. The engines below were grinding at top speed. You could only hear a shout directly into your ear.

"Gum?"

I jumped.

Sergeant O. J. Marion was the platoon guide which meant he went in front of everyone. He was also from Marion, a small town in the mountains

of North Carolina. He was also either brave or
crazy. I was leaning towards the latter at the
moment because he was handing me a stick of Juicy
Fruit and smiling like he was heading for a hot
date.

He leaned into my ear again and shouted, "Kind
of quiet."

I was overwhelmed by the sounds. He must have
read my eyes.

"No Jap shells coming at us. Crafty bastards
holding fire."

In the middle of something so massive I'd
missed the one point it took a veteran to appreciate. I put the Juicy Fruit in my mouth and
smiled back. It may have been a weak grin. There
are some things you can't learn in basic training, or at a newspaper desk.

A pair of Wildcats did a flyover. They came in so low, I could see the
pilots clearly. Our boats rode the waves onto the beach. That's when I
heard machine guns.

The boat hit sand and Marines started bailing over the side and hitting the surf. I followed the sergeant. I landed in water up to my thighs
and ran like hell in a crouching position. Men fanned out, ran thirty
yards and dropped in a defensive line. There was a lot of shouting and
some firing into the tree line. There was no incoming fire.

"Ceasefire!" Mead called.

Silence. Down the line men looked at each other.

"Marion take two men and go into the trees."

Three men took off running.

Lying on my back I could hear two different worlds. From the ocean
there was the surf and the sound of landing craft grinding into shore.
Men shouting and running and splashing. From land there was silence
except for the sound of bird calls and jungle noise.

The scouting team reappeared.

"No Japs lieutenant. There's nothing here."

A cheerful noise ripped down the line. A few men jumped up pumping their rifles into the air. One or two did impromptu hula dances. It sure as hell wasn't what they expected. But they'd take it. A landing where nobody died.

"Ok Marines! Into the woods. Set up a perimeter and dig in. Just because Tojo's late to the party doesn't mean he's not coming. Move out. There's a few thousand others behind us who need to use this beach."

The sergeants were getting the war back to business. I looked down the beach to Mead. He caught my eye and smiled, shook his head and walked towards a grove of coconut trees.

Guadalcanal
August 8

So far the heavy fighting had been across the water on another island known as Tulagi. We could hear that battle going on during lulls of off-loading on Guadalcanal. The guys with gold braids and brains decided there were too many ships together and were going to order them out. What supplies didn't make it to shore would go away. You could bet those boys were busting themselves to get every last tank, bullet and bean on shore.

Somebody must have sent word back to Jap headquarters that they didn't own the islands anymore. I wandered back down to the beach about mid-morning to see what kind of stuff it took to outfit some sixteen thousand marines. I wasn't the only one to drop in.

A flight of Jap Bettys was moving in to attack the ships. They dropped so low some were flying beneath the level of the bridge of most ships. Captains weighed anchor and made a run for it throwing as much lead as they could towards the incoming enemy planes. The attackers worked like wolves, like professional killers. Some targeted the big battleships while others went for the lone and slower moving ships like the transports. On the beach there was a frantic effort to get material ashore and squared away.

It was hard to take your eyes off the desperate speed of the battle. One Betty dropped to a couple dozen feet off the water and headed straight for a transport. Guns on both sides were blazing. The battery on board scored a direct hit and the Jap bomber exploded. But it was flying so fast and so close to the ship that the exploding mass collided mid-ship just aft of the superstructure.

"That's the Elliott," groaned an officer.

I borrowed his field glasses and looked just as an explosion showed above deck and a huge cloud of black smoke rose up into the sky. I handed the binoculars back.

"You know that ship?" he asked.

"I spent most of my recent lifetime on her."

We watched as she steered a jagged course through the other ships and out into more open waters. She was still under sail and didn't appear to be under an imminent threat of sinking.

"They'll probably send her out, abandon ship and scuttle her," the officer stared seaward. He seemed to know how these things went.

That kind of explosion and fire doesn't happen without men dying. I thought of the horror on board. I thought of Captain Patrick and a whiskey in Wellington. Life changes abruptly in war.

Finding and fighting the Japanese was a dangerous game of cat and mouse. The Marines landed and almost immediately captured the enemy airfield which was their main objective. It was just days away from being ready to host a killing field of enemy planes. Instead of standing and fighting most of the enemy ran for caves in the hill. All that the Marines came across were a few forced laborers and a Jap officer. His 'interrogation' consisted of all the whiskey he could drink followed by a congenial conversation. The prisoner reported there were a number of fellow soldiers sick, starving and willing to surrender just west of the Matanikau River.

Lieutenant Colonel Frank Goettge called together a twenty five man patrol to move quickly. They were ambushed. Only three survived and that was by running into the ocean and swimming miles in shark infested waters to avoid the enemy. Those three described watching as the Japs slowly tortured the Marines with bayonets.

George came to see me a few days later.

"Sam we're going out on patrol. We've been told to go inland and flank the Jap position on the Matanikau and try to hit him from behind. They suckered us. Now we need to go and get our Marines."

"Give me a second to grab a couple things. I'm coming with you."

"Nope."

"Hey. You can't pull that shit. If the top brass gave me the ok to land with a few thousand Marines on Guadalcanal here I don't see any reason why I can't go on a routine patrol."

"Two reasons Sam. The first; the presence of an unarmed civilian in a combat patrol under these circumstances could put my men at risk protecting you. You know what happened to Goettge's patrol."

"What's the second reason."

"This patrol is under my command. It's my decision."

"You're pulling rank? What the hell are friends for?"

"Maybe friends are for making the tough calls. My decision is based on what I think is best for my men. It's also based on what I think is best for you."

"This stinks George. You know it does. I can't write war stories sitting here on this beach getting a tan. I should have played you harder when I had you on a horse in Aiken. Next time we play don't expect mercy."

"I'll look forward to that. Can't say the notion of getting back to Aiken hasn't been on my mind lately. But if you want to take it out on me, we'll go for some high stakes poker when I get back. You'll have to wager something besides the cigarettes you bet with the boys."

"Deal."

We shook hands. I watched as he picked up his rifle and walked away and into the jungle.

Guadalcanal August 19,1942
Sam Marlow/New York Herald Tribune

It was approaching dark when the men of L Company, 3rd Battalion of the 5th Marines started coming back into camp. They looked like Marines who'd finally found their fight.

This night there was no rain. The moon was up. Through the palms a soft light filtered to the ground. That light was not in the eyes of the

Marines. Their eyes were black. They came and sat with a great weight.

The last Jeep came slowly. It carried two stretchers both covered by tarps. Four men stood and walked slowly to lift their comrades and carry them to lie beneath the palms in the shadow of the moon.

There are no ceremonies in a combat zone. No lone bugle to signal this Marine's day is done. It is for each to say goodbye in their own way.

One stood quickly and walked alone towards the beach. In his shoulders I could see the deep breaths that fill the space before the sobs began.

The second laid his hand on the chest of one body. The hand became a fist. He stood and walked past me reciting a litany of vengeance each ending with, "Sons of Bitches".

The third spoke softly to each dead Marine, then made the sign of the cross. He stood for a silent moment then lit a cigarette with a Zippo that cast a trembling light over the shadow of the moon.

Sergeant Marion was the fourth. He held a pale hand that had slipped from beneath the tarp. He spoke not as if in prayer but in conversation. As if death was not a hard separation but a thin line shared between men in war.

"I'm sorry sir, I should have stopped you."

"You did fine you lead from the front like a good Marine."

"The men are taking this kind of hard."

Those phrases drifted from a conversation that had only one voice. It was enough to confirm a dread I'd felt since the first man walked into camp. When the sergeant's voice fell silent I stood and walked slowly.

He saw me and started to stand. Instead I kneeled beside him. Marion said nothing but reached over and pulled back the tarp.

"Lieutenant Mead and Sergeant Branic."

The stillness of death is little different from that of sleep. One might think of peace, but not if you consider the chaos and courage of the moment that preceded death. Their faces were made more pale by the light in the shadow of the moon.

"The lieutenant saved the company. He picked some high ground yesterday. We snuck up there in the evening and dug in. The Japs spotted us this morning and threw everything they had at us. We had the better ground. They tried flanking us but the lieutenant saw it coming and took a platoon to cut them off. Jap sniper shot him. Our lines held because the lieutenant was smarter than those yellow bastards. We piled their bodies high. But it cost us two good men."

Dog tags were in one of the sergeant's hands. He put them in his pocket and pulled the tarp to cover the faces of the two men. Then he began to speak in a language I'd never heard. When he finished he stood and smiled just slightly.

"It's an old Cherokee blessing, 'May the rainbow always touch your shoulder'.

He executed a sharp salute then turned to join the platoon.

I stood alone looking at the dead and tried to imagine their last moments under fire. I thought of the other images I had of George on a horse, on the steps of 'The Pillars' and laughing with Kick Kennedy on his arm. The images wouldn't merge. The Big Picture was just as elusive at the moment.

Sitting on a crate by my bedroll I smoked a Lucky and felt the same. Maybe on this day it was the decision of a dead lieutenant that allowed this cigarette. It will take luck or god for any of us to walk off this island.

Soon I was asleep on the ground beneath the palms in the shadow of the moon.

CHAPTER 17

Darwin, Australia
Autumn 1942

BY NOVEMBER THE JAPANESE OFFENSIVE to retake Guadalcanal was running out of steam. So were the men of the 1st Division. Three months in the jungles with constant rain, constant battle and the scourge of dysentery and malaria dulled the edge of Marines who now fought and looked like hardened veterans. General Vandegrift wanted to go on the offensive, but he had the good sense to call up fresh troops from the army and 2nd Marine Division. That meant a bunch of marines were headed for an R&R tour in Australia.

This time a slow boat wasn't fast enough for me. You spend enough time hobnobbing with brass and making sure booze gets to their tents and you can stack up a few favors. I used a big one to hitch a ride on a general's Catalina that was hopscotching a few islands before heading to Darwin.

Guadalcanal from ten thousand feet is a glorious view, especially if the view is going away. From the air it was the image of a tropical paradise with a few bombed and burned areas. The island and the men on it have aged decades in the last three months.

Ashley was in Darwin. There were hotels with beds in Darwin. There were showers and hot food and cold beer in Darwin. And, I was going to have me some of all the above.

The town itself wasn't exactly a cozy little safe haven from the war. The Japs had put it on their 'drop in' tour earlier this year. In February they attacked twice in one day in what the Aussies called their 'Pearl Harbor'. In fact it was far less catastrophic in either the loss of life or military but a few hundred casualties and a burning harbor were enough to convince the continent of kangaroos and allies that they could be the next big target for the Empire. The U.S. Army Air Force sent in a fighter group to help support the Aussies. So far Japan seemed content with island grabs from the South China Sea to the Solomon Sea and wasn't quite willing to take on such a huge land mass.

Our approach took us over Melville Island and the Timor Sea on a course similar to the one the enemy would take on an attack. That probably explained the pair of P-40s that flew in hot and close for a view before pulling up with a waggling of their wings as they flew off. The airbase was inland and north of town but the Catalina allowed us to land right in Port Darwin and taxi up to a dock.

I stepped off the plane and into my dreams. Ashley was there on the dock. She was wearing something that looked like it would work well on the tennis court. I was thinking it would look better draped across a chair. My ensemble was simpler, the cleanest and best marine issue field clothes I could borrow before leaving Guadalcanal. Even those emitted a smell not for polite nostrils.

You've seen it in the movies. A man and woman separated by war, time, disaster, fate, or stupidity see each other again. They run and leap into the other's arms. It happens in real life. It's followed by a real kiss. A real long kiss.

"Excuse me have we met?" I asked?

"Actually I was looking for a writer. A famous war correspondent," Ashley responded.

"Would you recognize him if he was wearing a borrowed Marine's fatigues?"

"Not sure but I'd recognize his kiss."

"Then see if this rings a bell."

I kissed her in a way she'd remember when she was a grandma.

"Any bells?"

"Like a Chinese gong."

Our dockside love scene was drawing a few whistles and a smattering of applause along with some words of encouragement that in civilized times might be cause for a fight. These weren't those times and frankly

I'd already considered some of their suggested acts. It seemed best if we took the act someplace private. We started walking.

"How did you know I was coming in?"

"You hinted in your last letter. I heard some of the marines from Guadalcanal were rotating through for R&R. So I did a little checking."

"You have sources?"

"You wouldn't believe. The brass just loves meeting the USO tour."

"Oh I know the power of your charms. Do we have a destination beyond the end of this pier?"

"There's a place or two I'll take you, Mr. Marlow."

"Please call me Sam."

"Only if you'll call me Mrs. Marlow. That's the name we're registered under at the Hotel Darwin."

"Heavens! Are you using the war as an excuse to further your agenda?"

"No I'm using deceit with the hotel manager to get a place where I can be alone with you."

"In this case I'll applaud the desperate measures of war."

The Hotel Darwin might be considered quaint by New York City standards. But it had a few things no hotel in either place could offer. A large window opened to a balcony that overlooked the Timor Sea and a garden below with palms and trees with tropical fruit. The room also offered a tall teak bed and a tall beautiful woman who was walking my way carrying an open bottle of Champagne.

"Compliments of the house?"

"No by order of Mrs. Marlow. Drink this then hit the shower. I think it's time someone gave you a good scrubbing."

"I never imagined my wife would be so bossy."

"Your wife has a keen sense of smell and some very particular ideas."

She rationed me one drink then shoved me towards the bathroom. I turned the water up as hot and hard as I could stand it then stepped in. There is a difference between standing in a shower by choice versus standing for weeks in an incessant rain. Why both are described as showers is beyond me.

I was in the middle of lathering with my eyes shut when I felt a shot of cool air. The next thing I felt was a pair of hands massaging my back then moving downward. I wiped the soap from my face and turned to look into hers.

"Where is the dirty part you thought needed attention?"

"The part that's been on my mind for several months now."

She leaned back against the tile and pulled me towards her, pulled me into her and we attacked each other with a passion and desperation that neither seemed able or willing to control. I could hear the sound of her back hitting the tile. I could feel her nails clawing, as she pulled me closer and deeper. It was the most beautiful hand to hand combat with no declared winner. We both claimed victory and collapsed into the tub. I killed the shower and plugged the drain. She cried softly as her tears fell on the rising water. We held each other in a slippery, wet grip until the water overflowed. Then both started to laugh.

The shadows were deepening when we stepped out of the shower. Ashley threw on a robe and quietly opened the door looking both ways before pulling the dinner cart inside.

In towels and robes we sat and watched the last of the sunset while eating greedily from a plate of huge local prawns and fruit. It went well with Champagne. It went well with being away from the jungle.

When the darkness came it was complete up and down the Esplanade and even to the sea. The Australians were taking their blackout and threat of attack seriously. The dark form of a ship moved across the harbor. It was barely visible in silhouette. It's course was clearly visible in the luminescent wake it trailed.

Using the darkness to cover her course and intent, Ashley came and sat straddling my lap. Her robe open and pale body full of life. She began to kiss me slowly and with purpose. This time I was calling the shots, lifting her without breaking the kiss and carrying her to the bed. There was no rush and we committed from memory a long list of acts we'd both had months to prepare.

"Does it trouble you much?"

I exhaled and let my lungs and mind lay empty for a moment.

"Which?"

"What you've seen, the battles and the death."

"I hardly think of it at all, except when I'm awake, or asleep."

"Is it here now?"

"Yes even now in this quiet, perfect place with you so beautiful and the air from the ocean bringing a freshness that does not smell of gunpowder, or burning oil, or flesh. It will be here for a long time, maybe forever. It makes these moments more important because they are all we have. Because so many will never have a chance to live and love again as we have tonight."

"Then it is our duty to love."

"At the moment it is our highest purpose."

Some of the Marines from the 1st Division were beginning to arrive in Darwin. In a stark contrast to the oxymoron of military intelligence someone actually thought of splitting the Marines between Darwin and Melbourne for their R&R rotations. Maybe there was a concern about running out of beer if they were all in one place. For the most part the incoming Marines seemed content to spend their first days getting clean, getting sleep and walking in a place where you don't have to worry about snipers.

We were sitting outside having coffee watching small groups of men strolling and enjoying a day without a gun in their hands. A few still showed signs of a nervous eye, glancing left and right, up and down still looking for an enemy in hiding.

Ashley casually mentioned that there was a USO performance in two days.

"Really? Are you the headliner?"

"No silly boy. They're bringing in the big guns for this one. Bob Hope's performing."

I dropped my cup and spit coffee all in the same deft moment.

"Didn't Bob do that same spit take in the Road to Singapore?" she said, mockingly.

"Are you on a first name basis with Mr. Hope?"

"Hardly! But we are suppose to sing together."

"Try to remember me after you're famous and all."

" I'm just trying to keep up with my famous newspaper boy. I'm planning on a long and physical contest."

"When does 'Bob' get in town?"

"Tomorrow. We rehearse in the afternoon. The show is the next day. Can't do night performances because of the blackout rules and besides daytime is my best time."

"Well I was thinking of offering a daytime audition for a young rising star."

"Does it involve nudity and a feather?"

"As a matter of fact..."

By Wednesday morning the Hope word was all over town. Every uniform in every unit from every country was talking about the show. The excitement was tempered by two threats. The first was the Japanese. It seemed that crews were doing double checks on every gun placement in and around the harbor. The second and larger fear was the brass. A big show like this brings all the top brass and when the stars and bars start coming to town every rank feels the pressure. Everything has to be ship shape, squared away, spit shined and no-shit or the brass can make everybody's day miserable. Darwin was getting a dress up, so no one would get a dressing down.

Around noon a deep drone came in from the ocean. We walked out on the balcony to see specks with wings incoming. It looked like a squadron of bombers. Heavy bombers. I was about to grab Ashley and head for a bunker when I saw her smiling. Then I noticed no sirens.

"Some friends of yours dropping in?"

"When there's a big star in the show sometimes they like to make an entrance."

She was right. The B-24's were inbound with a fighter escort of P-40's leading the way. The group flew straight towards town then made a sharp turn to fly broadside along the beach. They P-40's dropped low and came in fast about a hundred feet above the water. The big B-24's came in close enough to see their insignia. It was the 380th Bomber group coming in to support the Aussies in Darwin. They were called the Flying Circus. On the nose of each of the bombers was painted cartoon figures.. including that of a pissed off Donald Duck. The entire air show took another hard turn to make a heading for the air base north of town.

"Quite the entrance."

"You cover war. I do the show business. Which means it's time to get to work. I'm going to rehearsal. The stage is being set up just down the Esplanade in the park. Come over in a bit and meet some of the crew. If your press credentials don't get you in, use this spare USO badge. Pretend you're a dance girl or something."

"Pretend you're a comedian, funny girl."

The sound on the other side of the door was her laughter going down the hall.

I found my own company less than amusing so I walked out to see what the Hope Invasion was doing to Darwin. Or maybe I just wanted a beer.

The Victoria Hotel up on Smith street was where a lot of the military was bivouacked. It also had a pub. There were a dangerous few blocks in between. Jeeps were racing all through town. A block further up the streets were lined on both sides with soldiers and civilians. As I walked up I saw why. A parade of Deuces with their canvas tops pulled back were making a slow trip through town. In the lead was Bob Hope himself. He drew a big cheer. The next vehicle was packed with showgirls. It had a military convoy either side. The only time I've seen a Marine on his knees begging was when that truck went by. In a few minutes the begging was over. It was time for crying into a beer. I followed a few Marines into The Vic.

It was dark and cool inside. I paused for a second so my eyes could adjust before walking to the bar.

A voice came out of the corner.

"Marlow..."

It sounded familiar. It did not sound like a challenge. I walked in the direction of the sound. It was Sergeant Marion sitting at a table with most of his platoon.

"Fancy seeing you here," he grinned from behind an almost empty pint.

"Not much fancy here but I hear the Aussies take their beer seriously and I'm seriously interested in one. Looks like you're in need of one."

"Got a lot of needs sir, but another beer's a good start."

I walked to the bar and ordered a round for the table. The bartender said the Marines were drinking on the tab of the Australian people and the town of Darwin. The Aussies were pretty glad to have an ally with arms show up for this little war. Churchill with his troubles at the front door pretty much left the whole of Australia at the mercy of the Japanese and/or good will of the American people. The Yanks showed up. Bloody island to island combat with the Japs.. gets you free beer. Sometimes you have to look at the positive. I thanked him and left some money on the bar for the 'home fund'.

The beers came and I raised mine in a toast, "Here's to L Company."

Glasses clinked and most downed a half pint in the salute. It was not a toast to sip. It was one to drink deeply for the dead.

"You get a new lieutenant?"

"Yep. Not the same. When we came over here we'd spent a lot of time together. We knew Mead and liked him, maybe too much. Now it's best not to get to know the lieutenants too good. Some don't last too long."

"They last longer than some of them Japs," that from a corporal in the corner.

"Stow it Byrne," the sergeant smacked him with all affection across the back of the head, "All you want to do is talk about killing Japs. You're on leave you oughta be thinking about chasin' girls instead of Japs."

He looked at me, "You'll have to excuse the boys. They're a little, how would a fancy writer put it? A little socially deprived. They could stand to meet some girls."

I hesitated a second weighing the risk of promising something I might not be able to deliver.

"What if I could introduce them to some of the showgirls from the USO?"

All at the table stood like I'd walked into the room with three stars on my helmet.

"Marlow, you got connections?"

"Just one, my girlfriend is singing with the USO. She's here. Just told me she's doing a number with Bob Hope."

"You got a girlfriend here? One that sings with the USO? Damn, Marlow, I gotta get out of this Marine business and take up writing. Can you help a few lonely Marines out?"

"Ok you guys. Let me think about this. There's a rehearsal going on this afternoon. Let's stroll down there. Let me do the recon for a change and see if we can sneak in."

They pounded their beers and ushered me out the door. I felt like Dorothy. Now all I had to do was find the Wizard... or I would find myself in the company of a platoon of pissed off Marines.

The perimeter of the stage area was roped off and secured by a patrol of Air Force MPs who looked like their sole purpose in life was to keep people like us on the outside. My plan was simple and stupid. Take the offensive.

I handed Sergeant Marion my USO badge.

"Take this pretend and like you're assigned to the tour group. Security or something like that."

"Protecting show girls. My dream job."

We walked up to what appeared to be an entrance point near the stage. It looked like where the performers would enter. We were close. There was a string of trailers. The lead one had a star on the door. Beneath in military stencils, Bob Hope. At the entrance was a small table manned by an officious looking little Air Force corporal.

"Hello corporal. I'm Sam Marlow with the New York Herald Tribune. These fellows are part of a security detachment assigned to the USO performers."

He looked at me. I could swear he sniffed, then looked down at a stack of papers.

"I don't see no Marlow on my list and I know there's no such thing as a Marine security detail. This is a US Army Air Force operation here. You're lucky if we even let any Marines in for the performance tomorrow. So why don't you fellows just go back to the bar that you've obviously just left and let the us take care of business here."

Uh oh. Marion brushed me aside.

"Listen here you little bitch. These Marines just came off Guadalcanal. They spent three months fighting Japs hand to hand in jungles so thick you couldn't even find your prick to piss with while you sat up here sipping tea with the Aussies and knitting at night."

The rest of the platoon was starting to circle closer. The little corporal called for some MP backup and we were one punch short of good old fashioned fist fight. Behind us a door opened and slammed against the wall of the trailer. General Vandegrift stepped out of the trailer with Bob Hope at his side.

"Marines!" the general bellowed.

Sergeant Marion spun around. Under his breath he muttered, "Holy shit".

Then much louder, "Ten-CHUN!"

All spun to attention.

"What the hell is going on here?" the general was walking down the stairs, "Who's in command here?"

Before anyone spoke the air force corporal started, "General these men..."

"Shut up corporal. I'm talking to these Marines."

Marion started, "General, sir. Sergeant Marion, L Company, 5th Marines."

Hope was behind the general. He was starting to smile, just a bit.

"Ahh, sir, we were with Mr. Marlow here. He said he knew one of the singers in the show and we thought we might just come down here and appeal to our Army Air Force brothers to get a little preview of the show."

He looked at me for the first time.

"Marlow. Dammit I didn't even see you. You been on that island so long with these boys, you're starting to act like a Marine."

"Thank you, sir," I smiled.

"Sergeant Marion it didn't look like brotherly love that was about to break out here. Looked more like a fist fight."

"Ah, sir... the corporal didn't seem to appreciate our service over the past few months. We were just about to share our experience with our friends in the Air Force."

"For the love of god, Marion. Didn't you get enough fighting on that damned island?"

Hope broke in.

"General, were these men on Guadalcanal?"

He looked at Hope, "These men were first on the island. Some of the first to fight and two of their leaders were among the first to die."

Hope looked at the men.

"Fellows. You are American heroes. You are the first to put the Japs back on his heels. You are the reason I'm here and the reason America has hope again. And I don't mean that as some wordplay for a joke."

He was just warming up and he already had an audience. Several doors had opened from other trailers revealing some of the most beautiful women America could offer.

Hope looked at the offending corporal.

"I want you to give these men a pass. They are my PERSONAL guests. They sit on the front row. They go backstage. And if they want to come in my trailer and drink my booze, you'd better make sure there's enough. Are we clear?"

"Yes sir, Mr. Hope."

Hope turned back towards the trailers.

"Ladies we have a show to rehearse but first, come on down and meet some heroes."

General Vandegrift slapped Hope on the back then executed a sharp salute to his men. They saluted back just as they were being swarmed by a dozen girls who seemed equally in awe of the Marines. I'm not sure I've ever seen a happier group of men. They deserved all they got.

I felt a hand on my arm, "Not a bad little entrance youself."

Ashley was steering me towards the stage. Behind us was a large and happy group.

"Well, that could have gone a couple different ways."

"Where'd you find those guys."

"In a pub of course."

"Are they George's platoon?"

"Yes."

"I'd like to meet them."

The band was starting to warm up as we walked in. They were playing 'Waltzing Matilda'. The unofficial Australian anthem was being adopted by the 1st Marine Division. The band was certainly playing favorites with General Vandegraft.

Hope took to the stage and took command going straight into his act.

"Hello everybody. I'm Bob 'that's not my scotch that fell out of the airplane' Hope.

"Good to be here in Australia. As a matter of fact, I just came back from a billabong and I can tell you what the waltzing Matilda and I did there had nothing to do with sheep."

"Was that a laugh, or just nervous Marine on the front row?"

The boys were seated in the front row for a Bob Hope show. Some of the girls were sitting with them. They were laughing at the jokes, laughing with the girls. It was a story they'd tell around the fireplace on those long winter evenings when they were old and grey.

"I was just over in Guadalcanal.."

The fellows stood and cheered.

"The weather there is a little different. They have light sprinkles. Light sprinkle is South Pacific for 'lookout boys the island's disappearing again."

They were on their feet with applause.

"You know I heard Crosby just went over to England. I heard they needed some entertainment for the older soldiers."

He paused and gave that famous Hope smile to the audience.

"It's been great to be on tour here in the South Pacific. Marines toast me wherever I go.. a guy can stand getting hot footed for just so long."

"But you know, the great thing about these USO tours is you get to work with some of the most talented performers in America. Give a warm Down Under welcome to Miss Ashley Chambliss."

Ashley walked out onto the stage as the band started playing 'Embraceable You'. Now the Marines grew quiet and I wasn't sure if their attention was for the music or the five foot ten woman in slacks and a simple blouse unbuttoned enough to make me feel the first hint of jealousy. She dispelled that with a two fingered salute directed towards me. The Marines saw it, too and elbowed each other pointing at me.

On the last line of the song Hope eased back on stage.

"Wow. Isn't she great?" He said clapping. "Take a bow Ashley. She'll be back in a bit. She's going to let me butcher a song with her."

She took a comic bow towards me and stood just off center stage. Hope kept going, running through the acts.

"You know General Vandegrift has been very supportive and very protective of me to bring this show into combat areas. He even promised to keep a supply of my blood type on hand... even if he had to kill the chicken himself!"

He took that patent pause again, waiting for the crowd.

But another sound cut into the Marines' laughter. Sirens could be heard out on Melville Island. Then the wailing sound started in Darwin. A low buzz could be heard during the tail end of the siren call, before it revved back up again.

I was up the stage stairs in a sprint to grab Ashley. The general and one of his colonels walked calmly on stage towards Hope.

"You know general, I really hope you don't have to kill that chicken. Which way do I run?" Hope asked.

"Those Japs probably had a spotter who reported those B-24s coming in yesterday and thought they'd catch them napping on the ground. The Air Force boys have a little surprise for them. Let's get you underground. There's a bunker about a quarter mile from here. It wouldn't do to get you killed, that'd be a bigger victory for the Japs than a whole squadron of bombers. Colonel, get that jeep up here. Sergeant Marion!"

Marion came running up the stairs.

"Secure those women. If you find a deuce with keys in it get them to the underground. If not find a foxhole nearby. Don't waste time. Those Japs are probably headed for the airfield but it doesn't mean they won't strafe something moving if they see it."

"Secure the women. Aye General," the two exchanged the briefest of smiles.

Vandegrift was herding Hope towards the jeep.

"General is there any scotch in the bunker? Fellow might need a little nerve remedy."

"It'll be over before you know it Bob. I promise we'll be back in your trailer with a whiskey in an hour."

"I like a General who can schedule cocktails in a war zone. They could use you in Europe. God knows Hitler has a way of screwing up a party."

Time for jokes was wearing thin. In the distance the leading wave of Zeros were beginning to split into two groups for their attack.

"Sam!" It was Sergeant Marion, "Foxholes about 50 yards that direction. Move out!"

You don't argue with a Marine sergeant. I grabbed Ashley and headed out to an area near the beach where it looked like someone did a little planning after the first Jap attack on Darwin to dig plenty of places to take cover. The shore guns were already starting to lay some welcoming flak for the Zekes.

All of us on the run for cover stopped in our tracks. A voice was coming from the microphone on stage.

"Ladies and gentlemen welcome to the second part of our show."

"What the hell?" I kind of led the collective question.

"That's Corporal Byrne," Marion scratched his head, "The idiot thinks he's a comedian."

"Is he crazy?"

"Probably no more than any of us now. He had a couple tough nights in the jungle. Seems to come back at him at different ways, different times. You people head for cover. I'll go back for Byrne."

We went in separate directions. Just as luck would have it for the Marines when we got to the foxholes they were all small. It ended up being boy and girl to each. Just like date night. Above the increasing sound of the AA batteries and the approaching planes Byrne continued talking.

"We'd like to welcome Tojo to beautiful downtown Darwin. You bastards didn't kill me in Guadalcanal you sure as hell aren't going to now! But wait Tojo there's more. What do I hear coming from backstage to greet you for the show?"

Almost on cue from directly behind the stage a dozen Warhawks thundered over at treetop level to meet the Zeros head on. It was incredible.

"Hello Mr. Zero, meet Mr. Warhawk. Surprise!!"

He actually seemed to know what he was talking about slipping into a play by play of the battle.

"Oh there goes a Zeke into the water. First score for the US Army Air Force."

"Up in the sky Tojo! There's another squadron of good old US fighters heading for your bombers which are now without cover. Oh ladies and gentlemen what a lovely airshow you're missing."

In a sense he was right. From the foxholes we were all watching. Somehow Byrne's announcing seemed almost natural. I was beginning to enjoy it. I was beginning to think we all might be crazy.

One Zero went down to the deck. He was coming in fast no more than 20 feet off the water and it looked like he was intent on hitting something before someone hit him. It's twin 20mm cannons were firing cutting a path across the water and straight towards us.

"Oh you slippery little devil... here comes Tojo!"

The line of fire was chewing up vehicles parked on the perimeter of the stage area. In an act of pointless chivalry I threw myself on top of Ashley.

"Come on you dirty bastard!!" Byrne was challenging the Zero pilot.

Over the microphone came the steady shots of a .45 calibre pistol. The crazy bastard was trying to shoot down the airplane. There was a growing roar coming out of the microphone. Part of it was the Zero's guns. Part of it was coming from Byrne's throat. I looked up to see the machine gun fire ripping through the stage. From the speakers came a huge sound that was like grunt and scream combined followed by a shrill blast of feedback through the mike and silence.

I looked down at Ashley's face. She'd heard the same thing and had come to the same conclusion. Marines scrambled out of their foxholes towards the stage and I pulled away from Ashley to join them.

"Ladies and gentlemen, that flying tackle and near miss was brought to you by Sergeant Marion. Who tells me we now conclude our broadcast."

We all stopped and started laughing. The girls came out of the foxholes and we gathered to watch the end of the air battle. It looked as if the Japanese had flown into a trap. After more than a year of unchallenged attacks on Darwin the flyboys showed them just what the Marines had demonstrated on Guadalcanal. The fight was on.

The one Zero had done a pretty good number on the area where the USO was going to perform. A few trucks were burning. Ambulances were coming into the area to pick up any wounded.

Sergeant Marion came walking towards us holding Byrne by the scruff of the neck. Byrne was smiling. Marion was trying not to.

"The first one of you who encourages this idiot's actions by telling him he did a great job with that announcement is gonna get a backhand."

Two jeeps came ripping into the area. Vandegrift got out and took a sweeping assessment of the area.

"Sergeant Marion any casualties."

"No sir, not that I can tell. My platoon is all accounted for as are all the ladies, sir."

"Good work sergeant. This place is a mess."

"I'm sure it's nothing the combined forces of the the Marines and Army Air Force can't fix by morning," Hope was climbing out of the jeep.

"We've got a show to put on."

"You sure Bob? I doubt the Japs will try anything foolish like coming back tomorrow.. but there is a risk."

"General, there's only one thing that scares me more than the Japanese and that's Crosby hearing that I cut and run from a performance. He'd show up in Hollywood carrying a chicken called Hope. No sir we'll do a show. By the way where's that guy who was doing the announcing while we were running for cover?"

"That would be Corporal Byrne sir," Marion half shoved him forward.

"Son I want you to emcee the show for me tomorrow. You were great!"

Marion slapped himself in the forehead.

Then unlike MacArthur's bogus promise of 'I shall return'... General Vandegrift fulfilled his.

The bar opened. We drank.

CHAPTER *18*

USS Rochambeau
March 1943

THE ROCHAMBEAU WAS THE PERFECT rogue ship to be carrying the unconventional crews of the South Pacific's PT squadrons. Like the motor torpedo boats themselves, the Rochambeau came to war with a questionable past. She sailed under an alias. Her original name was the Marechal Joffre, a French ship sailing in the Philippines and manned by Vichy French forces. While in port she was taken over by a downed group of US Navy fliers and a handful of French sailors who mutinied and took a stand for the Free French. When the ship sailed into San Francisco, the Navy took her and renamed the ship to honor the nobleman who commanded French troops under George Washington. Now she was heading for the New Hebrides carrying fresh Navy pilots and new crews for the casualty hit PT commands.

Jack Kennedy and the other officers bunked on the A deck of the ship that afforded a few more comforts than the decks below. The shared quarters were small staterooms where days of sea passage left long stretches for rambling discussions. One topic popular on all decks was girls, girlfriends and girls most wanted. The other was the war.

The Rochambeau and all on board were headed to war. It was a different front from just a few months ago. The Japanese had conceded Guadalcanal. After months of bloody fighting with the Marines they managed to move nearly 10-thousand troops off the island in the dead of night. Now the question on many minds is whether they were going to war or a backwater.

"Guadalcanal done. So what's next?"

There was a circle of chairs around a table where a card game was going on. There was something about playing cards during the daytime that could never quite rise to the level of a serious game. Those games came after dinner in the short hours before lights out.

"There's still a war somewhere. Nobody's turned this ship around yet."

With a group of lieutenants and ensigns, a cacophony of conversations ran non-stop. The only change came when a new player sat down at the table.

"You might consider a second front in this Pacific war and it's not with the Japs," Kennedy interjected.

"The Army and Navy are going at it over who's getting the lead in the fight. Seems like that battle started in Casablanca. Churchill was holding to the 'Defeat Germany First' plan. Admiral King called him a liar for promising to send troops to defeat Japan. Now King and General Marshall are trying to put their own men in charge of two different tactical wars."

"Nimitz and the Marines are the ones who started turning this war in the Pacific," offered a Navy pilot who dropped a three of a kind on the table and swept the winnings towards his end of the table.

"Dugout-Doug would not be a strong contender in running this war," Kennedy said in reference to Douglas MacArthur.

"He sat safe in Australia while the dirty work was going on in Guadalcanal. He was suppose to send relief as soon as the Marines landed and established a beachhead. Three months later - no Army."

"He should stick that corncob pipe up his ass," mumbled a PT officer standing against the wall. The Army was not winning any points on a ship full of Navy men.

"The point Dug-out isn't getting is that an island to island fight in the Pacific is going to create a long and costly war, in ships, equipment and men instead of making a more direct thrust to take the battle closer to the Japanese mainland. It's similar to the war in Europe, to the campaigns in Italy and Africa. They are sideshows. If Hitler's being attacked in Berlin he might curtail the other campaigns."

"Who invited Roosevelt's war advisor to the table?"

The question came from an ensign sitting at the table. He was playing, though not well, and his sense of humor was disappearing along with his stack of chips. One of the other players leaned forward and whispered a few words in his ear.

"Oh! So you're Jack Kennedy. That explains your knowledge of the European theater," the surly ensign stated. "Though it's kind of odd that the son of an appeaser would press the issue of war."

"My father offered the President his opinions in the lead up to the war. He was not the only person who felt at the time that American interests might be best served by not entering the conflict. He and I differed in our opinions as many Americans took opposing sides on the issue. I came to this war to fight. I don't think you'll find any appeasers in this room."

The ensign thought for a moment, "You know I heard your father speak once on the radio. He made a good case, but I was most surprised that he didn't sound like the rest of the Irish trash from Boston."

The stateroom fell silent. Jack fixed his eyes across the table on the ensign. A few of the fellows standing around the poker table stepped back allowing more room. It felt like the moments before the first shots at the OK Corral.

Kennedy smiled. You could hear heavy exhales.

"I believe it's my deal. Everybody in? Let's double the ante and double the wagers."

In a friendly and steady manner he destroyed the man opposite.

The long trip on a ship filled with troops was a journey of mind boggling boredom. Jack spent much of his days in the stateroom reading and continuing to build a pile of correspondence that he would mail on the first stop.

Remembering his last night with Inga was more than motivation to stay in touch. It was a motivation to survive and come home.

Inga Binga,

Are you settling down to the life of a single woman? Hopefully not fighting off too many dashing Hollywood actors who play warriors in movies, while the rest of us do the dirty work. Do you remember a certain remark about dinner and breakfast when I get back? Just give me the straight dope on that will you, so I'll know if this whole thing is worth fighting for. You don't need to get too nervous...It will be a few months but I'll be there with blood in my eye.

Jack

In letters home he described a cruise of another kind.

From the SS Rochambeau

Must be short in this missive. Cruise schedule is packed with activities. The Naval dress whites are perfect for the dances on the afterdeck and quite a hit with all the ladies, or at least I imagine them ladies. After lights out on ship you can't see who your partner is. Cuisine not to be matched by New York or Palm Beach. Healthy servings of bologna fried anyway you like it. Yesterday a bit of beef appeared for dinner and caused quite a stir.

I think my favorite activity is gazing at the sunbathers on the deck below. It might be a lovely view for a woman, which being not, means the scene...like the endless ocean, remains the same.

Your son.

Jack

Solomon Sea

The Navy LST that was lumbering across the Coral Sea did, in fact, make the Rochambeau seem like a cruise ship. Kennedy and the other sailors destined for Tulagi were riding atop a ship filled with gear, fuel and explosives heading to troops in the Russell Islands. The three day journey from Espiritu Santo seemed more slow and dull than the weeks crossing the Pacific. Boredom is underrated.

"What the hell is all that?" A sailor down the deck was pointing towards the island.

Coming dead at them was an enormous landing fleet. Troop transports and destroyers were at full steam out of Tulagi harbor and racing for open water.

"I don't think that's a yacht race," Kennedy said looking astern over his shoulder.

The sky was filled with incoming aircraft. Apparently, the Japanese had changed their strategy. If they couldn't take and hold Henderson field they would destroy it and anything they could hit from the air.

"Ninety one, ninety two.."

"What the hell are you doing?" Two sailors asked in unison.

"I'm trying to count Jap planes but I ain't even half way finished."

The call to battle stations changed everything from dull to duty in seconds flat. LST 449 was mounted with over a dozen guns from fore to aft that all started to pepper the sky towards the approaching planes. But the captain must have had some call to glory or a death wish because instead of steaming towards the support of the destroyers he turned the slow moving ship filled with enough fuel and ammunition to blow everyone sky high into the leading edge of the attack.

Call them what you will but the Japs are quick on changing a game plan. Several squadrons of bombers kept their altitude and direction for the island and Henderson field the rest split off and started dropping altitude. One group of bombers dropped low to attack as glide bombers, flying a couple thousand feet off the surface to target and release in their bombs with deadly accuracy if the anti-aircraft guns didn't get them first. A second group of bombers kept their altitude at about 10-thousand feet. They were headed directly over the ships for a sudden drop at 80 degrees in a terrifying and difficult-to-defend dive. Buzzing all around were the Zekes looking for our boys and a dogfight.

The first flight of Bettys went over our heads heading for the main Henderson field. Maybe the LST was lucky to be such a small prize when a whole fleet was only a few miles away. A pair of fighters made a half hearted strafing pass but pulled up quickly to join the rest of the pack. With the attack now astern the captain came about and pointed the ship towards the battle that was still heading in his direction.

The fight on the sea was intense. The high-low tactic of the Japanese kept the ship gunners looking in all directions for incoming threats. Every American airplane that could fly came up to meet and fight the Japanese. Like the ships in the harbor anything on the ground and not fighting was simply a target. The Americans split their formations with half flying high to poach the bombers and the rest fighting low and close in to the ships to stop the Bettys before they could release their loads.

   The USS Aaron Ward ran at flank speed ahead of the other ships to offer protection to LST 449. Both started a zig-zag course to try to make themselves poor targets. Cutting her speed to match the LST's made the Aaron Ward an attractive target. Three Japanese planes thought the same. They spotted the bait and flew around to attack with the sun directly at their back. The captain spotted them and turned hard to port and opened fire with 20 mm and 40 mm guns. Coming in sequence plane each releasing their loads.

   All three bombs hit close to the ship. Close enough to blow holes in her sides and crippling her engine rooms. She was still afloat but dead in the water. In the distance the dark smoke of burning oil told a similar story for a tanker. The USS Kanawha took a direct hit and was burning furiously. Then like a summer shower the battle was over. Flight and fuel time puts a finite limit on duration but not destruction.

   Jack Kennedy stepped off a gang plank late in the afternoon to the remnants of a battle and his first experience of war.

   Dear Sam,

   Seems the Japanese welcome wagon is still hard at work here on Guadalcanal. To give you an idea of what we are against---the day I arrived, they had a hell of an attack. As we were carrying fuel oil & bombs--and on a boat that was a tub---I thought we might withdraw + return at some later date, but the Captain evidently thought he was in command of the (USS) North Carolina as he sailed right in. Well, they dropped all around us--and sank a destroyer next to us but we were O.K. During a lull in the battle--a Jap parachuted into the water--we went to pick him up as he floated along--and got within about 20 yds. of him. He suddenly threw aside his life-jacket + pulled out a revolver and fired two shots at our bridge. I had been praising the Lord + passing the ammunition right alongside--but that slowed me a bit--the thought of him sitting in the water--battling an entire ship. We returned the fire with everything we had--the water boiled around him--but everyone was too surprised to shoot straight. Finally an old soldier standing next to me --picked up his rifle--fired once--and blew the top of his head off. He threw his arms up--plunged forward + sank--and we hauled our ass out of there. It brought home very strongly how long it is going to take to finish the war.

Moving into quarters at the PT base. Why don't you come back this way for some stimulating pieces on the PT command. Besides we need to go over and visit Mead's grave.

Jack

CHAPTER 19

Calvertville/Tulagi

THEY SAY AN ARMY MARCHES on its stomach. I'm not sure what floats the Navy but the supply boat I was riding across Iron Bottom Sound was loaded with Vienna sausages and toilet paper. Just the basics.

Coming up the channel towards the base the most welcoming sight was a crude sign hanging from bamboo poles: Calvertville:Through These Portals Pass The Best Motor Torpedo Boat Flotilla In The World. All units tended to brag about their exploits. This one was spinning pure fiction.

Bulkeley did a good job of selling the Mosquito Fleet to the public and the White House but the exploits of the PT crews and their commanders had made them the misfits of the navy. To date the fleets biggest 'kill' came when a flotilla of six boats surrounded the flagship of Admiral Turner and, ignoring signals from the USS McCawley opened fire. 'Sighted ship, sank same' to coin the popular phrase. The same ending came to Lieutenant Commander Robert Kelly who was demoted from command.

Jack stepped onto the island and into the chaos of command and duty. He inherited one of the oldest boats in the squadron. The *PT 109* was an 80-foot Elco Patrol Torpedo boat that saw hard duty during the Guadalcanal campaign and needed serious refitting for duty. Kennedy took command of a boat barely afloat and with three 1500-horsepower engines that weren't fit for trolling much less patrol. His first months as skipper were spent more in drydock than at sea.

My supply boat pulled into the dock and tied up. We could have been a Jap patrol or the Queen Mary. No one was on the dock to guard or greet us. The skipper blew one blast on his horn and a couple young sailors, half dressed in shorts and boots, started down the walkway. I grabbed my kit and walked towards them.

"You fellows know where I can find *PT 109*?"

"Far dock, outside boat. Think they put her back in the water this morning. Those might be here engines starting up," said a dock hand.

"Thanks."

I headed in the direction of the deep rumble of the Packard engines. It was the *109*. She was docked, like a gem in a gift box, facing proudly toward the shoreline. Kennedy stood at the helm - skinny, suntanned, shirtless and smiling. The engines were revving and roaring. Shouting seemed pointless so I dropped my bag and started waving my arms overhead to get Jack's attention. He looked up and waved me on board.

"Man you newspaper guys know something about timing," he shouted.

"We just got these new engines running. Look at this old tub. Fresh paint, scrubbed hull and 4500 horsepower. Get on board we're going for a test run."

I tossed my bag on board and followed as the crew was casting off.

"Stow your gear below. Anything above deck tends to go airborne if not strapped down."

We pulled into the narrow channel and moved slowly past the docks. As soon as he saw open water Jack eased the throttles until the boat's bow raised to block the horizon then settled back square on the water. The sea was calm and the old PT felt and looked like the little warship she was supposed to be.

The grin on Jack's face was getting wider. The crew fell into their duty positions. All were wearing the same smile. It was a good day to be in the Navy.

Jack waved his executive officer over, "Lennie I'm not going to have any confidence in these engines until we've got a few hours of straight run time on them. We've waited long enough to get on patrol, let's just take a run across the sound and make sure they're squared away."

"That's good. I'll tell the boys we're making a run and make sure they run all the checks on this shakedown cruise," answered the XO. "We going to the Canal?"

"I think so. I've got a friend there I've been meaning to visit. By the way, this is another friend, famous war correspondent Sam Marlow. Sam, Lennie Thom my executive officer."

If you were picking skippers by appearance the assignments would have been flipped. Lennie Thom was a tall, muscular man with the build and features of a Nordic god. Next to him Jack looked like a skinny, sickly little brother. The XO went forward to fill in the crew.

"Lennie looks like a poster boy for the master race," I began,

"Tall, blonde, muscular.. I'm sure Hitler would love to put him in his breeding pool.. but he's all American. He was an All Star tackle and guard at Ohio State. He's about as apple pie as you get and as solid an XO as you could ask for."

"The fellow you mentioned visiting..."

"I said we'd go see George. Seems like as good a time as any."

Running at full throttle we were across the sound and arrived at the pier in less than an hour. Jack went below and came back topside wearing a shirt, slacks and shoes.

"Around here if you want to be an officer you have to dress like one or some semblance of one. They don't give our outfit a lot of respect."

"Lennie, we're running ashore for a few minutes. Don't intend to be here long. The dock seems a little underpopulated today. Send a couple of the boys around to see if the Navy's left anything unattended."

We'd docked at Lunga Point where the brunt of the US force came ashore the summer before. It was where a few thousand Marines and myself had found our first experience of war. Many of those Marines had rotated out. The rest were buried near the beach where the battle for the Pacific became a land war.

I didn't recognize much.. There were a few palms left, very few. The island where we had come ashore was now conquered. It had become a key forward post for the battle against Japan. Less than a year ago the sandy beach and coconut trees led to the thicker edge of a tropical forest. The Seabees had done their job to transform the landscape. Now the jungle was pushed back and cleared. In its place were anti-aircraft batteries, roads and large open areas where cargo and supplies were stacked. They had done their job so well there was a line of sight down a well worn road that went all the way to Henderson Field. An invasion might work better if we simply sent the Seabees in first.

The bulldozers had cleared one other area. It was near the beach where we first landed. It was where many Marines were buried. It was not Flanders Fields. No flowers between the crosses row on row. The symmetrical and symbolic beauty in death comes years after a war. Where war is still living the dead take their place as best they can be managed at the time. Here there was a large field prepared and a population that was still growing.

"Here he is," Jack stopped and turned to face the simple cross.

One a piece of metal that looked like it had been hammered from a mess kit was a battlefield epitaph:

Lt. George Mead USMC.
Died Aug. 20
A great leader of men
God Bless Him.

"You were with him weren't you?" Kennedy asked.

"Not in the battle. It was his command. He would not authorize me to accompany them. He ordered me to stay in camp."

"To be a leader you have to accept risk and responsibility. He did. But part of his responsibility was to spare you from unnecessary risk. Maybe he sensed something that night. His decision may have saved your life, maybe not. He wasn't the arbiter of life or death. He was just a damned good man who should not be dead...just like many alive today who will not be here when this war is over."

"We lived, felt dawn, saw sunset glow..." I picked up the famous poem from the First World War.

"Loved and were loved, and now we lie..." Jack followed.

"In Guadalcanal," we both ad libbed a new finish.

"Damn. Let's get outta here."

We walked with purpose. We wanted that hallowed ground behind us. It was not time for a memorial when the main idea in your head is that you could soon be joining those thereunder.

Our conversation had moved beyond death to women and how war plays hell on one's love life. Fifty yards from the docks we saw Lennie waving his arms above his head then motioning us to come along. We broke into a dog trot and came within earshot.

"Let's go Skipper. Time to make a quick exit." He said.

Coming alongside he used both of his huge arms to encourage us to pick up the pace.

"What's going on Lennie?"

"Well, you told the boys to go scouting."

"And...?"

"They found some cargo that must have been sent for the brass. They have 'appropriated' a few cases of good whiskey and some canned food that is neither Vienna sausages nor Spam. Real canned hams Skipper, beef stew and peaches and cigars."

"Real beef and ham. That'll make us the heroes of the hut. Why the rush."

"Well, Skipper.. one of the dock boys spotted them and called the Shore Patrol.

"Hope you've got the engines running."

"And lines on board.."

We could hear a jeep coming up fast. We ran faster.

"This is going to be close," Jack said with half a laugh.

Lennie was in much better shape and ran ahead. He lept from the dock to the middle of the boat and went straight to the helm. The jeep was already on the dock racing towards us. The SPs were blowing their whistles. Jack and I both took the literal flying leap and landed just as Lennie gunned the engines. The boat was moving as we landed and sent us both sprawling. We grabbed the 20mm guns to pull ourselves up just in time to see the dock disappearing quickly to stern while the two military policemen shook their fists at the escaping PT crew. To their credit the entire crew stood and saluted the pair who returned the salute with a single finger.

The pirate's booty was spread about the open deck. One of the crew was already carving a ham and handing out chunks to all on board. It tasted like the best ham I'd ever had in my life.

"A drum of aviation fuel?" Jack asked.

"We were running a bit short back at the base. If they left it sitting out there they couldn't of needed it that bad," the answer from a shirtless sailor in a navy crew cap.

"Sam this is Edgar Mauer. He's the quartermaster. If it passes through the Navy supply chain he can generally find a way to get his hands on it."

"You mean like these three new engines, Skipper."

"Damn right I do. How they running, Pappy?" He asked a grease stained sailor who came up from below and was so hungry he didn't seem to mind mixing the engine oil on his hands with his sample of ham.

"Good sir. We maybe ran them a little harder than what the break-in period says on the books but they sure got us away from that dock fast enough. Oh, and any of you monkeys who break out those cigars with that tin of high octane fuel right there better hope the explosion kills you because if you blow up my boat... I'll feed your tender parts to the sharks."

"Pappy's right on that. You boys stow that stuff.. .not the fuel... below deck. If anyone on base finds out we 'appropriated' a stash like that we'll have to post guards outside the hut to guard the hooch."

Jack took the helm and continued to run the boat near top speed into a second channel that the Seabees cut as an escape hatch for the PTs to use if the base came under an air attack from the Japanese. This channel led straight to the PT docks. Jack kept the boat at a high speed until about 20 yards out then cut the throttle back. The boat sat down hard, then came to a gentle drift the last few yards where Jack pulled her into a perfect mooring.

"That was a hot approach," I said, as we stepped ashore.

"It's just how we do things here in Squadron Two. Come on... let me show you Shangri-La."

The path to Shangri-La was paved with deck plating from ships - not a carpet of exotic flowers. It looked more like a summer camp for juvenile delinquents. We walked past a couple work huts and crew bunks before coming to a small row of tents.

"Behold the Royal Palm Club. It's our own humble, and let me repeat the word humble, Officer's Club. The most extravagant of concoctions are served here and are largely drawn from the torpedo tubes and known as torp juice. Every night about 1930 hours the tent bulges, a few men come crashing out blow their lunch and then stagger off to bed. This torp juice makes the prohibition stuff look like Haig and Haig but probably won't do anyone any permanent harm as long as their eyes hold out."

The tour ended at a row of thatched huts. As much as any man might fantasize these huts were not the intricate work of native craftsmen and surrounded by their nubile daughters in scant if any clothing, wearing leis and offering the same. These were more like poles thrust into dirt floors, with a roof of thatched palm leaves.

"Sam, welcome to Shangri-La. Please leave your South Pacific dreams at the door. Oh, sorry there is no door." Kennedy said sarcastically, "Take that bunk over there. Lennie bunks here. The crew has a couple of tents closer to the boat. I think after that shakedown cruise the *109* is fit for duty. Make yourself at home settling in. I'm going to run up to Lieutenant Cluster's quarters and put us on the roster for a patrol tonight."

He was back in fifteen minutes.

"Cluster gave us a go. We'll go out with *PT 48* on a two boat patrol. You might as well just fall in with this screwball schedule we keep. Now that we're back on the duty roster we'll go out on patrol every other night. During the days we work on the boats. If something hasn't broken on the boat then we're just as likely to be fixing some modification made by Jap gunners. These plywood boats tend to take on bullet holes pretty easily. Somewhere in between we try to grab a few hours sleep. 'Try' being the operative word because slumber here in the daytime heat of Shangri-La is precious. At five-forty-five little John over there wakes us up."

He pointed towards a small native boy squatting in a corner of the hut.

"Wakie, wakie, John?" Kennedy pointed towards the boy speaking in a pidgin English that the two seemed to share.

"Wakie, wakie, bye borty bibe," John stood and pointed towards his watch.

"A native with a watch?" It looked a little out of place.

"You'd be surprised what a few trinkets will get you from the natives. For that watch I could have had his sister and all the fresh meat I wanted. I passed on both."

"But if canned ham is considered a delicacy here then why pass on fresh meat?"

Kennedy broke out in a fit of laughter. Lennie walked into the tent about that time and growled and stomped.

"Because you never know who might be in the pot. As if the Japs aren't enough to worry about this island is crawling with cannibals. John is a favored name by a lot of the local men. They like the Christian name but not many of the practices. John likes his Man meat. Says Japs are tasty, though he seems to like the looks of Lennie."

"Little heathen better stay on your side of the hut. If he comes close to me I'll shoot him," Lenny looked warily, "Gives me the creeps looking at me like he's looking at a butcher chart in a meat market."

That started Jack laughing again.

"He'll bring us something to eat when we wake up. Blackout begins at 1830 and it's enforced. As you see the tents and huts have no sides and the Japs love to fly over looking for something to shoot at."

"Hey Sam," Lennie broke in, "Just make sure if that little heathen brings you something to eat it comes out of a can or package. And at any point if you don't see me for more than a couple hours, find this fine young cannibal and make damned sure he isn't smiling with a full belly."

John looked at Lennie with an eye of adoration. Or maybe it was hunger. The XO heaved a shoe across the hut.

We went each to our cots and dropped the mosquito nets to create our sheer cocoons. Jack had explained their odd hours of duty. He'd been here a couple months. Most of us had already done a tour, or two. For anyone at home, a hut, a cot and mosquito net might seem a bit primitive. Compared to the months on the Canal this was Shangri-La.

The other thing about battle is that when bullets aren't flying, you can go to sleep anytime, anywhere. I was out in an instant.

"Bye borty bibe." I heard loudly.

I launched off my bed like I'd heard an air raid siren. The process wrapped me in the mosquito netting like an insect caught in a web. I heard two people laughing. It was triangulated by the eyes of young John who was close by and watching me. The notion of prey trapped in a spider's web didn't seem inappropriate.

"Welcome to the menu, Sam," Lennie seemed particularly happy, "Maybe I'm off the top of the entree list."

"Does John watch us while we sleep?"

"Used to be just me. Now you, too. He sleeps by Jack's bed but the big Bwana - he be safe."

"Great, just great. I actually dreamed last night of African missionaries and a big kettle cookout."

"John. Mangia, mangia," Jack picked up on the food theme.

"You've taught him Italian?" I asked.

"Somehow it sounds more civilized than teaching him to "fetch, eat" and it's all the same to him. He's learning, bright little fellow. Maybe we'll keep him as part of the crew."

"Over my dead body," Lennie started.

"Don't get the boy's hopes up," Jack finished.

It was raining outside the hut. The kind of rain that came and went on schedule this time of year. The kind of rain that made a ground war miserable. The kind of rain that made PT skippers nervous.

We cast off and started slowly up the channel. The crew had pulled a tarp over the cockpit so we stood in a spot that was protected from the direct rain. Nothing on a night like this could keep you dry. Jack ran the boat at a low throttle. The rain and the darkness combined to create total blindness. There was no horizon, no land, no visible markers.

"We can run a basic course heading out into the open water. After that it gets pretty lonely, pretty quick. Most of these boats don't have radar. We don't use radio unless it's an emergency. In the rain, in the dark it doesn't make much difference. Patrol is mainly a game of chance. Hoping that we see them before they see us. The Jap cruisers can outrun and outgun us so those aren't usually very positive encounters. If we come up on a barge we might have a chance to hit them and run. On the positive side, this cloud cover will keep the seaplanes from tracking our wake."

Lennie came up from below carrying coffee.

"Nothing like a pipin' hot cup of joe on a moonless cruise," the XO handed out coffee.

"Thanks Lennie. This rain is starting to slacken up a bit. Let's get all hands on deck for now. If no Jap planes show up in the next couple hours we can go to two hour watches."

"Aye. I'll send somebody up to stow this cover. It's good for the rain. Not so great at stopping bullets."

"Thanks Lennie, and for the coffee, too. Tell the crew to stay sharp."

The canopy was folded back. It opened to a clearing sky. I walked aft to look at the wake. Even running slow using the center, deeper screw the boat was putting out a wake the glowed with the brilliant light of the tiny creatures disturbed by the turning propeller. I looked from the luminescent trail up to the sky. The clouds were clearing and I could see the Southern Cross. Such constellations can steal the eyes and the imagination. It not only directs sailors, it comforts them. In the Southern hemisphere it is a constant, like the Northern Star.

"Of whose true fixed and resting quality there is no fellow in the firmament," Jack spoke behind me.

"You're reading my thoughts."

"I think of Caesar's lines often when I look at the Cross. The Northern Star runs deep in the history and mythology of the North. Here, below the Equator, the Cross may be even larger in lore."

"Woe to those who try to command its dedication to the heavens and to man. It didn't bode well for Caesar."

"Caesar created his own fate and was felled by friends. Here our fate hangs on chance and circumstance. It is framed by men sitting in much safer places, placing men and destiny at the whim of a decision. Even worse, putting men at risk to advance their own schemes of grandeur. It happened to Caesar. It's happening now. It will happen again in the future. Shakespeare's plays are for the ages. All you have to do is change the names."

In the middle of the ocean, in the middle of a war this young lieutenant observes the stars, quotes Shakespeare and sees the future. He may be remarkable if he survives. It was a wonderful moment. I contemplated for an instant if any of the 'appropriated' whiskey might still be on board. As my eyes moved from the sky to the deck I thought I saw a shooting star. The crew saw something else.

"Battle stations!" Jack called as he ran towards the helm.

Now I saw other the fiery tracers making their way from an attacking plane towards the boat. If we didn't move he'd have us targeted in seconds. I ran forward to the cockpit as the PT took up the attack.

"Full throttle!" Jack yelled from below.

The boat began to build speed and go into a zig zagged pattern. Gunners on the twin 50 caliber and the 20mm machine guns began shooting back towards the tracks of the tracers. Off the tail the smoke generator was throwing up a black cloud to cover our well lighted path. It seemed both sides had run this drill before. The noise from the guns and engines made it impossible to hear how many planes were attacking or where they were coming from.

To the port side a splash was followed by a huge explosion. I heard the same to starboard, but it was closer and so strong it lifted the boat out of the water.

"Kill the engines. Ceasefire," Kennedy called.

We came to a dead stop in the water.

"Kill that smoke."

Lennie came into the cockpit. Dead silence.

"Keep the crew quiet. Let him think he got us."

"Playing possum? It might work," Lenny looked into the darkness.

The plane circled. If it dropped a flare the game would be over. The gunners were following the sound of the plane with their barrels. I heard the sound of moans, someone wounded, just forward near the torpedos. The Jap dropped altitude and tightened his loop. No one on board was breathing. He sounded so close. I knew the gunners just wanted to paint the sky. When he seemed like he was as low and close as he could get, the pilot steered off. The sound of his engine began to fade in the distance. We all took a deep breath and then let out a collective cheer.

"Check for wounded. Let's wait a few more minutes then head back to base."

It was a close call. That doesn't mean being straddled by two bombs doesn't trigger a chain of consequences, like the age old connection between sex and death. I was sitting in the hut working on a long and lusty letter to Ashley when Jack came back up from the boat.

"How's the boat?"

"Nothing we can't patch. Fortunately most of the bomb's blast went to the fish."

"What about the men?"

"Couple of minor injuries. Nothing we can't patch, physically. The close encounter rattled one. Andy Kirksey, the torpedoman, who thinks his number's up. I think we all had that thought last night."

"What did you tell him?"

"I'm sure you saw it on the Canal. They're spooked and it doesn't really help to explain destiny, or fate, or the law of averages... which aren't really good for PT boats anyway. So I gave him the old Irish lucky charm."

"Lucky charm?"

"It's all hocus pocus. Religion, faith, belief but it's what keeps a lot of people going. So I dug into my kit and found some old Catholic trinket my sainted Mother sent me and gave it to him."

"Did it work?"

"Who knows in the long run. For now his eyes lit up like kid at Christmas. Maybe it'll work. Or maybe he just needs a change in scenery."

"You mean Tulagi isn't beautiful enough?"

"Guess not. We're being detached from Shangri-La. They want us to up in Rendova to try to stop the Tokyo Express from supplying the Japs in New Georgia. It sounds like a great time. We'll be going up against ships we can't stop and from all reports the commander is the biggest shit in the Pacific. That base makes this one look like Plaza Hotel. So let's find one of those bottles of whiskey and enjoy our last night in paradise."

With that he walked over to his prized Victrola, dropped the needle down on a Sinatra record and started another in a long string of letters to Inga.

CHAPTER *20*

Hollywood, Ca.

Dear Inga Binga,

Word must have gotten around that the country club life was getting too good here on Tulagi, so we're shipping out to Rendova. MacArthur's brilliant plan from his dug-out in Australia to send both the Army and Marines island hopping is going quite well, for the Japanese. They've dug in and gone on the defensive which is making it hard for our boys. So they send in the Mosquito Fleet because, as our motto proudly claims: They Were Expendable.

A number of my illusions have been shattered, but you're one I still have, although I don't believe illusion is exactly the word I mean. By an illusion I would mean the idea I had when I left the states that the South Seas was a good place to swim in . Now I find that if you swim there is a fungus that grows in your ears. Thus, fungal infections are not just for bad boys, or girls. Some of the crew were down at a lagoon the other day for a swim when a few native girls appeared out of the bush and went for what the natives likely consider an innocent naked swim. Under my command I cannot condone mingling with the natives and I didn't ask any questions, but my hut boy seemed to sum up the story with a gesture that looked a lot like a native mating dance. Leaving the lurid lagoon behind will be a sad loss to the crew. However, I shall return with a fungus growing out my ears to a heroes welcome, demand a large pension which I won't get, invite you to a dinner and breakfast which I'm beginning to have my doubts about you coming to, and then retire to the old Sailors home in West Palm Beach with a lame back.

Love, Jack

She put the letter down gently and smiled. His letters always made her smile. She could see the skinny sailor and his grin that masked the brilliant mind and lusty man. It was difficult not to be impressed by the wit and bravery of a man in the middle of a war. It was difficult not to continue to love him. But Inga was practical. She might love Jack but she also knew that it was a love with diminishing returns. Papa Joe would never change his mind and at the moment Jack was one of millions of men at war who might never come home. Besides on the homefront Inga had a war of her own.

Her phone rang. She looked at it. Thought about the possibility of cutting the cord and tossing it out the window. It would probably only fall and hit the agent on the street below and he really wasn't the problem.

"Hello. This is Inga."

"Inga Binga."

"Director Hoover. How pleasant to hear from you."

"Don't lie to me Miss Arvad. I can detect a liar with each of my six senses."

"And I thought humans only had five."

"I'm special, Miss Arvad, didn't you know?"

Sometimes it almost seemed like he was flirting with her. When he wasn't being a complete asshole.

"Now here's why I called you."

"Please share, Mr. Director."

"You will receive a visit from a young woman by the name of Joan Barry. Did I mention she was a -young- woman? She's also pregnant. Claims the father is that molester Charlie Chaplin."

"And what would you like me to do?"

"Listen to her then write a story. You can break the story that Charlie Chaplin is going to face a paternity suit. Even better since he flew her to New York for an 'audition' and sex we're going to charge him under the Mann Act for transporting her across state lines for immoral purposes."

"Defending the morals of America.."

"Don't get smart with me. It's a good story and it might help shut down that little pervert and his commie filmmaking."

"Mr. Hoover you would have to admit that The Great Dictator has put Hitler in a context that millions of people can understand."

"You would know about Hitler, you perfect little example of Nordic beauty and don't try to lecture me on film or propaganda. I deliver you the subject. You make the propaganda. Get it?"

"As always Mr. Director a pleasure talking with you."

She dropped the phone lightly on the cradle. He made her wish she kept an office bottle in the bottom drawer of her desk like the tough detectives in pulp fiction. She made a note to get one.

There was a knock at the door. The sound was so faint you were unsure if it was an actual knock or the anticipation of the knock you knew was coming. It came again. Then another.

"Come in."

"Miss Arvad?"

"Yes, please have a seat."

"I was told to come see you. You're a columnist aren't you?"

"Yes. And who told you to come see me?"

"A man told me. A man who was in my lawyer's office."

Inga walked over and looked out the window. She could just imagine who that man might be.

"So you're here to tell me about your relationship with Charlie Chaplin."

"How did you know?"

"A man told me."

For an hour they talked. Inga made tea. There was no reason to hate the girl just because Hoover was using her. It was clear Chaplin used her. She had no idea what she was in the middle of or who was pulling the strings that would change her life. It's how dirty deeds get done. You're either the player, or you get played. Inga was somewhere in between. Which meant she had no play. She wrote the article.

It had unintended consequences.

Whatever Inga's experience had been at the Times Herald in Washington writing amusing personal pieces on people about town her position and prominence turned radically on one headline: **The Little Tramp Gets a New Suit: Paternity and Fed Sex Charges Face Chaplin.**

She wrote it like she owned it. And she did. When the piece hit the streets the town erupted. Charlie Chaplin was Hollywood. His career began by bringing humor and relief during the grim years of the First

World War. The Little Tramp found laughter in poverty in the midst of the Depression. He lampooned a dictator bent on ruling the world in these modern times. Chaplin owned studios, ran huge film budgets and was wealthy beyond measure. George Bernard Shaw called him 'the only genius to come out of the movie industry'. Americans loved their Little Tramp.

Hollywood was not unlike Washington where politics, fame and power combine. Sex is a plaything, a toy of the mighty. Chaplin had a history of teenage attraction. His first and second wives were skirting seventeen when they married. The Hollywood version of a shotgun wedding, one step ahead of the baby. This time he seemed to be skipping the wedding part. Perhaps because Joan was safely in her twenties. Perhaps because after three divorces he found the process too costly.

Charlie Chaplin in a paternity suit was no shocker to anyone in Hollywood. Federal sex charges were something else. A conviction could end his career.

Inga's piece hit the papers before the charges were formally filed. Her phone was ringing non-stop. Suddenly everyone wanted to know who she knew and who wanted to bring down Chaplin.

The phone rang again. She looked at it. Did it sound different? Her intuition told her this call was different. She answered.

"Hello this is Inga Arvad."

"Miss Arvad. I read your piece this morning with some attention. It saddened me to think of someone as smart and attractive as you jumping on that bandwagon. You know, Miss Arvad, it is only the unloved who hate."

His voice was soft, refined. It sounded a bit sad. He was also quoting himself from The Great Dictator.

"Good morning, Mr. Chaplin."

"I was wondering to myself this morning over coffee and your article why the ex-wife of Paul Fejos would come to Hollywood to torment me."

"You know my husband?"

"Of course, we've both done films for Universal. I was a big fan of The Last Moment."

"We are divorced. Paul has nothing to do with any of this."

"I thought not. He didn't seem to be one to pursue personal agendas."

"I have nothing against you, Mr. Chaplin."

"But your column seemed to suggest otherwise. Unless it was the work of someone else."

"This is not a wise conversation to have on the phone."

"Of course not. I was actually calling to invite you to lunch. Meet me at the Chateau Marmont at one if you please." Chaplin demanded.

He hung up without waiting for an answer. He knew she would be there.

The FBI agent took off his headphones. The Director might want to know about this. He went up the line in a telephone daisy chain until he hit the top.

"Who is this?" Hoover demanded.

"Agent Smith, sir."

"Well agent Smith, this better be important."

"Miss Arvad, sir. Just got off the phone with Mr. Chaplin. They're meeting for lunch at the Chateau Marmont."

"Arvad and Chaplin together? Ha! This might be interesting. You get some agents down there. Chaplin will probably get the hotshot table. Try to get a mike planted. Call me back when you get something.. and you'd better get something. What'd you say your name was?"

"Smith, sir. Harry Smith."

"Harry Smith. Ha! Bet that's on the registry at the Marmont about a dozen times. Ha!"

"Yes, sir."

The phone went dead. Hoover hung up without another word.

Smith jokes. Ha! The agent thought. Very original.

The Chateau Marmont sits high on a hill above Sunset Boulevard . It is styled after a structure in the Loire Valley. It is a hotel filled with all sorts of sex and intrigue and fitting of the French motif.

Inga arrived a few minutes early to scout the surroundings. She was looking for Hoover's men. They were there scattered about doing a worse job of acting nonchalant than a B grade actor playing King Lear.

"Good afternoon ma'am. May I help you," the maitre d' inquired dismissively. "I'm here to meet Mr. Chaplin for lunch."

"Mr. Chaplin?"

"Charlie."

"But of course ma'am. Right this way," He led with ruffles and flourishes.

The table was the best in the room. It was in a corner by a large window that looked out over the city. She settled in.

Chaplin strolled into the room, not twirling a cane. A stroll like a man with a purpose and no real rush. He was short. His hair was almost white. Lita Grey, his second wife, was said to be the cause of it. Paulette Goddard had just become ex-wife number three. He was alone now with a long string of failed relationships in his wake.

The maitre d' was suddenly smitten. He looked like he was going to pee on himself with joy.

"Mr. Chaplin so nice to see you again. There's a lovely lady waiting at your table."

He approached and bowed admiringly.

"Oh Jean Paul, it's such a lovely day, let's sit outside on the terrace. Miss Arvad, would you join me." Chaplin said.

He extended his arm and they walked together onto a terraced garden where they were alone. Inga looked around, then looked at Chaplin.

"Yes my dear, we are alone. Ahh, let me look at you. You are lovely. I understand why the gentlemen of the Reich found you so appealing."

"Mr. Chaplin, if you would agree not to torture me about my past. I'll agree to avoid yours. There are others more threatening than you who take pleasure, or purpose, in exploiting my past associations in Germany."

"Miss Arvad, Inga if I may, if you think about it what you have just said describes my situation as well. Instead of antagonists we should be allies. We have a common enemy."

"Hoover."

"Exactly."

As if they were each acting on cue, they looked over their left shoulders to make sure they were still alone.

"But what can we do to J. Edgar Hoover?"

"He uses his power to blackmail and control people from the White House to the West Coast. Sex is how he leverages others. Sex between adults, sex out of marriage, sex between men and women, sex between women, sex between men.. he may even have a file on sex and animals.. if he can find a way to compromise someone of use to him he will."

"But he seems to hold all the cards. He's the head of the FBI for heaven's sake."

"Only because no one has ever gone after him."

"He would destroy you. He will destroy us."

"That seems to be his current plan anyway. I have little to lose. He has power and he is evil. We need kindness and gentleness. Without these qualities life will be violent and all would be lost."

"So you believe what you said at the end of The Great Dictator."

"That was not acting."

"How on earth can we stop The Great Director?"

"Come closer my dear. Let me describe a plan."

CHAPTER *21*

Lumbari Island

THE SUN WAS ALREADY ABOVE the horizon. Daylight on the open sea was not a good place for a PT boat. Kennedy's boat was trailing another's wake on the way back to base. Getting off the water was one motivation to move faster. The second was sleep. The first boat back to the dock was the first boat to refuel, the first crew to go off-duty and the first crew to hit the sack. Sleep was a premium for PT crews after a long night on patrol. I watched a subtle signal between Jack and Lennie. It was followed by a call.

"Full speed."

Kennedy steered the PT out of the wake and pulled alongside the other skipper.

"Hello ladies... see you in bed."

It's doubtful the crew on the other PT heard the taunt. The tip of his cap was a call to the races. Suddenly it was summer in Hyannis Port.

Both skippers pushed their boats to full speed and were in a race for the base. Each tried to cut the angle on the approach to gain an advantage. *PT 109* gained a half boat lead as the fuel dock came into sight and was closing fast. It was a game of chicken. From experience I knew Jack would not be the one to back down. Both crews seemed to be bracing when the other boat cut and reversed engines. Jack saw their speed drop and called below for Pappy to cut the engines. They stopped. They did not reverse. We were still close to full speed and headed for a collision.

"Hang on boys," was Jack's warning.

Then we crashed into the dock. The plywood bow plowed into a structure built for convenience and not the ages. That probably spared the boat. Several of the crew went sprawling. We were picking ourselves up. Jack was sheepishly inspecting for injuries and damage.

"Kennedy! What the HELL is going on here?" Commander Warfield came out of his duty quarters shouting.

"Seems the dock slipped up on us sir," Kennedy replied.

"Seems like dereliction of duty to me Kennedy! You could have killed people here. Don't think I won't bring you up on charges. What have you got to say for yourself?"

"Well sir, you just can't stop that *PT 109.*"

Warfield's face went brilliantly red. He looked like he'd been out in the sun too long.

"Kennedy maybe a court-martial would wipe that grin off your face. You PT skippers are nothing but a bunch of hooligans!"

"Commander.."

"Frat boys.."

"Commander Warfield.."

"Rebels.. without any regard.."

"Ah.. Commander Warfield.."

"WHAT Kennedy?"

"Look over there. Isn't that PT boat adrift?"

Two docks over a boat not on duty rotation had somehow slipped its lines and started drifting away from the dock on the tide.

"Goddammit! What kind of navy is this? You PT people can't even make fast your own boats!"

Warfield and all hands made a dash for the dock in order to secure the boat before it drifted out to the channel. The diversion gave the crew of *PT 109* a chance to heave their boat out of the splinters, refuel, secure and scatter while Warfield and the others were otherwise occupied. Jack, Lennie and I led the safe retreat to our tent.

"Jack. Jack Kennedy," Lennie started, "I never really felt the two names flowed together."

"Well Lennie you'd have to speak with Mother Rose about that."

"Maybe you just need a nickname. Pappy has a nickname."

"I'm thinking you have an idea."

"Inspiration that's what that incident was. A better name for alliteration... think I'll call you Crash Kennedy."

"It does have a ring to it."

PT bases and their commands weren't too different from families. Tolstoy's opening to Anna Karenina says it best: *'Happy families are all alike; every unhappy family is unhappy in its own way.'*

At Tulagi the squadron included some of the PT commanders and crew Jack had known at Melville. Cluster was a young commander but he was one who understood and was capable of leading from the front. He went to sea on combat patrol. Cluster may not have been a big defender of PTs or their strategic use in the war but he went out and took his chances with the rest of the men.

Warfield had another approach to fighting in the navy. He did it by land. Like MacArthur he adopted a bunker campaign against the Japanese. He stayed in his fortified hut and used an 'appropriated' radio transmitter to command his fleet. Safely ashore he was gradually sending more boats out in ever larger groups on patrol.

The boat crews had little use for Warfield's tactics, however, his high powered radio provided more relief than a case full of torpedo juice. When not on night patrol, crew conditions at Lumbari were about the same as any other forward base. Lights went out early and when Warfield went away, the radio began to play. For the first time in months we had a connection to the outside world and it allowed for a few laughs.

> *"From somewhere in the South Pacific we offer the Bob Hope Show. Ladies and gentlemen, the men have been through some bitter campaigns.. what they're about to face now is ridiculous, here he is now - Bob Hope."*

"Hey Sam, there's your buddy Bob Hope," Kennedy enjoyed breaking my tender parts over the stories of the USO show and the Jap attack in Darwin.

"Think your girl Ashley could help out the crew of the *109*?"

"If she can get dates for a bunch of Marines I don't think there would be any problem for the dashing men of the Mosquito Fleet."

"Good evening this is Bob 'Mosquito Network' Hope...." The reception was scratchy but audible.

"They don't need to be stars, though you could save one of them for the Skipper, just make sure they're a little better looking than John's sisters."

That was another sore point between Kennedy and Warfield. Jack had declared his hut boy an honorary crewman of the *109* and smuggled him from Tulagi to Lumbari as a special envoy to the native tribes.

"Bunga, bunga John."

The young cannibal made a familiar motion, the international symbol of the mating man. Jack had broken the language barrier.

> *"Here we are in the beautiful and romantic South Pacific,"* Hope started his monologue, *"Aren't these islands beautiful? Wait'll I see that Dorothy Lamour. What a liar."*

His 'Somewhere in the South Pacific' shows were rebroadcasts. After Darwin the brass realized how close they'd come to losing an American favorite and now kept his tour in the same top secret files as future invasion plans. A live broadcast would be just as risky. The Japs were getting better at triangulating radio signals. Another attack on a USO show could shut down the tour. That would be a terrible blow to the men's morale. It might even spook Hope.

> *"We had a very fast trip coming down, flew all the way from San Francisco. Didn't scare me a bit. I read a novel on the way down. On the way back I'm going to read the second page."*

The men's laughter drifted out and into the night.

When the USO show was over we turned the radio back over to the assigned radioman. Tonight he was from the *109* crew, John Maguire. Maguire was one of those wizards who could do more than spin dials and set frequencies. He had a way of discovering useful information by separating the noise from the nuance. Less entertaining, though more important, than Bob Hope, were the frequent broadcasts from the coast watchers. Intercepting those made Maguire a favorite of Warfield's. That helped keep Warfield off Kennedy's back.

The Coastwatchers were likely the bravest and loneliest men in the South Pacific. Many of them were Australians who were on the islands before the Japanese invaded and who remained afterwards hiding in the hills and jungles to radio reports of troop movements and actions. They used native scouts as spotters. The Japs put all of them on a wanted list. If captured they faced torture and beheading. They ran a high risk game of hide and seek and in doing so saved thousands of American lives if not the battle in the Pacific.

If the Japanese hated them - Admiral Halsey loved them. In the early days of the Guadalcanal landing their reports saved the campaign. On the first and second days radio warnings allowed our troops a chance to prepare for attacks. On day two it was Coastwatcher Jack Read who saved the day. He and his native carriers were trekking up the a steep ridge on the north side of Bougainville. The Japanese had several bases on the island to launch attacks against American forces. As he was climbing he heard aircraft overhead. It was a large number of Jap Bettys and Zero fighters heading towards Guadalcanal. He coolly stopped, set up his radio and sent a simple message: "from J.E.R., forty bombers heading yours". The Navy was waiting. Most of the attacking bombers were blown out of the sky.

Once our forces had taken and reinforced Guadalcanal the Japanese began entrenching on islands between the two points. The only way they could survive was through daring nighttime supply runs by Japanese destroyers and supply barges.

From his perch on the mountain of Kolombangara Island Coastwatcher Arthur Reginald Evans could see the nightly runs between Rabaul and Guadalcanal. The stretch of sea separating the Solomon Islands into two parallel island chains was called "The Slot". The Navy called the nightly supply runs bringing fresh troops to fight the Marines the "Tokyo Express".

Lumbari was the most northern PT base. When word came from the Coastwatchers that ships were heading south the PTs went out.

"Good evening. This is London," Evans had his own humorous opening. It took a pair of brass ones to be funny in a jungle surrounded by thousands of Japanese who wanted your head on the end of a sword.

"In the land of the setting sun, all seems quiet. Tojo must be honoring the Festival of the Dead and we wish him many more. Forecast for tomorrow? Look for planes early and a heavy run down the Slot. Things seem busy on the ground. Good night and good luck."

Maguire sent a copy of the message to Kennedy. The first copy went to Warfield. He wouldn't be happy to know that Jack was getting the straight scoop. Knowledge was power. In this case it could also save your life. Warfield was the sort who thought that only his interpretation was valid.

"Funny guy that fellow, playing Edward Murrow in the jungle," Jack laughed at the message, "What a brave son of a bitch. Anytime I think this job on a boat is the worst in the war, promise to remind me of this guy."

"What do you think the message means?" Lennie asked from his bunk.

"I think it means we won't go on patrol tonight for one," replied Kennedy. "Second it looks like tomorrow might be a little busy, so third, seems like we ought to distribute a beer ration to the crew."

"What do you think Warfield will make of it?" Lenny followed.

"Well I just laid out one chain of logic. My guess is that he'll run in the opposite direction."

"Which means we should expect something stupid."

"It wouldn't be PT duty if it wasn't stupid," Jack was warming up. "But I've been thinking.. we keep going out and sinking nothing. We know the torpedoes are useless. Our machine guns are ok for spraying barges or airplanes. We could use something with a bit more punch. Let's get Mauer and Bucky to go scouting and get us something we can strap on the forward deck."

"How big?" Lenny asked.

"Big enough to do damage. Not big enough to sink the boat."

"I'll get the boys started on it."

Lennie walked out into the night.

"So you just decide you want a bigger gun and go get it?" I asked.

"It's kind of the way things work out here; 'The Lord protects those who protect themselves'."

"Think they'll find one?"

"I'll double the poker losses I owe you and will throw in a bonus bottle of whiskey if they don't by noon tomorrow," Jack put his losses and liquor where his mouth was.

"Wow. That's some tidy sum. You have a lot of confidence in your crew."

He paused for a minute, "They're a great crew. A good bunch of men. It takes a lot to go out there night after night. You spent one night under fire. We've spent well, I've lost count. It's not good to count. But they're good sailors in this navy and good pirates on the side. You should get to know them better."

"I think Jack, the country could stand to know them better."

A full night's sleep felt strange. The sounds of the base and sounds of the jungle co-mingled like a morning alarm. My eyes opened to the vision of John crouched on the opposite side of the tent by Jack's bunk. He was smiling in my direction. Jack was already up with a cup of coffee in his hand.

"Don't worry, I wasn't going to leave you alone here with John, although I don't think you really have to worry about becoming his favorite flavor. I don't think."

"That's reassuring."

"Come on let's walk down to the dock."

I'm not the quickest first thing in the morning. As I was pulling on pants and boots his grin was giving something away. John held up a cup of coffee with both hands like he was making an offer to the gods. I took the coffee and exited the tent backwards watching him. Jack was cheerful on the walk. The boat wasn't in its usual dock position. We kept walking down a path beyond the last dock where the *109* was tied to a tree and drifting on the tide. In the clearing beneath the tree was a 37 mm anti-tank gun still on wheels.

"Beauty isn't she?"

My mouth was hanging open.

"That erases the 400-dollars I owe you and you can throw in a bottle of Haig and Haig at your convenience."

"Where.."

"As Skipper of the *109* I have no knowledge of how this gun got here.. Maybe Bucky can tell you."

Bucky was Gunner's Mate Third Class Charles Harris from Watertown, Massachusetts. He was standing like a proud father at the business end of the gun. Jack started walking away towards the boat.

"For the record, I was not present when this conversation took place," Kennedy said.

"Can I tell him, sir?"

"Bucky I would never get in the way of the American press trying to do their job. That's First Amendment infringement."

"Yes, sir. Whatever that means," the gunner's mate scratched his head.

"So Bucky did the weapons fairies deliver this in the night?" I asked.

"That's a good one sir, I might keep that."

"Then what's the real one?"

"Well sir, it's not like there aren't plenty of these around the islands," Bucky started his story. "They're really kind of useless for their original purpose. They've pretty much been all shipped out of Europe because they can't stop the new Kraut tanks, so they sent a lot here. But the Japs don't have a lot of tanks, so half the time we load them with canister shot like back in the Civil War days."

"So where did you find it?"

"It was just kind of sitting all lonely like at the supply depot. I know a fellow there. He really appreciated some of that good whiskey we found at the Canal. Now if you'll excuse me sir, as they say possession is nine tenth of the law and the sooner we get this strapped on the *109* the harder it's going to be to take her away."

A couple of the crew were already stripping the wheels off the carriage. The rest of the crew was on the bow clearing a life raft and strapping two large timbers to the deck. If 'Necessity is the Mother of Invention' this crew was trying to reinvent the PT boat to make it something other than a hapless target for Japanese practice shooting. They were in high spirits. They were a crew in the cohesive structure formed by war.

Lumbari Island, August 1, 1943
Sam Marlow/New York Herald Tribune

"I have not yet begun to fight!" Were the
words of Captain John Paul Jones when some of
his men called for surrender in the face of the
overwhelming fire of the HMS Serapis. Here in the
frontwaters of the War of the Pacific the tiny
Mosquito Fleet is forging similar mettle. There
is no question of courage among these crews. They
were told at the beginning not to count on coming
home alive. But they signed up and continue to
show up for duty night after dangerous night. You
might think cruising around South Pacific islands
in a fast boat would be a great way to spend the
war. I'll take a foxhole with a Marine and his
chances any day. At least he's got someplace to
hide.

These PT crews hang it out in plain sight day
and night. During the day they're easy targets by
air or from Jap surface vessels. At night they
churn up a wake that's lit up like a runway or a
target arrow for the Emperor's airplanes.

Then there's the boat itself. It's plywood.
That doesn't stop a bullet very well. On top of
that they're powered by three huge Packard engines that suck down high octane fuel. These boys
are riding a rocket where a well placed round
could blow them all the way to Tokyo.

But the question they're asking themselves is
not, "What the hell am I doing here?". Instead as
I heard last night it's "How the hell can we find
a better way to kill the enemy?"

Absurd bravery.

```
There are a dozen men in the crew of    PT
109. The skipper is an ambassador's son from
Massachusetts. This boat just happens to have
three other crew from the Bay State. It's a won-
der they haven't converted it to a lobster boat.
Instead today they converted it to an anti-tank
boat by affixing a 37 mm gun to her bow.
    Gunner  Bucky  Harris  from  Watertown,
Massachusetts now swears the 'weapons ordinance
fairy' dropped it during the night. Quartermaster
Ed Mauer from St. Louis says he asked for it last
Christmas, but the requisition must have gone
to the South Pole Santa. Motor Mechanic Pappy
McMahon from Wyanet, Illinois and Motor Mechanic
Gerard Zinser from Belleville, Illinois bolted
two timbers to the bow and strapped the cannon
down. Now the 109 has a weapon that may surprise
the steel plated enemy.
    There is much out here that doesn't go by the
book because there is no book for this kind of
war. But some day the book will be written of
these men and both their antics and heroism.. and
how they took their wits and courage against the
odds to defeat the Japanese. Just like John Paul
Jones did in his victory against the Serapis.
```

I was sitting in the tent banging away on my typewriter. Jack was play-ing Sinatra again on his Victrola while writing another letter to Inga. We seemed a pretty urban pair to be on the edge of the jungle. It seemed almost peaceful. That feeling doesn't last long in war.

A blast came from the direction of the *109*...as Sinatra played in the background.

> *And if I fell under the spell of your call,*
> *I would be caught in the undertow...*

"Ahh, the cannon's calling. It's the sweet sound of an anti-tank gun test."

"Don't you think that might attract attention?"

"Those sailors talk like hairdressers. Word's already out about the gun. I'm surprised Warfield hasn't come calling yet."

Jack was prescient.

"Kennedy! What the hell is that coming from your boat?" Warfield was red in the face.

"Why sir, I'm as shocked as you. That crew of mine is very resourceful."

"Resourceful. Is that what you call it? I heard at 37mm anti-tank gun went missing last night."

"I know nothing about that, sir."

"Don't think you can screw with me Kennedy. Let's go see what's going on with your crew."

Sinatra was still singing through Warfield's rant. Somehow it took the edge off his threat. The sound of the anti-tank gun was still hanging in the air when the sound of several of the twin 50's on the boats cranked up. That sound was followed by the low drone of the air raid siren. Warfield made a sprint for his reinforced hut. The rest of us scrambled for the slit trenches outside our tents. Kennedy was so skinny there was room to spare. He squared his back to the muddy wall and looked up to the sky.

"The Japs don't usually waste their time bombing over here. I guess Evans called it straight last night. What I'm also guessing is that Warfield ignored it. I got nothing from him and if my guess is right all the boats tied in their usual spots are clustered for easy hits."

Jack called it. As soon as the intense attack cooled there was a scramble for the docks. It wasn't pretty. Medics were moving in to treat the wounded. Some were beyond help. Brave lads who stuck to their guns died with them. Two of the PTs were destroyed, blasted to splintered pieces and in their death throes discharged torpedoes that were churning circles in the harbor. *PT 109* was spared. Sneaking the boat away from the docks for its retrofit put it out of the line of fire. Both the crew and their charge hunkered down beneath the tree and managed to avoid being spotted from the air.

Warfield was wandering about. He was neither flustered nor furious that the Japanese had just shot the shit out of his base. In fact he seemed ponderous. I was walking with Jack and Lennie back from the *109*.

"Look at that," Lennie nodded towards Warfield.

"Not a good sign," Jack joined in.

"What?" Was the best I could offer.

"Warfield. He's thinking. That never amounts to anything good," Jack explained.

He walked our way.

"Kennedy. I want you and all the other skippers in the briefing tent in thirty minutes."

"You mean the surviving skippers?" Kennedy tossed a taunt.

"A wiseguy and the commander of a pirate crew. You're a real asset to the Navy, Kennedy. Be at the briefing."

"Aye, sir."

Warfield stood in his war room. He looked like he was trying to impersonate Churchill. There were maps on the wall. The only chart that mattered was the one detailing The Slot and every skipper was pretty familiar with that by firsthand experience, unlike Warfield who had yet to see combat. He ruled his domain from inside his fortified bunker.

"Men, that attack this morning made me think," he started his briefing. There was a cough and Warfield narrowed his eyes and looked to the group.

"Tonight Commander Burke is going to take a group of destroyers -north- of Kolombangara. Admiral Wilkinson thinks the Tokyo Express is going to run to the northeast of the island. But if the Japs are so concerned about our base to the south that makes me think they're going to to fake north and head south in our direction."

He seemed impressed with his genius and paused to wait for someone to recognize his acute grasp of tactics. All he got was another cough. Phlegm was his only friend.

"If the Japs think they're going to sneak around us we'll show them we won't be caught napping."

He was facing the map.

From the back of the room, someone said "Like today?"

Warfield spun, "Who said that?"

Silence.

"Here's the plan. We have fifteen boats that are patrol fit. Tonight we send the entire force out. It will be the largest deployment of PTs in the Pacific. We'll deploy in four groups. Each hunter pack will seek the enemy and fire every torpedo at our disposal. Since we don't want the Japs to get wind of what's coming at them, every boat will maintain radio silence unless absolutely necessary. Any questions?"

"Will you be leading the operation from a command boat?" Quipped an officer in the back. He sounded a bit phlegmy.

"An operation of this complexity will be best managed from a central command point. I'll be here where I can monitor traffic on multiple frequencies." Warfield continued

"Aye, sir."

The briefing broke up. Several skippers reconvened down at the dock before briefing their crews.

"So let me get this straight," it was the lieutenant who torpedoed Warfield with the last question, "He's going to stay in his bunker. We're going out in four groups with only four boats equipped with radar, with radio silence and no way to coordinate our own groups much less the main body."

"That sounds pretty accurate, Lieutenant Keresey," Kennedy agreed.

"And we're suppose to go against the destroyers with our torpedoes that have yet to sink a ship?"

"Yep."

"This is going to be a cluster fuck," Keresey stated.

"You should put that in proper Navy language."

"A SNAFU, sir."

"Aye."

"Kennedy did I hear something like a 37 firing from the bushes before the Japs attacked?" Keresey asked.

"I would have no official knowledge of that lieutenant."

"Well good luck with that you might be the only boat to hit anything tonight."

We walked on down towards the small channel where the *109* was still tied to a tree. Passing the docks Lieutenant Barney Ross joined us. He was the skipper of *PT 166*, but at the moment he was a skipper without a boat.

"Hey Jack.."

"Barney."

"I was in the briefing and unlike Warfield I really don't want to sit this out tonight with my ass on shore. You got room on your boat for another body?"

"Well Sam's been going out with us though we do have that new gun on board and I don't really have anyone to man it. You know how to shoot one of those things?"

"Not really. I'm guessing it works something like, you put a shell in and pull the trigger?"

"Barney you just made gunner's mate. Sam do you mind if I get you on another boat tonight? Probably wouldn't hurt for you to ride with another crew. I'll try to get you on one of the radar boats. They always fire off first and run for base. You'll be back in sipping a scotch by midnight."

"Well it won't be with Warfield. What do you think of this mission?"

"The mission is idiotic. It runs against everything every seasoned PT commander has learned about the effective size of patrol and the firepower of PTs. This is his 'Charge of the Light Brigade.' He's the biggest asshole in the Pacific!"

CHAPTER 22

K ENNEDY GOT ME A SLOT on the flagship for his patrol. The commander of the unit was Lieutenant Hank Brantingham. He'd been on one or two PT sorties before. Brantingham was XO for Bulkeley when the PTs helped MacArthur escape from the Philippines. Like Bulkeley he was dedicated to the gunboats and spreading the word. In other words he was happy to have a reporter on board.

All fifteen boats moved up to different positions in the Blackett Strait off Kolombangara. Our group of four boats was at the northern-most point. *PT 159* was the lead and *PT 109* the tail. It was a pitch black night. On radar we could see the faint blips of the other PTs. Without that the crew was totally without sight of land, or friend, or foe. It was hard to keep sharp. Everywhere you looked was the same an impenetrable black wall. The crew kept contact with quiet chatter fore to aft. An observation to be followed by a taunt, escalating to the kind of insult only shared by trained seamen. The men had obviously been together long enough to have a deep source of personal knowledge. You just can't say those sorts of things to a stranger.

The hours began to slip into stretch time. That's when an hour is more than an hour. It is the direct opposite of quick time when you wish every second could last for hours. Quick time is when you're with the one you love. When the light of a candle illuminates a universe you wish you could freeze, stop, contain and never leave. I was on a boat with a dozen men I barely knew in a black box that could have been in the Solomon Sea or some deep dark hole in space. Time stood still. Brantingham would occasionally pick up on parts of his monologue about the wonders of the Mosquito Fleet. The only thing I was wondering was how more boats and men weren't lost in maneuvers like tonight's. I was wondering how that cannon on the *109* might work tonight. That was actually a better story if that pirate crew actually switched armaments and tactics and made the PTs effective. It annoyed me. I'd missed the boat, literally. It was now a matter of settling back to ride out a long night.

Around midnight I was getting drowsy. I was propped up against a rear hatch and one nod away from dreams of Ashley. There was a rumble in the forward part of the torpedo boat and I felt the engines coming to life.The boat was bolting forward when I entered the cockpit.

"Hello Marlow. Thought you might sleep through the war," Brantingham was at the helm. I was already disliking this guy..

"We have four blips on the radar, probably barges. We're heading toward them to get close enough for a staffing run."

I went below for a look at the radar. I saw the four targets. We were closing in on them. Back up on deck, I looked forward and saw nothing. Without radar we would have no idea they were there.

"Prepare to launch torpedoes," came the call.

Even without a clear sighting of the targets, all four torpedoes were launched. . One of the tubes caught fire. They were lined with grease that sometimes caught fire when the torpedoes were launched. It wasn't a problem except the fire on deck created a perfect target for the enemy. A shell splashed and exploded astern. It was followed by another, closer.

"Shit! Those aren't barges. They're destroyers. Lay smoke and let's get the hell out of here!"

The *159* started a high speed zig-zag in the opposite direction. To the stern I could see another boat with a tube on fire that was turning and taking the same counter measures to cover a hasty retreat. We ran hard and fast for ten or fifteen miles before slowing and pulling behind a small island. The other boat was still with us and pulled alongside. It was the *157.* We both cut our engines to talk over the side.

"Any hits?" Brantingham asked.

"I saw one flash but I'm not sure if it was a hit on a ship. Didn't seem wise to stick around to find out," said Liebenow, skipper of the *157.*

"You see anything of *162* or *109?*"

"Nope. They were behind us and I doubt they knew anything until they saw flashes from the destroyers."

"Well I fired all my torpedoes. I'm heading back to base," Brantingham stated.

"I've still got two. I'm going back to try to find the others," Liebenow replied.

"Remember keep radio silence. Be careful out there. See you later."

Brantingham went back to the cockpit and steered the boat on a course to Lumbari. I stood looking aft as the three screws churned a lighted trail behind us. We were the command ship with one of four radars and we were heading back in leaving fourteen boats behind. It didn't seem to make sense to me. So I did what I do so well. I played dumb and asked question.

"Lieutenant Brantingham why are we heading back in?"

"Orders Marlow pure and simple. Warfield doesn't see any point in PTs on patrol without torpedoes."

"But it seems with our radar you could help direct the other boats."

"Orders again. Radio silence Marlow didn't you hear me? Warfield thinks he can direct any necessary logistics from base."

I walked aft. Except for the pitch darkness someone would have seen me shaking my head. Bulkeley has backed the PT commands ever since Corregidor. He was the one who won the Medal of Honor. Brantingham was cut from the same cloth. They were both key characters in the best-seller, '*They Were Expendable*', based on their exploits in the Philippines. I'll be damned if it didn't seem to me all in the PT chain of command were doing their best to make the title come true.

0010 hrs Off Kolombangara Island
PT 171

On another radar screen, the same four blips continued down the shore of Kolombangara. Lieutenant Berndtson commanded the second group.

"Damn. Whatever that is is moving at about 30 knots which means destroyers. Let's run straight on them and see if we can launch before they see us. Maybe this darkness will actually help."

The boat raced alone towards the destroyers. It doesn't take too long to cut a few miles when two objects are racing towards each other at a combined speed of over sixty miles an hour. The destroyer fired first. Star shells burst overhead. The cover of darkness was yanked back and the advantage went to the destroyers. They opened fire with their main batteries and automatic weapons. In the lead the *171* was still fifteen hundred yards out when she launched all four torpedoes. The flash in the PT's tubes tipped off the destroyer and she turned and avoided all four of the fish.

The three other boats in the patrol knew nothing of the destroyers until they started shelling. By the light of the star shells they could see the *171* directly between them and their targets. Their targets were putting out heavy fire. All turned and ran.

0015hrs Ferguson Passage
PT 107

As the Japanese destroyers continued south they'd cleared two groups of PTs unmolested. They were facing the third. Lieutenant Cookman was the lead boat in his patrol. Like the rest he was the only one with radar on board. Cookman saw two targets on his radar screen. He moved at a high speed towards the destroyers and fired all four torpedoes. Unlike the others, he was not spotted. With empty tubes he reversed course and sped for base passing his three other PTs. They continued patrol but did not engage.

0025hrs Kolombangara/Blackett Strait
PT 174

To the north flashes of gunfire lit the night. Lieutenant Rome's patrol saw a fight in the distance. A flair and bombs were hitting about a mile to the west. A destroyer continued to fire as it drifted in their direction. Close to the island it was protecting the entrance to the Blackett Strait at the head of the Ferguson Passage. The ship came closer, then turned on a powerful spotlight continuing to fire towards the west. He had them blindsided. Motoring slowly, he fired four torpedoes at a thousand yards. The skipper saw two explosions on target.

"We got a hit! Take that you bastards!"

The cheers rose up on the crew deck. Then stopped short. A shell from the destroyer went overhead. Their hit wasn't critical, if they hit the ship at all. There was no secondary explosion or fire visible, except from the guns on board. A plane joined the ship in a combined attack on the *174*.

"Let's get the hell out of here," Rome commanded the crew.

Like every other lead boat she'd fired her torpedoes and was clearing out fast and under fire. Hauling past the other boats in her patrol one of the PTs broke radio silence.

"Where is the target?" The call came from Lieutenant Keresey on *PT 105*.

"I'm under fire from a Japanese destroyer and running," Rome responded to the open frequency.

"Where is the destroyer?"

"Keresey get out of there! You're in a trap!"

Another voice came across the radio.

"Dammit Keresey, can't you hear the man? You're in a trap. Get out of the area." It was Warfield. The absent commander was getting into the game.

0030hrs Lumbari Island/Command Center

"What in the hell is going on out there?" Warfield tossed the mike down on the table next to his radio operator.

"The Tokyo Express just cruised past fifteen PT boats and we didn't stop a single one."

No one in the room outranked Warfield so a candid response was not likely. If a PT boat on this night or any other had actually succeeded in sinking a Japanese destroyer it might reset the game for the Navy. But so far neither the boats nor the tactics had changed much. That was not likely to create a different outcome.

"Give me that mike," he snatched that which no one would likely try to take from him.

"Now hear this commanders. If your boat still has torpedoes you'd better get in this fight.

The Japs just a sailed right through us and we missed one big chance. But we haven't lost yet. Tojo has to come home. You'd better find him on the way back and when you do you'd better send him to the hell he came from."

Warfield delivered his message then turned to the charts on the wall. He started making marks where he thought the PTs were, where he thought the Tokyo Express went and where the two may meet again. He drew nice lines and trajectories. He didn't have a goddamn clue.

0031hrs Blackett Strait
PT 109

Kennedy listened to the radio and smiled. There was no real reason to smile. His boat and several other boats were still on patrol with no radar to assist them and no coordination coming from the base. All he heard was a rather poor sideline speech from a coach who was totally unfamiliar with the game. As rally speeches go, Warfield's sucked. Pat O'Brien did a much better job as Knute Rockne. Rally the Irish, 'Win one for the Gipper'. At least Rockne was with the team.

"Hey Barney can you see anything up there?"

"I can see the barrel of this gun and that's about it."

"Great you're my radar and you're blind as a bat."

He called down to the radio room, "Maguire see if you can raise any of the loose PTs in our area. If we're all flying blind out here maybe we can cover each other."

"Lennie what do you think?"

"On the whole I'd rather be in Philadelphia."

"Or New York.."

"Or Chicago.."

Then together, "Any place but Kolom-BANG-ara." They laughed.

"We should replace Hope and Crosby. Start our own 'Road' series..."

"As long as it's someplace with roads and not a pitch black ocean at night."

"But since we're here.."

"Well we've got the *162* in the area. If we can find another boat we can set a patrol from north to south in the Strait. The one point I'll concede to Coach Warfield is that if the Express went down, it's got to come back up. We might catch them."

0218hrs East of Gizo Island/Blackett Strait
PT 169

Lieutenant Potter on the *169* saw the ship closing on Kennedy's boat. He fired two torpedoes at close range. The ship was so close the torpedoes couldn't arm in time to explode. It didn't matter for the *109*. The destroyer rammed the PT from the starboard bow and sliced straight through. The Jap warship sailed out of an explosion from the destroyed boat and left a fire burning on the water. Then like some dragon emerging from her own special hell she opened up her guns on *PT 169*. Shells straddled the boat as Potter went to full throttle and blew smoke off the stern to hide her escape. The destroyer raced onward into the night.

0218hrs East of Gizo Island/Blackett Strait
PT 109

"Ship at two o'clock," the call came from the forward gun turret.

"General quarters," Kennedy called, then below, "Full speed now!"

He spun the helm to turn facing the destroyer. The captain of the destroyer was doing the same. The huge ship was keeled over at forty five degrees and bearing straight for the *109*.

"Barney, shoot that damn gun!" Kennedy screamed.

"Fire torpedoes. Let's hit that sonofabitch!"

The hit came from the destroyer.

For a frozen instant the division of life and death was a simple matter of place.

The bow of the destroyer plowed into the *109* on the starboard side slicing through the forward turret. Gunner Harold Marney is the first to die.. The deadly cut continues straight back to the right of the cockpit and through the crew quarters below. Torpedoman Andrew Kirksey died in his bunk. When the bow hit the rear fuel tanks the boat exploded spreading a sheet of fire across the water. A large piece of the PT was still afloat. Kennedy and the boat's radioman are thrown against the side of the cockpit in the collision. Several of the crew managed to cling to their positions and struggled to stay on the boat and out of the surrounding fire. With the burning wreck to stern the destroyer opened her guns to finish off any survivors.

"Into the water!" Kennedy yelled to any who could hear.

He heard several splashes. The guns from the ship stopped almost immediately. The one gift from the departing Japanese was the draft of the destroyer pulled the worst of the flames away from the wreckage. What settled over the remains of the boat and crew was a frightening silence.

Kennedy, Maguire, the radioman and Mauer the quartermaster were floating near what was left of the boat. They swam back and climbed onto the wreckage. Kennedy climbed to the highest point and started calling out names.

"Over here!"

"Harris?"

"Yeah. Pappy just came up. He's burned pretty bad."

Kennedy started stripping off his clothes.

"Where you going Skipper?"

"Out to get Harris and Pappy. You two stay here and see if you can find any of the others. Mauer see if you can get together what gear you can salvage. When we get the survivors together we'll figure out what we're going to do."

"Got it. Call back here if you need help with those two."

Kennedy swam towards the voices. Pappy was in pretty bad shape. How he got clear from below deck was a miracle. His lifejacket popped him to the surface. Without that he'd be dead because he was in no shape to swim.

"Harris I'm going to help Pappy back to the hull. You ok to swim?"

"Not sure, Skipper. Banged my leg up pretty bad when I got launched off the boat. Might be broken."

"You can swim with a broken leg."

"I just got run over by a Jap destroyer. My leg's broke. I can't swim."

"Well Harris there aren't any pretty nurses going to come pick you up. Maybe some cute little Jap sailors will be along to help."

"Go to hell, Kennedy."

"Harris you sure are putting on quite a performance for a guy from Boston. We gotta show we're tougher than the rest. Get rid of some of those clothes so you can swim easier and let's get back to the boat."

Maguire found a battle lantern first and used it to try to pinpoint anyone in the water. He spotted three people adrift behind the wreckage that was starting to move with the current. Barney Ross, Lennie Thom and Zinser the engineer were trying to catch up. Maguire jumped into the water and swam in their direction.

Zinser was burned. Maguire secured him by tying a rope around his waist and began swimming. Reality was slipping away from the engineer.

He was beginning to scream,"Bring the boat!" It became a chant of wavering intensity.

After a few minutes it wore through Maguire's nerves, "Goddam it Zinser, there is no boat!"

He was beginning to scream,"Bring the boat!" It became a chant of wavering intensity.

After a few minutes it wore through Maguire's nerves, "Goddam it Zinser, there is no boat!"

Lennie was rattled in the collision but rallied enough on the swim back to find and retrieve Johnston. The gunner had sucked down enough gas fumes to put him in a stupor. Lenny swam pulling Johnston behind him.

By the time they reached the wreck Kennedy was counting heads. The torpedoman Starkey and gunner Albert arrived while Maguire was rounding up the others. There were eleven survivors.

"Mauer, what could you salvage out of the cockpit?" Kennedy asked.

"Got a signal gun, machine gun, a couple of .45s and .38s."

"That may not be enough to hold of the entire Jap army. The way I see it we were patrolling between Gizo and Kolombangara. Gizo has a few hundred Japs at the dock there. Kolombangara has maybe ten thousand. I don't think we want to use that signal gun and invite any to visit. It's so dark I don't think they'll spot us until daylight. Hopefully by then one of the PTs or a rescue patrol will pick us up."

"Skipper's right," Lennie backed Jack, "Let's secure the wounded and hunker down as best we can. There must have been a half dozen PTs still on patrol when we got hit. We had visuals on both the *162* and *169* they must have known we were hit. Help's got to be on the way."

Eleven men clung to the debris and their hopes. All suffered from being run down by the destroyer. Some worse than others. Alone and exposed in enemy territory a few prayers were offered into the darkness. It would be a long and lonely four hours until sunrise.

CHAPTER 23

Lumbari 0400hrs

I MADE MYSELF SMALL IN THE corner of the command center. Several of the skippers and some of the crew were jammed into the room listening to the radio traffic from the boats still on patrol. For almost two hours since the frantic traffic from PTs *162* and *169* nothing had been heard of Kennedy's boat. During that time Warfield had continued scattered chatter with the boats exhorting them to seek and engage the Japanese ships that they had clearly already missed. He had not commanded any boat to return to the area where the *109* may have been hit to determine what happened or if there were any survivors. I wanted to ask him why but that would get me kicked off the island. His inaction made me want to grab him by the throat, though in his megalomania he'd have me hanged from a yardarm, if he could find one. If he knew what one was.

"Go down to the dock and check those incoming boats," Warfield snarled at one of Brantingham's crew who was lingering in the command room, "Tell the skippers to come up here asap."

The room began to empty of crew members except the skippers and their XOs. Lowrey of the *162* and Potter from the *169* were the last to come in. Warfield did a head count.

"I count thirteen. Where's Keresey?"

"Down at the dock, sir. He's refueling the *105* says he's going out to look for Kennedy and his crew," Potter replied.

"I said I wanted all skippers here. Someone get him. NOW!"

No one jumped. One man walked with ease out the door. A few minutes later he was back with Keresey."

"Now that we're all here.."

"Except Kennedy,"interjected Keresey.

"Stow it, Lieutenant," Warfield barked back.

"What I want to hear are reports from Lowrey and Potter on the *109* then a complete debrief from the rest of you for my report in the morning."

Lowrey started with their first sighting of the destroyer. Then the failed attempt to launch torpedoes. He continued with their narrow miss and the collision between the destroyer and the *109.*

Potter continued in a matter of fact tone.

"We turned and fired at the ship about the same time it hit Kennedy's boat. There was an explosion. The destroyer sailed right through it and began to fire on us. We took evasive measures."

"Did either of you go back to look for survivors?" Warfield asked.

"We did sir," Potter said, "We cruised the area for about a half hour and saw nothing." "You're a liar, Potter," Keresey said softly.

"Keresey you'd better watch yourself.." Potter stiffened.

"How is it possible that on a protected stretch of water between two islands you could find nothing? No debris, no bodies." Keresey asked.

"We crossed that Strait for about a half hour," Potter explained.

"You cut and ran when the destroyer fired on you."

"Can it Keresey," even Warfield could see this fight coming.

"I want to see detailed reports from all of you by 1200hrs tomorrow. It's been a tough night. We fired a lot of torpedoes and the only casualty appears to be one of ours. Everybody go to your huts. Get some rack time. We'll deal with the rest of this in the morning."

I slipped out unnoticed and walked slowly down the dark path towards the hut. Jack wouldn't be there. Lennie wouldn't be there and I didn't feel like sleeping with John staring at me all night. Keresey caught up with me.

"Hey Marlow - you bunk with Kennedy?"

"Yeah."

"Warfield's an asshole. He's incompetent and some kind of chicken shit to do nothing about that crew."

"No argument here. He pretty much stopped you cold."

"He actually told me to mind my own business. Taking care of each other, that seems to be our business."

"Any ideas?"

"A couple. The first as soon as he's out of that radio room I'm going to get a message off to Cluster. He's actually Kennedy's commanding officer. The *109* was detached for duty up here because she's one of the larger boats. He may be able to get a search plane up later today."

"Anything I can do?"

"I had two ideas. One if you can communicate with that native boy who served their hut, those people have a strange network that stretches across most of these islands. Some of them work for the coastwatchers. If he can get word out maybe they can keep an eye out for survivors. Second Kennedy's father has some influence. If you can get a message to him he might be able to shake something from the top down."

"I'll give both a shot. I don't know his father personally and would hate to be the one to break this to him."

"It's either you or a telegram from the War Department. At least from you he might have a chance to do something to find his son."

"Good point."

We separated to follow our own devious paths. At the hut I found John sitting and waiting. He looked at me then looked back out with a curious eye. Jack and Lennie were supposed to be coming back from patrol. I was not supposed to be coming back alone. In the most ridiculous form of pantomime and pidgin English I managed to communicate what happened. He looked heartbroken. That caused me to pause.

It had yet to settle in.. the Real and Final outcome of the collision. Jack was likely dead along with a dozen other members of his crew. Maybe it was Warfield and his irreverent dismissal of thirteen lives. That's a lot of light and laughter and lives unfulfilled to dismiss without a rescue effort.

Somehow I knew that John felt the same. At the end of my comic/ tragic tale he nodded solemnly and forced a smile Then he jogged off into the jungle.

I went to my single cot in an empty hut and stretched out to stare into the same darkness we'd entered almost eleven hours ago.

CHAPTER  24

Day One
Blackett Strait 1000hrs

SINCE SUNRISE THE EYES OF those able scanned the skies for a search plane which never came. What was left of the *109* was gradually sinking. The changing current swirled them ever closer to the Japanese held island of Gizo. At almost eight hours adrift it was time to make some decisions. All morning long the talk had been about whether to fight or surrender if discovered by the enemy. We knew what surrender meant. That made almost any option a better choice. For much of the morning Kennedy listened to the men talk about their choices. He listened and offered opinions but not orders. Now it was time to return to duty.

"Ok guys. We need to make a few decisions. The first being do we continue as a crew? Or do we split up and make it every man for himself. If we do that some may have a better chance than others. Pappy here and those of you who can't swim will almost certainly die. I'll only say one thing about that and then you can make your own call. In my mind we've been abandoned by our own command. Maybe that's Warfield's decision. I don't know. But I'll tell you this, that's not the Navy I signed up for and whatever decision each of you makes I'll die before I'll abandon a single one of you."

The crew looked from one to the other.

Lennie spoke for all, "What's your plan, Skipper? We're with you."

"Since we don't want to surrender or be captured then what we need to do is escape, find a safe place and try to find a way to contact friendlies. The Japs have the main islands around us. Let's pick a small one. One they wouldn't even bother with."

To the south there was a small strip away from Gizo and in the general direction of Lumbari. It was several miles across open water. The question was how to get there with wounded men and almost half a crew who couldn't swim.

"I know she was the pride of the ship but let's cut the 37 millimeter loose. Free up one of those timbers for a raft. Lennie you take the timber and strap the gear to it and anyone who can't swim. It's your ship sir."

"Aye," Lennie offered a fake salute and got started on his command.

When the raft and her crew were ready to push off Lennie looked back at the wreck and Jack.

"What about Pappy? He's too hurt to hang on."

"Pappy's with me."

The burns on his face and arms looked even worse in the light. Kennedy slid him gently into the water, took the strap on his life jacket and putting it between his teeth began swimming with the wounded crewman in tow.

Tulagi 1200hrs

Lieutenant Commander Al Cluster got the report on the *109* in his early briefing. It was the first time he'd lost an entire crew on patrol. He decided to hitch a ride up to Rendova then to Lumbari. Word leaked out before he could leave the base. The loss of an entire crew hit hard. Thirteen men leave an imprint behind. They were well liked. Kennedy, Thom and Ross were all officers respected by their crews and by the fellow officers who shared card games during the day and patrols at night.

Cluster was headed for the dock when a group of men surrounded him.

"Is it true sir? Did a Jap destroyer sink the *109*?" asked a sailor.

"That seems to be the report," the commander replied.

"What about the rescue mission?"

"There doesn't seem to be one."

"That's bullshit, sir."

"It's Warfield's command."

"He's full of shit, sir."

"That seems to be the unofficial report. I'm heading up there now to see if I can 'assist' in any way."

"Kennedy was Catholic. Shouldn't we talk to the priest?"

"I'm not sure how they handle such things. We don't know for sure that they're dead. Find the priest and let him know."

"Good luck sir. Kick Warfield in the ass."

"Thanks fellows. That might take some restraint."

Lumbari 1600hrs

The afternoon shift in the radio room was manned by one of Keresey's crew. Radioman Ford held his commander's contempt for Warfield. Even he though, balked at my request.

"Sir, you want me to do what?"

"I need you to get a telegram out to Kennedy's father outside the regular channels."

"You know if Warfield found out he'd have me court martialed?"

"Or send you out on another patrol. Which is worse?"

"You've got a point, sir."

"Look I know it's a risk but surely you know a way and if you do, I have a girlfriend who has some girlfriends in the USO. Maybe we could get you a date."

"A date with a USO girl? A showgirl? Damn. Let me think a minute."

He thought, about as long as it took me to smoke a cigarette and write what I hoped wouldn't be too shocking a note to a father who may have just lost a son.

"Here's an idea. The coastwatchers use ham radio signals to send their messages. There are some ham operators I talk to in Australia when nobody's around. If your message is short I could send it to an Aussie buddy who could send the telegraph from Darwin."

"You're a genius Ford. Here's the message."

AMBASSADOR KENNEDY, AM FRIEND OF YOUR SON JACK. AM IN SOUTH PACIFIC. REPORTS HE AND CREW MISSING AFTER PATROL. ANY PRESSURE APPLIED CMDR WARFIELD LUMBARI BASE FOR RESCUE NEEDED. SAM MARLOW

The message went out and I was out the door almost as quickly. Walking down the path to the docks I saw Warfield and Cluster walking toward me.. The conversation appeared tense.

"Tom I'm not trying to step on your command but Kennedy is still part of my squadron. I simply asked for an air patrol to fly over the area."

"I've got two reports from two boats that they saw a collision and a fire. You're wasting time and resources."

"Look, Kennedy was a good skipper.."

"And I've got about fifteen other good skippers who don't need to be distracted by false hopes."

"Hope is what keeps them going out there, plus the hope of returning, and the hope that if they get in a fix, somebody's got their back."

"I don't need a lecture on motivation Cluster. There's a briefing in fifteen minutes if you'd like to attend. The mission is their motivation."

They came abreast of me .

Cluster nodded, "Marlow."

Warfield glared and continued walking to the briefing hut.

"You were on the patrol last night?"

"Yeah. Though I was on the lead boat. We fired torpedoes at radar blips, turned and ran."

"I heard some of that. Keresey briefed me when I came in a little while ago. He also said you were going out of channel to see what you might be able to do. Officially I don't know a damn thing about what you two are up to. Unofficially keep me in the loop and I'll do what I can."

Keresey was walking up to the briefing and joined us. He was looking at a note.

"Ford slipped me this report from a coastwatcher. It's from the Aussie named Evans on Kolombangara. He saw the explosion early this morning. He decoded a message saying that it was the *109* and he sent out some natives in canoes to look for survivors. At least somebody's making an effort."

Let's not get any hopes up. It would be a miracle if anyone survived the impact of that collision."

"War's all about miracles, Lieutenant, miracles and fate and horror."

"That's why you're the writer Marlow. Let's go to this briefing, see what Warfield's got up his sleeve for us tonight."

We filed into the briefing room. Warfield's fixed his eyes on me. I was beginning to feel my welcome was wearing out. He was standing in front of his maps again with a pointer in one hand and a note in the other.

"Gentlemen, he began, I have a report from an aerial reconnaissance flight requested by Lieutenant Commander Cluster. It spotted a small piece of floating debris this afternoon in the Blackett Strait. It reported no survivors and no bodies."

He stopped there, making no mention of the Aussie's report or efforts. I looked at Keresey and he shook his head.

"Now men after our unsuccessful effort last night in the Strait, tonight we're going to send six boats around Gizo and up to Vella Lavella. Maybe we can surprise the Japs by sneaking in from a different direction."

He went through the details of the mission using his pointer for direction and emphasis. The six skippers who were named for patrol didn't look pleased. The others looked like they'd be showing up for beer call in the very near future. Warfield finished his briefing and took questions.

"Sir," Keresey couldn't hold himself back, "If debris was spotted shouldn't we send a couple boats through the Strait just to look for survivors?"

"Drop it, Keresey. I'm not putting any more crews at risk to look for survivors who aren't there."

"Sir, I'd be glad to lead a second patrol through there."

"One more word and you're going on report, Keresey."

That sucked all the air out of the room. The hut emptied like it was an 'abandon ship' drill. Cluster pulled me aside.

"Marlow I don't hold out much hope. Some of the fellows back on Tulagi want to have a memorial service tomorrow. If you want to come down I'm sure a boat will make the run."

"Thanks Lieutenant. I'll try to come down, though I'm not feeling like it's quite time to commend his soul to the deep."

Plum Pudding Island 1600hrs

"How far do we have to go?" Pappy asked. He'd been floating on his back, towed by Kennedy for four hours.

"We're almost there Pappy, just a short swim through the reef. How you feel?"

"I'm ok Mr. Kennedy. How about you?"

"Doing great Pappy. Hang on, we're almost there."

He swam the last few yards and half carried, half dragged Pappy across the beach and into the bushes, then collapsed on the sand. He breathed heavily then laid exhausted on his back, looking at the sky. Land felt good under him. The smell of the trees and bushes around him were worth sucking in a few deep breaths. He was exhausted but he pulled himself up, checked on Pappy and did a quick recon for Japs in the area. The others were close behind. Jack went back to the water to help them ashore.

"Welcome to my island, Lennie. Cocktails on the veranda at seven."

"Thanks Jack. I thought you'd have scouted some women for us. You've already been here ten minutes." Lennie smiled back.

"Thought we might scout for Japs first. Let's get the wounded up in those bushes and have a look about."

Pappy was clearly the worst off. His burns looked horrific, but he was conscious and still talking through the pain. Johnston seemed to be getting worse hacking and retching from the fumes he inhaled along with the saltwater. Harris was the one positive. His leg did not seem to be broken but just badly bruised from the hit he took in the collision. They made the crew as comfortable as possible then did a quick check of the island. It didn't take long.

The island was about a hundred feet across with a few trees. Some were coconut with fruit too high for exhausted men to reach. There was no sign of Japs. No food. No water.

After fifteen hours in the water without rest some of the men fell asleep almost immediately. Kennedy and Lennie were barely awake when they heard a boat.

"Listen something's out on the water," the XO heard it first.

"Well if it's the Navy they could have come a little sooner and spared us that swim."

The crew grew excited.

"Heads down everybody," Lenny warned. "Chances are a lot better that's a Jap patrol than a rescue."

Kennedy crawled forward to the edge of the bushes and looked out. He was right but even so, his hopes sank. The patrol kept on going.

He crawled back, "It was a patrol. They moved on. We we need to stay sharp in case they come back."

The daylight was fading. They were on land, though one that would not sustain them. With the injured men there was no time or luxury to rest.

"We're not getting anywhere just sitting here," Kennedy barked at Lennie and Ross.

"These flares are still more likely to bring the Japs running than our boys," Lennie offered.

"You're right about that. Here's what I'm thinking. Every night we've been going out on patrol and spending part of every patrol in the Strait. I'm going out there tonight to see if I can signal one of our boats."

"Swimming...?" Ross started.

"Out into the Strait." Lennie finished.

"Right. Unless somebody has a better idea."

No one did.

Kennedy stripped to his shorts, tied a .38 around his neck, grabbed the battle lantern and looked towards the ocean.

"If I find a boat I'll flash the lantern twice. The password will be 'Roger'. The answer will be 'Wilco'."

He stood up and walked towards the reef, walking like it was the journey of a thousand miles and he barely had energy for the first step. Walking on the reef would take him to the Strait. He could walk some distance out and swim the rest.It would not be easy. The reef was uneven and jagged. They were stumbling steps with each stumble adding a cut and each cut bleeding into water that carried the scent to any host of creatures who would gladly have him. By darkness he came to the end of the coral pier and slipped into the deeper water. Swimming with the current he made it in an hour and begin his lonely vigil.

He could hear the sounds of the Japanese camps. It was not comforting. What he wanted to hear was the deep rumble of the big Packard engines on a friendly PT. By midnight he'd come to a conclusion. For a reason unknown to him, it was apparent that Warfield sent the patrol in some direction other than the Strait. Jack began to swim back towards the island. He was fatigued and shivering. August was winter season in the Pacific islands and the nighttime water temperature was barely in the 70's. Cold enough to sap heat from a human body.

Kennedy made his way back to the reef. Returning was more difficult than going out. The current was stronger. He was weaker. The current finally won and swept him off the reef and into the deeper water. He was being carried past the island, past the hard earth that had felt so good just a few hours earlier. In desperation he flashed the lantern calling, "Roger, roger."

From land he heard, "Wilco, wilco," as the current carried him back towards the Strait.

"Was that Jack?" Asked Lennie who was on the beach with some of the crew.

"It was the call sign. Maybe he found a boat."

"There, the lantern is flashing again."

"I'm not sure that's a lantern. Might just be the water. Maybe we're seeing things."

"I might be seeing things but I'm not seeing and hearing things."

"If it was the Skipper where is he?"

Ross turned and walked away from the beach, "If it was Kennedy he was just swept back out to sea."

The remaining crew returned to their rough camp off the beach. They were torn between the loss of Kennedy and their loss of hope. It was the second night without any sign of being saved.

CHAPTER 25

JOE KENNEDY HELD THE TELEGRAM. It elicited a rare reaction from the ambassador. He wasn't quite sure what to do. It was not an official notice from the War Department saying that his son was dead. But he interpreted it that way.. Missing though, not dead and this Marlow seems to be playing outside channels. Smart move. He'd heard of the writer, read his columns and knew he and Jack had spent some time together.

He sat in a chair to sort things out. Jack was missing. In this war missing typically meant dead or captured - which in the South Pacific was about the same. Both Jack and his older brother had been set on going to war. Joe Junior got his wings first. That seemed to spur Jack to seek an assignment in a combat zone. Rivalry or patriotism or both? Joe was strong and sailed through training. Jack was sick, always had been. It took work to push those records aside and get him into PT training. But he wasn't suppose to end up in the South Pacific. He'd managed to end-run his father's plans to keep him in the backwaters of the war. Two boys off to war and one may now be dead. He'd wanted a hero to promote their political careers after the war. But a dead hero was no good to him.

There could be no talk of dead, yet. He didn't want anything getting out to the press. This was something he had to play close for now. No need to tell Rose. Just the thought of his death would send her into mourning. The thought that he might have died in war without a priest by his side would make it worse. She would worry about his soul. He was just worried about his personal legacy.

Joe ran the realities through his head. The telegram and Jack, in whatever state, were on the other side of the international dateline. He was already a day behind. Any chance of a rescue decreased with time any idiot knew that except perhaps, the idiot Marlow mentioned in his telegram. Joe Kennedy picked up the phone and called Washington. If Senator Walsh used his influence to get Jack into the PT command maybe he could do something to get a search started for his son.

Blackett Strait 2400hrs

Kennedy was floating in the water, in and out of consciousness. Although he hadn't given up, his body had given out. The current had carried him away from the island and back out into open water. It had carried him beyond the point of caring.

He tried to focus on the horizon, on small objects to keep from losing consciousness because if he did that would be the end. Thoughts of Warfield helped for a change. He thought of what he would do if he ever saw him again. Most of the acts were outside his training as a proper son of a prominent family. Hatred is a good motivator, so is love. He thought of Inga and their short and intense love affair and how much he wanted to see her again. A peace came as the tide carried him away.

Plum Pudding Island 0800hrs

Ross and Thom stood on the beach looking towards the ocean. With Kennedy gone one of them would have to take command. Ross had merely been along for the ride on the *109's* fated patrol. He was a skipper and ranked Lennie.

"We can't just sit here and wait," Lennie began, "Bucky found some Jap papers on the other side of the island. They've been here before. You can be damn sure they'll be here again before the Marines come storming ashore."

"We could wait until we see a fighter patrol fly over and use the flare gun," Ross offered.

"The Japs would get here first. It's not like Warfield's got round the clock patrols out looking for us."

"That sonofabitch."

"Royal asshole."

Both men spat to seal the insult. It was no small task as neither had had any water other than the dew licked off the leaves of the bushes around camp.

"We need to look for some food. Maybe we should send a couple guys out to the reef to try to spear some fish."

"Not a bad idea. I'd eat fish, even raw about now. It shouldn't be too hard to do. They seem to be feeding out there now."

"Holy shit. Barney that's not a fish."

Both men raced across the reef towards Kennedy who was making tough progress towards the beach. The current was helping carry him in the direction of safety this time. They carried him the final distance to shore where he fell exhausted and began to retch. The men gathered around him on the sand. Kennedy finally sat and looked up at them.

"Ross you try it tonight."

Then Kennedy collapsed on the beach.

Lumbari 0900hrs

Warfield's brilliant plan worked only slightly better than the night before. All the boats came back. One bore the body of George Cookman the skipper of *PT 107*. The patrol came under fire from Japanese floatplanes. Half turned and went back to base. Cookman and the rest found and engaged some of the heavily armed and armored barges. It was another mismatch for the PTs. The *107* was shot up pretty badly but managed to get back to base.

It made my day easier. Instead of catching a ride to Tulagi for a memorial service I could just stay at Lumbari. The crews were organizing a service for both Cookman and the crew of the *109*.

The hut was still waiting for Jack and Lennie to return. Their lockers and gear remained by their empty bunks. I was writing a few notes and thinking my welcome was wearing thin with Warfield. It would be hard to argue staying much longer with my editors in New York. John walked into the hut. He still looked like he'd misplaced something.

"Paper," he pointed at my notepad.

I handed him both pad and pencil. He started sketching furiously. When he finished he had a rough but accurate map of the surrounding islands. As a matter of fact he had a few islands not on the briefing maps up on Warfield's wall.

"Gasa, Kumana go here," he pointed in an area of islands south of Gizo, "Watch-man Evans he know. Him look."

"Coastwatcher Evans," I asked to be sure.

"Yes. Him look."

What I took from that was the coastwatcher Evans on Kolombangara was sending natives out to check the smaller islands in the area where Kennedy and his crew might have reached. That meant at least one person was actually orchestrating an effort to find survivors.

"Boys find Jack," John pointed at his map with conviction.

I looked in his eyes. They harbored no doubt. He also offered the first hope I'd felt in the last thirty two hours.

"Find Jack," I repeated back to him. He offered a solemn nod and walked out.

There's nothing more solemn than the Navy hymn, or more depressing when it's being played over a tinny loudspeaker for the benefit of the base. Warfield was pressed to do something. He seemed to be making as minimal an effort in the memorial as he did in the rescue. I steered clear of the gathering. It would be difficult to stomach his hypocrisy. After the encounter with John I was nowhere near ready for giving them up for lost. The music floated down to the docks.

> *Oh hear us when we cry to thee,*
> *For those in peril on the sea.*

Keresey was down by the *105*.

"That just pisses me off," he volunteered while listening to the lyrics. "No one upstairs would have heard a call come up from this command. Warfield is our Captain Bligh and he's not even a captain."

"Before you plot mutiny..." I then told him of our new allies in the search for the crew.

"When you want something done around here, you call up the cannibals. Damn right. Evans and his crew know more about what's going on in these islands than the whole damn Navy. Screw Warfield."

My thoughts exactly.

CHAPTER 26

Day Three
Plum Pudding Island 0800hrs

Ross WAS FAST ASLEEP UNDER a makeshift lean-to. His effort to swim into the Strait went no further than the end of the reef. It was the same slow, painful process but after a few nicks from the reef and an encounter with a school of sand sharks he spooked and headed back to the island. The end result was the same as Kennedy's only less harrowing. They were no closer to rescue and still without food and water.

"We can't stay here," Kennedy was talking to Lennie.

"We won't make it more than another couple of days unless we find something to drink. That island to the south is larger and further away from the Japanese bases. Worst case there are more trees on the island. Maybe we'll find coconuts on the ground. That'll at least keep us alive."

"It's going to be tough on Pappy," Lennie looked towards the wounded man.

"He'll die here. We'll all die here if we stay. Let's get the men together. Wake Ross up - he's had his beauty sleep."

For the second time the crew of the *109* set out on a swimming marathon through shark and enemy infested waters. Nine swam or clung to the familiar timber from the deck of the boat. Kennedy swam with a life jacket strap in his mouth towing Pappy, again.

They made the island after three hours. Kennedy made better time with one passenger than Lennie did with only a couple swimmers pushing the timber. The first ashore were the ones to find a store of coconuts on the ground. Kennedy hacked into one and gave it to Pappy who thirstily began to gulp the water. By the time the others found them they were already puking from drinking too much coconut juice.

"I hear that stuff packs a bad hangover, too," Lennie could afford the humor at Jack's expense. The coconuts meant they could survive.

"The rest of you guys take it easy with this stuff. Just drink a little at a time."

"I thought if I drank enough I'd see girls in hula skirts," Jack groaned as he rolled over.

The crew set up a rough camp, drank their first liquid in days and fell asleep.

Kennedy awoke and began a restless walk around the island. It was better than the first one but they still faced little to no chance of rescue by staying put. He could see other islands to the south hopscotching towards Rendova and a better chance of contact. That was the direction they needed to go. Ideas and options were running through his mind as he approached camp. The sound of a hammer being cocked on a .38 pistol stopped him.

"Friend or foe?"

"It's me, Kennedy. for Christ's sake don't shoot!"

"Dammit you coulda gotten shot," Lennie said.

"I am a bit tall for a Jap. Sorry I shouldn't have wandered off. I just needed to think a bit."

"We are all exhausted. That could get us killed. We need to set up regular watches. Who knows there could be a tall Jap named Kennedy lurking out there."

"You're right, and you're in command," he turned to Ross, "Barney I've got a bit of wanderlust and thought we could swim to that next island and see what's going on."

"Which island?" Ross asked as if it mattered.

Kennedy pointed like Christopher Columbus seeing another shore. "That one," he said.

Naru Island 1600hrs

They approached the island with caution. It was larger and strategically closer to the Ferguson Passage which meant a greater chance for a Japanese encampment. Both men swam through the surf with only their heads above water, crawling on the beach and making a low dash for the brush above the waterline. They crept keeping as much cover as possible while moving across the island towards the beach on the Ferguson Passage side. Jack was first to the edge of the bush line. He froze.

"Stop. Barney get down," he whispered, "There are two men out there."

He pointed towards a barge that had run aground on the reef. Two native men in a canoe were looking over the wreck for what the Japanese may have left behind.

"Are they friendlies?" Ross wondered.

"It's a risk. Most of the natives hate the Japs. John told me most of them are connected to the coastwatchers. They go about their business but report what they see. The Japs kill most of the ones they catch."

"What do we do?"

"Let's try saying hello."

Kennedy stood up and walked out of the brush and onto the beach. Ross followed.

"Hey!" Kennedy waved towards the two, "Americans!"

For a moment the four men stared at each other in silence. Then the two in the canoe looked at each other and turned their boat around and paddled into deeper water and around the corner of the island.

"Shit. Dammit," Kennedy said.

"Well at least they didn't shoot us."

"Now we don't know if they'll paddle off to report us to the coastwatchers or the Japs or forget they ever saw us," Kennedy sat thinking, "Either way I still think the odds are better, if they report anything, they'll report it to ally rather than enemy. One of us is going to have to stay here in case somebody comes back."

"If that barge ran aground you can bet the Japs have been on this island. Let's get back closer to cover and scout up the beach," Ross started moving.

Halfway up the beach Ross pointed. The tip of a canoe was barely visible in the scrub. They approached a few feet at a time stopping to listen. When it seemed safe they pushed the bushes aside. The canoe was a one man dugout, a smaller version to the canoes that connected the natives across all the islands. But inside the canoe was a treasure.

"FOOD!" Both said at once.

A small crate contained Japanese provisions that natives at some time or another stashed with the canoe. There was also a tin of rainwater.

"They must have been looking for more Japanese loot on that barge. I'll bet they've made emergency stashes like this all over these islands," Kennedy said.

"Good idea Skipper but let's eat," Ross got to the point.

In the crate was some Japanese hardtack and candies. It made for an odd meal but washed down with fresh water, at the moment it was better than a Thanksgiving dinner.

"Ok so one of us needs to stay in case the natives come back. Agreed?" Kennedy seemed energized by the first food in days.

"Agreed."

"Then let's flip a coin to see who takes the canoe and the food and water back to the crew."

"Ahhh, I don't happen to have a coin, Jack."

"Ok then you lose. I'll take the canoe."

By taking the canoe across open water Jack was taking the larger risk. He knew that. He was also not hugely impressed by Ross's timid efforts the night before. The food and water needed to get to the crew. He set out, a white man in a native canoe who would stand out as clearly from the air as a mermaid on a rock.

He returned to Plum Pudding Island bringing the crew a surprise dinner. They had a bigger surprise waiting. The same two natives who were surprised by Kennedy and Ross a few hours earlier, paddled their canoe straight into the lagoon just yards from Thom and the others.

"We were on the beach. A couple of the guys, your Massachusetts boys, were in the water figuring they could find some sort of native clam. Said they were going to make damn clam 'chowda'. Around the edge there come these these two boys in a canoe and nobody moved. I start yelling, 'Americans' and 'U-S, U-S' and they keep looking at me dancing and waving my arms," Lennie described the sighting.

"The sight of you dancing on the beach should have scared anybody off."

"Then they start coming in a little closer and I yell, 'Hey, you know John from Lumbari?' They come in closer. 'Lumbari John?' They ask. 'Yeah and I hold my hand up about this high to show how short he is. 'Lumbari John! They start smiling and paddle right into the beach."

Somehow between a big, blonde headed Nordic looking man dancing on the beach and the mention of John, the hut boy, the natives decided the men on the beach weren't Japanese. They warned the crew that the next island over they'd seen two Japanese jump out of the bushes.

"I said those were our guys. The Skipper. The Boss-man," Lennie continued, "They said all white men look the same to them, including Japanese."

"Where'd they go?" Kennedy asked.

"Not sure. They seemed to be on some sort of mission. I tried to find something to write a note on but there's nothing here."

"So they know white men, Americans are on two islands and they know John. They must be working for the coastwatchers. I'd better get back to Naru and tell Ross and keep an eye out for them."

"Jack it's dark and feels like there's a bit of a storm coming. Why don't you wait until tomorrow," Lennie warned.

"White boy in a canoe more obvious in the daytime. Besides the natives took off into the dark."

"They've spent their whole lives in these islands they know them like the back of their hand."

"Bet they never swam laps between the islands," Jack smiled.

"I'm not going to stop you am I?"

"Nope. Sorry Lennie. We can't let a chance like this slip away."

Kennedy was not content with testing Fate. Sometimes it seemed he wanted to piss it off.

He paddled the canoe out of the lagoon and towards open water edging on Ferguson Passage ignoring a stiffening wind and Lennie's warning. It seemed to him if he was out in a canoe it was better than being out with nothing better than a life jacket. Maybe this time he'd get lucky and catch the PT's heading out on patrol. No such luck.

The wind was kicking up five to six foot waves. Even Kennedy was starting to think it was a bad idea. He tried to turn towards the island and was hit broadside by a wave. When he came to the surface the dugout was being carried away by the sea.

Once again he was alone in the ocean, buoyed by a life jacket but not on a current in a calm sea. He bobbed from trough to crest. The high seas had robbed him of all sense of direction. There was no island in view. Unlike the first night in the Strait he was not drifting on the edge of consciousness. He was floating in a fury. So close to the chance of a rescue and he'd taken a stupid risk. He'd survived a collision with a goddamned Japanese destroyer, carried his crew through two dangerous transits to find the basics of survival: food and water. Then tonight he made contact. The crew would be rescued and he'd be a corpse floating and damned to haunt this Strait forever.

At the top of one crest he thought he saw his canoe in the distance. If he could catch it he might ride out the storm. From wave top to wave top he seemed to be gaining on it. Then he realized it was gaining on him.

It was a two man canoe headed in his direction. They were making progress rowing in perfect rhythm to ride the waves instead of fighting against them. As they came alongside they looked like they might be the two natives from earlier that day. Or they might be two cannibals out looking for dinner. Then one of them reached out, grabbed his collar and pulled him on board.

"Lumbari John say get Kennedy. You Kennedy?" Someone said in a native accent.

"Yes." Kennedy replied.

The two natives looked at each other and nodded without breaking stride or stroke of their paddling. Kennedy hunched down and held on to the sides as the natives paddled in harmony with the sea. Soon the sound of the wind was mixed with that of waves breaking on shore. They rode the surf straight up onto the beach where he'd left Ross hours ago. While dragging the canoe on shore there was a rustling in the bushes.

"Kennedy is that you?"

"Can you say that in Japanese, Barney?"

"Jesus, don't kid with me Kennedy." Barney stepped out of the bushes and jumped backwards, "What the hell is going on here?"

One of the natives led the four into the woods to a small hut the Japanese had left behind. There was a Japanese gas mask and a few figurines carved out of wood. Some Jap had spent a lot of dull hours sitting in the shack. There was also another small crate of food. The two natives picked up a couple of twigs and started a small fire.. Jack watched in amazement and felt a new and profound respect for the men who could row a primitive craft through rough weather, survive the Japanese around them and bring comfort to two white men lost in the middle of what they considered nowhere. He wondered if the few phrases he'd learned from John would help now.

"You know Lumbari John?" he asked.

"Yes."

"Your names?"

"I Baiku, he Eroni."

Kennedy communicated with a few common words to indicate he wanted to send a message.

"There's nothing around here to write on," Ross offered, "I looked all through the crates."

"Paper wouldn't work anyway, it'd get soaked and destroyed in this weather."

Baiku looked at Eroni and said a couple of words. Eroni left the hut and came back a couple minutes later with a coconut. Baiku took it and using his hands showed how to carve into the surface. Kennedy pulled out his pocketknife and carved a simple message:

NAURO IS NATIVE KNOWS POSIT HE CAN PILOT 11 ALIVE NEED SMALL BOAT KENNEDY

CHAPTER 27

WARFIELD SAT AND LOOKED BLANKLY at the maps on the wall.

"I don't bloody believe it," he spoke simply verbalizing his thoughts.

"It's pretty amazing, sir. Eleven survivors from the *109*," It was the radioman Ford on duty who had just set up the conversation between the coastwatcher Evans from his island post and the commander at Lumbari.

Warfield jerked around like a ghost had spoken, "Ford that was a classified conversation. If any word of that leaks out I'll put you on one of those islands and leave you."

"Yes sir, didn't hear a word."

"Get Cluster on the radio for me. I'm going outside for a smoke."

"Yes sir."

As soon as Warfield left the room Ford jotted a short note to Keresey that he'd send with the first runner he could get past Warfield. He got Cluster's radio op to muster his commander and called out to Warfield.

"Sir, commander Cluster's on his way."

He returned and waited, saying nothing until he heard Cluster come on the line.

"Al, we've got a strange one here."

"What are you talking about Tom?"

"Evans radioed this morning. Said some of his natives found Kennedy and ten survivors on some islands off Kolombangara. Said he had a damn coconut with a carved note from Kennedy."

"Well I'll be damned. Have you had any patrols in that area checking for survivors?"

"No. My boats have been on duty patrols nothing else."

"Tom, I saw the order from Admiral Halsey to step up search efforts. That pressure to look for Kennedy came from the top, from Washington."

"And we both saw the other order from Halsey to keep the PTs out of the Slot because he decided to send destroyers after the Tokyo Express. I'm not going to go against an operational order just because Halsey is getting pressure from Washington to save the son of some damned ambassador. Besides this whole thing smells like a Jap trap to me. I think those wiley bastards are trying to lure a rescue party out in the open," Warfield said defiantly.

"God Dammit Tom! Halsey's order to step up the search efforts has nothing to do with night patrols and you know it. You are not at liberty to pick which orders you want to follow and which ones you don't. I'll give you this is pretty strange but we're going to follow it through. I'm going to catch a boat up to Lumbari. Let's get a plan together with the Coastwatcher."

Naru Island 1100hrs

Kennedy sat on the beach looking like a caricature of man deserted on a tropical island. His clothing was torn. He was sunburned and scraggy. He was also on watch and determined that his coconut carving would be their salvation.

"Hey Barney! Get out here," he called into the bush. Ross had gone off watch and was sleeping. He walked painfully out on the sand. The coral cuts on his feet were blistering and becoming infected.

Jack was heading to the water just as a huge war canoe was coming to shore with eight natives on board.

"We're either about to be rescued, or we're going to make the most handsome pair of shrunken heads in their collection."

One man stepped out of the canoe and walked with some formality to Kennedy.

"I have a letter for you, sir," he said in perfect English with a British accent, " from Leftenant Evans."

Kennedy tore open the note.

On His Majesty's Service

To Senior Officer, Naru Is.

*Friday 11 p.m. Have just learnt of your presence on Naru Is +
also that two nativeshave taken news to Lumbari. I strongly ad-
vise you return immediately to here in this canoe + by the time you
arrive here I will be in Radio communication with authorities at
Lumbari + we can finalise plans to collect balance of party*

A.R. Evans, Lt.
RANVR

P.S. Will warn aviation of your crossing Ferguson Passage.

"You've got to hand it to the Aussies," Jack laughed as he handed the
note to Ross.

"Sir, we have food and provisions for your crew."

"The way you guys have come through I'm surprised the *Queen Mary*
isn't anchored outside the reef and holding brunch for us. Come on
Barney let's go eat with the boys."

When the war canoe rowed ashore with two white men sitting like
odd tokens among the natives, the nine survivors scrambled to the
beach.

"Did somebody order lunch?" Kennedy called out.

The English speaking native was Benjamin Kevu who was Evan's
right hand man and coordinator of the local tribes who served as an un-
dercover network for the coastwatchers. Kevu and his crew made short
work of setting order to the rough camp. They built a better shelter for
Pappy and started a fire. Soon the crew of the *109* was sitting down to
their first real meal in days: rice, potatoes, boiled fish, yams and C rations with roast beef hash. They were fed and happier but not yet safe.
Pappy's burns were infected and starting to emit the odor of gangrene.
Almost every member of the crew was dehydrated and suffering from
cuts and wounds that were also reaching dangerous stages of infection.
Kennedy wanted to make sure the rest of the rescue went off properly.

"Benjamin," he gestured to Kevu with a bow, "Take me to your
leader."

Half of the natives stayed to take care of the crew. That made room in the canoe for Kennedy to lie flat on the bottom while they covered him with palm leaves. Paddling across the strait with a white man in the middle would likely end about mid crossing with a Japanese air attack. Beneath the cover listening to the rhythmic sounds of the paddles across much calmer waters Kennedy felt comfortable for the first time in days. He fell asleep.

Two hands pressed down hard on his shoulders.

"Lieutenant Kennedy do not move," It was Kevu.

The sound of airplanes was overhead. One came close on a low pass. The rowing stopped. A paddle was placed across the gunnels above his head. Through the fronds he could see Kevu standing up and waving his arms.

"Hello you crazy Jap bastards," which sounded a bit charming with his accent, "Can't you see? You stupid fools. We are just innocent, ignorant natives carrying coconuts and a navy commander, beneath your noses."

He sat down. The sound of the planes grew distant.

"No worries Mr. Kennedy. They like to fly low and make sure we're the savages they think us to be."

"Well I'm glad they can't read lips when they fly over."

"Good point, sir."

The rowing continued. Jack was relaxed enough to begin feeling the different parts of his body that hurt. He'd begun an inventory and considered a healing process that may or may not include contact with nurses at the base hospital when he felt the canoe crunch into shore. At this point he didn't move unless Kevu told him to move. He heard a voice with an Australian accent.

"Benjamin where is the American?"

Jack instantly sat up.

"Hello, I'm Kennedy," Jack said offering his hand.

Evans reached out and helped him from the dugout. The Aussie wore a collared shirt, shorts, boots and a bush hat. Jack was barefoot, ragged and wearing what was left of a tattered uniform and several days worth of scruffy beard. They greeted each other with a smile.

"Well mate, why don't you come up to my tent and have a cup of tea."

Lumbari 1800hrs

The briefing room was full. Once Cluster arrived on base Keresey knew something was going on and started spreading the news. If everyone showed up, Warfield couldn't suspect he was helping to paint him into a corner where he would finally have to do something to rescue the crew of the *109*. Keresey had pressed his way towards the front. I was a spider on the wall.

Warfield and Cluster stood at the head of the group. This time Warfield held neither rank nor command of the meeting. Cluster held rank. A group of three small, dark men held command.

"Send boats. Men sick. Get Kennedy," John started.

Baiku held up the coconut, "Kennedy. Need help."

Eroni was the strong silent type. He carried a machete and tapped the edge of the table occasionally. His eyes never left Warfield.

"I'm still not buying this thing. This could be a trap."

"The coconut pretty much seals it for me," Cluster said firmly, "Let's put together a rescue."

A cheer went up from the room. Keresey was up front for a reason.

"Sir, permission to lead the mission with *PT 105*. "

Every other skipper chimed in.

"Quiet!," Warfield yelled, "This ain't no debutante ball. This is a dangerous mission close to enemy positions. Here's what we're going to do. I want three boats to go straight to the island, take rafts and send rescue teams in.."

"Lieutenant..." the radioman tried to get Warfield's attention.

"And when the teams secure the island..." Warfield continued.

"Lieutenant.."

"Why are you interrupting me ensign."

"Leftenant Evans is on the radio, sir. He has Lieutenant Kennedy with him."

The room erupted in cheers like someone had just hit a homerun in the World Series, for the home team.

"Well put him on," Warfield sounded less than pleased.

"Hello Chaps," Kennedy's voice sparked another cheer. "Was just sitting here having a cup of tea with my new friend Leftenant Evans of the coastwatchers and we thought we'd ring up and say hello."

It was Jack alright. The Boston accent and sense of humor were intact.

"We were hoping you might throw a little party tonight and wondered about the plans."

Warfield clenched the mike and his jaw, " We're sending three boats out to rendezvous at your island approximately 2300hrs."

There was a pause on the other end.

"Sir, with all due respect," Kennedy began.

I thought Warfield might bust his jaw - he was biting down so hard.

"I think Commander," Kennedy continued, "it might be better if two boats came, one with radar to stand guard off the island. Let's set a rendezvous for 2200hrs near Patparan Island. I'll be in a dugout with natives. Fire four shots as a signal. I'll return with four shots. Once you've got me on board we'll proceed to the island for the crew. And bring the natives with you. They know the reefs better than anyone."

Warfield looked like he was going to rip Kennedy for countermanding his rescue mission.

"Hang on Tom," Cluster stepped towards the radio, "It's his crew and his command. He's been out there and probably knows the area and conditions better than we do."

"You mean we're going with his plan?" Warfield bellowed.

"I think it's a good plan."

"Then perhaps it's better if you command this mission," Warfield handed the mike to Cluster and walked out the door.

"Ahh... roger that Jack," Cluster said.

"Commander Cluster, nice to hear your voice. Where is Lieutenant Warfield?"

"He stepped out for some air."

"It's a lovely evening for that. You should come up to our island for a visit. It's lovely after midnight."

"I'll see you then. And Jack.."

"Yes commander?"

"Good to hear your voice. Well done."

"Thank you, sir."

There was cheering, hand clapping and foot stomping. It was a hoe-down. Cluster held the mike open for just a moment, just so Kennedy could hear it.

There were six PT boats going out that night. Four were going further up the passage to run interference for destroyers on a wolfpack mission to stop the Tokyo Express. The navy had given up on the notion that PTs could effectively fight enemy destroyers. Warfield would command that group from his bunker on base.

Cluster would lead the rescue mission while Berndtson and *PT 171* with a radar would be the spotter boat to protect the evacuation. Keresey and *PT 105* would carry Cluster, a navy corpsman for the wounded and John, Biuku and Eroni. On the way out of the room Cluster caught my eye.

"You should come along, Marlow. Not often these things work out this well. Might make a good story."

"Might. Hell it's a great story. Thank you."

"Oh damn," Kennedy remarked to Evans.

"Sounded kind of cheery to me mate. What's to damn?"

"The signal for tonight. I said four shots. I've only got three in this pistol." Kennedy said, scratching his head.

Evans looked around his tent. He travelled light, it was kind of a requirement when the Japanese hunted you on a regular basis.

"Well I don't have any .38 ammo. You can take that old Jap rifle over there. Fire off your fourth round from that."

"That should work. It can double as a souvenir after the war. My kids will ask me, "Daddy how did you get that Japanese rifle?" I'll tell them I got it sipping tea with an Aussie hero."

"You might have trouble selling that last bit." Said Evans, with an accent that ended in upswing, almost a question.

"Not when I tell them about you."

"Well here's to the end of the war and wives and kids and grandkids and sitting by a warm fire with something better than tea," and he raised his cup, "Now off with ya. The lads are down by the water with a canoe. You have a crew to rescue tonight."

"Reg, thanks for your help. Without you there'd be no rescue. Hope to see you after the war, because without you my war would have ended this week."

"Just take care out there tonight. Don't give the Japs a second chance."

Jack headed out in the canoe with two of Evan's crew well ahead of the appointed hour. He didn't want to run the risk of missing the rendezvous and leaving the crew on the island even one more night.

On *PT 105* Keresey's crew was looking like some strange assembly from *Treasure Island*. The corpsman's main medicinals were small bottles of rum and brandy that he thought would fortify the crew. Below the cook was planning to lay out enough food for a pirate's feast and on the aft deck were the three small men who played the largest role in tonight's adventure. When the big Packard engines came to life and the PTs started out into open water the three looked afraid.

"Boat too fast," John managed bravely.

None of the natives had ever travelled any faster than a well stroked canoe. It was too much for Biuku and Eroni. They both went below where the speed and the waves died down. Around eleven the PTs neared the meeting point and cut their engines. The moon was setting. Darkness would support their cover. Drifting quietly, Keresey stepped to the bow and pulled out his revolver. Bang. Bang. Bang. Bang. The sound of the last shot drifted out across the water.

On the canoe Kennedy heard the sound he'd been waiting for. He stood up and fired. Bang. Bang. Bang... then a pause while he grabbed the rifle.

On the PT they heard the delay and had a moment of concern. Then the fourth shot, which was followed by a splash. The recoil from the rifle had knocked Kennedy into the water.

The boat and the canoe drifted towards each other.

"Hey, Jack!" Cluster called.

"Where the hell you been?" Kennedy half joked.

"C'mon aboard. Let's get you out of that water. We've got some food for you."

"No thanks. I just had a coconut."

I was standing on the aft deck listening. At the moment of rescue Jack showed both wit and the anger and annoyance at a navy that had abandoned he and his crew. A ladder went over the side and Cluster and Keresey leaned over to help him up. On seeing these men he warmed and it was handshakes and hugs all around. When he'd worked his way through the first few men he stopped and looked.

"Good evening, Mr. Kennedy," John said in a very practiced English.

Jack moved to the three men and used his practiced pidgin English to thank them for the rescue. He thanked them pointedly in front of the rest of the rescue party that was following up on their initiative. He then leaned over the side of the boat and thanked the two men in the dugout. The boats parted ways and the PT picked up speed towards the island and remaining crew.

Jack relaxed and accepted a medicinal offering of brandy from the corpsman. That worked well enough that he asked for another and then got one for me. The two of us were sitting on a hatch cover, sipping like we were taking a summer cruise around Boston harbor.

Biuku summoned his courage and finally came topside when we neared the island Keresey needed their help through the reefs. The *105* slipped through a passage. The *171* stayed in deeper water where it could fight if needed.

Cluster walked back to us as they were lowering a small boat off the stern.

"Jack, you come with me," he began. "Biuku will lead us in. Maybe your men won't shoot us if they hear your voice."

He stood up, weaved a bit and smiled back at me. It was the Kennedy grin, all teeth and mischief. The brandy, on an empty stomach, was do-ing its job.

The three cast off with Cluster rowing into the dark. We were at the most vulnerable part of the mission. The crew was on shore. A rescue party was away from the PT boat which was positioned inside a coral reef like a sitting duck. The crew on the *105* was nervous. Keresey had all at battle stations. Their guns were pointing outwards and pivoting back and forth.

"Lennie. Hey, Lennie where are you?"

It was Jack's voice howling like some frat brother calling a buddy out for another run on the pub.

"Lennie. Hey, Lennie!" he repeated.

I expected to hear an oar smack Kennedy upside the head. Someone tried to quiet him down. Then there was quiet. Finally, we heard the sound of oars returning. Cluster and Kennedy saw to the wounded first. Pappy was the first back. He looked terrible. He didn't refuse the corpsman's brandy on the way to a berth below.

They came in one by one.. Each arrival from the beach brought a new round of cheers and celebration. Finally, Jack and Lennie and Biuku and Cluster all climbed up the rail and all were together and as safe as you could be on a gunboat surrounded by ten thousand or so Japanese. By this time we kind of figured if there was a Jap within ten miles, he was deaf anyway.

"Let's get the HELL out of here," Keresey commanded from the helm.

He steered us back through the reef, into open waters and then made that PT fly as fast as she could go. The corpsman was making the rounds like a cocktail waitress on a cruise ship and soon there was little distinction. The rescue that none thought was coming, was beyond imagination. With spirits high and flowing the men started singing the only song the natives knew, from their contact with missionaries. It was 'Jesus Loves Me'. Out of the darkness and into the dawn *PT 105* sailed towards home on the repeating chorus of:

> *Jesus loves me, this I know,*
> *For the Bible tells me so;*
> *Little ones to him belong,*
> *They are weak, but He is strong.*
> *Yes, Jesus loves me; yes, Jesus loves me..."*

CHAPTER 28

London, England
October, 1943

Dearest Sam,

How might I induce you to leave your islands and infections to pursue interests in other parts of the world? I could seduce, to rhyme with induce, but know that a dedicated journalist like yourself might be more interested in headlines of war. Perhaps the trick would be to offer you both.

The Tour is in England now. Bob 'These Bombings Make a Good Shaken Martini' Hope thought Crosby needed to hit the Pacific, which he did.. getting as far as Malibu.

We flew over with the 8th Air Force. Those boys are doing a huge and brave job of taking the fight to Hitler's home turf. Seems Adolph sent most of the Luftwaffe to Russia. They're bombing London less. We're bombing Berlin more. It's not that the air raid sirens never go off. I still have my skill for finding a shelter during a raid. They're so polite here when they head for the undergrounds and I have no brave reporter-boy to throw himself on top to spare me from the bombs.

Of rescues, seems the piece you wrote on Jack's risk and return down there has pretty much made it around the world (did they really sing 'Jesus Loves Me'?).. as have the other Kennedys. Kick is here. So is Joe Jr. They had a little party the other night at Devonshire

House on Piccadilly. Sound impressive? The party had a purpose. Kick announced she was going to marry Lord Hartington. She may be a Duchess someday. She's charmed the Duke and Duchess and most of London. There was no toast in Palm Beach. The Lord is Anglican. Mother Rose is said to be in a state of shock and mourning that her daughter would marry a non-Catholic. Guess Kick has seen the benefits of Catholic marital bliss and has opted otherwise. Love her for that. Looks like Joe Jr. is going to have to give her away and it's probably going to happen soon.

There were toasts galore last night, to love, the progress in the war (Lord Hartington is a major in the Coldstream Guards) and heroes. To their honor a glass was raised for the Kennedy hero, of legend made by our own favorite war correspondent. An odd reaction from the older Brother, who raised a glass but barely sipped. Methinks sibling rivalry. Brother has completed enough missions to go home. He signed up for more when he heard about Jack. War is not a competition and this could end poorly.

For your own good you should try to get here. The war is turning and could use your brilliant writing. Besides if the wedding occurs before I see you, I'm going after the bridal bouquet like a rugby player, all fists and elbows. If I catch it the next shotgun wedding will be yours.

Love and laughter, and peace ever after..

Ashley

Lumbari

Jack was back in his bunk. It was the one that sat empty for days. The one where John would sit and watch at odd hours willing Jack home. His plan had worked. Jack was on the mend. John was back to being number one hut boy.

Meanwhile, I was packing to leave.

"I heard through channels that Cluster offered you a ticket home." I offered.

"It was part of a conversation. I was more interested in another part of the conversation," Jack deflected.

"On the conversation of the first part, why don't you take him up on it. You did your job here. You'd be returning home a hero. What's wrong with that?"

"I'm not finished here." John added, "Two of my crew aren't going home as heroes. They're not going home at all. Maybe I feel like I have a score to settle."

"By staying here on these pointless PT patrols? Give him enough time and Warfield will kill off the whole squadron."

"It's not Warfield, that SOB. Cluster has seen the genius of our pirate plans. We're going to convert a few PTs into real gunboats."

"You mean you're going to go out and 'appropriate' some more anti-tank guns?"

"Better than that, a forty millimeter fore and aft, six 50's plus the two twin 50's and two 30's on the forward quarters. These boats are going to have so many barrels they'll look like porcupines. Lennie's going to get command of one and a third is going to Johnny Iles from back at Melville. We're going to scrap those useless torpedoes and finally have a boat with some punch to hit the Jap barges."

"So you're staying."

"For a while. I can't walk away from my crew yet, just because some reporter wrote some story that made me a hero, though thanks for that. Which raises the question of where you're going."

"The paper thinks I've spent enough time here. That little story about Jack and the rescue seems to be getting around a bit. They think I need to head to Europe to find a few heroes there."

"That shouldn't be too tough. Every grunt with a rifle's a hero. Same with every crew in every bomber that takes off. They're kind of like us, doesn't take too much to knock one of those bombers out of the sky. I hear the casualties in the 8th Air Force are pretty high."

"Maybe they should steal your motto, 'They were expendable'."

"They can have that. Or better yet, we'll let the Japs use it when we meet up with guns blazing."

"Just don't go out in a blaze of glory." I warned.

"No my blaze of glory is going to be when I get back to the States. My plan is to get home before the war is over to help comfort a continent of women who have suffered through a man deficit and I'll start with Inga." Kennedy replied.

"I'll warn them on my way through."

"I'm guessing your plans involve a rendezvous with Ashley?"

"She's in London. I'm headed for London. Strange coincidence, huh?"

"I think not. You're pretty devious for an honest newspaperman. You should consider politics."

"I believe I'll leave that up to you, Jack"

"By the way, my father is wild about the piece you wrote. He'd like to see you. If you could manage a swing through Palm Beach on your way through."

"How could I say no to an invitation from Joe Kennedy?"

"If you happen to be a part of FDR's administration, saying 'no' to Joe is the most often used word in the dictionary. I'm sure he'd appreciate seeing you."

"And I'll see you back in the States, Kennedy. Don't do anything foolish here to disappoint all the women waiting for you."

"You can go ahead and make dinner reservations. Just make sure there are enough seats at the table for my dates." He laughed.

We shook hands as friends. I went to pick up my bags. John already held them at the ready.

"Mr. Marlow, this way please," he'd been working very hard to perfect a few phrases.

He led the way to the docks and to the supply boat that would take me back to Guadalcanal and the beginning of a long trip back to the States. There was a lot of activity on the pier and a lot of noise. Some of the noise was coming from an officer shouting at a crew. The officer was Warfield.

"What makes you think you're fit to be in this Navy?"

Our path was in his direction.

"You PT people think you're different. A bunch of goddamn pirates."

We were within a few feet.

"What is lacking here, is a little discipline."

John seemed to veer off a towards Warfield. The bags he was carrying were heavy. He was off balance and leaning forward towards the water. He clipped Warfield.

For me, there was a moment of opportunity that slipped into slow motion. It wasn't one of those scenes like you're supposed to have when you're dying, when your life passes before your eyes. It was more like a condensed reel of Warfield's asshole moments. The reel ended with the look on his face when he heard Kennedy's voice on the radio after being rescued. My arm went out to clutch the back of his shirt. I could have pulled him back, instead I pushed him forward and into the water. There was a splash followed by a roaring cheer that started at the PT boat and ran down the entire dock. Warfield bobbed up, spitting and sputtering. When he saw me he started shaking his fist and calling for the Shore Patrol. I faked a salute that ended with one finger pointing upward.

Hollywood, Ca.

Inga hung up the phone and sat with a sense of thrill. Hoover had taken her bait and accepted her invitation. Now she was in that heady, dangerous place where success would mean freedom from Hoover's grasp. Failure would mean her destruction. Trying to out wit The Great Manipulator' was a power play of the highest order. It was as good as sex. Funny how those two seem to go together.

Hollywood wasn't the only place where Ego ruled. On the west coast Ego was tied to the Industry: films, box office success, fan adoration. In the east it was tied to power. With Hoover it had been a matter of connecting the two.

Chaplin's creative genius was without doubt measured either by the money or the awards and acclamations. His comedy was not without an occasional dark side. When faced with Hoover he decided to embrace the diabolical. The plan began during their lunch at the Chateau Marmont.

"Hoover preys on people's sex lives like a spider preys on the victims of it's web," Chaplin explained, "He uses them for blackmail. He uses them for his own pleasure. He uses them to sustain him."

"As he has used my relationship to control me and yours to destroy you," Inga added.

"Precisely. Our task is to create a situation where we can get something on *him*."

"He's too smart. He'd smell a trap a mile away."

"I'm not thinking of a trap. I'm thinking about creating opportunities to create that spark, that moment that we can immortalize on film. Here's what I'm thinking. Eddie Sutherland has a film coming out soon. I gave him a break in one of my films some decades ago, now he's a director. The film is called *Dixie*. It stars Dorothy Lamour and Bing Crosby. Now in Hollywood it's common knowledge that Hoover has affections for Dorothy. On the East Coast everyone wonders but they say nothing of the close relationship between Hoover and his boy, Tolson. Like all great dramas I simply want to bring the actors to the stage and allow their emotions to emerge. Eddie will create a debut party. We'll create the afterparty... and I'll have that place wired like a film studio."

"Oh heavens do you expect a three way?"

"Oh! That's a disturbing image for me to carry. But I like your imagination.. It could be a cat fight if Tolson happens to be the jealous sort, or we could throw in a goat for good measure. For us, it's a matter of providing the fuel and letting the fire ignite itself."

The Chinese Theatre dressed up nicely at night. With your name on the marquee or a couple of drinks in you it could almost seem glamorous. For Bing Crosby both combined as he walked down the red carpet with Dorothy Lamour on his arm. It was not an unfamiliar walk for Crosby. He already owned a piece of the sidewalk. Kleig lights shot their beams into the clear California sky. Their arcs against the darkness were either a signal to the heavens or a shining path to the center of a glamorous universe. Flash bulbs along the red carpet exploded as the stars walked past. The frequency of the flashes could disorient the novice. For Crosby and Lamour they were simply the lights that go with stardom. When those lights fade, so does the star.

Another dark sedan pulled to the curb. Photographers gathered around to catch a shot of an emerging star. Out stepped Hoover. For a moment there was a stillness, while the photographers tried to determine the personality of the porcine man in evening attire.

"Hey! That's Hoover," came a call from the crowd.

Flashbulbs began popping. Behind Hoover, Inga emerged looking like a Hollywood beauty in her own right. She took his arm and they stepped onto the carpet. With the attention focused on them, a lone figure stepped out of the car behind them.. Clyde Tolson followed like an Arab's wife.

"Dixie" had about as much a chance of winning an Oscar as the South had of winning the war. It was a mediocre musical to showcase Crosby's crooning and Lamour's smoky, sexy persona. Hoover sat between Inga and Tolson laughing along with the audience, slapping his knees during a number where Crosby performed in blackface.

When the movie ended, the real show began.

The official after party was at the Roosevelt Hotel only a block away. Yet a string of limousines were waiting in front of the theatre. In the subtleties of Hollywood status you could be ranked by where your car stood in line. Hoover's was second. He noticed.

"You impress me, Inga," Hoover settled into the back of the limo.

"How is that Mr. Director?" she played charming as effectively as any starlet in Hollywood.

"The invitation to the premier, VIP status, the afterparty and a chance to talk with Dorothy Lamour. Pretty impressive."

"You have to play all sides when you're a gossip columnist in Hollywood. It can't be all about destroying people as you'd have me do with Mr. Chaplin. I've written plenty of pretty prose to stroke the egos in charge in this town.."

"Speaking of Mr. Chaplin, how was your lunch?"

"Perfectly civil."

"*Why* was your lunch?"

"If I'm to attack someone I find it easier to do so at close range."

"You could be a dangerous woman, Miss Arvad."

"Relax, Mr. Director. The party is just beginning."

The Blossom ballroom was decorated with the antebellum cast offs from the movie set. The room was populated with extras dressed in period costume. If the scene didn't make you want to whistle Dixie it certainly made you want to grab a bourbon. Eddie Sutherland swooped in on the Hoover entourage as soon as they hit the door. It was Inga's job to deliver the Director. It was Eddie's job to emcee the evening as designed by Chaplin.

"Oh Inga you ravishing Danish. You'd be so delicious for breakfast."

"Eddie you'd better save your charm for the stars. I'm just a columnist."

"You're a columnist who has become must reading for every studio exec in Hollywood. Not too bad for the new girl in town. I see you are a woman who isn't satisfied with a single date."

"Let me introduce Mr. J. Edgar Hoover of the Federal Bureau of Investigation and Mr. Clyde .. "

He cut her off abruptly, and intentionally.

"Oh my god. It's the G-Man himself," Eddie started fluttering. Everyone was an actor in Hollywood.

"We are -thrilled- that you came all this way for the premier. J. Edgar. Hoover, I can't believe I'm talking to you. You're a legend. I should make a movie about you. Oh my god. I'm a genius. Why haven't I thought about that? We need to think about a leading lady. Dorothy. I'm sure she'd like to meet the man gangsters run from. Come. You come with me let me introduce you. No! Better yet, let me get you a seat at her table."

Eddie wrapped his arm around Hoover's shoulder and they formed a flying wedge through the crowd. Tolson and Inga were left behind in the wake. She looked at him and smiled. Clyde looked at a waitress and grabbed a drink and threw it back. He picked up another.

"Well Inga. They also serve who only stand and drink. Let's try to catch up to the limelight. Maybe we can warm ourselves on the edge."

The edge was in his voice. The normally inseparable pair had been separated. Inga walked with Tolson towards the celebrity table. They were seated nearby. It was the Thanksgiving equivalent of being seated at the children's table. Inga watched with delight as Hoover sat and supped alongside the stars. Tolson sipped and strolled back and forth between the bars. Inga's eyes scanned the crowd in anticipation. Along the wall next to a door a short man in period costume and blackface smiled and winked. Chaplin was directing in plain sight.

The lights dimmed and a small group of support actors began a spoof sketch for the amusement of the cast. Tolson was at the far end of the room having another sullen drink.

Eddie walked around from his position at the table and leaned between Hoover and Lamour. The three stood laughing at some private joke and walked to the door where the short man was standing offering up a tray of drinks. Hoover grabbed one, glanced briefly at the man, then Lamour's hand touched the side of his face and he disappeared down the hall.

Arvad had the last scene in this second act.

Tolson returned to the table with a fresh glass of bourbon. He sat, looked around, then noticed the two empty seats where Hoover and Lamour last performed as starstruck lovers.

"Where'd they go?" Clyde pressed, somewhere between panicked and pissed.

"I'm not sure Clyde. They went through that door and haven't returned." She did innocence proud.

Tolson flew through the door past a little dark man who danced a jig as soon as the door closed. He held his serving tray aloft and walked in Inga's direction, lowering the tray in offering, offering a whisper in her ear.

"Beautifully played my dear. Meet me for lunch tomorrow, same place, same time."

Chaplin walked through the service door. She walked through the front door. Stage left and stage right.

California mornings always seem bright. Some more than others. Inga walked into the Chateau Marmont and straight into to the same maitre d'. Same man, different reaction.

"Why hello my dear. So nice to see you again. Mr. Chaplin is waiting for you. Right this way."

They walked through the dining room to the table by the window. The same table they'd shared before.

"Inga my dear good afternoon. You look lovely as always."

"Charlie did you have trouble removing the blackface, or are those dark circles under your eyes?"

"I'm afraid my dear it was a busy night. I've had no sleep but have never felt more refreshed. Here this is yours."

It was a large manila envelope. She opened it and started flipping through photos. There was Hoover and Lamour *in flagrante delicto.* Enter Tolson. Exit Lamour. A fight, a makeup and two men together in bed.

"You are brilliant, sir. It turned out just as you'd planned."

"Well I'm glad we didn't have to introduce the goat."

"I notice there are no FBI lingering about today. It's the first time in ages I feel like I'm not being followed."

"And that should continue for awhile. We stayed up all night developing those photos. There's film as well but it wasn't necessary to make the point. This morning a similar packet was left for the Director. He had an uneasy breakfast alone. Mr. Tolson joined him then they both packed and left rather hurriedly. His packet contained a note informing him that three copies of these photos existed. One in my hands, one in yours and another in an unnamed third party's possession. There was a simple request to cease and desist or they would be released. If anything happened to either or both of us, they would be released."

"Oh," Chaplin reached inside his jacket and pulled out a single sheet of paper, "Though this is hardly usable as he'd declare it was a forgery, my people inside the hotel found this note which must have been overlooked in a hasty retreat."

He handed the note across the table:

> *Words are mere man-given symbols for thoughts and feelings, and they are grossly insufficient to express the thoughts in my mind and the feelings in my heart that I have for you. I hope I will always have you beside me.*
> *JEH*

"What a romantic apology to poor Clyde," Inga mused, "It seems so simple now I wonder why no one tried something similar before?"

"All traps are not the same my dear. I don't think this would have worked in Washington or New York or even Miami. Hollywood is different. It's all about playing the ego. We made him a Hollywood big shot for a night. In building his ego he felt impervious. In Washington he is impervious but not in this town. This is my town not his. For one moment he was like Cagney in 'White Heat', "Top of the world?".. only he was atop Dorothy Lamour. Then it all blew up. You really should come to my house sometime for the feature length movie. It's all very amusing if you have a strong stomach. Which I do. Now my beautiful cohort let's order lunch."

"Only, my brilliant companion, if it starts with Champagne."

CHAPTER 29

Dearest Inga Binga,

Rec'd your letter at long last today, and while I'm still mad as hell that you didn't answer before, this will keep me for awhile. You still have the knack of making me feel one hundred per cent better after talking with you or hearing from you. You know, I wrote you about a week ago. It was unfortunately written when I was a little under..so disregard it. I've gotten a new boat and am up the line again. We had a small celebration after we had some luck, we got the alcohol out of the torpedoes, but anyways I think that an indignant, incoherent letter to you was the result.

The war here is dirty business. It's very easy to talk about the war and beating the Japs if it takes years and a million men, but any- one who talks like that should consider well his words.

I received a letter today from the wife of my engineer, who was so badly burnt that his face and hands and arms were just flesh, and he was that way for four days. He couldn't swim, and I was able to help him, and his wife thanked me, and in her letter she said, " I suppose to you it was just part of your job, but Mr. McMahon was part of my life and if he had died I don't think I would have wanted to go on living.."

There are so many McMahons that don't come through.

Inga Binga, I'll be glad to see you again. I'm tired now, we are riding every night, and the sleeping is tough in the daytime, but I've been told that they are sending some of us home to form a new squadron in a couple of months. I've had a great time here, everything considered, but I'll be just as glad to get away from it for awhile.

Now that I look back, it has been a hell of a letter. It isn't what I was going to say at all.. I think it's great about your job in Hollywood, this should really be a great chance for you. When I get relieved, I'll come down to L.A. if you are going to be there. Write me when you can.

Much love,

Jack

The command back at Tulagi split the three new gunboats up and deployed them to different operating bases. Jack and *Gunboat Number One* went to the most forward PT base on Vella Lavella. Cluster went up to see the operation and new gunboat in action.

Kennedy and the crew of *No. 1* were back at the dock after their first night patrol when Cluster trotted down the dock.

"Jack get as much fuel in that thing as you can quickly. You need to go back out."

"What's going on?"

"There's a bunch of Marines from the 2nd parachute battalion locked down by Japs on Choiseul. They're surrounded and got nowhere to go but the sea. You need to get up there and help get them out."

"*Gunboat Number One* ready and looking for action. The boys have been looking for a chance to let those guns loose."

"Just get in and get them out. No need to play hero here. You've got that covered already."

Kennedy turned towards his boat and yelled, "Wind 'er up, we're heading back out."

Two boats left Vella Lavella. *PT 236* was fully fueled. *No. 1* had less than half a tank.

The Marines had gone on to Choiseul as a recon and feint to draw Japanese forces away from Bougainville. It worked, to a degree.. the Marine's had attracted a much larger force of Japs who were converging on several flanks and bent on payback for Guadalcanal.

Approaching the shore Kennedy brought his boat down to an idle and listened. There was gunfire coming off the beach. He signalled the crew to ready and gunned the engines in the direction of the fight.

Marines were retreating under heavy fire. Some were trying to hold a position on the beach while others were swimming towards a landing craft a hundred yards offshore that had come to their rescue.

"Covering fire!" Kennedy yelled, "Put everything we've got into that treeline."

He drove the gunboat into a point between the landing craft and the beach. Sixteen guns opened fire. Kennedy's boat spit fire like a Jap's worst dragon dream. *PT 236* came in opposite and added to the salvo. The Marines began to evacuate the beach. Those helping the wounded swam to the closest boat, others swam past to the landing craft. With a dozen Marines added to an already crowded gunboat Kennedy steered towards the landing craft. He was surprised by the officer who hailed him as he came alongside.

"Kennedy!" Keresey stood on the gunwales, "I wondered who was crazy enough to come in with guns blasting. John Wayne's going to want that white hat you're wearing back."

"Dick what the hell are you doing out here on a LC?"

"I came up and scouted the forward base your operating out of. I've been working with the Marines on this operation to get into the Jap's backwaters a bit. These guys we just pulled off the beach blew up one of their supply depots. The also walked away with charts that are far better than what we have. I think we might finally have a chance at stopping some of their supply barges."

"That's what we came for. *Gunboat Number One* at your service. Are there more Marines who need to evac?"

"This is it for now. There are more on another part of the island."

"I've got some wounded on this boat and damned little fuel. We should get the hell out of here."

"With the Skipper's permission I'll come on board with you. We'll get the wounded on the PTs and back to base as fast as we can."

"Let's go."

The crew fed the Marines canned peaches and a bit of torpedo juice. It was a tough ride home. One of the wounded died in Kennedy's bunk. Halfway home the gunboat ran out of gas and was towed back to the base. Cluster was there to meet them.

"Once you've got these guys taken care of and the boat squared away come up to the tent and let's have a look at some of these maps.

When they walked in Cluster had the charts spread across a table studying them. He stood and smiled.

"Gentlemen what we have here is the Jap playbook for their supply runs. HQ is going to love this. Come here and look."

He pointed out the routes and drop points for the supply sorties the enemy had been making for months right under their noses. The Tokyo Express had played a major role in keeping the Japanese troops both manned and able to fight. Stopping the supplies could considerably shorten the fight in the Solomons.

"Sir," Kennedy began in a formal manner, "I've finally got a boat that can do some damage to those barges. I'd like permission for a little payback."

"Jack how long have you been awake?"

"Not sure sir, thirty hours maybe."

"You and your crew go get some rack time. We'll talk about assignments later this afternoon. You'll get your chance."

Jack had his chance. Gunboat One and those skippered by Lennie, Thom and Johnny Iles went out night after night on a duck hunt. Then the ducks became scarce. Losing the maps cost the Japanese dearly. The Marines pulled out of Choiseul under fire again. Their job was done there.. They killed scores of Japanese, blew up hundreds of tons of supplies, burned one supply base and sank two new barges tied to their pier. Between the Navy and Marines the Japanese supply missions were all but stopped and boots were on the ground in Bougainville.

After more than a week of nightly sorties, Cluster called Kennedy to his tent.

"Jack you look like shit."

"Top of the morning to you, too, Skipper," Jack sat slowly in a chair. His back was in constant pain now. It was bad before the collision that sank the *109*. It was much worse now.

"You haven't stopped since the rescue. Now you're going out *every* night on patrol. Don't you think you've proven your point?"

"What point is that, sir?"

"That you can kill as well as be killed. That you've somehow added balance to the stupid scales of war. They killed two of yours and you've now taken your toll on them. The war became personal for you Jack. You've settled the score. It's time for you to go home."

"Sir?"

"Home Jack. Where the pretty girls are. Where stories circulate of the hero Kennedy. Girls love heroes Jack. You shouldn't miss out on that."

"Al, I appreciate what you say. All I'm trying to prove here is that I'm a good Skipper for my crew."

"You are, Jack, one of the best in my command. Your crew would follow you up a one way river surrounded by Japs. But you're worn out, Jack. You need some rest and you need better medical attention than we have here in the jungle. Hell they can't even cure crotch rot here. How are they gonna cure what you've got?"

"How do you know what I got, Al?" He smiled.

"I don't want to know what you got, Kennedy."

Cluster stood.

"Jack you're going to see a doc this afternoon. He's going to recommend a rotation home and a thorough examination."

"The same doctor who cleared me with flying colors two weeks ago?"

"The same."

"Amazing how quickly the medical profession advances."

Jack stood and saluted, then offered his hand.

"Thanks, Al. See you back in the States."

"If you get tired of chasing girls you can always come back. We'll still be fighting Tojo on some damned island ever closer to Tokyo."

CHAPTER 30

Palm Beach, Florida
November, 1943

IF THERE WAS A WAR going on there was little evidence around the Kennedy breakfast table other than the headlines in the newspaper. The headlines served up news on the Tehran Conference. It was the first time the Big Three allied leaders sat to discuss the future of the world if, and *if* was a big word, they were to prevail. Roosevelt, Churchill and Stalin made for an impressive photo. They made for a precarious balance of powers.

The Kennedy table served up items rationed in most American households. There was a full pot of coffee, a heaping sugar bowl, ham and eggs. If it was on the table I wasn't holding back. I'd been eating out of cans for the past few months.

This breakfast was about all I could spare for time and that took some creative arguing with my bosses in New York. They wanted me in Europe. Joe Kennedy meant about as much to them as he did to Roosevelt.

"Roosevelt thinks he can hobble his way into a meeting with Stalin and command the agenda."

I let him talk. He was the former diplomat. These were areas where he was the expert, albeit an expert in exile. I'd been living in and out of a jungle for most of a year. I listened and kept stirring sugar into my coffee.

"Stalin is the only one who's making real gains against Hitler. We're just starting to put points on the board. Britain is done as an empire.

Churchill is lucky to have a place at the table. If Roosevelt lets Stalin walk all over him then the Soviets will end up the winner after this war. If it isn't Hitler."

I had to say something, "I would hope that Roosevelt and Churchill together can manage to protect our mutual interests and the recarving of Europe after the war. The three have to find some common ground. It will take all three together if we're going to get out of the war without learning how to goosestep or eat with chopsticks."

"In the end you are right. The question for all time will be whether the devil we end up with is better than the one we're fighting."

He still clung to his old appeasement ways.

"But I don't want to bore you with an old man's opinions of foreign policy. I want to thank you for the piece you wrote on Jack and his heroism."

"I'm not sure he'd see it that way."

"He's too modest for his own good. That's what I'm here for."

He reached to a side table and picked up a couple of newspapers.

"Here look at these. The New York Times and the Boston Globe both with the same headline: 'Kennedy's Son Is Hero in the Pacific'. I can't tell you how much that means to our family."

"I'm just a writer Mr. Kennedy. Your son is the hero."

"There are thousands of heroes in the war Sam. You made my son a hero in two newspapers that may influence his future."

"How do you mean sir?"

"I won't be subtle with you Sam, it's not my way. I want my sons to enter politics and be successful in a way that I'll never be able to achieve now."

"What is that sir." I asked, anticipating his response.

"The Presidency of the United States."

It was the kind of title that bears pause. I used the pause to refill my coffee cup and was absent mindedly adding sugar.

"Sam, you might leave room in that cup for the coffee."

"Sorry."

"Joe is certainly the more likely candidate. He's tall, handsome, smart and straightforward. Jack is smart certainly, but the boy has been sickly all his life. Though, now Jack's a hero. That's a good start for wherever we campaign him. Now about your article. Would you object if I shopped it around a bit? Maybe we can get *Life* or *Reader's Digest* to pick it up. Then it would be seen by millions of people."

"I certainly have no objection if my newspaper's ok with it. However, if there is a negotiated placement with any payment coming my way, I'd like for that to go to a fund for the families of the two men who were killed on the *109.*"

"You sound like Jack."

"We spent a little time together. Maybe his better qualities wore off on me."

"I hope none of your bad ones wore off on him. The boy can be a little girl crazy."

"Doesn't make him a bad person."

"Let's hope not. Now I know you have a train to catch and a long way to go to get to London. It seems you have a chance to see more of my family than I do."

"It seems the Kennedys are spread pretty far and wide. Perhaps that's your foreign policy."

"That's funny. But they're more my *future* policy. Try to look up Joe if you can maybe do one of your profile pieces on him. I think he feels like he's taking a backseat to his younger brother. You know he's flown his missions. He's eligible to come home. I think he's taking a risk by asking for more missions trying to prove something."

"A wise person once said, "War is not a competition.""

"That's pretty smart. Who said that?"

"My girlfriend."

"The one in London?"

"The only one at the moment. How'd you know?"

"As you say we Kennedys are all over. Please give Kathleen my love if you see her. Unfortunately her marriage did not please her Mother. It's created a bit of a rift."

"So I've heard. It seems she's not the first Kennedy to fall in love without parental approval."

"Indeed, Mr. Marlow. Have a safe trip."

Beverly Hills
January, 1944

Her apartment was a sign of her ascendance. It looked down on Los Angeles. Inga's column continued to grow in readership and influence. She was no longer the outsider. She was as inside Hollywood as you could get. Inga was not the same woman she was just a few months ago. Neither was Jack.

She stood at the window and looked at the lights below. A cab was winding it's way up the Hill on a serpentine path, back and forth like their relationship, this time to a final destination. It stopped outside her door. The bell tolled.

"Lieutenant Kennedy welcome home," Inga greeted him with a kiss on the cheek.

"Inga Binga. You've certainly kept this sailor awake many a midnight watch. You're as beautiful as ever."

She stood back and held him at arm's length.

"Sailor you look a few pounds shy of fighting weight. I guess you weren't fed a steady diet of steak, mashed potatoes, peas, carrots and ice cream."

It was a polite description. He looked skeletal, skin the color of saffron and he walked with the gait of an old man.

"I don't think food like that exists in the South Pacific except on the menu in the Admiral's mess. As for fighting weight we fight lean in the Navy. We love lean, too."

He took her by her fingertips , their hands entwined as he pulled her close. The doorbell rang. Inga bolted for the door.

"Jack, this is Bill Cahan. He's a doctor in the Navy. He's working on a film here. It's called *Winged Victory*. I thought I'd invite my two favorite sailors to dinner."

Kennedy looked from Inga to Bill. He walked over and extended his hand a sad smile on his face.

"Good to see another sailor. I've been away from them for so long. So you're here on the frontline in Hollywood? I hear it's a pretty ruthless town." Jack's smile turned to a smirk.

"Gentlemen, care for a drink?" Inga offered. When awkward arrives rally the booze.

"I've grown rather fond of torpedo juice as you could tell from some of my letters. Lacking that any Haig & Haig would be fine."

"Bill?"

"Martini please."

Kennedy could have won a best acting award that night if one was handed out for concealed emotions. Through cocktails, dinner and dessert he carried the conversation with stories of Harvard football, foreign policy and the antics of life on PT boats. When the topic of his heroism arose, he dismissed it. The dishes were cleared and Inga returned to deafening silence.. It was clear that one of the men would have to leave. Jack made the first move.

"Well I suppose I should be off," He said, awkwardly. "I need to make arrangements to go to Palm Beach. Believe I'm going to take up residence by the pool for awhile."

"Let me walk you to the door." Inga said.

They left Cahan at the table and walked outside into the cool evening air.

"Well that wasn't quite what I expected."

"I know it wasn't Jack. It wasn't what I really wanted either. A year ago I would have been your war bride waiting and hoping for your return. But your father stopped all that. When you left the last time I knew that I could never have you. Between the war and Big Joe you were as good as dead to me. So I moved here. It broke my heart. You can survive in Hollywood without one."

"So is this where the broken hearted hero walks away into the night?"

"Do come see me tomorrow. We need to talk. It's important."

Daylight meetings are a more controlled environment. They doesn't require candles or cocktails. It is conducted largely in an upright position. They are generally less, emotive. Heartbreak and passion tend to be creatures of the night. She was straightening magazines and pillows for the eleventh time when Jack arrived.

"Lieutenant Kennedy reporting as ordered ma'am."

"At ease lieutenant. Come in."

She led him into a living room that was decorated like an art deco Hollywood set. Some sweet fellow made a bundle off her. The furniture was angles and inlays, colors and clean edges. All that was missing was a comfortable place to sit.

"I didn't bring it up in front of your doctor friend last night. I kept looking around your apartment wondering where your friend Hoover has hidden his listening devices."

"Have a seat Jack, that's what we're here to talk about and this time you can be assured he's not listening."

They sat on a pillow perfect couch. On the coffee table were recent issues of Life and Look magazines and a manilla envelope which Inga picked up.

"Jack, while you were gone I had to face some realities. One was the fact that you were gone and I had to accept that. The other was that Hoover had me in his grip and was never going to let go. He was pressing me to work for him and become part of his network of blackmailers and manipulators. I could no more do that than be a German spy. So I had to do something."

"You? Had to do something to stop J. Edgar Hoover. What was that?" She handed him the envelope.

He looked at the photos one by one then put them back in the folder.

"You. Have blackmailed the nation's Blackmailer-in-Chief."

"I suppose I have but started it."

"How did you get these. Were the.. were the.. "

"Germans involved? No, but that hurts Jack. I'm not sure Himmler could even have pulled this off?

"Then whom?"

"You'll never know. But you have to trust me that he is an American who was threatened by Hoover, too."

"If you won't trust me with *whom*, then why tell me?"

"Remember so long ago when we were in love and together in Charleston? When you were honest and open with me and shared your dreams? I believed them. I believe in you. I believe some day you'll be the President of the United States."

She paused. The calculated control in daylight thing wasn't working too well.

"There are three other copies of these photos. This one is for you. Take it with you today and put it someplace safe so that when that time comes in a few years when Hoover tries to bully you, as he did me, you will have something to stop him," Inga touched his hand.

Kennedy raised and kissed her fingers, "You know, in Hoover you have made a powerful enemy. In me someday, perhaps, you will have a powerful friend. Wow. A war and a few months have changed us. I go off, get a couple of my crew killed, save the rest and come back a scraggly assed hero. You alone put together a plan to outwit J. Edgar Hoover."

He stood gently taking her hands and looked into her eyes. Tears were forming barely held on the tips of long lashes.

"Inga Binga," he held her close and took a deep breath, "We could have been perfect together. There will never be a woman the measure of you."

She looked up knowing it would be the last time she saw him so she abandoned her self discipline and kissed him gently.

A week later Jack was sunning by the pool in Palm Beach. His father walked out with a cup of coffee in one hand and a newspaper in the other.

"I thought you were through with that Arvad woman."

"We are. Through, that is."

Joe dropped a newspaper in his lap. It was *The Boston Globe.* Jack's picture was on the front page. Below and smaller were photos of Churchill and Eisenhower. He got the headline:

TELLS STORY OF PT EPIC:
KENNEDY LAUDS MEN, DISDAINS HERO STUFF.
Exclusive Interview by Inga Arvad.

His father said, "I guess she finally gave you something better than a blow job," and walked away.

Jack scanned through the article. She was a better writer than she was a year ago. He remembered some of her questions as they were in bed that afternoon. She'd taken pillow talk and spun an exclusive that made its way to papers across the country.

"That Inga Binga, he thought, she just keeps on giving," he said to the empty chairs around the pool.

CHAPTER 31

Spring/Summer, 1944

London
Sam Marlow/New York Herald Tribune

England is an occupied country and they're pretty happy about it. The Yanks are here in force like an invading army. But the Brits know their island is just a stopover. The real invasion is coming and coming soon.

In the countryside outside London the daily business of war continues with the regular schedule of a well run factory. The planes go up, they drop their bombs and most come back. It goes on around the clock. The Americans run most of the daylight missions because our Nordon bombsights are more accurate for precision bombing. The Brits bomb at night. They call it 'area bombing' because whatever they hit is the target. Some decry the civilian casualties of the night attacks but British Air Marshal Arthur 'Bomber' Harris says, "The Germans sewed the wind, now they will reap the whirlwind." For the Germans it's the Apocalypse, delivered daily.

You wouldn't know the horror of war by spending time with the bomber crews on the ground. I visited with the 579th Bomb Squadron in Norfolk.

It's as bucolic a setting as you could imagine, a picture perfect English countryside where the runways and ramps of B-24s are surrounded by farms and grazing cows. The boys like it here. The folks in a tiny village of Beeston (pop.400) like them here. When the crews get leave they hop on their bicycles and ride into town. The local pub does good business. If you think the only attraction is dark English beer. It's not. Fifteen fellows from the squadron have already married local girls. That's how allies are made.

Crews live in Nissen huts, eight men to a hut, two pilots and two co-pilots from two crews. The floors are concrete and the huts are drafty. In the center is a coal burning stove that sees active duty. But there were no complaints. The men know they are living in a palace compared to the infantry who sleeps on the cold ground in a pup tent.. if they are that lucky.

The B-24 is a modern marvel. It can fly faster, further and higher than any other bomber. Crews have a love-hate relationship with their aircraft. If you're flying a B-24 you can call it a 'Flying Boxcar' because of her slab-sided fuselage and heavier payload. But only her crews can call her that. Anyone else making fun of the B-24 will probably end up in a fight.

Crews are flying more missions deeper into Germany. They now have P-51 fighters to fly escort all the way there and back. What's left of the Luftwaffe is finding it tougher to pick off our bombers. That makes the boys happy. That makes a lot of wives and mothers a lot happier.

Covering the war in London is a far different affair from the South Pacific. You sleep in a bed. Your clothes are not soaked by either rain or sweat. The food is better. The most serious challenge is making sure you get to the mess in time for an early round of rationed whiskey before dinner. And it's nice to see women again.

American officers in London had a choice of places to eat. The largest by far was a place called 'Willow Run' in Grosvenor House in the West End. It was thought to be the largest officer's mess in the world. Transients from different theaters were often there but it was also where you could run across almost anyone from any unit serving in England. They required proper dress. They allowed war correspondents and they welcomed anyone with a USO headliner on their arm. In this town Ashley far outranked me. With her we could have dined at the 'Old Men's Club' where major was the entry level rank. It was populated with colonels and generals with big bellies and war ribbons from the last war with Germany. They were not the people I wanted to talk to about the war. The closest they'd come to it was in a bunker during an air raid. I was hunting the lower ranks, like lieutenants named Kennedy.

The most dangerous place to be in London was at the front of the scrum when the bar opened. It was a cheap ploy but with a woman on my arm we navigated our way easily to the front and collected our ration. Whiskey was in short supply in Britain. The mess managed the demand by opening the bar for fifteen minutes then hanging a sign politely stating "all out". The crowd would wander on to dinner then the bar would reopen for the second seating.

We were carefully cradling our cocktails on the way to a table when we saw a small group of men in navy uniforms. One of them was Joe Kennedy, Junior.

He was a Kennedy, alright. With the eyes and toothy smile. But there was much more to him than his younger brother, in height, in weight and in presence. I had never spoken with the man. There seemed to be substance. Compared to the elder brother, Jack was a skinny kid. In politics image can mean everything. Perhaps Joe Senior had a point. We steered in his direction.

"Lieutenant Kennedy," I offered, "I'm Sam Marlow with the New York Herald Tribune.

"Ah, Mr. Marlow," he offered a half smile, "The same who gave such great ink to my brother's heroics?"

"I spent time with your brother in the South Pacific now I'm covering this war. It's a very different war. I was out with a B-24 squadron yesterday. I believe you fly the same plane on your missions."

"Yes really good planes only I'll still take carrier duty with a fighter. Things happen there. You don't fly 1700 hours and see nothing. You don't make 29 trips, 10 to 12 hours each, and see nothing. Yeah I've made 29. The next one is my 30th. You know what happens after you've made your 30th? You go out on your 31st. But not me, not this time. The next mission is going to be a little different. Let's talk in a couple of days. Maybe I'll have an exclusive for you as interesting as my brother's. A pleasure meeting you Mr. Marlow. Now if you'll excuse us I believe we're off to dinner."

He must have been standing with his crew. After a few dozen missions they develop a sixth sense for each other and they clearly read his intent to move on. I watched them walk away in unison and turned to Ashley.

"My! Is it just London or does it seem chilly in here?" she mocked.

"Seems that mighty Joe Junior has a chip on his shoulder. His father asked me to look him up, so I did. Though his father also seemed concerned that young Joe might try something foolish to one-up his brother. I feel something foolish coming on."

"So do I but it doesn't have anything to do with Junior."

Dinner at "Willow Run" was probably better than most in London had eaten in some years, American pork chops, mashed potatoes and local vegetables that the farmers probably sold to army purveyors at a solid profit. But it wasn't worth lingering over. A private room with clean sheets on a soft bed is where time is better spent.

We stood looking out the window at the darkened city. Thanks to her endless sources we sipped a nice claret and listened to the bombers flying outbound on their night missions.

"Oddly romantic isn't it," Ashley mused, "We drink wine and make love in a nice hotel and those bombers go out to face flak and fighters to drop bombs on German cities."

"Love and war," It's a writer's theme for the ages he thought, "In the face of death, sex is the affirmation of life. To love is to live."

"I hope you don't use that eloquent phrase as a pickup line in all your war zones," she smiled.

"Don't you worry. This is my first war zone with women. How'm I doing?"

"I feel a need to offer you affirmation."

"Does that mean what I think?"

"You lucky writer boy."

The other good thing about being a war correspondent in London was room service for breakfast. When you've awakened in the jungle for months on end with spam as the best you could hope for the simple elegance of an egg, toast and coffee with the morning papers across the table from a mussed and beautiful mistress requires a pinch just to make sure you really didn't die in some other warzone the night before.

Headlines were all about the bombing of Berlin. The Eighth Air Force was dropping the first American bombs on the heart of the Third Reich. When the Germans bombed civilian targets in Britain the strategy was to destroy the English will to fight. The Eighth Air Force and the RAF were bombing to destroy the German's industrial capacity to sustain a war. One plan didn't work the other was showing signs of success.

Every paper in every city on several continents now contained an extended obit page to include locals killed in the war. I had neither kith nor kin in England but always scanned the notices for the footnotes of lives in passing.

"Holy Shit!" I pulled the paper closer to my face.

"What Sam?"

"Tommy Hitchcock was killed."

"Oh my god... that's two from the Aiken weekend to be killed. First George Mead, now Tommy. It seems so long ago."

"*U.S. Ambassador John Winant regrets to inform,* the death notice continued, '*famed World War One pilot and hero killed during a test flight of a P-51 near Salisbury, Wiltshire... Hitchcock was an assistant air attache to the Embassy... instrumental in bringing the long range fighter into combat.. greatest polo player to come out of the Colonies.. all England thankful for the sacrifices of Mr. Hitchcock to preserve Britannia during two World Wars..*"

I dropped the paper on the table, "That just caps it."

"How so?"

"You can survive being shot out of the sky flying a plane made out of canvas and wood, walk across half of Europe to escape the Germans, live a whole and storied life playing the most dangerous game in the world..only to die in a test flight."

"Don't expect me to throw in some half witted euphemism that would include any of combination of: life, fate, war, man, woman, birth, death or infinity."

"That might be why I love you. I got rid of my last girlfriend for using half witted euphemisms."

"I'll keep that in mind.. only time will tell... about this relationship."

"If we're lucky to be alive.."

"Truce."

"Tommy though, damn. I hope he gets credit for what he did on the P-51. That plane is going to save a lot of bomber crews and allow them to strike deeper into Germany. Funny how one man's efforts can have such a large impact on the war."

"You keep tempting me with that kind of talk and I'm going to come back at you with fate or destiny."

"Why don't you come at me with a cocktail. I think Tommy needs toasting. It's almost noon, surely we can get a drink somewhere."

"Actually I have the perfect place."

"Where?"

"At Devonshire House with the Marchioness of Hartington."

"With whom?"

"Kick. Hurry and get dressed. She's sending a car in a half hour."

Kathleen Cavendish, the Marchioness of Hartington, the former Kick Kennedy and forever sister to Jack, greeted us at the door. Fancy title, same Kick. She seemed to stir, attract and command as large a social circle as she had in Washington. It was just a few notches higher. Apparently in such circles lunch is an occasion. We were introduced to Lord 'Such' and Sir 'That'. My only real connection to them was a desire for an early afternoon cocktail. So we stood and sipped and chatted and when asked about my title I mentioned a book I'd written once... and they all guffawed over that.

Ashley was circulating with Kick. William, Kick's husband, was off with his troops. His command was in the oldest regiment of the British Army. That goes back a ways.

Kick left one conversation and walked over to me.

"Oh Sam, Ashley told me you'd read about Tommy. We heard last night. The Ambassador called to tell me."

"Was he calling the daugher of the former Ambassador or the Marchioness of Hartington? Congratulations by the way."

"Thank you. Pity it was no cause for celebration at home. I hear you saw Father. Was he well?"

"He seemed so. Was quite interested in promoting Jack as a hero. And worried your older brother might do something foolish to become one."

"That's one concern we share."

"Have you heard from Jack?"

"Got one of his usual letters. He's been in and out of hospitals trying to mend his back. Except for the nurses, he's not too happy with the whole process, claims if the Japs didn't kill him the doctors might. I heard he's out and heading to Hyannis Port to recuperate though not sure how much rest he'll get since Father will be there, too. Now it's time for lunch. I'm going to keep your Ashley for support and throw you to the men. There are a few American generals and a smattering of colonels. Maybe you can find a story or something."

So it became a working lunch for me. For the generals I'm not sure how much the war effort was furthered by a two hour lunch. Though they were aware of my work from the South Pacific and ever aware that good press brings good backing from the politicians back home.

When lunch was finished I went back to the hotel. I needed a nap. This war correspondent business can be exhausting.

It was past mid-afternoon when I awoke. You could tell without looking at a watch because the American bombers were returning from their day raids over Germany. In a few hours the Brits would be heading out. They ran like clockwork.

I threw some water on my face and was thinking how the notion of afternoon tea was a point of brilliance that had kept this Empire in balance. There was a knock on the door. Thinking it was Ashley, I quickly put on a tie, then loosened the knot and rolled up my sleeves to give the impression I'd been hard at work. It was a weak defense against being caught napping in the afternoon. Ashley was not the one knocking.

"Mr. Marlow?" Inquired a major wearing the badge of the Eighth Air Force.

"Yes Major."

"May I come in?".

That seemed a bit odd, "Of course I was expecting.. well, nevermind."

He walked in the room and looked around.

"You war correspondents do pretty well." He observed.

"Well Major, since you seem interested... in the spirit of the war effort I'm sharing this room," I looked in the direction of his gaze to a nightgown that Ashley had left draped across a chair.

"Indeed, sir."

"How may I help you, Major."

"I'm here at the request of General Doolittle."

"Really."

"Yes, sir. You had lunch today with Brigadier General Thompson."

"Of course. We had a pleasant conversation."

"He thought the same and spoke with General Doolittle about an invitation."

"To another lunch? I'll have to check my social schedule... very busy what with the Lords and Earls and such that I've been meeting."

"No, Mr. Marlow, an invitation to a top secret mission."

"Please Major, sit down. My apologies for sounding a bit flip."

It was a short conversation. The Major gave few details other than to say the mission was important, top secret and dangerous. I would only be able to write about it if it was successful and that would have to be cleared by Doolittle himself.

"A car will pick you up at 0500 hours. Are you interested, Mr. Marlow?"

"Of course and thank the generals. Where will I be going?"

"You'll find that out in the morning."

The car and the early morning sun arrived with military precision. Daylight comes early during English summers. We headed north out of London. It was a rural setting that made me want to return after the war. I had the notion that if I stopped the car and walked across a pasture and into a barn where the morning milking was underway, it would be difficult to believe that just nearby mighty armies were preparing for the greatest invasion known to man.

Some of the surroundings looked familiar and I knew we were somewhere in Norfolk. The car pulled into an air base. The sign read RAF Fersfield. We stopped outside a briefing hut on the edge of a long runway.

"End of the line, sir," the driver turned around to face me. They were the first words he'd spoken since he picked me up.

"There are people inside expecting you."

"Thank you. I'd tip you but imagine that's frowned upon."

"No tip, sir, but you can buy me a pint at that fancy hotel if I drive you back."

There was something I didn't like about the way he said 'if'.

When you walk into a military situation your eyes naturally go first to the top rank.

At the front of a briefing was General Thompson whom I recognized from our lunch, beside him was his major and then there was a tough looking, short man who had three stars on his shoulder.

"Mr. Marlow, good morning," Lieutenant General Jimmy Doolittle motioned me over and stuck out his hand.

He leaned over and whispered, "Nimitz said you're ok. That makes you ok with me."

The room paused when he spoke, "Carry on people. We have a mission this morning."

The briefing continued. I leaned against the wall and looked at the crews seated in front of the maps. On the front row was a familiar face. Lieutenant Joe Kennedy was the lead pilot. He nodded and turned his eyes back to the maps.

It was not a normal mission. I'd sat in on regular bombing briefings. They were pretty standard; setting out rendezvous points for the flight groups, altitude, fighter escorts, targets and any intel on enemy threat or defense available. This mission involved five planes. They were using words like 'drone', 'remote control' and 'mother planes'.

The one word that stood out to me was the target: *Mimoyecques.* It was an underground German fortress in the north of France where Hitler was launching missiles at London. No attack against *Mimoyecques* had been successful.

"That's about it gentlemen any questions?" The Major was leading the briefing.

From the back of the room,"If we hit the target, who buys the beer?" That brought a laugh.

Doolittle stepped forward, "Gentlemen if you hit the target you're drinking on my tab at the best hotel in London. Good luck out there. I'll see you all back here for a de-brief this afternoon."

At least he was positive about it.

As the crews walked out, Kennedy stopped for a second.

"Sam this is the mission I was hinting about. I'll give you the exclusive when we're back in London tonight having cocktails."

"Seems like it'll be a pretty exciting story."

"Knocking out Hitler's missile base? I think that's a little better than getting run over by a Jap destroyer." He walked out with a confident grin on his face.

A colonel followed Kennedy, "Mr. Marlow I believe you'll be flying with me today. I'm Elliott Roosevelt."

I put on my best poker face and still lost the bluff.

"Yes the President's son," Roosevelt smiled. "We'll see you out at the flight line."

He left me before I could come up with a smart reply. Doolittle was watching from the sidelines with an amused look on his face.

"Little confused Mr. Marlow?"

"Big and dumb would be closer General."

"Walk with me to the flight line. There's a lot we couldn't tell you earlier and parts of the briefing we couldn't let you in on. Let me tell you what I can tell you while we get you some flight gear."

The mission was called Operation Aphrodite. The goal was to deliver a shit-load (official military term) of explosives on the hardened fortress. Kennedy and his co-pilot would fly a *B-24* stripped of all non-essential gear and loaded with over ten tons of the British high explosive Torpex. When Kennedy's plane was aloft he and the co-pilot would engage an electronic autopilot that was controlled by two motherships then parachute out. The motherships and a navigation plane would direct the flying bomb to *Mimoyecques*. A British *Mosquito* would serve as a chase plane carrying Colonel Roosevelt who was to film the whole event.

"Sound like fun. Is this the first attempt?"

"We've had a few trials.. and problems. But we think we have all the kinks worked out now. All these high risk runs are for volunteers only and these guys volunteered. You don't think I'm going to send the President's son and an Ambassador's son up along with one of the country's most highly read war correspondents up on a suicide mission do you?"

That was coming from a man who had a Medal of Honor tucked away somewhere for flying the most daring raid yet in the war. Some called his raid on Tokyo a suicide mission.

"Ahhh, no sir. I guess not."

"Well suit up son. You'll either be reporting history or become part of it."

"That's a good way to look at it sir, though I do intend to join the crew and do damage to your tab tonight."

"I'll be at your elbow at the bar. See you in a few hours." He said, slapping me on the shoulder as I left.

I pulled on a pair of flight boots, jacket, life preserver, earphones and parachute and walked over to the plane. One of the boys boosted me up through a hatch in the bottom. The engines started. Vibrations and noise filled the plane. I went forward to the cockpit. Roosevelt was set in the co-pilots seat with a camera. There was just enough room behind the seats for me to wedge a small box to sit on so I wouldn't bounce around.

We were last in line for take off. The first to take off were the two Lockheed Ventura mother planes, then the navigation plane. Kennedy's *B-24* was next. It was starting down the runway when our pilot came on the headsets.

"Watch this. They've got more than twice the normal payload on that boxcar. This runway's over a mile long and it'll use every inch. Dollar says the wheels clip the tops of those trees at the end of the field."

"You're on," came Roosevelt.

The *Mosquito* pilot revved the engines and sat on the brake. And sat. The big rolling bomb was three quarters down the runway and still on the ground. We started rolling and were in the air before we hit halfway and as the *B-24* slowly climbed from the last feet of tarmac.

"Oh Jesus, Oh Jesus.. get up boys," I'm not sure if I said it or if it was on the headphones.

The treeline was coming up quickly.

"Come on, come on.."

Kennedy cleared the treeline. His wheels didn't. They clipped the top branches as he pulled it into the sky.

"Yahoo," yelled the pilot.

Roosevelt stuffed a dollar in the pilot's top pocket and grabbed a pack of cigarettes.

"Damn. Smoke 'em if you got 'em boys.." and Roosevelt handed out the pilots cigarettes.

We all lit up. Elliott was filming as we flew. Good thing he didn't have a sound recorder. The five planes banked and turned towards the south setting a course towards the Channel and France. The pilot was giving a running aerial tour of the landscape below.

"Whoa. There she goes," he sounded excited. The *B-24* was starting a slow turn inland.

"That's her first radio controlled turn. We're only a few minutes from the crew bail-out now."

"Let's get up a little closer," Roosevelt pressed, "I want to get a good shot of them jumping."

We pulled in tighter on their tail and a little higher so there'd be no chance of catching their chutes. At 300 feet the bomber looked huge.

"Ok, any minute now we should see them climbing out of the cockpit."

A white flash filled the sky.

"Holy sh.."

The impact hit us before the phrase was out of his mouth. The *Mosquito* was lifted up by the explosion. I went from looking forward to looking straight up. The little plane was practically standing on her tail and flying through what had been Joe Kennedy's plane. Flaming debris punched holes in our wooden fuselage. The pilot was struggling for control. If he couldn't get the nose down we would stall. Roosevelt was helping to level the *Mosquito*. I tasted blood in my mouth and wished I'd asked a few more questions about how to parachute from a crashing airplane.

"Anybody hit?" Roosevelt called over the headset.

"Got a scratch on my arm," the pilot said.

He was being modest, that was where the blood came from on my face. The metal box I was sitting on was the medic kit. I pulled out some bandages and patched his arm as best I could while he continued flying. Roosevelt put his hands on the co-pilot controls to assist.

"Marlow hate to yell at you like crew, but go back and see if any of that debris started any fires. These wooden planes just love to torch off."

That reassured me. I grabbed a fire extinguisher and headed aft. There were a couple hot spots that looked like they might flame up with the extra air flowing through the plane. The chunks of metal had been parts of Kennedy's plane. I doused them and went back forward.

Four planes made a slow circle over an area where debris was burning on the ground. There would be no remains.

Hyannis Port

A broad drive winds gracefully to the summer home of Joe Kennedy in Hyannis Port. A black sedan stopped by the green lawn in front. Two priests stepped out. They carried a telegram. Both knew the Ambassador, the house and knew that the surrounding porches and lawns were places where the family found happiness. Their feet were heavy on the steps. The knock light on the door.

"Good afternoon gentlemen," a housekeeper answered the door.

"We'd like to see Ambassador Kennedy, please."

"He's retired for an afternoon nap."

"Would you please wake him. We'll wait on the porch."

They walked down the length and turned the corner to look out over the ocean. A thin young man was stretched out on a chaise lounge reading a book. He looked up and saw the men and the envelope.

"Father Patrick, Father O'Connor. Why are you here."

"We need to talk to your father, Jack."

Footsteps were coming. They were slow and measured. Joseph Kennedy Senior turned the corner and saw the priests. The yellow telegram stood out against their black garments. The older of the two stepped forward.

"Joe, could we talk for a moment alone?"

"Father Patrick whatever you have to tell me you can share in front of Jack. He's familiar with death. There's no need to shelter anyone on this porch."

"The Secretary of the Navy asked us to bring you this with his sincere regrets."

The priest's eyes wend down. He handed the former Ambassador the telegram no father wanted to receive. Kennedy reached out with a hand that rarely trembled.

> *The Navy Department deeply regrets to inform you that your son Lieutenant Joseph P. Kennedy, Jr. was killed in action in the performance of his duty and in the service of his country. The Department extends to you its sincerest sympathy in your great loss. Although I cannot divulge the specifics related to his mission he is to be awarded the Navy Cross:*
>
> *For extraordinary heroism and courage in aerial flight as pilot of a United States Liberator bomber. Well knowing the extreme dangers involved and totally unconcerned for his own safety, Kennedy unhesitatingly volunteered to conduct an exceptionally hazardous and special operational mission. Intrepid and daring in his tactics and with unwavering confidence in the vital importance of his task, he willingly risked his life in the supreme measure of service and, by his great personal valor and fortitude in carrying out a perilous undertaking, sustained and enhanced the finest traditions of the United States Naval Service.*
>
> *James Forrestal*
>
> *Secretary of the Navy*

The elder Kennedy leaned against the railing of the porch. It was the only sign of the staggering blow delivered by the telegram in his hand.

"Jack I'm going to go and tell you Mother. Father Patrick, she may want to spend some time with the two of you. We must be brave. It's what he would have wanted."

Then he looked directly at Jack, "He died trying to be a hero. You lived and became one. Now it's up to you."

He walked slowly back down the porch into the house and into days of seclusion.

For years Joe Kennedy spent money to attract major newspapers to print positive stories. Even at the height of his grief he made sure they got the story of a second Kennedy hero.

The Boston Globe: August 14. "Ex-Envoy Kennedy, Crushed by Son's Death, Remains in Seclusion. " 'What can I say?' the father szaid tonight. 'We received word yesterday. All my younger children are here.' "From the time the family received the Navy telegram, the ex-Ambassador has kept to his room. His grief is deep. He hasn't learned yet details of how the oldest of his nine children --the first son-- died."

August 15. "Countless messages of sympathy from national leaders were arriving.. as the nation shared his grief in the loss of his oldest son. It is now known that Lieutenant Joseph Kennedy had volunteered for a secret flying mission, had completed some 50 combat missions and had twice refused leave home under the rotation plan after completing his first 30 missions."

August 16. "Kathleen Kennedy, last of her family to see Lt. Joe Kennedy Jr. before he died at his Navy plane controls on Saturday, arrived here from London by plane yesterday to join her family--her first visit since her marriage in May

> **to Lord Hartington... She ran up the ramp alone,**
> **to be greeted by her brother, Lt. John F. Kennedy,**
> **holder of the Navy and Marine Corps Medal for her-**
> **oism aboard a PT boat in the Southwest Pacific."**

Boston, Massachusetts

"Hello Kick," Jack called to his sister.

She saw him and ran ahead into his arms. For a moment they stood still as she wept quietly in a way that most would hardly notice, then she stood back and smiled.

"Hello handsome. How are things on the homefront?"

"You'll feel quite at home, positively British. Keep Calm, Carry On--keeping up the Kennedy tradition. The Old Man insisted I invite some of the old crew for the weekend. The sailing regatta must go on. I believe the only sign of solemnity is a one drink ration before dinner."

"Say it isn't so..how else are we to get through our mock normalcy?"

Ashley and I came up the ramp to join them.

"Hello you two," Jack shook my hand and gave Ashley a lingering hug.

If possible he looked worse than he did in the Pacific. He couldn't have weighed more than a hundred and twenty five pounds. His skin showed the yellowed signs of malaria.

"Hal heard you pulled a few strings to get Kick home so fast," Jack said.

"General Doolittle helped. He felt bad about losing your brother," I added, adding little comfort.

"Later tonight I'd like to hear the whole story. I'm glad you made it through."

Jack was not exaggerating the forced normalcy of the family. Dinner was served with a polite single cocktail before and polite conversation during which ranged across all topics except the largest one on everyone's mind. The only apparent acknowledgement of the loss of his first son was an empty place at the dinner table. It was set waiting as if Joe Junior would soon join the table. When the last dishes were cleared Joe retired to his room and Rose to hers.

"Let's go downstairs to the wine room," Jack whispered to willing conspirators.

There was little of either the Palm Beach or Hyannis Port homes that didn't speak of taste and money. The wine room was no different. It was comfortable and well stocked.

Kennedy pulled out a bottle of Champagne, "I'm not overly fond of this stuff. Joe merits a proper toast."

We did. Then pulled out a bottle of bordeaux as a more suitable fit for the conversation that followed.

"Tell me about his last flight," Jack asked.

I ran through the whole day to the burning debris on the ground and our tricky landing with a shot up plane.

"Sounds like you just barely walked away from that one yourself."

"Well it's not like getting rammed by a Jap destroyer."

"You might want to be a bit more careful Sam.. I don't think they give journalists any medals."

"Listen to the lieutenant there writer boy," Ashley added, "We need to keep this shrinking circle intact."

"Tell me Sam," Kennedy returned to the subject, "How did he look in your last conversation?"

"Look? He looked like he was about to take a walk in the park."

"That's Joe. He knew he had it nailed. One way or another he was coming home a hero."

There was a noise behind us on the stairs.

"Hello.. who's there," Kick called.

Young Bobby walked into the room. He was enrolled in a midshipman's course at Harvard and wearing a uniform that made him look like a little boy in a sailor's suit.

"You know Father would be pretty upset if he knew you were down here drinking wine. His order was one cocktail."

"And how would he know?" Jack asked with little humor.

Kick stood up, "Bobby, can we have a word?"

They walked out. She returned in less than a minute.

"Quick fix, Kick?" Jack asked.

"I told him if he said a word he would never visit me in my castle."

"Nicely done."

We picked up our conversation catching up on all the adventures and loses. There was a toast to George Mead and one for Tommy Hitchcock. There was another to Kick and her titled husband. Then one to love in general.

"You know Sam," Kick started, "Ashley was at my wedding."

"So I heard."

"She caught my bouquet."

"That I had not heard."

"Seems you might want to do the honorable thing," Kick was taking this to the limit.

"Well Kick it seems if I remember my basic classes in honor, doing the honorable thing is what a gentleman does when he finds his girlfriend pregnant," when the word came out of my mouth, I shut it.

"No, I'm not," Ashley added to my relief.

"Well Sam," Kennedy stood, "As a decorated hero of this war I'd say let's not let honor get in the way of good sex. I'll see myself off to bed, alone."

We all started up the stairs. Ashley and I continued to our billets on the second floor. As a matter of propriety Rose had assigned us separate rooms. We were holding each other between clean, crisp sheets listening to the sound of the ocean.

"I hope Kick's little joke didn't make you feel pressured," she whispered.

"No. It's not something I haven't thought about."

"Feel free to share those feelings at any point."

"This war is a bit inconvenient."

"More so for some than others."

"But it's coming to a close in Europe. I need to get back soon. There will be a race to get to Berlin and I need to be able to write the final chapters. It won't be long and then maybe your Father and I can have a little discussion on the veranda."

"Oh he's been waiting some time for someone foolish enough to show up for that talk."

"And I can assure you I'm just that fool."

The next night while Jack and I were standing on the porch after dinner Joe came around the corner.

"Sam, I hear you're leaving tomorrow."

"Yes, sir. Someone told me there's still a war going on over there and I should go cover it."

"Orders from the boss, eh?" Kennedy quipped.

"Otherwise I'd be happy to sit on this porch for a while.. like a few years."

"You're welcome here or in Palm Beach anytime you like. You've been good to this family. You made Jack a hero. Go back to your war if you must but come home soon. You're an honest man unlike so many of the newspaper people on my payroll. I think Jack could use the support of an honest man when this war is over."

CHAPTER 32

Charleston, S.C.
May, 1945

A ZALEAS IN SPRING BRING A heartbreaking beauty to Charleston. They color the streets in celebration for a victory in Europe, for love and survival.

A white MG TB comes fast around the corner, downshifting into the turn and accelerating before it straightens and heads south. A few people scurry to the safety of the curb. A thin young man wearing a morning coat throws a salute to a pedestrian he barely misses. I knew his tricks by now and stepped back from the curb just in time. Jack parked and climbed slowly out of the car.

"Maybe you should give up the low slung sports cars and try a sedan," I offered..

"Just because I have the body of an old man doesn't mean I've got to look like one. I need to look sexy for the bridesmaids. Ashley did a superb job selecting them."

"She said it was the only way I could get you back down here to be in the wedding."

"I hope in future years you don't regret marrying a woman who's smarter than you are."

"And I hope in future years you find one smart enough to manage you."

"I did once. She's gone. That's why I'm interviewing new candidates."
My hand went to pull a cigarette out of my case. It trembled slightly.
"Nervous, old man?" Kennedy seemed to be enjoying this.

"Haven't had a lot of practice."

"Well even a man facing execution gets a last cigarette."

The pipe organ started inside the church. The sound was clear across the street. So was the message.

"Time to face the music," Kennedy slapped me on the back.

I remember battles where I had fewer butterflies. All of the courage I'd either shown or faked over the past three years seemed to disappear. I trembled at Ashley's beauty. I managed my vows. I don't know how. We were Man and Wife. I kissed her like a school boy, a timid first embrace in an inappropriate place. The bells began to chime, as they have tolled for two centuries to mark both hardship and happiness in this historic town.

"They toll for we," Ashley grabbed my arm tightly as we walked out of the church.

Horse drawn carriages lined the front of the church. We all climbed aboard for the short trip down Broad Street where the reception was being held at her parent's home. Besides being one of the most beautiful homes it was one of the few with an adjacent lot that served as a garden. In marrying off his daughter, father Chambliss had spared no expense.

In the courtyard the party was in full swing. I held Ashley while we looked out over the same harbor view we shared on a simple afternoon so long ago.

"Maybe history should be written in love stories instead of war stories," Ashley mused.

"I'd be happy to volunteer to cover that."

"We can start on that story as soon as we get away from here."

There was raucous laughter coming from inside. Kennedy stepped out onto the porch with a bridesmaid on either arm.

"Ashley your bridesmaids are far too charming for one evening. I'm trying to talk them into coming up to visit Hyannis Port this summer."

"Ladies consider yourselves warned," I wagged my finger at both.

"And to you Jack, I surrender all the world of single women and all the privileges and dishonors that may entail."

Kennedy saluted, "Aye, sir. And I'm just the man for the assignment. And what about you two. Where do the two happiest people of the moment go after the party's over?"

"Not far my friend. We kind of think we've travelled enough over the past three years. There's a quiet beach house not far from here where we hope no one will find us for a week or two."

"It's my intent," Ashley added, "To make the famous war correspondent a prisoner of love."

"Well I can't imagine anyone trying to escape from that," Kennedy's eyes turned a bit more serious, "But when you do, come up to Boston for a few days. There's a seat open in Congress. Someone thinks I should run for it."

CHAPTER 33

Quincy, Massachusetts
July, 1945

THE FORE RIVER SHIPYARD WAS packed with press. You don't usually get this kind of a turnout from the nation's biggest newspapers for a ship launching. The event was seeded by a mass mailing of invitations to every major politician and paper in the country. Then there was the name of the ship: *USS Joseph P. Kennedy, Jr.*

I sat in the rows reserved for the press listening to the candid conversations of my fellows describing Joe Senior's return to relevance. He was pressing for economic development in Massachusetts, buying the world's second tallest building in Chicago, making the covers of *Time* and *Life* and buying out a corrupt congressman to open a path to the Capitol for his second son.

The VIP platform was almost double the normal size for a launch. It was only fitting for the Secretary of the Navy and the new Secretary of State. The number of Kennedys alone would have filled a normal dais.

All stood while a navy band played the 'Star Spangled Banner'. From my seat I could see tears in Jack's eyes as he stepped to the microphone.

John Kennedy, the candidate for Congress, wore a dark suit and a striped tie. It was somber. It was a different look from the many I'd seen him wear during the war. His face was different as well, solemn and sincere.

"Ladies and Gentlemen, Distinguished Guests.. This new destroyer is named for my brother. Joseph P. Kennedy, Junior died as a hero of this war. He died with honor. In death he received the Navy Cross.

This ship carries the most advanced weapons of our age. It is my most sincere hope that she never has to fire them in war. It is my hope that our leaders will forge a military so strong, that in the face of our enemies we will appear so mighty, none would dare to raise arms up against us."

There were cheers and whistles drifting up to the platform. He paused. Across the shipyard all work had stopped. Workmen standing on other warships dropped their tools to the side while they applauded.

Kennedy looked to them, then up and out far beyond that Massachusett morning.

Quincy, Massachusetts
Sam Marlow/New York Herald Tribune

Jean Kennedy closed her eyes and swung a bottle of Champagne against the bow of the USS Joseph P. Kennedy, Jr. and launched the destroyer that carries the name of her brother.

Another Kennedy stood on the stage today, a war hero of unlikely stature. He offered words of warning and remembrance and launched a campaign for Congress.

John F. Kennedy received the Navy and Marine Corps medal. Joseph P. Kennedy, Junior was awarded the Navy Cross. Two heroes. One survivor.

War changes men. The changes are less profound for those who survive. Our veterans will return home soon to their wives, to their lives and they will carry on as best they can. Their dreams replaced by nightmares of war. They are things only understood by their brothers in battle.

A generation of young men rushed off to war. We were afraid we would be too late, miss the battles, fail to find glory. Now they dedicate ships and monuments to friends who gained glory and gave up life.

Kipling wrote of the hubris of war and ar-
rogance of empires... Lest we forget--Lest we
forget!

The Secretary of the Navy said: "We need men
who understand the causes of war and conflict,
who understand the fundamentals of our aims and
ideals.. We must find and train such men--out-
standing citizens who have served their country under arms.. If we don't.. we will lose our
shirts as we have in the past--and then what
avails the sacrifice of life, blood and treasure
that we have made?"

John F. Kennedy has seen the horror-- and the
glory. Now he sees a world he must try to change.

EPILOGUE

JACK KENNEDY WAS ELECTED TO Congress in November of 1946. He served as a Congressman for six years. In 1952 he ran for the Senate and won. Those were stepping stones to the presidential election of 1960, which he won, defeating Richard Nixon in one of the closest races of the twentieth century. The musings in love letters between Jack and Inga came true and JFK became the 35th President of the United States.

For many months I debated whether to take on the task of writing a novel that touched on any part of the Kennedy story or legacy. Scholars would find it shallow. Other projects have run afoul of the family and been shut down. One major publishing house said they'd publish the book, if I wrote more sex scenes involving the ensign-who-would-be-President.

I declined that offer.

What appealed to me about the story was Kennedy's real wit, determination and bravery that propelled him into war and on to the Presidency. They are the same qualities mentioned in the eulogy offered by Mike Mansfield, Majority Leader of the United States Senate, November 24, 1963, "He gave us of a good heart from which the laughter came. He gave us of a profound wit, from which a great leadership emerged. He gave us of a kindness and a strength fused into a human courage to seek peace without fear."

Printed in Great Britain
by Amazon.co.uk, Ltd.,
Marston Gate.